Girl with the Origami Butterfly

A Sidney Becker Mystery Thriller

LINDA BERRY

To my mother and father,
who taught me the magic and beauty of books.

Other books by Linda Berry:

Hidden Part One

Hidden Part Two

Pretty Corpse

To learn of new releases and discounts,
add your name to Linda's mailing list:

www.lindaberry.net

ACKNOWLEDGMENTS

A wonderful community of friends and family assisted in making this a suspenseful and entertaining work of fiction.

I owe a debt of gratitude to my editors, whose fearless comments kept me on the straight and narrow when I wanted to veer off course—including Denice Hughes and my husband, Mark Fasnacht. A heartfelt thank you for the amazing editorial talent of JT Gregory, who invested countless hours identifying stress fractures in the construction of the story. Trish Wilkinson, with her remarkable eye for detail, applied the final gloss and sparkle.

A warm thank you goes to my muse, LaLoni Kirkland, who joined me in the trenches with good cheer and enthusiasm, exhaustively drumming up plot and character ideas until the final choices rang true.

I greatly appreciate the assistance of criminal investigator Mark Rogers, Chief of Police Jim Doherty, Officer Jason Oviatt, and legal expert John Gragson for their insightful counsel on law enforcement procedures.

A big thank you to my dear sister, Francine Marsh, and Cathey Kahlie for reading *Girl with the Origami Butterfly* in its final stage and giving it two thumbs up.

CHAPTER ONE

BAILEY'S LOW, INSISTENT growls woke Ann from a dreamless sleep. She found herself sprawled on the overstuffed easy chair in the living room, feet propped on the ottoman, drool trickling down her chin. She swatted at the drool, half opened one eye and peered at the antique clock on the mantle: 11:00 p.m.

Ann heard Bailey sniffing at the front door, and then the clicks of his claws traveled to the open window in the living room. She opened her other eye. Her sable hound stood sifting the breeze through his muzzle with a sense of urgency. She didn't want to fully waken but she knew what was coming. Sure enough, Bailey trotted back to the front door and whimpered while gazing expectantly at her over one shoulder. *Damn those big brown eyes.*

Normally Ann would be in bed by now, but she had passed out after dinner, exhausted from carting her boxes of organic products into town at sunrise and standing for hours in her stall at the farmers market. By the time she loaded her truck and headed home, the pain in her calves had spread up her legs to her back and shoulders, and she felt every one of her forty-five years.

Bailey whined without let up. He knew how to play her. Ann looked longingly toward her bedroom before returning to the hound's pleading eyes. This was more urgent than a potty break. He'd no doubt caught the scent of a deer or rabbit. Now he wanted to assail it with ferocious barking to assert his dominance over Ann's small farm. Then he'd settle in for the night.

Since the unsolved murder that rocked her small town three years ago, Ann had refrained from going out late in the evening. Still, she felt a pang of guilt. She and Bailey had missed their after-dinner walk. She was determined to sleep in tomorrow, but if the spirited hound didn't exhaust his combustible energy, he'd be circling her bed at dawn, demanding that she rise.

"Okay, Bailey, you win." Ann heard the weariness in her voice as she heaved herself from the chair and shuffled to the front door. Fatigue had settled into every part of her body. Her limbs felt as heavy as flour sacks. "But only a half-mile up the highway and back."

Bailey sat at attention, tail vigorously thumping the floor.

Still dressed in jeans, a turtleneck sweater, and solid hiking shoes, Ann grabbed her Gor-Tex jacket from the coat rack, wrestled her arms through the sleeves, pulled Bailey's leash from a pocket, and snapped it onto his collar. The boards creaked softly as they stepped onto the covered front porch into the damp autumn chill. The moist air held the promise of the season's first frost. Her flashlight beam found the stone walkway, then the gravel driveway leading to the highway. A good rain had barreled through while she slept, and a strong wind unleashed the pungent fragrance of lavender and rosemary from her garden. Silvered in the moonlight, furrowed fields of tomatoes, herbs, and flowers sloped down to the shoreline of Lake Kalapuya, where her Tri-hull motorboat dipped and bobbed by the dock. A half-mile across the lurching waves, the lights of Garnerville shimmered through a tattered mist on the opposite shore.

Following the hound's tug on the leash, Ann picked up her pace, breathing deeply, her mind sharpening, muscles loosening. Steam rose off the asphalt. Scattered puddles reflected moonlight like pieces of glass. The thick forest of Douglas fir, red cedar, and big leaf maple engulfed both sides of the highway, surrendering to the occasional farm or ranch. Treetops swayed, branches dipped and waved, whispered and creaked. The night was alive with the sounds of frogs croaking and water dripping. The smell of apples perfumed the air as she trekked past her nearest neighbor's orchards. Miko's two-story clapboard farmhouse floated on a shallow sea of mist, windows black, yellow porch light fingering the darkness.

Ann didn't mingle with her neighbors, few as they were, and she took special pains to avoid Miko, whose wife had been the victim of the brutal murder in the woods adjacent to his property. The killer was never found, but an air of suspicion had hovered over Miko ever since. Ann detested gossip and ignored it. She had her own reasons for avoiding Miko—and all other men, for that matter.

When they reached the narrow dirt road where they habitually turned to hike into the woods, Bailey froze, nose twitching, locked on a scent. He tugged hard at the leash, wanting her to follow.

"No," she said firmly, peering into the black mouth of the forest—a light-spangled paradise by day—black, damp, and ominous by night. "Let's go home."

Bailey trembled in his stance, growled with unusual intensity, tugged harder. The hound had latched onto a rivulet of odor he wanted desperately to explore.

Ann jerked the leash. "Bailey, home!"

Normally obedient, Bailey ignored her. Using his seventy pounds of muscle as leverage, he yanked two, three times until the leash ripped from her fingers. Off he bounded, swallowed instantly by the darkness crouching beyond her feeble cone of light.

"Bailey! Come!"

No sound, just the incessant drip of water. Ann's beam probed the woods, jerking to the left, then right. "Bailey!"

She heard a steady, muffled, distant bark.

He's found what he's looking for. Bailey's barking abruptly ceased. *Good. He's on his way back.* She waited. No movement.

No appearance of Bailey's big sable head emerging through the pitch.

Ann trembled as fear took possession of her senses. She bolted recklessly into the woods, her light beam bouncing along a trail that looked utterly foreign in the dark. Her feet crushed wet leaves and sloshed through puddles. Her left arm protected her face from the errant branch crossing her path. A second too late she saw the gnarled tree-root which seemed to jump out and snag her foot. She fell headlong, left hand breaking the fall, flashlight skidding beneath a carpet of leaves and pine needles. Blackness enveloped her. Shakily, she pulled herself to her feet, trying to delineate shapes in the darkness, left wrist throbbing, the moist scent of decay suffocating.

The forest was deathly still, seeming to hold its breath.

Soft rustling.

Silence.

Rustling again.

Something moved quietly and steadily through the underbrush. Adrenaline shot up her arms like electric shocks. Ann swept her hands beneath mounds of wet leaves, grasping roots and cones until her fingers closed around the shaft of her flashlight. She thumbed the switch and cut a slow swath from left to right, her light splintering between trees. Her beam froze on a hooded figure moving backward through the brush dragging a woman, her bare feet bumping through the tangled debris.

The man kept his face completely motionless, eyes fixed on hers in a chilling stare. The world became soaked in a hideous and wondrous slowness. He lowered the woman to the ground and hung his long arms at his side. He was quiet; so was Ann. He radiated stillness. The stillness of a tree. It was hypnotic.

Ann felt paralyzed. Tongue dry. Thoughts sluggish. Then threads of white-hot terror ripped through her chest and propelled her like a fired missile into motion. Switching off the beam, she turned and sprinted like a frightened doe back along the trail.

His footfalls crushed the earth behind her, breaking through brush, snapping branches, closing the space between them, his breathing thunderous. Any moment, he would yank her by the hair, pull her down.

Ann's world narrowed to a pinpoint. Everything except survival ceased to exist. She darted off the trail, skidded down a steep ravine, hobbled and splashed across Deer Creek, heard the man bulldoze through thickets, plummet down the slope, stumble, fall, curse, regain his balance, resume crashing after her like a bear through a woodpile, heaving, staggering, steps slowing down as he splashed through the creek.

Ann ran light-footed and sure, shoes springing off the deep mulch of the forest floor. She understood the features of the marsh that lay ahead. The smell of peat moss and a current of frigid air guiding her steps. Her footsteps sank deeper into wet earth and soon she was wading into the black shallows through dense clumps of reeds. When she reached a monstrous fir that lay like a great beast across the wetland, Ann crawled beneath the carcass of rotting wood. She backed into the hollow where Bailey once hid and refused to come out. Jagged wood scratched her skin and cold water swelled through her clothes and hair, shocking her flesh. Imprisoned, she listened, trembling. No sound. Then the heavy weight of a man splashed into the marsh and sloshed along the full length of the fallen tree, circled back, and stopped.

Ann's body went rigid. Threads of nausea reached up around her throat and she tasted bile on her tongue.

With a short guttural sound, the man hoisted himself onto the trunk of the tree and it compressed a few inches into the bog. The ceiling of Ann's hiding place pressed down upon her. Water crept higher, and with effort she kept her nose in the desperately thin space above the water line. The weight of her prison shifted as the man marched up and down the length of the tree. Agitated. Did he know she lay within? Was he taunting her? Or was he using the tree as a lookout to scan the surrounding wetland and woods?

A ghastly creeping terror rose from a place beyond thought. Her heart knocked so furiously against the cage of her chest she felt certain the man would hear. She heard him jump off into the shallows with a big splashy crescendo and the tree bounced up higher above the water line. For a breathtaking moment she didn't hear him move, and then he waded away and the tree settled firmly into the oozing earth. Silence sealed itself back over the forest.

CHAPTER TWO

AT 11:43 P.M. THE RADIO crackled and the scratchy voice from dispatch erupted into the cab of the Yukon. "Hey, Chief?"

"Yeah, Jesse."

"We got an elk collision on Old Garner Highway. Just past mile marker thirty-four. West shore. Hit and run."

"I'll take it." Police Chief Sidney Becker glanced at the clock on the dashboard. Almost midnight. "I'm a couple miles away. Notify Vicki."

"Already done. She just got there. She was in the area."

"Copy that. Over." Sidney turned on her strobe, hit the high beams and punched the gas pedal, accelerating into a corridor of tall trees. Forest flashed by on both sides of the Yukon. An earlier storm left the highway slick as grease but the tires of the SUV grabbed the asphalt like talons. Sidney soon spotted the animal control vehicle parked off the road ahead, its red strobe fracturing the darkness. Pulling in behind, she scoped out the scene. Vicki Slope was on the job, reflective strips on her canvas uniform brilliant in the headlights. An elk with four-foot antlers lay twisted on the shoulder of the road between the two vehicles, a trail of blood leading from the point of impact on the highway.

Sidney lowered the window, adjusted the spotlight to illuminate the area, killed the engine, and climbed out. A cold wind bit into her skin, encouraging her to flip up the collar of her uniform jacket. Pinesap seasoned the moist air. Not much moonlight shone through the dense cloud cover.

Vicki had attached chains to the carcass and was winching it up the ramp to the flatbed. Sidney hated seeing the senseless loss of an animal, especially one as magnificent as this. Thank God it was dead and she didn't have to put it out of its misery. Sidney took photos as the elk was loaded, then she joined the Linley County worker at the rear of her truck.

"We gotta stop meeting like this, Chief," Vicki said, her long horsey face and limp blond hair pulsing crimson.

"Got that right." Large animal collisions happened a dozen times a year and caused more accidents if the carcass wasn't promptly removed. Though gruesome, Vicki's job was critical to public safety. She'd been scraping animals off Oregon roads for six years, and nine in Alaska before that. "Damn shame," Sidney said, turning her eyes away from the elk.

"Yeah, damn shame this good meat's going to waste." Vicki peeled off her thick leather gloves and stuffed them into an oversized pocket on her work pants. "God knows, there's plenty of folks around here who could use it. When I worked up in Alaska, I delivered all road kill to churches and charities. It went a long way in feeding the poor and homeless."

Though Sidney agreed with Alaska's policy, she kept her viewpoint to herself. She had a sworn duty to uphold the laws of Oregon. "Lawmakers here think if we let folks eat their road-kill, it'll encourage them to poach."

"That's bullshit," Vicki snorted. "Nobody deliberately hunts animals with a vehicle. We've seen the damage a large animal can do."

Sidney had seen the damage, all right. Deer and elk pulverized cars and could launch over the hood through a windshield, mutilating and killing passengers. "Who called it in?"

"Passer-by. He put flares around it and waited until I got here, then he helped me drag it off the road. Must weigh five hundred pounds. He left just minutes ago."

"Decent of him. He see who hit it?"

"Dunno. He wasn't up for conversation."

"Whoever the culprit was, he must've smashed the hell out of his hood and bumper. You see anyone driving by with one headlight?"

"Nah. Pretty quiet this time of night." Vicki shoved her hands deep into her pockets. "Pisses me off the hitter didn't call it in."

"Yeah, me too. Probably drunk or high or has priors. He'll call it in tomorrow when he finds out a police report is needed to file an insurance claim. Did you recognize the good Samaritan?"

"Too dark. He had his jacket hood over his face. He was strong, though. He did most of the pulling. But I got his license plate." She tapped her temple.

Sidney pulled out a notebook from her breast pocket. "Shoot."

"It was a silver Mercedes." She spouted off the license number.

Sidney scratched it on the pad, shoved it back in her pocket. "You should be working for the FBI with that memory of yours."

Vicki laughed. "No, thanks. I like what I do. Autonomy is priceless." At five-foot-four, she had to crank up her neck to meet Sidney's eyes. "You getting taller, Chief?"

"Nope." Sidney spread her feet slightly apart and hooked her thumbs on her duty belt. "Still six feet. It's these new shoes. Thick tread."

"Uh huh. If you say so. You still working out?"

"Faithfully."

"You might want to cut back on those protein bars. Eat more junk food. Sugar. You grow outward, not up." She patted her sizable paunch, laughed heartily, and turned toward her truck. "Gotta get this load to the compost center. At least they'll make good soil out of it."

"I'll see you at the gym sometime," Sidney called after her.

"Don't hold your breath."

As Vicki pulled out, Sidney walked slowly around the point of impact, studying the wet asphalt with her flashlight. She snapped more photos, pulled a couple of evidence bags from her duty belt, and bagged pieces of a broken headlight. Looking more closely, she noticed large chips of red paint. She scraped up a few pieces with one of her business cards and placed them in another bag.

She got back into the Yukon just in time. An eighteen-wheeler blew past, creating a rush of wind sufficient to shake the vehicle. It would have pulverized her evidence. Sidney took out a marking pen and dated and labeled the bags. No crime had been committed. Still, she documented everything. Old habits die hard.

Time to call it a night. Sidney headed toward town. It had been a fairly uneventful day, as were most of her days as chief of police of a town of two thousand residents. Just the usual rash of minor disturbances. Far cry from her life as lead detective of a homicide unit in Oakland, California. Admittedly, she missed the excitement of working with the best minds in law enforcement, out-witting killers and getting them off the street. But she didn't miss the frenetic energy of urban life, or the unceasing murders: acts of heated passion, gang members protecting their turf. But the worst, were depraved individuals who killed for pleasure. If offered the chance to go back to her former life, she wouldn't hesitate to decline. Fifteen years in that psychotic city left her battle-weary, haunted by blood-spattered crime scenes, and ready to give up police work entirely. She believed, unequivocally, that anyone could commit murder if faced with the right circumstances. Luckily, those circumstances were almost non-existent here in Garnerville.

Two years ago, at the firm request of her sister, Selena, Sidney took a three-month hiatus and returned home to Garnerville to help care for their mother who suffered from early onset Alzheimer's. Watching her mom's beautiful mind disappear in slivers day by day was brutal, and the two sisters made the gut-wrenching decision to place her in a memory care facility.

The slower pace of life, the small-town morality, and neighborly kindness rekindled Sidney's faith in humanity, and helped her recover from cop burnout. Police Chief Kirk McDonald retired during that period, and his position came up for election. The town's power players urged Sidney to run. She did, winning easily against an officer from another town who had a fraction of her experience. It didn't hurt that her father had been a highly respected police chief in Garnerville for eighteen years.

Chief Clarence Becker was still a vital force when Sidney left for the police academy seventeen years ago at age eighteen. Though he appeared to be in robust health, her father died abruptly a few years back of cardiac arrest, catching everyone by surprise. His spirit still burned strong in the memory of the townsfolk, and his photos graced the walls of City Hall, the police station, and the historical society.

Static on the radio yanked her attention back to the present and she focused on her dispatcher's alert voice. "Report of a possible homicide, Chief. West shore, Lake Kalapuya."

"Who called it?"

"Ann Howard."

Sidney blinked. *Ann Howard?* "Is there a body?"

"Not at this time. She saw a man dragging a woman in the woods. When he saw Ann, he chased her."

An alarm sounded in Sidney's brain. Ann Howard wasn't the kind of woman who conjured scary stories. "I'm on it, Jesse. Tell all units to respond."

"All? Officers Woods and Cruz are off duty."

"All units," she clipped. "I want the K9 unit out there, too."

"Copy that. Over."

Her stomach tightening, Sidney turned on her strobe and gunned the engine, high beams carving a tunnel in the night. Only three homicides had taken place in Garnerville in the last decade. None on her watch, but she took all threats of violence seriously. Three years ago, a woman was brutally murdered in the Siuslaw Forest bordering Ann's farm, and the victim's husband was Ann's immediate neighbor. Sidney knew she should be better acquainted with Ann, considering the woman had been in business with Sidney's sister, Selena, for seven years. But Ann had a reputation for being standoffish, and something of a recluse, rarely coming to town except to sell at the farmers market, allowing Selena to do all the public relations.

The crackling voice of her dispatcher filled the car again. "Officers Cruz, Woods, and Wyatt are on their way, Chief. A K9 unit is heading over from Treehorn."

Forty-five minutes away. "That's the best they can do?"

"Sorry. Busy night."

"Tell them to step on it."

CHAPTER THREE

OFFICER GRANGER WYATT'S Dodge Ram pickup arrived right behind hers as she pulled to a stop in Ann's gravel driveway. Sidney shared the evening shift with Granger, while officers Amanda Cruz and Darnell Woods worked the day shift. Hustled out of bed, and driving from town, they would arrive within twenty minutes. Though a rookie, on the job for only six months, Granger was a Marine vet with combat experience. He was disciplined, accustomed to a chain of command, and had good instincts in a crisis. Raised on a cattle ranch, just a few miles up the highway, Granger was all-American handsome, and his perpetually tanned face and neck gave him the look of a rancher even in uniform. He caught up to her as she crossed Ann's covered front porch.

"Chief," he said hurriedly in greeting.

She nodded and rapped on the door.

Residual rain dripped from the eaves, and the moist air felt thick and heavy, almost like a presence. Pots swollen with herbs and flowers crowded the porch, scenting the air.

The door swung open and a sturdy-looking young man with pleasant, even features appeared. He was in his mid-twenties and wore a worried expression, his brows knitting together beneath a deeply creased forehead. "Hi, Chief Becker. I'm Matt, Ann's son." Matt ushered them into a spacious great room, tastefully decorated with overstuffed furniture and farmhouse antiques. The kitchen was at the opposite end of the room, separated by a granite-topped island lined with stools.

Ann rose from her seat on the sofa; a pretty woman with a slender build, large frightened blue eyes, and dark hair hanging in wet tendrils across her shoulders. Though dressed warmly in a brown turtleneck, corduroy pants, and sheepskin boots, she visibly trembled.

Ann looked directly at Sidney but showed no flicker of recognition. Not unexpected. Selena had shared a confidence—her best friend had facial blindness, a cognitive disorder that prevented her from distinguishing the features of one person's face from another's. If her own son passed her on the sidewalk, Selena had told her, Ann wouldn't know it. The humiliation of not being able to recognize people was the primary reason Ann kept to herself.

"Ann, it's me, Chief Becker, and Officer Wyatt. My dispatcher said you saw a man dragging a woman in the woods. Then he pursued you. Is that correct?"

"Yes." Ann's eyes seemed feverish, and her skin was ghostly pale.

"We need to go check it out. Can you give me exact directions?"

"No. It's in the thick of the woods." A chilling terror rose in her eyes. "Please don't ask me to go back there."

"Ann, I need you to show us," Sidney said. "A woman's life is at risk. You'll be safe with us in the car." She glanced at Matt, who stood by his mother's side, body tense. "Matt can come, too."

"Sure thing." Matt's eyes flashed grave concern to Sidney.

"We need to go. Now." Sidney put a firm hand on Ann's arm. "You can do this."

Ann swallowed, nodded.

Sidney hustled mother and son out to her Yukon, and Ann chose to sit with Matt in the rear seat, basically a steel mesh cage. It seemed to make her feel safe.

"Granger, follow me," Sidney ordered. "Let Amanda and

Darnell know where we're headed."

"Copy."

Sidney opened the trunk, took out her Remington 870 shotgun, loaded it with shells, climbed into the driver's seat, secured her weapon between the seats, and drove out of the driveway.

"Turn right on the highway," Ann said.

Sidney glanced at Ann in the rearview mirror. Her face looked ashen, the muscles so tight it looked like her jaw might snap. "You okay?"

"Yes," she said in a voice barely above a whisper.

Sidney saw the bleating strobes of two SUVs racing toward them and heard Granger on the radio, telling the officers to fall in line behind their vehicles. She turned her full attention to Ann. "Why were you out here so late?"

"My hound was wired, so I took him for a walk," Ann answered in a tremulous voice. "He caught the scent of something in the woods and yanked the leash out of my hand. He ran off and wouldn't come back. I worried he'd been attacked by a wild animal, so I went after him."

"Where's your dog now?"

"I don't know," she said with a touch of panic.

They passed Miko Matsui's farm.

"Turn here, Chief," Ann said. "The dirt road on the right."

Angling onto a road hardly wider than a hiking trail, Sidney had the sensation of driving into a tunnel. Bushes crowded the sides of the vehicle, a thick canopy of branches hung low overhead, and the headlights bounced over ruts in the road. The wheels spun in a deep puddle, seeking traction, then caught and moved on. The headlights of the three other vehicles bobbed behind her, evenly spaced. Sidney breathed easier when the trail widened to the width of two cars and the ceiling of the forest opened above them.

"Tell me about the woman the man was dragging," Sidney

said.

"I didn't see her clearly. She had dark hair. A white blouse. A skirt. Her legs and feet were bare. That's it."

"Was she alive?"

"I couldn't tell. She wasn't moving. I focused on him."

"Can you describe him?"

"He was huge. A giant." Her voice quivered. "He wore dark pants and a dark hoodie. Long arms. He looked right at me and lowered the woman to the ground. But I blinded him with my beam. I'm sure he never saw my face."

Sidney glanced at her in the mirror. Ann looked as if she were reliving the moment.

"I turned and ran for my life," she continued. "I know these woods. I headed to the marsh and crawled inside a hollowed-out Douglas fir."

Terrifying, Sidney thought.

Ann expelled a ragged breath. "Seconds later, I heard him splash into the water. He climbed on top of the fir. I could feel him walking up there." Ann's eyes squeezed tight. "After a long while, he left. I was wet. Cold. I waited maybe fifteen minutes before heading home, taking the back way, to the shore of the lake. It's longer, but there's more cover. I kept stopping to listen, to make sure he wasn't following me. When I got to my driveway a man stepped out of the shadows. I screamed holy hell, I can tell you. But it was Matt. I'd never been so happy to see my son in all my life. While I changed into dry clothes, Matt called 9-1-1." Ann pointed into the woods. "That's where I saw him."

Sidney peered into the forest but saw nothing that served as a distinguishing landmark, just columns of trees connected by tangled underbrush. She wondered how Ann could tell one bend in the road from another. After easing the Yukon to a halt, she studied her passengers over her shoulder. They sat huddled together, hands locked, Ann's white-knuckled. Matt, she noted, wore dark pants and a dark Hoodie, and had a muscular build. "Where exactly was the man standing?"

"About thirty feet in." Ann pointed again. "Between those two alders."

Sidney zeroed in on the spot. "We're going to take a look around. You two stay put." Grabbing the shotgun, she climbed out of the Yukon, leaving the spotlight burrowing into the woods and the motor running to provide heat for her passengers. The exhaust formed a billowing white ghost behind the truck.

The three officers joined her, armed with AR-15 patrol rifles, Kevlar vests bulking up their uniforms.

Officer Amanda Cruz was a six-year veteran of small town crime, transferred from Auckland two years ago. Her ebony hair was pulled into a ponytail, and her fragile Latin features belied the grit of her character.

"Amanda, stay here and watch over the vehicles. Stay out of the headlights."

Amanda nodded, brown eyes steady, muscles tight around her mouth.

Sidney sized up Darnell, a young black man who bore a striking resemblance to Pharrell Williams. Clean cut, lean build, father of two toddlers, two-years on the force. He'd never been placed in a situation where he had to discharge his duty weapon. Beads of sweat gathered on his forehead and upper lip. Sidney sensed his adrenalin pumping, as was hers. "You good?"

"Yes, ma'am."

"A sniper could pick us off one-by-one, Chief," Granger said. "We need to spread out."

"Copy that," Sidney said, appreciating his military training. She'd had her share of urban warfare, which required a different skill set and was just as dangerous, but she had no experience hunting a perp in a forest. "Darnell, circle to the right. Granger, go left. I'll take the middle ground where Ann saw the suspect. Look for any disturbance on the ground or bushes. Stay alert. Let's roll."

Their beams darted over the forest floor and burrowed through pillars of gleaming trees. The wind had died down, but a piercing chill hung in the air. A musky dampness breathed off the leaves and lifted off the spongy carpet beneath their feet. The only sound came from the rustling of footsteps.

Sidney's light found drag marks in the debris between the two alders pointed out by Ann. She also spotted snapped twigs and crushed bushes where the suspect must have barreled through to get to Ann.

She and the two men continued deeper into the woods, beams sweeping through the mist. "Over here," Darnell shouted, a stunned tone to his voice.

Sidney and Granger joined him, their beams merging and spotlighting a ghastly sight. It had been a while since she had witnessed a crime scene, and it struck her with a force that stole her breath. The staging of the body looked hauntingly familiar. The woman sat against the trunk of a massive tree, her skirt and blouse neatly arranged, one ankle jauntily crossed over the other, arms lying at each side, wrists slit, hands immersed in pools of blood. What struck Sidney as especially chilling was the relaxed appearance of the woman's face—calm, with a Mona Lisa smile, eyes wide open, staring back as though this was a practical joke, and at any second she would spring to her feet, laughing.

Granger stepped forward. As a CLS Marine, trained to save lives in combat situations, his instinct was to provide emergency care. Sidney brought her hand down on his arm and stopped him. "She's dead. Don't contaminate the crime scene."

Granger lowered his head and shook it. "You're right. No one could survive that kind of blood loss."

Darnell looked shell-shocked; his first murder scene. He turned away from the body and she thought he was going to lose it. But after a long moment, he composed himself and turned back, face tight.

He and Granger turned expectant faces to Sidney.

Though she felt a tension inside her, like a cold hand squeezing her chest, she forced herself to speak in a calm voice. "Darnell, call dispatch. Tell Jesse to get the M.E. out here with his crime scene specialist. Find out where that K9 unit is."

"Got it, Chief."

"Granger, tell Amanda to bring the crime kit. Set up a perimeter around the body. I want only one footpath in and out of this crime scene. Mark any footprints and tire tracks that may belong to the suspect."

"What about Ann and her son?" Darnell asked.

"Tell them to sit tight. Do a background check on Matt."

The two men left, single file.

Sidney turned back to the victim, trying to close off her emotions and study the scene with intellectual objectivity, her shoulders and neck burning with tension. The staging of this victim was identical to the crime scene photos she had reviewed of Mimi Matsui. When Sidney became police chief, she carefully studied the homicide case, uneasy that a killer in her district had not been caught. No forensic evidence had been discovered at the time, and all possible leads had been pursued to no end. The case went cold.

Now it appeared the killer had struck again.

The weariness Sidney felt welled up from a place in her psyche that reviled humans who could kill others in such a cold-blooded manner. This was not a crime of passion. The killer had carefully planned this murder. The extent of blood loss told her that the woman was alive when brought here.

The way the victim was posed told Sidney several important facts. The killer carefully arranged her clothing to give the victim an appearance of modesty, yet he deliberately dragged her bare feet over the ground as a form of punishment, allowing them to get scratched and bloodied. Her bare legs and feet gave the woman a heightened sense of vulnerability. The violent act had been interrupted by Ann, a witness who could potentially identify him, yet the killer's inability to catch her did not deter him from completing his mission. He returned, staged the victim, sliced her wrists, and let her bleed out, knowing the police could arrive momentarily.

From years investigating homicides, profiling murderers, and getting a ringside view into the workings of a psychopathic mind, Sidney recognized this murder to be an act of cold, calculated revenge, spurred by hatred. The killer perceived he had been the target of some threat, some injury by the victim, or she was a surrogate for a woman who wounded him deeply in his past. Sidney suspected the killer stood and watched as every moment of life seeped from his victim's body.

While standing guard, Sidney made a mental checklist of what needed to be done. A small town, with a tight operating budget, demanded that law enforcement personnel have several areas of expertise. Sidney and her three officers served as detectives as well as patrol cops. Darnell had IT experience, and Amanda was certified to conduct crime scene inspections. Collecting forensic material was a race against time before weather or the victim's physiology degraded evidence.

Amanda and Granger arrived and set to work preserving the crime scene, which freed Sidney to talk to Ann and Matt. When she returned to the vehicles, Darnell was sitting in his Jeep Cherokee patrol vehicle under the dome light, head bent over his computer. He rolled down his window when she approached.

"Find anything?" she asked.

"Not yet. Matt's clean."

"K9 unit?"

"Fifteen minutes away."

Sidney walked to her Yukon, slid into the driver's seat, and looked at her two passengers over her shoulder.

"What's going on?" Ann asked, anxious. "She's dead, isn't she?"

"This is now an active crime scene," Sidney said gently.

"Did you find Bailey?"

"No. Sorry."

Ann looked stung.

"It's possible Bailey got frightened and ran away in a panic. Not unusual for a dog."

"He knows his way home," Ann said, her expression lifting slightly.

"Ann, I need to talk to Matt." She turned to face him in the back seat. "Will you accompany me to another car?"

"Why does he have to leave?" Ann asked.

"Police policy. Just routine questions," Sidney said in a soothing tone, but she needed to rule him out as a suspect. "It'll only take a minute."

"Mom, it's fine," Matt said. "Chief Becker is just doing her job."

Ann nodded and released Matt's hand. He accompanied Sidney to Granger's truck, and they climbed into the front seats.

Sidney momentarily studied the young man. Matt had a handsome, angular face, shadowed by dark stubble, dark hair, which fell over his brow, and his mother's blue eyes. He sat with his hands relaxed on his lap, yet she sensed his tension. "Thanks for your cooperation, Matt. Like I said, these are just routine questions. Mind if I record our conversation?"

"Go ahead," he said, frowning.

She placed her cell phone on the console between them and turned on the recorder. "Tell me what you do for a living."

"I have my own business—Greenlife Landscaping."

"I've seen your trucks around town. Many clients?"

"We stay busy."

"How many employees?"

"Nine."

"When your mom came home from that brutal experience, she sounded surprised to see you. Why'd you show up at her house so late tonight?"

"I store supplies in her shed. I need turf builder and fertilizer for work tomorrow."

"You couldn't pick them up in the morning?"

A muscle twitched slightly near his mouth. "We're on site at six. I didn't want to get up any earlier than I had to."

"Did you go into the house?"

"No, I didn't want to wake Mom."

"The lights must've been on. She was out walking Bailey."

He hesitated, broke eye contact, and met her gaze again. "I figured she fell asleep with the lights on."

"Why were you standing in the shadows when she arrived home?"

"I was walking to my truck when she came tearing in, soaked to the skin, frightened out of her mind." His eyes narrowed. "Holy hell, Chief, you don't think I chased my mom through the woods, do you? Whoever that psycho was, he meant to hurt her, to shut her up." He paused for effect. "I'd never do anything to hurt my mom. I know she can't recognize faces, but the man in the woods didn't."

Matt had a good point, but she wasn't ready to rule him out entirely. Something about him disturbed her. He was in the area during the time of the murder, his dark clothing fit the description of the suspect, and with his muscular build he could have easily dragged or carried a woman a long distance. Matt and the victim were about the same age, which meant he may have known her, maybe even went to school with her. In his favor, he had no criminal background. It seemed unlikely Matt would chase his mother, but psychopaths operate from their own playbook, and many had been known to terrorize, even kill their parents.

Headlights appeared in the rearview mirror. The medical examiner. "Matt, I'll get one of my officers to drive you and your mom home. It's not advisable to leave her alone tonight."

"I plan on staying with her."

"How can I reach you if I have more questions?"

He recited his cell number and address, and they both left the truck.

Sidney tapped on Darnell's window, and he rolled it down. "Get anything else?" she asked.

"Other than parking violations, they're both clean."

"Drive them home, then come back and help process the crime scene beyond the taped perimeter with Granger."

"Got it. How you holding up, Chief?"

"Good. You?"

He made the okay sign with thumb and forefinger.

She smiled, then headed to the M.E.'s van. Garnerville was fortunate to have an M.E. Most small towns had to hire a pathologist from the county, but Dr. Linthrope had moved here from Portland twenty years ago for the same reason she did—big-city burnout. The doctor had worked under both Chief McDonald and her father and had since overseen the removal of every dead body in Garnerville. If a death was even remotely suspicious, his scrupulous post-mortem examination revealed the cause—natural, accident-related, suicide, or the rare homicide. Her father had thought highly of Dr. Linthrope, and so did she.

Dressed in field scrubs, the doctor and his assistant rolled the gurney out of the back of the van. Florid-faced, with wild white hair, Linthrope looked like a portly version of Albert Einstein, and at age seventy-one, his intellect was still scalpel sharp.

"Sorry to get you up this time of night, Doc."

He pushed his bifocals higher on the bridge of his nose and smiled. "Morning's more like it. We're closing in on two a.m."

"I feel it in my bones."

"I brought you coffee." He lifted a chrome thermos off the gurney and handed it to her.

"Bless you, Doc." Sidney opened the thermos, poured a cup, and sipped. Strong, rich, hot.

She nodded at Linthrope's assistant, Stewart Wong, a studious Chinese-American with thick glasses and a slight frame. An introvert through and through, with a hyper focus for minute details. She suspected his single mindedness was due to OCD, which made him an excellent forensic specialist—but socializing, not so much. He'd barely spoken five complete sentences to her during her tenure.

Stewart nodded back, solemn-faced. A Digital SLR camera hung from his neck. "The body?" he asked.

"We have a Jane Doe." She screwed the cap back on the thermos. "Follow me."

The wheels on the gurney bounced over the ground as the caravan carved its way through the underbrush. Granger and Amanda had illuminated the area with generator-powered lights and marked off a wide berth with black and yellow tape. Amanda was on all fours, her gloved hands sifting through the damp debris around the body. Granger was searching outside the perimeter, placing an occasional plastic marker on the ground.

The doctor's eyes widened when he viewed the victim, and his gaze met Sidney's.

"Same as Mimi Matsui?" she asked.

"The very same."

His confirmation chilled her. Possibly, she had a serial killer on her hands. Spirals of memories unraveled in her mind of past investigations where her team hunted down serial killers with specific traits: highly intelligent, calculated, organized—essentially invisible. Sidney had been a relentless investigator—compulsive, her colleagues said—but her doggedness paid off. Some tiny oversight the killer missed often broke the case.

The doc and Stewart snapped on latex gloves and ducked under the yellow tape. Stewart photographed the area surrounding the body, then the body itself, and finally moved in closer to check for marks and trace material. Ignoring the popping camera flashes, Sidney watched closely as Linthrope methodically examined the victim.

Jane Doe appeared to be in her mid-twenties, pretty in a round-faced, cherubic way, her perfectly highlighted brown hair brushing her shoulders. She might even have been beautiful, if not for her bloodless pallor. Her big hazel eyes stared at Sidney, seeming to follow her movements, as though challenging her to find her killer. Sidney made her a silent vow. The killer made a mistake by moving back into her district. She *would* bring him in. The bastard was heading straight for a lethal injection.

Linthrope searched the folds and pockets of the victim's gaily-flowered skirt for identification but found nothing. He carefully searched all exposed skin. "No sign of restraints on her wrists or ankles. No sign of a struggle. No bruising, defensive wounds, or broken nails. Same as Mimi Matsui."

"How was Mimi constrained?" Granger asked, watching from outside the taped perimeter.

"Injected with a neurotoxin that paralyzed her." He glanced up at the officer. "Mimi's killer wanted her fully conscious. She knew exactly what was going on, but could do nothing about it. Not even twitch the smallest muscle. Mimi's expression looked peaceful, just like this young woman, but on the inside, she was quietly screaming."

Sidney broke out in goose bumps, imagining the woman's last terrifying minutes on Earth.

"Why are her eyes open, Doc?" Amanda sat back on her heels with an evidence bag and tweezers in her hands.

"It appears, like Mimi, her lids were glued open."

Amanda gasped. "He forced her to watch while he killed her."

Granger's eyes flashed with anger. "Sick sunnuvabitch."

Her two officers had been listening to every word. Just as well. They needed to know every grisly detail. Still, even to Sidney, this killer seemed especially pitiless and inhuman.

Amanda brushed debris from her pants and stood. "Nothing from Mimi's autopsy could identify her killer?"

"Unfortunately, no. Mimi had been dead for almost twenty-four hours. It rained. Forest scavengers had access to the body."

"Thanks for the Norman Rockwell images, Doc," Amanda said.

"Death is a natural part of life, Officer," he said calmly. "Flesh goes back to nature. The deceased are at peace, unlike the living."

"Too peaceful for my taste."

"Our Jane Doe died within an hour of you finding her, Chief." As he spoke, the doctor lifted the woman's hair on the left side of her neck. "Just as I suspected. Here's the injection site."

Sidney leaned over the doctor's shoulder to view the angry red mark on her skin.

"If this is the same neurotoxin, it's extremely powerful. It doesn't take much, just a pinprick. Her killer must have come up behind her and jammed in the needle."

Amanda visibly shuddered.

They were all silent for a moment. The rain dripping from nearby branches tapped out a steady, morose melody.

After Linthrope and Stewart bagged the victim's feet and hands to preserve trace evidence, they proceeded to stretch a shiny black body bag on the ground with a clean sheet on top. They gently wrapped the woman in the sheet, placed her in the bag, and zipped it. The imprint of her body remained pressed into the forest debris between two wide pools of blood.

Sidney was grateful the victim could no longer peer at her, but she knew Jane Doe's wide-eyed stare would live in her memory.

"Let me help you carry her." Amanda stepped forward, and

she and Stewart carried the body to the gurney.

"Stewart will stay to help process the crime scene, but my work here is done." Linthrope stripped off his gloves, his good-natured expression undaunted, hazel eyes bright beneath his bushy white brows. A man who unraveled the mysteries of death from corpses without losing his composure brought a sense of calm to the ghastly event. "I'll start the autopsy today and notify you with the results."

"Appreciate it, Doc."

Granger and Amanda negotiated the gurney back toward the van. The doctor lagged behind. "A miracle you found this body so quickly. Who called it in?"

"Ann Howard." Sidney shared the details of Ann's flight for her life.

"Harrowing. Poor woman. Ann's had more than her share of violence." He shook his head. "First her husband, now this."

Sidney's antennae shot up. "What happened to her husband?"

"Why, she and Matt killed him, eight years ago." His brow furrowed. "You didn't know?"

Sidney felt ice touch her spine. "No. Their background checks came up clean."

"Ah, of course. No record. It was ruled self-defense. I'm surprised your sister never told you. Selena and Ann are like Siamese twins."

"Protecting Ann's privacy, I guess."

"I did John Howard's autopsy. We can go over his file tomorrow when you come by." Linthrope cast his gaze toward the gurney, now disappearing into the darkness. "I better get moving."

"See you tomorrow, Doc."

He nodded politely and hurried away.

Only Stewart remained behind, his camera flash popping at the edge of her periphery. The sudden sharp barking of dogs back where the vehicles were parked told her the K9 unit had arrived.

Hopefully, they'd find some evidence leading them to the killer's identity. At least his entry point into the woods.

CHAPTER FOUR

AS DAWN CREPT ABOVE the tree line, Sidney drove down the empty streets of Garnerville feeling the fatigue and deep chill from a long night in the woods. Downtown looked peaceful in the golden morning light. Many of the red brick buildings, built in the late 1800s, had been perfectly preserved, and it was easy to imagine life as it was back then—dusty streets bristling with commerce, wagons transporting goods, ranchers, lumbermen, and women in long dresses and bonnets patronizing small merchants. Many of the descendants of the original settlers now occupied the town's rolling green hills, leafy suburbs, and shoreline properties of Lake Kalapuya, named after the Native Americans who once inhabited the region.

Sidney slowed in front of the red brick storefront that had been her mother's shop for twenty years. Molly's Thrift and Gifts. Her father brought in a comfortable salary, while the store barely broke even, but her mother's core objective had been altruistic—providing low-income families with clean, functional merchandise at minimal cost. The Becker family benefitted as well from the constant stream of "lovingly used" items that found their way through their front door. The repurposing of commodities taught Sidney to respect the planet's limited resources and to be charitable to those less fortunate. After she and Selena moved their mother into the memory care center, her sister took over the space. The increasingly neglected, dusty, and cluttered thrift store morphed into Samara Yoga Studio—light, spacious, airy—and Selena prided herself on filling her classes mat-to-mat with students seeking a dose of mindfulness with a challenging yoga workout.

Sidney turned into the driveway and drove behind the studio. The family home, which she shared with her sister, stood hemmed in by flower and vegetable gardens, the colors now turning with the changing season. Heartwarming memories flickered through her mind; her dad flipping burgers on the grill, her mother knee-deep in flowerbeds, the endless parade of neighborhood kids who eventually traded roller skates and bikes for cars and plans for college. Most of those friends were now married with children of their own.

She pulled into her father's old parking spot, fondly picturing Chief Clarence Becker sitting behind the wheel of his Crown Victoria cruiser. He used to pull pieces of candy from his pockets for his two daughters when he arrived home. Sidney recalled the feel of his starched uniform against her cheek and his big warm hands holding her close.

She found the door to the house unlocked. Again. Sidney needed to warn Selena that lax habits had to change as more strangers moved into the area. She bolted the door, stowed her Glock 19 sidearm in a gun safe in the laundry room, climbed the stairs to her childhood bedroom, stripped off her uniform, and sank into a dead sleep within minutes.

~ ~

The alarm went off at 9:00 a.m. Sidney woke with a jolt and gasped, suffocating. One of Selena's four cats, an orange tabby, was draped across her throat, purring like a motor in neutral. "Off, Chili." As she lifted the limp ball of fur from her neck, the gruesome memories of Jane Doe came rushing back, and she remembered the task force meeting she'd scheduled for 10:00 a.m. Three-and-a-half hours of sleep would have to do. Rubbing the sleep out of her eyes, unable to stifle a jaw-cracking yawn, Sidney headed for the shower.

Fifteen minutes later, dressed in a clean uniform, hair damp around her shoulders, she headed downstairs. She followed the smell of coffee and something delicious baking, through the living room—decorated in her sister's bohemian style with bright reds and yellows, comfortable furniture, Tiffany-replica lamps, and a worn Oriental rug—to the dining room where two calico cats sprawled in a shaft of sunlight on the hardwood floor. The fourth cat, a gray angora, sat on a deep windowsill among pots of African violets, hypnotized by the sprinklers spraying water to and fro in the yard.

Selena stood cutting up veggies with a large chef's knife at the kitchen island. Sidney was struck by how different she and her twenty-eight-year-old sister were in appearance. While she had a muscular build, auburn hair, freckled skin, and hazel eyes like their father, Selena had inherited their mother's Scandinavian coloring—pencil-straight blonde hair, pale skin, celery green eyes fringed with dark lashes. A Mexican peasant blouse and long tapestry skirt hung gracefully on her slender figure. The only physical similarity between the two sisters was their lofty stature; six feet, give or take a half-inch.

"You're up." Selena's perfectly shaped eyebrows knitted together. "When did you get in?"

"At dawn." Sidney made her way to the coffee pot and filled a big ceramic mug to the brim.

"Not much sleep."

"Not even close."

"Sit. Let me get you breakfast." Selena set down the knife and pulled a bowl from the cabinet.

Happy to let someone take care of her, Sidney sat at the heavy oak table and watched Selena move around the sun-drenched kitchen. Copper pots hung over the stove, potted herbs crowded the windowsill, and Selena's state-of-the-art appliances—food processor, blender, espresso machine—reflected her passion for cooking.

"Here, this will revitalize you." Selena placed a bowl of chunky granola in front of Sidney and added cashew milk. She went back into the kitchen, and the blender sounded like a boat motor for half a minute, then Selena returned with the dreaded green smoothie. "*Voilà.*"

Sidney ignored the smoothie and poked dubiously through the granola. "What's in here besides oats and nuts?"

"Acai berries, ground hemp, flax, and chia seeds."

"Sure that's food?"

"It's energy food. Has a high vibrational level."

"Energy. Right. Good vibrations." Sidney flashed her a peace sign, chewed, and found the cereal surprisingly tasty. Everything Selena made was fresh, usually straight from her garden, with emphasis on health, if not always on flavor. Unlike her sister, Sidney never cultivated domestic skills. In school, she concentrated on sports, while Selena migrated to cooking and gardening with their mother. Eventually, her sister evolved into a natural foods guru, packaging organic products with Ann Howard in Ann's big barn. Her website, Selena's Kitchen, boasted myriad recipes, colorful photos and videos, and had thousands of subscribers.

"Try to eat healthy today," Selena said, leaning against the island. "You're stressed. You need live food."

"Will do." Sidney knew the drill. No additives, preservatives, or sugar. Nothing deep-fried. Groan. She kept up the façade at home, but unlike her sister, she excluded nothing from her diet, and she had a soft spot for pizza and greasy cheeseburgers. So what if she died a few years early? In the meantime, she would make full use of her taste buds.

Selena stood hugging herself, hands clutching elbows, muscles tightening around her jaw. "I talked to Ann this morning."

That got Sidney's attention. She gazed at her sister's troubled face.

"She told me everything. Some psycho dragging a woman through the woods. Chasing Ann into the marsh. She's a wreck." Selena swallowed. "Was a woman really murdered?"

Sidney expelled a breath. "Yes."

"Someone we know?"

"A Jane Doe." Sidney didn't have to tell Selena the information was confidential. With a police chief as father, discretion was imbedded in their DNA, along with an unquenchable passion for mystery solving. They grew up theorizing around the dinner table about crimes their dad was investigating, coming up with hair-brained conclusions, which made their parents laugh uproariously. Comparing notes with Dad after the fact made for some colorful conversations. Sidney fished her phone from a pocket and sorted through the crime scene photos until she found a head shot of the victim. "Recognize her?"

Grimacing, Selena studied the photo. "Don't think so."

"She's close to your age."

Selena shrugged. "What's with the bug eyes?"

"Glued open."

"Yech."

"He injected her with a neurotoxin that paralyzed her but didn't knock her out. She had no muscle control, couldn't even twitch an eyelid."

Selena shuddered. "He wanted her to see what he was doing. That's sick, and very, very creepy."

"Between you and me, Ann's lucky to be alive. This perp is sadistic and ruthless. It appears he also killed Mimi Matsui."

Selena's skin paled. "Yippie. A serial killer's moved to town."

"Or he's been here all along and knows how to blend in."

"All the better. Now I have to suspect every guy in town. The barista at Crazy Beans? The mailman?"

"Please be extra careful," Sidney added soberly. "Don't go anywhere alone, especially after dark. Lock the doors."

"You're scaring me."

"Good. My job is done." She drained her coffee.

Visibly shaken, Selena brought over the pot and poured Sidney another cup.

"Ann is going to need a lot of support, Selena. Matt's staying with her, but I think you should spend time with her, too."

"Already planned. This afternoon."

"Did her dog come home?"

"No."

"Too bad." Sidney felt a pang of sadness.

"We've called the shelters. Hopefully, if anyone finds him they'll call the number on the collar."

"No doubt."

"Do you think Ann's in danger? The psycho surely thinks she can recognize him."

"She believes she blinded him with her flashlight, and he didn't see her face. So he'll only know who she is if her name gets printed in the paper. That info won't be released."

Her sister's shoulders relaxed.

Sidney pushed her chair back from the table. "I better get going. My team's waiting."

"And I have to teach my yoga class."

"Hell of a commute."

"Yeah, I'll try not to trip over the sprinklers."

The timer went off.

"What's baking, anyway?"

"Rosemary cheddar cheese scones." Selena donned mitts, opened the oven, and pulled out a cookie sheet laden with scones browned to perfection. "I'm taking them to Ann. I'll save you a couple."

"You better." Sidney snuck behind her and emptied the

smoothie down the kitchen drain. Experience told her it would taste like pulverized lawn clippings.

In the laundry room, Sidney clipped on her duty belt and removed her sidearm from the safe. Her sister stood framed in the doorway, cradling the tabby in her arms like an infant. Sidney reflected on the closed door to the nursery, all the furnishings inside collecting dust. Selena's last miscarriage had crucified her. Being abandoned by her loser husband didn't help, either.

"Sidney…"

"Yeah?" She met her sister's light green eyes.

"I have something for you." Selena put down the cat, pulled a small pink crystal hanging from a silver chain over her head, and held it out on the flat of her palm. "Wear this. It will keep you safe."

Sidney believed her pistol and bulletproof vest would keep her safe. "That's your special necklace. You never take it off."

"You need it more than I do right now. Rose quartz has high energy, but its vibe is also calming and soothing."

Sidney humored her sister and pulled it over her neck, tucked it between her uniform collar, felt the warm stone against her skin. "Thanks."

"Be careful out there."

Sidney shot her what she hoped was a reassuring smile. "That's my motto."

CHAPTER FIVE

IN THE WARM MORNING LIGHT, the town looked awake and lively. Antique stores and gift shops displayed their wares on the sidewalks, the new art gallery had rainbow banners waving out front, and people sat enjoying coffee and pastries under the umbrellas of trendy coffee shops. It still surprised Sidney to see out-of-towners in brightly colored shorts and T-shirts strolling down the streets, but she was thankful tourist dollars were revitalizing the economy. The town was coming out of a decade-long downward spiral. Sidney applauded Mayor Burke for being a visionary and reinventing the town as a vacation destination. Garnerville offered an opportunity to experience living history in a perfectly preserved turn-of-the-century mill town. At least, that's what the brochure said. She wondered how the headline of murder would impact the jovial spirit of Garnerville when it appeared in the paper tomorrow.

Sidney drove six blocks down Main Street to the old Garnerville Bank building. Circa 1910, it featured the original red brick exterior and elegant Doric columns on each side of the brass-plated front door. The interior had been gutted and renovated in 1960 into a functional police department—three cells and four small offices, offshoots from the central lobby. She parked behind the station, grabbed her laptop, and stopped at the front desk to get her messages from Winnie Cheatum, administrator extraordinaire.

Buxom and middle-aged, Winnie was an exotic beauty and had a memory like a steel trap. She once confided to Sidney that when she was younger, she didn't know which box to check on applications under race. "My grandpa's black. My grandma's Japanese. They had my dad, who married my Mexican mom, and…" Her hand gestured down her curvaceous body. "This is what they got."

"You won the genetic lottery," Sidney had replied with a smile. "Women would kill to have your cheekbones and that figure."

Now Winnie smiled up at her from behind the computer screen. "Morning, Chief. Everyone's in the conference room. Fresh doughnuts and coffee. Your messages have been forwarded to your email. I have all your appointments on hold."

Sidney grinned. "If you were a man, Winnie, I'd marry you."

"You couldn't afford me." Winnie winked. Her face sobered and she cast Sidney a sympathetic glance. "Heard you had a rough night."

"Understatement. And it's just getting started."

"FYI. Jeff Norcross from the *Daily Buzz* has been over here hazing everyone. We've all been tight as clams."

"Jeff can smell blood a mile away."

"Yep. Part shark."

"Stay mum."

"You got it, Chief."

Sidney entered the conference room; barely large enough to accommodate an oak table with a seating capacity of eight if you didn't mind rubbing elbows. This morning, Granger, Darnell, and Amanda sat on one side with coffee and half eaten doughnuts, laptops open in front of them. Linthrope's forensic specialist, Stewart Wong, as solemn-faced as he was last night, sat at one end of the table with bottled water. He wore a white button-down shirt and black bowtie, hands neatly folded on a single manila folder.

Historical photos and portraits of past police chiefs lined the walls, and it was Sidney's habit to lock eyes with her father before seating herself at the head of the table. Chief Becker gazed down with an enigmatic smile, and she heard his voice in her head, sharing one of his many philosophical musings. *"Life's an infinite cycle of creation and destruction, Sidney. Bad guys replace bad guys, but a force of good will always stand up to evil."*

"And that's you," she replied.

He grinned, ruffling her hair.

"Morning," she said. "How's everyone holding up?"

Stewart sat mum, but her three officers greeted her pleasantly. Darnell looked like he'd slept in his uniform. Granger's face was red in spots from razor burn, and his hair looked like he'd hurriedly combed it with his fingers. Amanda's dark hair was pulled into an unruly ponytail. She usually wore light makeup but had skipped it entirely this morning. Though operating on minimal sleep, their alert eyes told her they were eager to get to work on the case.

"Let's get started," Sidney said. "Last night you all got a taste of homicide. Crime scenes aren't easy to look at, or process, and this one was especially gruesome. We put in long hours. Be prepared to put in a lot more." She turned to Stewart. "Do we have an ID on our Jane Doe?"

"Yes, ma'am." Eyes bloodshot behind his thick glasses, Stewart opened his file and passed out copies of his report.

Sidney followed along as he read.

"Fingerprints identified the deceased as Samantha Ferguson. Five-foot-five, twenty-three years old. Moved to Garnerville seven years ago with her parents. She had several drug-related priors. Opioid and heroin addiction. Her last job was waitressing at Hogan's. Quit to go to rehab. Got out two weeks ago. She rented a small apartment downtown." He looked up at Sidney and cleared his throat. "Her phone hasn't been located. No cell pings. It must be dead. Her car still hasn't been found. Don't know if she was abducted and transported to the crime scene, or if she knew her killer, met him somewhere, and voluntarily got into his car. County Sheriff put out a BOLO and his deputies are scanning the countryside for her white BMW 320i, year 2015."

"Nice wheels," Amanda said.

"Her family has money," Sidney said, reading the report. "Parents live in Maple Grove. Father's a retired surgeon." She turned back to Stewart. "I don't see anything on the suspect."

"Didn't get much. The plaster casts I made from his footprints identified his boots as Standard Timberland, size twelve. From the depth of the prints, we guess he's about one hundred-ninety pounds. Officer Cruz found a small piece of cloth torn from his hoodie. It's being analyzed. For now, that's it."

"Let's hope we get something from the autopsy," Sidney said.

"I enclosed a few Facebook photos of the victim with friends and one of her parents." Stewart closed his file and passed it down a row of hands to Sidney. "I need to go. Dr. Linthrope wants to start the autopsy."

"Thanks, Stewart. Get any sleep?"

He shook his head. "Nada. Part of the job." Without a smile, he slouched out of the room.

Sidney pulled Samantha's photos from the file. A few selfies depicted an exceptionally pretty woman with a contagious smile, laughing gray eyes, and an athletic figure. There were a few shots of her posing with friends, and one of her parents sitting in a golf cart in front of a posh country club. Sidney passed the photos around the table.

"Now I recognize her," Amanda said sadly. "She waited on me a bunch of times at Hogan's."

"I recognize her from Hogan's, too," Darnell said. "She went by the name Sammy. She always joked around with my kids."

"Of course. Sammy. She was very outgoing," Granger said.

"It's nice to remember her with a normal face."

"Got that right," Darnell said. "I've been haunted by her death mask."

"I'd never guess she was strung out on drugs," Amanda said. "She was always so upbeat. Joking around."

Sidney didn't have the benefit of memories. She never ate at the family-style restaurant. Too many screaming kids. But this beautiful young woman was known to her deputies. Their impressions added dimension to the victim's life and brought the woman out of the shadows of anonymity. "Samantha Ferguson. Twenty-three. Privileged background. Upbeat. Funny. Addicted. Trying to get clean," Sidney summarized, then turned to Granger. "Anything from the K9 unit?" Granger had been out in the woods with the county deputies and their dogs when she'd left for home.

"Not much. The killer's scent led to tire tracks on a dirt road a quarter mile from the crime scene. We also trailed him to the marsh where he chased Ann, and where he circled back to Samantha to finish… what he started. The sheriff's investigator ran the tire tracks through their system but found no unique features. They're a brand commonly used by many vehicles in the county."

"Dead end." Sidney poured a cup of coffee from the carafe on the sideboard, grabbed a glazed doughnut, and reseated herself. "Darnell, do you have the file on Mimi Matsui?"

"I do. I've been here all morning. Put a slide show together."

That surprised her. "You came straight here from the crime scene?"

"Yeah. Had to." His dark brown eyes shadowed with emotion. "This case is eating at me."

She shot him a sympathetic smile. The shock of murder close to home and the sudden, compulsive drive to get a killer off the street was something she understood well.

"No worries," he said. "I caught a little shut-eye in one of the cells."

No wonder Darnell looked like he slept in his uniform. He had. Two years on the force, the young rookie was a hardworking cop, absorbing everything, going the extra mile, and even working in the community coaching kids on his days off. "Let's see what you got."

Darnell dimmed the lights and pressed an arrow on his keyboard. All heads tuned to the screen on the opposite wall. "A warning, these photos are graphic."

The first image to fill the screen was Mimi's three-year-old crime scene, shot from a distance of about thirty feet. The next few images, shot from different angles, showed Mimi propped against the base of a massive tree in a heavily wooded area. The similarities to Samantha's crime scene chilled Sidney. Mimi's arms were at her side, slit wrists facing up, legs out-stretched, one ankle crossed over the other, barefoot. Wisps of fog hovered over the ground, and a recent storm left the trees dark and slick with rain. The victim's wet dress clung to her body like a second skin.

"As you can see, Mimi's head is drooped over her chest, and it's covered from view with a beanie."

The next shot showed Mimi's head held upright by Dr. Linthrope's gloved hands. Drops of rain beaded the fabric of the beanie.

"We see here that the killer pulled the beanie down over her face to her jaw line. In his report, Dr. Linthrope said he believed the suspect wanted Mimi's head protected, knowing it might be days before she was discovered."

Darnell clicked through the next few shots, and there were audible gasps from Amanda and Granger. The hat had been removed. Mimi's face looked gray and bloated, and she gazed back at them with a surprised, wide-eyed stare. Wisps of hair clung to her forehead and cheeks. Darnell went on to show slides of Mimi's lacerated wrists and some of the damage done by foraging animals.

"Christ," Granger said, the color draining from his face.

Even Sidney felt sickened. She had gone through the photos when she studied the case two years ago and knew what to expect, but seeing the gruesome details enlarged on the screen in vivid detail had a sharper impact. "We've seen enough, Darnell."

"Sure thing," Darnell said with a relieved sigh. "Just a couple more photos of Mimi as a real person."

A picture of a dark-haired woman with a fresh, natural beauty filled the screen. Mimi had expressive, intelligent brown eyes, a full mouth, a flawless complexion and an unfussy haircut. In the next shot, she was posed in the woods wearing hiking clothes. She had a slender, athletic figure.

"Read us the lab report, Darnell." Sidney needed to refresh her knowledge of the case as well as get her officers up to speed.

Darnell clicked off the projector, brightened the lights, and turned his gaze back to his laptop. "Confirmed cause of death was blood loss from lacerations to her wrists. The wounds were clean, made in one swipe by a thin, razor-sharp blade. Tox screen found no alcohol or drugs in her system besides a trace of a neurotoxin injected behind her left shoulder."

"What kind of neurotoxin?" Amanda asked.

He shrugged. "A blood sample was sent to the best research lab in D.C., but they couldn't identify it. Might be venom from a spider or reptile."

Darnell's eyes darted back and forth as he scanned his screen. "Mimi was forty-three, five-foot-four, one-hundred five pounds, Caucasian. No police record. She was active in her church and a couple charities."

"Was she sexually assaulted?" Amanda asked.

"No sign of forced penetration," Darnell said, his eyes returning to his screen. "Seminal fluid was not found in the vaginal canal but there was condom lubricant. When questioned, her husband said he had relations with his wife the morning of her disappearance."

"Where was she last seen?" Granger asked.

"St. Mary's Episcopal Church. She and a few other women stayed late preparing for a rummage sale the next morning. Mimi stayed behind to paint a couple of signs. The church was locked, and the keys were in her purse in her car, still parked in the church lot. No prints or trace evidence were found in the car other than by family members. Dozens of people at her church and around town were questioned. No suspect was singled out during the investigation."

"I remember two men were brought in for questioning," Sidney said. "But neither was held or arrested."

"Who were the two men?" Granger asked.

Darnell scanned his notes. "Derek Brent and Tom Sevinski. Both active in Mimi's church. Tom worked closely with Mimi on fundraisers. Derek played keyboards. Mimi was a soloist in the choir. They practiced together quite a bit."

"Let's give these two men another look," Sidney said, fingers busy on her keyboard.

"Any relatives have a beef with Mimi?" Granger asked.

"No motive surfaced. She had been married to Miko Matsui for six years. Aside from Miko, now fifty-years-old, she was survived by a daughter, Tracy, twenty-seven, who lives out of state, and her stepson, Noah, age thirty."

"Do they have any priors?" Amanda asked.

"Miko and Tracy are clean." Darnell scanned his notes. "Noah was busted for sales of narcotics. Released from prison two months ago. Served thirty-six months."

"What kind of narcotics?" Amanda asked.

"Prescription opioids and heroin."

"Same drugs as Samantha," Granger said. "Possible connection."

"Needs to be checked out," Sidney said. "We have to find a link between the two victims. Why were these two women targeted? What did they have in common? Hobbies, friends, church, gym. Right now, the only common denominator is they were both exceptionally attractive."

While fingers tapped keypads, Sidney refilled her coffee mug.

When heads bobbed up, she continued. "These were not random murders. They were carefully planned. This perp stalked these women, found the right time to abduct them, and acted. What's clear is that he wanted them to suffer. If they died instantly, it missed the point."

"Motive, Chief?" Granger asked.

"My take, this was punishment." She looked around the table, letting the gravity of her words sink in. "Revenge. Payback. This killer targeted these women to relieve a simmering hatred bottled up inside him. He expressed his hatred in a slow, methodical manner over a period of many hours."

The faces around the table looked grim, postures tense.

"This case takes priority over all else," Sidney said. "We're spread thin with a lot of ground to cover, so we need to work fast and smart. Keep the county deputies informed and let them help anyway they can."

Sidney shifted her weight in her chair, drained her coffee mug. "Amanda, head over to Samantha's apartment. Go through each room with a fine-tooth comb. Canvass her neighborhood. See if anyone saw visitors at her place since she's been out of rehab, any suspicious behavior. Darnell, secure Samantha's computer, get into her social media accounts, her phone records, credit card purchases. Look for any communication that might appear threatening. Hit up Samantha's coworkers at Hogan's." Sidney tapped her fingers on her armrest, thinking. "Let's put together a comprehensive profile of this woman—her activities and the people she associated with. See if we can map out a timeline."

All hands in the room were busy typing, then heads looked up one by one.

"Winnie needs to get a press release to the *Daily Buzz*," Sidney said.

"I'll fill her in, Chief," Amanda said.

"Great. Bare facts only."

"Got it."

"Granger, you and I need to notify the Ferguson's of their daughter's death."

He nodded, his jaw tightening almost imperceptibly.

She understood. They were about to deliver news to a family that would shatter their world and from which they would never recover. Sidney reflected on the many times she had been placed in this excruciating position back in Oakland. Worst part of the job. The messenger always walked away from the fallout riddled with shrapnel.

Sidney dismissed her officers. As they filed out, she felt a swell of pride. They were acting as a cohesive unit, handling the demands and long hours of their first homicide with enthusiasm, diligence, and no complaint.

Winnie buzzed her. "Don't come through the lobby. Jeff Norcross is out here, watching my every move."

"Thanks for the warning." To avoid the pesky reporter, Sidney and Granger exited out the back door.

CHAPTER SIX

"TAKE A LONG, DEEP BREATH. Hold it. Slowly release. Repeat."

Barefoot, Selena quietly wove her way between the bodies sitting in the Sukasana pose in her yoga studio. She lightly touched random students between the shoulder blades to remind them of their posture. All eyes were closed. Faces relaxed. Soothing music quieted their minds, and Selena's organic candles brought the fragrance of a flower garden into the room. Within these walls, a healthy challenge to the body and a sense of peaceful mindfulness could be found. That combination brought Selena a loyal clientele. Five classes a week filled to capacity.

She returned to the front of the room and ended the class with her usual parting. "Open your eyes. Smile. Go out into the world and have a beautiful day. Be kind to all you meet."

Twenty students got to their feet, some stretching, some rolling up their mats and heading out the door, some idling in the gift section by the cashier counter, a few crowding around Selena to ask questions about meditation and yoga. When the last curious student had departed, and only one browsing customer remained, Selena blew out the candles and turned off the music, hinting she wanted to close up shop. Thoughts of murder had crept back into her mind, and she was anxious to get to Ann's farm to comfort her traumatized friend.

She studied the man who lingered. Derek Brent. A student for three months, three times a week. Seemingly planted to the floor,

Derek lifted products one-by-one and leisurely read the labels and ingredients. He had always been friendly, and he made a point of talking to her for a few minutes after every class. From past conversations, she learned Derek had returned to Garnerville after a two-and-a-half-year absence. He had made a slow recovery in a sunny beach town after a devastating car accident nearly killed him. She vaguely remembered him from his prior life when the choir from the Episcopalian Church gave public performances in the park. He had been their pianist. Her eyes traced his profile—a tall, handsome man with thick, dark hair and a strong jaw.

He turned toward her, and she tried not to stare at the left half of his face, a maze of burn scars stretched tightly over the skull bones. She focused on the products he was juggling; two vanilla scented candles, a jar of lavender honey, pomegranate vinegar.

He placed them on the counter, and she met his one good eye, warm brown, arched by a fine, dark brow. The other was embedded in a tilted seam of skin, the white of the eye permanently red, the iris milky blue. Despite his physical imperfection, Derek exuded an aura of confidence, and she found it admirable that he never acted like a victim. His persona was charming and appealing, and over time, she found the disfigured half of his face had become easy to overlook. "How's it going, Derek?"

"No complaints."

He had a nice mouth and sexy smile.

"Excellent class, as usual," he said.

She smiled back. "You're improving. More limber." She rang up his purchases as she spoke. "Stronger, too."

"No wonder. That three-minute plank pose is a killer."

"You're holding it without a problem."

"You obviously haven't noticed my grimace."

"I took it for a smile."

"That's me, the happy yogi."

Derek always covered his body in baggy pants and long-sleeved shirts. She sometimes wondered how extensive his burns were. Visible scars traveled down the left side of his neck and the back of his left hand, up his wrist. The crash, he once told her, had left him mangled, burned, and in an induced coma for days. Suffering from a brain injury, broken collarbone, a broken arm and shattered ankle on the left side, and a series of painful skin grafts, he'd made an intensely painful but miraculous recovery.

She placed his purchases in a bag, took his money, and dropped his change into the palm of his scarred hand. When he hugged the bag to his chest, his sleeve rode up a bit, revealing a Daytona Rolex watch, made famous by Paul Newman, and crazy expensive. She smiled up at him. "Thank you."

He didn't leave. "Nice to come here and take my mind off the world's problems."

"Overwhelming sometimes."

"Too often." He swayed on the balls of his feet for a moment. "Look, I hope I'm not being too forward, but I notice you wear your wedding ring on your right hand."

Selena felt a little twist in her stomach. She smiled out of politeness. "My husband and I are taking a break."

"So, you're separated."

"Yes."

"Are you dating?" His good eye studied her face closely, as though looking for vulnerability, or a lie.

"No. Not dating." Her smile felt pasted on. She did not want to be having this conversation. Too sensitive. "I'm very much married. Randy and I are giving each other space while we work things out."

"I see." He smiled his sexy smile. The eye lost its laser stare, softened. "Well, I hope things work out for you."

"Thanks, Derek. I appreciate that."

"See you next week."

"Best place in town to be." She followed him to the door and locked it behind him, a faint residue of unease lingering. She hoped Derek would take the hint and not trespass into her personal life again. No doubt, he felt encouraged by her friendliness. Selena was gregarious by nature, but with Derek, she saw she needed to tone down the wattage a bit. She felt a piercing ache when she thought of her husband. Randy had been the one true love of her life since she was sixteen, and she wasn't close to being ready to give up on him. After ten years, their marriage was in limbo—a precarious balancing act that could sway either way with the slightest zephyr. Hopefully, back to terra firma.

She watched Derek climb into his silver Mercedes sedan, pull into the traffic lane, and head north on Main Street. He was a man of means. The luxury car put him back six figures, and at forty-two, he was retired and made no mention of going back to work. At another time, in a different world, she might be interested in Derek, but for now, the concept of romance with a stranger seemed as cold and remote as Siberia.

Selena turned out the lights and left through the side door. It opened onto the driveway that led back to the house. Turning to lock the door, she heard a sudden scuffing of feet. Pulse racing, she turned to face the tall man standing directly behind her, boxing her in against the door.

Christ. Jeff Norcross from the *Daily Buzz*. The gangly reporter was dressed in his normal uniform; khaki Dockers and a polo shirt, and a ball cap shading the top half of his face.

Selena huffed out a sigh of relief. "You should never creep up behind a woman in an alley, Jeff. You scared the holy hell out of me."

"Sorry." He pushed up his cap, revealing pale blue eyes behind wire rim glasses. He didn't look sorry. His features were sharpened with expectancy, and his eyes contained an eager gleam. Jeff had no doubt caught the scent of the murder and was going to try to shake her down. His phone was out, ready to tape their conversation.

"Just want to ask a few questions. Can you tell me anything about the murdered woman found in the woods? Do you know her name?"

"I don't know anything." Selena pushed against his shoulder, steered around him, and walked briskly up the driveway to the house.

"Your sister's police chief." He kept pace behind her shoulder. "She must have mentioned something."

"Nothing."

"How was she killed?"

She climbed the porch, opened the front door, and gazed back at him. He had followed to the bottom of the stairs. "Jeff, please go. I have nothing for you."

Selena stood watching him tuck his phone into his pocket, shoot her a frustrated smile, and walk hurriedly back down the driveway to Main Street. He turned the corner and disappeared.

CHAPTER SEVEN

WHILE Granger drove, Sidney pulled her hair into a ponytail and read Samantha's file thoroughly. When she finished, she turned her attention to Granger, wanting some personal conversation to get her mind off the case. "How's life at the ranch?"

"Busy." He glanced at her, his hands relaxed on the wheel, his blue eyes reading her mood. "Just harvested our last crop of hay for the season."

"You mentioned a while back you were selling off part of your land."

"We did. A third of the property, and half the livestock. With Dad's health declining, my brother and I are phasing him out of ranching. Conner's a forest ranger. I'm a cop. We have great pension plans. Neither of us want the ranching life anymore."

"Why's that?"

"Full-time job, Chief. Twenty-four seven. No vacations. You ever pull a calf out of a cow in freezing weather at three in the morning?"

"Not lately." She grinned. "Builds character, right?"

"If you say so." He smiled back.

The last time Sidney saw Granger's father, at the Fourth of July parade, he and his wife rode beautiful Palominos and were decked out in classy western wear and white Stetsons, reminding her of Roy Rogers and Dale Evans. A casual observer would never have guessed Jeb suffered from Parkinson's. "Your dad looked great at the parade."

Granger shrugged. "He has good days and bad."

"How's it feel to be living back at home after being a Marine?"

"Beats sleeping in a ditch. Food's better. I'm not getting shot at every day."

"Always a plus."

"I've got the bunkhouse, so I have my privacy."

Third-generation ranchers, the Wyatts were well liked and respected in town. Good people who held American values close to heart. The brothers grew up in 4-H, scouting, and rodeo, and when they came of age, they didn't hesitate to enlist in the Marines to fulfill their duty to country. Both were promptly sent to the Mideast. Conner to Iraq, Granger to Afghanistan. Now back home, they were helping their parents through a difficult transition. Granger never talked about the grim details of life in a combat zone and the buddies he'd lost—only the good memories, the camaraderie with fellow Marines. Sidney hired him because of his outstanding service record and leadership abilities.

They threaded their way into the hills through a forest blazing with color. Scarlet, gold, persimmon. Shoals of clouds swam through a sea of deep blue sky.

Granger parked on a leafy street in the town's most upscale neighborhood, Maple Grove. Sidney gazed across a long stretch of manicured lawn at the Ferguson's Victorian-style mansion, one of a dozen built at the turn of the century that overlooked the lake and valley. Giant maples shaded the house and a tennis court was visible behind the garage. While growing up, Sidney knew all the folks who lived up here, but over time, kids left home, and parents wanted to downsize. Wealthy families moved in from out of town, several using the estates as second homes.

A dull dread had been growing in Sidney's chest on the ride

over, and she sensed Granger's growing tension.

"How does a woman from a family like this end up on drugs, viciously murdered?" Granger asked, his eyes searching hers.

"Murder doesn't discriminate," she said quietly, quoting a dictum her father often used.

"When I was in Afghanistan, my job was fueled by anger at atrocities by terrorists, but always in another country. When a killing happens right in my own backyard…" His voice drifted into silence.

"It's more personal," Sidney finished for him.

He nodded.

"Ready?"

"Never ready."

They got out of the car and started up the paving stone walkway.

CHAPTER EIGHT

AFTER TUGGING a dozen red tomatoes and two plump eggplants from their vines, Ann snipped sprigs of basil, oregano, and thyme for the pasta sauce she would make for Selena. Everything in her garden was fragrant and thriving. Butterflies, hummingbirds, and bees darted in and out of flowers, feasting on pollen and nectar. On a good day, there was something infinitely soothing about pulling weeds, deadheading wasted blossoms, and feeling the sun warm on her back. On a good day, the pain and suffering she had endured during her fifteen-year marriage could be pushed to the back of her consciousness, a dull throbbing ache, localized behind the modest screen she showed to the world.

But the nightmarish episode in the woods last night split open an old wound. Memories of her husband's abuse resurfaced like sharp glass slicing her skin. Every small sound—a shovel falling over, the branches of trees clicking together in the wind, made her flinch and look up, as though her drunken husband towered over her, ready to strike.

A low buzz of anxiety hummed along her spine. She missed Bailey. Normally the hound shadowed her every move and slept on the other side of her bed at night. His absence felt like a part of her had been torn away.

She parked her basket on the porch and crossed the clearing to the old gabled barn. An amber glow filled the interior of the cavernous structure and dust motes swirled in shafts of light. Ann climbed the creaking wooden stairs to the loft. Over the past seven years, the barn had been converted into a factory of sorts. From the loft, she could view the whole operation; the laboratory kitchen where she and Selena experimented with recipes, the four-gallon stainless steel vats used to melt beeswax for candles, the distillery equipment that reduced hundreds of pounds of flowers into oils, and in the back, rows of herbs and flowers suspended on drying racks. A bouquet of fragrances lifted into the air and combined with the sweet, musty smell of old wood.

To make the loft homey, she and Selena had moved in a rust-colored sofa, which provided a place to curl up and read or nap. The sofa faced two overstuffed chairs dragged home from a garage sale and redressed in chenille slipcovers. One wall, lined with shelves, displayed beautifully packaged natural products labeled "From Selena's Kitchen"—scented candles, potpourris, huckleberry vinegar, lavender honey.

Ann's desk was strewn with orders that needed to be processed. Selena's desk looked the same. Lots to do, if she could only focus. This was where she normally felt safe, but today she felt like she would never be safe again.

Ann bypassed her desk, crossed to a window, and stood gazing at her neighbor's farm, three times larger than her own. Miko's tidy orchards and corrugated fields stretched down to the shoreline, with tall pines and maples blurring the border between their properties.

If not for this vantage point, Ann would never see a sign of life from her neighbor. She often distracted herself by watching Miko, like some enthralled bird enthusiast observing the habits of an exotic species. Ann knew his seasonal routines—plowing the fields in the spring, tending his vegetable fields in the summer, picking fruit from his orchard with a handful of migrant workers in the fall. In the winter, he hibernated, and if she was lucky, she caught a glimpse of him trudging through the snow to the shed for firewood. Though she had never seen him up close or exchanged a word, she felt an affinity for Miko—a man who had lived in solitude since the brutal death of his wife, who worked doggedly over the land as Ann did, grinding out a respectable living.

Ann picked up her field glasses, scoured his property, and found him chopping wood outside a sun-bleached shed. The muscles in his back bunched up when he lifted the ax, and his forearms rippled when he swung it down and sliced through the wood. A wide-brimmed hat shaded his face. Since she lacked the ability to coordinate facial features, it made no difference whether Miko was handsome or homely. Faces were irrelevant.

When he put down the ax and started organizing the split wood into a pile against the shed, Ann realized the man wasn't Miko. Her neighbor had a distinctive gait with a slight limp to his right leg. This man was wider in the shoulders, narrower in the hips. With a sharp intake of breath, she realized the man was Noah, Miko's son, whom she hadn't seen in three years. The last few months before he went to prison, she recalled with distaste, Noah had become a disturbing presence in her life.

He'd started stopping by her stand at the market when she was alone, and spoke to her in an arrogant, flirtatious manner. His tattoo-covered body and muscular build were easy to recognize. She always responded to him coldly, and eventually, he'd leave, uttering a crude remark. Once he stole into her stand from the back entrance and quietly stood behind her. When she backed into him, he wrapped his arms around her, held her tight, and murmured, "You feel good."

She'd roughly pulled away. "Please go!"

He lingered long enough to say, "Just trying to help." He nodded toward her parked truck. He had unloaded a few crates of vegetables while she was engaged with customers.

"I don't need your help."

Ann shivered, remembering his unwanted touch. And now he was back.

She pulled her eyes away from Noah and gazed across the countryside. Mirrored in the lake were billowy white clouds and the brilliant reds and yellows of the forest. A flicker of movement at the edge of the woods caught her attention. A lone figure stood in the shadows and then disappeared. A man. She felt a sudden thud in her stomach. The walls of the barn shrunk inward for a moment and then swelled back out.

Was she hallucinating? Or had she seen someone?

Downstairs, the barn door opened. Ann went rigid.

"Ann, are you up there?"

Selena. Ann sighed her relief. "Yes. I'm coming down." She had been so intent on Noah, and the male form she thought she saw, she missed Selena driving up to her house. Her friend stood silhouetted in the open doorway against the bright afternoon light.

Selena pulled her into a warm hug and Ann allowed herself to be comforted.

"How are you?" Selena asked, pulling away.

"Not good," Ann said. "I'm worried sick about Bailey."

"Me, too." A pause. "I didn't see Matt's truck."

"I told him to go to work."

"You've been here alone?" Selena sounded alarmed.

"I don't need a babysitter. And he can't afford to lose a day's work." Ann linked arms with her young friend and guided her in the direction of the house. "Let's eat. I'm making you a special lunch. Italian."

"It better be marinara sauce over angel hair, with grilled eggplant."

Ann smiled.

"Yum. Suddenly I'm starving." Selena grinned. "I'll throw a salad together."

CHAPTER NINE

SIDNEY'S STOMACH TWISTED as she and Granger climbed the stairs to the front porch of the Ferguson home. She pressed the doorbell and braced herself when she heard footsteps on the other side of the door. It swung open, and Samantha's parents stood facing them.

Dressed in golf clothes, the couple looked as though they had just stepped off the course or were about to leave for one. Jack's eyes widened when he saw their uniforms. A big man with broad shoulders, he appeared to be in his late fifties, with a gray, close-cropped beard and fashionable tortoiseshell glasses. Terry was petite and looked a decade younger than her husband. A tan visor shaded her hazel eyes, and reading glasses hung suspended from a gold chain around her neck.

After exchanging introductions, Sidney cleared her throat and said, "I'm afraid I have some bad news about your daughter. Maybe we could sit down with you for a minute?"

Jack's face tightened and he made a sweeping gesture with his arm. "Please, come in."

"Thank you." She and Granger stepped into the spacious foyer and the four stood awkwardly staring at one another. The Fergusons glanced at each other and frowned, then ushered them into a sunlit living room decorated with elegant Victorian antiques. A lot of velvet upholstery, ornate furniture, polished hardwood. For a moment, Sidney felt as though she'd stepped back in time.

Jack and Terry sat stiffly together on the damask couch as though bracing themselves for bad news. Sidney and Granger seated themselves across from them in matching wingback chairs.

"Christ, don't tell me," Jack said sternly. "Samantha's using again."

Gathering her thoughts, Sidney glanced out the large window that provided a sweeping view of well-tended gardens, the tennis court, a swimming pool and the vibrant colors of the forest. She found the easiest way to convey bad news was to get straight to the point. "I'm sorry to tell you that your daughter was found dead last night."

Jack and Terry recoiled as though hit by bullets. Terry covered her heart with a hand and gasped.

Jack found his voice first, and asked, "Did she OD?"

Sidney cleared her throat. "I'm afraid she was murdered. She was found in the woods on the west shore of the lake around midnight."

"You're sure it's Samantha?" Jack asked.

"Yes. The fingerprints match."

He drew in a sharp breath and closed his eyes for a moment. One of his large hands moved down to his knee, which had begun to tremble. Terry bowed her head, and a curtain of blonde hair fell over the right side of her face. She pressed a fist to her mouth and sobbed almost soundlessly, her shoulders shuddering.

Sidney sat frozen, her eyes darting away from the raw anguish that threatened her own composure, then drifting back.

"Do you know who did it?" Jack's voice, almost a whisper, sounded inordinately private.

"Not at this time," she replied. "But we're focusing all our efforts on finding her assailant."

"Please tell me she didn't suffer," Terry said, voice tremulous, face streaked with tears.

"We're still putting the facts together, Mrs. Ferguson. We've arranged for the M.E. to do a full examination."

Jack pulled a handkerchief from a back pocket and gave it to his wife.

Terry dabbed her eyes, blew her nose, but the tears kept streaming. "When can we see her?"

"I'll call as soon as that information is available. Late afternoon, I imagine. We're so sorry for your loss." Sidney paused. "I know this is difficult, but we need to ask you a few questions that could help us find who did this. Would you like us to come back at another time?"

Jack exchanged a glance with his wife. She nodded.

"If it will help, we'll do it now," he said.

Terry wiped tears from her flushed face and sat straighter on the couch. She looked like a smaller, older person than she had minutes ago.

"Do you know anyone who would want to harm your daughter?"

Jack exhaled deeply, his eyes vacant with shock. "Samantha didn't confide in us much. She lived a private life. Other than old family friends, we don't know who she associated with."

"Can you give me a list of those friends?"

Granger pulled out a notepad and pen from his breast pocket.

Jack stammered a few names.

She heard Granger scribbling. "Do you know if your daughter was seeing anyone?"

"No one we approved of." His voice croaked. He looked away for a long moment and then continued in a husky voice. "Someone named Jason Welsh. A druggie. I think they broke it off before she went to rehab."

"Does the name Matt Howard mean anything to you?"

Jack shrugged, shook his head.

"I remember Sammy speaking of Matt." Terry wiped tears away with trembling fingers. "They went out a few times."

"Do you remember the time period when they dated?" Sidney asked.

"Back in April or May. Didn't last long."

"Why is that?"

"Probably because he didn't party, like her other friends, or use drugs."

"So, she broke it off?"

"Yes."

"How did he take it?"

"Not well. Sammy told me he kept calling. Showed up at her apartment. She threatened to call the police."

"What about Noah Matsui?"

Terry blinked and the muscles in her thin neck tightened. "He's the one who got her into drugs. He went to prison." There was a spark of anger in her now, as though she were fighting to keep control of herself. "I heard he's out. I prayed he'd stay away from Sammy."

Sidney met Granger's gaze for a moment. He raised a brow. Matt and Noah just moved to the top of her suspicious persons list. "Was Samantha staying out of trouble?"

"Yes. She got out of rehab two weeks ago. She was a new person. Optimistic. Hopeful. She enrolled in school and was going to start next month. She wanted to be a teacher."

Sidney glanced at her hands to disconnect from the profound loss and anguish in Terry's eyes.

Jack reached over and covered his wife's hand with his own.

Granger kept his eyes on his notepad.

"How did Samantha pay her bills? Waitressing at Hogan's?"

"Yes. She made enough to get by. We refused to help until she went to rehab. Then we paid all her expenses," Jack said. "As long as she stayed in school, we were going to continue."

"Samantha had been in rehab several times. Was this time different?"

"Yes. They approach addiction differently. Like a disease. Not a crime. A lot of therapy, a lot of structure. It wasn't in-and-out treatment like before. There's a satellite clinic here. She's…" He paused to correct himself. A frown tugged the corners of his mouth. "She had been going to sessions five times a week."

"Sounds like she was very committed."

Jack nodded.

"Did Samantha have a relationship with Mimi Matsui?"

"Noah's mother?" Terry looked puzzled. "I don't know. We're not church goers, but Sammy and I went to concerts at the Episcopal church on occasion. She had a lovely voice. Poor woman. Murdered, like my baby." Her face contorted with grief and she covered it with both hands.

Time to go. Sidney rose from her chair.

Granger shoved his pen and notepad back into his pocket and stood to leave. Sidney took a moment to scan a row of gilt-framed photos on the mantle above the fireplace; a chronicle of Samantha's life from infant to lovely young woman, and the gradual aging of her parents. The smiling faces and affectionate poses portrayed a warm, happy home life. A sanitized version of a family afflicted with the heartache of a drug-addicted child.

Sidney and Granger repeated their condolences and left, a cloud of gloom hanging over their heads. Driving away, she noticed a white SUV parked on the road that had not been there when they arrived. She spotted Jeff sitting in the driver's seat gazing intently at his phone, pretending he didn't know they were there. The reporter was relentless. There was no heavy crime presence in Garnerville. Jeff normally covered social events, obits, and petty crime. He was taking this opportunity for investigative reporting seriously. Murder sold papers. She hoped he had the decency not to invade the privacy of Samantha's grieving parents.

CHAPTER TEN

SELENA AND ANN busied themselves in the kitchen. Ann sautéed chopped tomatoes with garlic, onions, and fresh herbs, while angel hair pasta bubbled in a pot. Selena tossed baby spinach, Swiss chard, green olives, and crumbled feta cheese in a bowl with balsamic vinegar and olive oil. They swapped small talk about recipes, customers, and the paperwork that needed to be processed in the office. On the surface, life took on a semblance of normalcy.

"I need wine. My nerves are shot," Ann said, studying the wine in the cooler cabinet. She pulled out a bottle of Merlot.

"Pour me a glass, too," Selena said.

Ann uncorked the wine, filled two long-stemmed glasses, and passed one to Selena. By the time the pasta was finished, she was on her second glass. They carried their dishes out to the patio and sat at a wrought iron table in the shade of the eaves.

Cumulous clouds drifted across the blue sky, and sailboats glided on the surface of Lake Kalapuya, white sails billowing in the wind. The air smelled of damp earth. The lapping of water on the lakeshore sounded like a lullaby. Peaceful. But on the inside, Ann felt as if wild birds were clawing at her chest, trying to escape.

"Delicious pasta," Selena said, eating with gusto, soaking up sauce with the rosemary-cheddar scones she'd brought.

"Thank you." Ann pushed her food around her plate with her

fork.

"Try to eat a little," Selena said, her sensitive face puckering with concern.

Ann took a bite and chewed, but the pasta stuck in her throat like dry stones. She washed it down with a sip of wine. "Your sister's good at her job. I saw her in action last night. She seemed fearless. I sat cowering in the car while she tramped off into the woods like a Marine, armed with a shotgun."

"She can be a badass, for sure, just like Dad. I wish he'd lived to see her become police chief. He would've been so proud. They had a lot in common. Love for the law, helping people."

Ann watched her friend eat the last bite of scone. "You worry about her?"

"Not as much as when she was in Oakland." She bit her bottom lip. "Until last night."

"Did she tell you what happened?"

"Yes, but I can't talk about an ongoing investigation."

"I saw the coroner's van. I know that woman was murdered."

"Yes. She's dead."

"That could have been me, too." Ann shuddered and sipped more wine. For a long moment, they sat in silence listening to chimes tinkle in the light breeze. The trees moved gently, incessantly whispering. Life felt surreal.

Selena pushed her plate away and sat back in her chair. "I'm glad Sidney's on the job. If anyone can find this killer, she can. She closed a large percent of her murder cases in Oakland."

"Really?"

"Yes, really." Selena leveled her clear green eyes on Ann. "It took a toll on her, though. She gets compulsive. Can't leave a case alone until the rat's in the cage. I think she was on the verge of a breakdown when she moved back home." Selena shook her head. "Witnessed too much death. Too many crime scenes."

Ann felt a little lightheaded. "We need to take care of her.

Make sure she eats healthy."

"I've tried to get her to come to yoga, but she only laughs. She says people shouldn't do some of those poses without a chiropractor on the scene."

"I agree." Half-smile. "How're you doing? Have you heard from Randy?" Ann knew Selena's rodeo bum husband had moved back to town two months ago and was working as a baker at Katie's Cafe. The two had been separated for a year, but neither seemed to have the will to pull the cord and bail completely out of the marriage. Selena rarely brought him up in conversation. The corners of her mouth lifted slightly, but Ann sensed it was a sad smile.

"I've seen him once. He came over to pack up some of his belongings. He rents the guesthouse at Katie's farm, which is halfway to Jackson. So whatever he needs, he gets over there. He works nights. I purposely stay clear of Katie's Café."

"Why are you avoiding each other?"

"Trying to dodge the bullet, I guess." She stared into her wine as though reluctant to speak, then she met Ann's gaze. "He called last night. He wants to talk. Guess I can't avoid it any longer."

"Talk about what?"

Selena shrugged a slender shoulder. "Maybe he wants to patch things up. Move back in."

Ann felt a sharp stab of concern. Selena had a blind spot where Randy McBride was concerned. Ann wanted to tell her friend not to get her hopes up. Her ex was a loser and would always be a loser. Just weeks after her second miscarriage, he up and left her. Selena was crushed. But in Ann's estimation, it was a blessing. Once out from under his rigid control, Selena opened to life like a rose in full bloom. She became financially independent, learned to trust her instincts, and even relearned how to laugh. "You sure that's a good idea?"

"I miss him." Selena stared gloomily into her glass, and the parallel lines between her brows deepened. She lifted her eyes to Ann's. "Or maybe I just miss having a man in my life."

"He can't go back to rodeo," Ann stated firmly. "He's thirty years old. Nursing chronic injuries. Can't believe he lasted as long as he did."

Selena nodded. "Don't I know it. He's broken about every bone there is. Men weren't built to be thrown off bulls, year after year. I kept telling him to train for another job, but would he listen? No. Too darn stubborn."

"Has he given you any money since he's been back?"

Selena shook her head. "He says he's in debt. I'm paying the bills."

Ann resisted the urge to roll her eyes. "You know I'll back whatever decision you make about Randy. Just promise me you'll think about it long and hard."

"I will. Thank you." Tears welled in Selena's eyes. "You've been such a good friend. I want to be a good friend to you, too." She swallowed. "I'm going to spend nights here for a while. You shouldn't be alone right now."

Ann felt a warm rush of gratitude. It was true. She desperately needed company, and she couldn't ask Matt. Her son labored hard from dawn until dusk and was exhausted at night. "I'd love it if you stayed."

"Sidney's not the only one who can be a badass. Dad taught us both to handle guns. I'm a pretty good shot. I have my .38 pistol in the car."

"I don't like guns, Selena, but right now I'd feel safer if I was armed, too."

"I'll bring you my twenty-two. It's small. You can attach the holster to your belt. Wear it all day while you work. We could set up some cans in the pasture and practice."

"That'd be great."

They were interrupted by the loud flutter of wings and a big shadow passed over the table. With a graceful hover and descent, Arthur the raven landed on the back of Ann's chair, his ebony feathers glossy in the sunlight, arriving right on time for his midday snack.

"Hello, Arthur," Ann cooed.

"Hello," Arthur repeated, imitating Ann's diction perfectly.

The magnificent raven had been a daily visitor for four years. At first, he watched her from the trees, then the bushes, then he advanced to the porch railings, enticed by the variety of treats she set out for him. Often, he trailed her in the garden, bouncing over the grass, hopping from perch to perch, making little cawing sounds in conversation. One day she was startled when he repeated her greeting. Ever since, Ann chatted with him regularly, putting special emphasis on a handful of words, repeating them over and over, building his vocabulary.

Arthur gestured with his beak toward the box of Cheerios she kept on the table. "Treat."

"Treat. Yes, Arthur. Good boy. Coming right up." With a chuckle, Ann grabbed a handful of Cheerios and lined them across the end of the table. The raven cawed softly, jumped from the back of Ann's chair to the table, and crunched the treats one by one. When finished, he bounded back to the rail, watching them closely, eyes as shiny as onyx beads.

"The wisdom of a sage," Selena said.

Arthur cocked his head. "Evermore."

Selena laughed, clapping her hands.

"Evermore," Arthur repeated.

"You clever, clever bird!" She turned to Ann. "How many words can he say now?"

"About a dozen."

"Did he bring you a gift today?"

"Didn't look. He usually leaves them on the birdbath."

They shielded their eyes and peered across the garden.

Something brightly colored sat on the lip of the birdbath.

"Is it a flower?" Selena asked.

"Arthur's never brought me a flower before."

As though on cue, the raven burst from the rail, flying fast with deep strokes of his powerful wings. He circled the birdbath, then in one elegant swoop, snatched the shiny object in his beak, returned, and dropped it at the side of Ann's plate.

"It's an origami butterfly," Ann said with a touch of wonder. Picking it up by the tip of one wing, she admired its delicate construction. Twice the size of an actual Monarch, the paper had a pattern of scarlet flowers on a bright yellow background. "This is amazing. The folds are so intricate, so precise."

"Whoever made it is an origami master," Selena said, leaning in, awe in her voice. "Where on Earth did Arthur find it?"

"I don't know, but he's outdone himself today."

In reply, Arthur cawed, "Evermore."

"Here's your reward." Ann laid out more Cheerios. While Arthur crunched, she turned the butterfly over and frowned at a thick, reddish-brown spot on one wing. "This looks like blood." She glanced at Selena.

"Oh dear. You're right."

"Seems far-fetched, but could it be from the crime scene?"

Selena's eyes narrowed. "The paper's unsoiled. If that's blood, it's fairly fresh. Put it in a baggie. We'll give it to Sidney. She can have it analyzed."

Ann jerked up her chin at sudden distant barking. "Do you hear that?" She froze, listening intently.

The barking grew louder.

Her breath caught when Bailey bounded around the corner of the house, limping and panting heavily, his big pink tongue lolling out of one side of his mouth.

"Bailey!" Ann stood so suddenly her chair fell over backward.

The dog charged into her arms with enough force to knock her on her rump, whimpering, body wriggling, tail wagging ferociously, oversized tongue frantically mopping her face. Ann's tears streamed down her cheeks and mixed with Bailey's drool.

Selena knelt beside them, and the three had an ecstatic reunion, Bailey delivering sloppy kisses to both. When the hound finally calmed down, Ann ran her hands over his body, looking for injuries. "Where have you been, my poor boy?" She sucked in a sharp breath when her fingers traced a sizable lump on the dog's head, above the right ear. "He was hit. Hard. Must have knocked him out. That's why he stopped barking."

"There's blood on your shirt." Selena gasped. "From his paws."

The front of Ann's t-shirt was stamped with bloody paw prints. All four of Bailey's paws were cracked and bleeding. "He looks like he ran a marathon."

"Poor Bailey. Where have you been?" Selena stroked his head.

Ann rose to her feet. "I'm going to treat these wounds."

"We need to get him to the vet. Have some tests run. Who knows what he's been through."

"You're right... the vet," Ann stammered. "I'm not thinking straight."

"I'll drive. Where's his collar?"

Ann frowned. "He had it on last night."

Realization widened their eyes. The psycho in the woods must have kept Bailey's collar.

"Is your phone number on it?"

"Yes," Ann said with a stab of fear.

"Sidney needs to know. Let's get to the vet. I'll call her from the car."

"I'll grab my handbag." Ann made a quick tour through the house, put the butterfly in a baggie, grabbed her handbag, and locked the door.

CHAPTER ELEVEN

SIDNEY AND GRANGER STEPPED from the sharp midday heat into the cool lobby of the small community hospital. A few patients sat reading magazines in the cramped waiting room. Sidney caught a whiff of disinfectant drifting in from the two sterile hallways. Nested inside the building were three doctor's offices, an ER ward that was often empty, and half a dozen patient rooms. Anyone needing trauma care was rushed by helicopter to a hospital in Salem. Thanks to Dr. Linthrope's tireless quest for grant money, there was a well-equipped morgue and forensic lab in the basement.

Sidney greeted Alice Friedman, the stocky, brown-haired administrator who kept the doctors' schedules running smoothly. Dressed in green scrubs, she stepped out from behind her counter. "Hi, Chief. Dr. Linthrope is expecting you. Right this way." After crossing the polished linoleum in the hallway, she ushered them into a small break room reserved for medical staff. "He'll be with you shortly." Smiling, she closed the door behind them.

The white walls, flat gray cabinets, and faded linoleum floor had a bland, institutional look. A sideboard held the standard offerings—coffee, tea, bottles of water. A vending machine promoted chocolate bars, chips and pretzels, and a small refrigerator purred quietly in one corner. Sidney and Granger seated themselves in plastic chairs at the gray laminate table, and

Granger opened his laptop.

Sidney's phone buzzed, and she slid her finger across the screen. "I only have a second, Selena."

Her sister rushed her words. "Couple things. Bailey came home."

"Great. Is he okay?"

"His feet are bloody. Looks like he traveled a long distance. We're on the way to the vet."

"Tell the vet to get a sample of Bailey's DNA to Dr. Linthrope ASAP."

"Will do." A pause. "The killer kept his collar. Ann's phone number is on it. Can he get her address from her phone number?"

Hearing the strain in her sister's voice, Sidney kept her voice calm. "Yes. She doesn't need to answer if she doesn't recognize the caller. Tell her to stay alert. Keep doors and windows locked."

The door swung open, and Dr. Linthrope entered the room hugging a few manila folders to his chest.

"Gotta go. Call me when you're done with the vet." Sidney clicked off.

The doctor wore a white lab coat over a blue shirt and gray slacks. His hair was an electrified white halo circling his scalp, his intelligent gray eyes were clear and bright. One would never guess he spent the morning cutting apart a corpse.

"Good afternoon," he said pleasantly. "Coffee?"

"None for me, thanks," Granger said.

"No, thanks, Doc," Sidney said. "I've had four cups this morning." What she and Granger really needed was lunch. Coffee swishing around in her empty stomach made her nerves jittery. "I'll take water, though."

Linthrope handed out plastic water bottles, poured himself coffee, and carried the Styrofoam cup to the table. He arranged the files in a neat stack, sipped his coffee, and peered up at his visitors. "Let's start by reviewing the autopsy report."

He opened his top folder, passed out photocopies, and continued with a distinctive edge of authority to his voice. "As we surmised last night, Samantha's death is indeed a homicide. She died from massive blood loss due to severed radial arteries on both wrists. Other than minor lacerations to her feet, sustained from being dragged barefoot, there was no other trauma to her body. Old needle tracks were found on both arms, but no evidence of recent drug or alcohol use."

"She was staying clean," Granger said.

"Yes."

"What about the neurotoxin? Is it the same as Mimi's?" Sidney twisted off the bottle top and took a swig of water.

"Don't know yet. I've sent blood, urine, and liver tissue to the lab for testing. Some material always leaks around the injection site, so I also sent a sample of the tissue surrounding the needle mark. Let's hope they can identify it this time." The doctor sipped his coffee and continued. "There were traces of soil on her clothes that don't belong to the crime scene. A very specific, nutrient rich soil."

"Something a professional landscaper or a farmer might use?" Sidney asked, immediately thinking of Matt Howard and Noah Matsui.

He nodded. "Most definitely used by pros." Linthrope pushed his glasses higher on his nose and light from the window briefly caught the lenses. "The small piece of fabric Officer Cruz found probably came from the killer's sweatshirt. Ann said he was wearing a hoodie. It has no human trace on it, but it does have DNA from dog saliva."

"Bailey must have grabbed it with his teeth," Granger said.

"Most likely."

"The vet will get you Bailey's DNA sample today."

"Perfect."

"Any sign of sexual assault, Doc?" she asked.

"Can't say for certain. No bruising or tears on the skin. I found seminal fluid, a trace of condom lubricant, and a single pubic hair belonging to a male. Samples were sent to the lab. She may have had consensual sex before her abduction. But if the killer did assault her, and he left his signature, let's hope his DNA is in our database."

Sidney sharply exhaled. "Hallelujah. That would break the case." She turned back to the autopsy report. "Partially digested ham and eggs were in her intestines. Does that give you the time of her last meal?"

"Eight to twelve hours before her death. Noon, or early afternoon."

Sidney paused, reflecting. "There was no mention of rape in Mimi's report."

"Again, we don't know for sure. I found a trace of condom lubricant in Mimi, too. Her husband told us they had intercourse the morning of her disappearance. They routinely used condoms, but different brands, so we couldn't trace the lubricant specifically to him." Dr. Linthrope paused for a moment, his bushy brows lowering. "I don't believe sexual assault is this perp's primary motivation. There would be more evidence of physical contact."

"Revenge?" Granger asked. "Like you suggested before, Chief?"

Sidney tapped the water bottle with her fingertip, thinking.

Granger watched her, waiting.

"I believe our killer was reacting to a real or perceived threat by these women, which prompted a devious urge to punish them."

"Certainly, a need to assert control over a helpless victim," the doctor said.

"Right. No immediate, passionate response would serve his purpose. He needed to draw out their suffering over many hours."

"Payback for the suffering he endured at their hands," the doctor said.

"He had her all afternoon and evening?" Granger asked.

"That's what the evidence suggests."

Granger's eyes sparked with anger. "Where did he keep her? What did he do to her?"

Dr. Linthrope peered at Granger over his file, his face flickering for an instant with unaccustomed emotion. "Whatever he did, she was conscious, helpless, and terrified."

"We need to nail this bastard." The vehemence in Granger's voice matched Sidney's feelings exactly. "He can't do this to another woman."

The three fell silent. Sidney's gut knotted, and she saw from the doctor's tight expression, he, too, felt anxious. A sadistic killer lurked in their town, and until he was caught, no woman was safe.

"Where's the link between Mimi and Samantha?" Sidney asked calmly and firmly, a technique she used to distance herself from gruesome images and an attempt to cool the temperature in the room. "They had different lifestyles, different habits. One was very involved in her church. The other in the drug scene. One was twenty-two, one forty-three. They don't fit a pattern."

"I agree," Linthrope said. "No similarity outside their appearance. Both quite pretty."

"He may have been attracted to them," Granger suggested. "And rejected."

"Very possible. To some men, rejection is the worst offense," Linthrope said. "But a psychopath is more apt to act on feelings of abandonment and betrayal."

Sidney put down the report. "Were there any personal effects, Doc, at either crime scene, besides clothing?"

"None from Samantha." Linthrope's eyes widened momentarily. "Wait… there were a couple items found on Mimi." He pulled out his bottom file, opened it, and thumbed through a dozen photos. "Ah yes. Here we are." He handed over two eight-by-ten glossies. One showed a silver earring with an amethyst stone. The other picture surprised her. An intricately folded origami butterfly, brightly colored. Somewhat wilted and faded on one side.

"That earring was still in her ear," Linthrope said. "The other was missing. The butterfly was tucked into her panties. My guess, the killer planted it there."

"An origami butterfly." Sidney rubbed her chin, trying to make sense of it. She passed the photos to Granger. "He wanted us to find it. Why? What does it symbolize?"

Linthrope handed her a photo of the butterfly unfolded into an eight-by-eight-inch sheet of paper. "There was handwriting inside, but as you can see, it got too washed out from the rain to read."

"There's a little symbol on it. Six lines."

"A hexagram. Two lines broken. Four straight."

"Maybe a watermark."

"We had the paper analyzed, but couldn't identify its source," the doctor said.

"Too bad about the writing," Granger said, frowning. "It could have given us some insight to his motive."

Linthrope nodded. "I believe so."

Sidney handed back the photos. "Doc, you said you'd share information about the death of Ann Howard's husband. You said Ann and Matt killed John in self-defense. What did the autopsy reveal?"

Linthrope stared off into the distance as though gazing back in time. "I remember being interrupted at dinner by a call from your predecessor, Chief McDonald. He told me to come out to Ann's farm right away. There was a body. When I arrived on the scene, I found John lying face down in the garden. A ghastly sight." Linthrope breathed in heavily through his nose. "Head completely bashed in."

Sidney shivered. "What led to his death?"

The doctor's eyes met hers. "According to Ann's testimony,

John showed up at her house stinking drunk. She was working in the garden. Didn't hear him. He came up from behind and attacked her, quite viciously. He locked his hands around her throat while ranting about killing her and Matt. Matt came up behind him and whacked him with a shovel. The force of the blow drove him to his knees. Reportedly, Ann then grabbed the shovel and administered several more blows, any of which could have killed him."

The hair rose on Sidney's arms. "Reportedly?"

Linthrope opened a folder and passed over photos of John lying in the garden, his scull bashed to a bloody pulp. Sidney was startled by the brutality.

The doctor ran a tanned, freckled hand through his hair. "I'm not sure Ann could have done that. Maybe incapacitate him, but pulverize his skull? Savage."

"You think she covered for Matt?"

He shrugged. "Hard to fathom where that kind of rage comes from. But if anything could trigger a son's fury, this is it." He passed out photos of the injuries Ann sustained from John's attack—one eye swollen shut, nose bloodied, bottom lip split open, purple and red bruises on her arms and torso, fingers imprinted on her throat.

"Jesus," Granger breathed.

Sidney was sickened, and speechless. It took a moment to calm herself.

"John's alcohol level was off the chart," Linthrope continued. "Those photos confirm she'd been brutally attacked. Matt saved her life. Self-defense. Plain and simple." He narrowed his eyes. "He was fifteen at the time. A miracle he came home when he did. He'd been at a sports event, but he left early. Wasn't feeling well." He paused. "Another few seconds…"

"She would have been a murder victim," Granger said.

Linthrope nodded. "Indeed."

"John had quite a police record," Sidney said. "DUIs. Drunk

and disorderly. Routinely picked fights in bars."

"The man was a violent brute. He used Ann as a punching bag for fifteen years." Bitterness entered Linthrope's tone, and Sidney picked up on the underlying sadness.

"We discovered she had racked up quite a list of ER injuries over the years, but she covered for John. Said they were accidents."

"Classic battered-wife syndrome," Granger said, shaking his head.

"Correct. Her self-esteem and will to fight back were beaten into submission. Obedience became her survival mechanism. After years of punishment, women like Ann suffer from a profound sense of helplessness. It was only when John turned on Matt, knocked him unconscious, that she was spurred to action. Her instinct to protect her son superseded her fear, and she had John arrested. While he was in jail, she filed a restraining order, bought the house on the lake, and tried to rebuild her life."

"A restraining order is pretty useless if someone is determined to kill you," Granger said.

"True. A court order isn't armor. John was barely out of jail before he tried to make good on his promise." Linthrope took off his glasses, rubbed his eyes, and looked drained of energy. "Both Ann and Matt, of course, were traumatized. No doubt, still are. These things stay with you. Layered in the psyche. Ready to surface with any small provocation." He shook his head. "Poor woman. What she's been through…"

The sunlight on Dr. Linthrope's face showed the fine lines of anxiety around his eyes and mouth, and the deeper marks of pain. This case was intensely personal to him, and to Sidney.

"Samantha's parents came to view the body," the doctor said, returning to the current investigation. "I didn't give them specific details."

"Appreciate that." She took a long, cool drink of water.

"I'll contact you as soon as I have the lab reports."

"When will that be?"

He squinted. "Let's see, today's Thursday. Probably Monday."

"Thank you for your time, Doc."

"And yours."

They rose from their chairs and filed out of the room.

Outside the hospital, Sidney felt the full brunt of the midday heat. Indian summer. Hot days were always scattered among the cooling temperatures this time of year. She slid carefully into the passenger seat of the SUV, which had been sitting in full sun, and felt the hot vinyl through her uniform. "Get that air going, Granger."

"Yes, ma'am." Granger put on his shades, started the engine, and pulled away from the curb with hot air blasting from the vents. "Where to? Burger Shack?"

"Sounds good."

"Noah and Matt are looking good as suspects," he said. "Both use commercial gardening soil."

"Right. Noah sold Samantha drugs, and Matt dated her. And he wasn't happy about the breakup."

"Sounds like he may have stalked her."

"And Linthrope believes he killed his father."

"Viciously."

She shivered, recalling the graphic images. "We need to get DNA swabs from both men. See if either had sex with Samantha before she died."

Driving down Main Street, Granger pulled to a stop at the only traffic light in town. Tourists dressed in summer clothes milled on the sidewalks. Parents pushed strollers. Kids carried ice cream cones. Folks strolled in and out of shops. Life was proceeding as usual. Innocent. Complacent. Unaware of the dark side of life cops witnessed every day. Through the storefront window of the Art Studio, which had been Moyer's Tack and Feed for fifty years,

Sidney saw a circle of students standing in front of easels facing the instructor. Art classes! It astonished her how fast the town was changing. No longer ardently blue collar with farmers and ranchers the bulk of the population. Pots of flowers brightened sidewalks, storefront windows displayed appealing merchandise, and trendy cafes had replaced shoddy greasy spoons.

The air conditioning finally blasted cold air, evaporating the sweat from her skin. She directed her thoughts back to the case. "What's Noah's last known address?"

"He's staying with his dad."

"Which puts him smack in the vicinity of the murder."

"What about Miko as a suspect? There are rumors he killed his wife."

"Chief McDonald rejected Miko as a suspect. Lie detector ruled him out." Sidney brought up Noah Matsui's police report on her laptop and read the details out loud to Granger until she was interrupted by the hum of her phone. Selena. "You back at Ann's? How's Bailey? Good. Good." A pause. "Okay. See you soon." She disconnected and said, "Turn around. We're going to Ann's."

"What happened to Burger Shack?" he said with a tinge of disappointment.

"Ann and Selena invited us to lunch. Want a greasy burger, or home cooking by a truly amazing chef?"

"Door number two. I'm starving. Can I put on the lights and siren and take this baby up to ninety?"

Sidney was glad to hear a smile enter his voice. "Starvation is a legitimate emergency. Cut 'er loose."

CHAPTER TWELVE

SIDNEY AND GRANGER rapped on the door and stood waiting on Ann's covered porch. The dark, ominous character of the previous night had dissipated with the sunshine, and today the farm looked like paradise. The air was fragrant with roses, she could hear the drone of bees, and butterflies fluttered over colorful blossoms. Sun glimmered on the surface of the lake, and clear blue sky arched overhead.

"Hard to believe anything ugly could happen here," Granger said, shaking his head. "That a man would come here to kill his family."

"Evil lurks beneath the thinnest of veils," Sidney said, quoting one of her father's often-used phrases.

The door opened and Selena stood in the doorway, still dressed in yoga clothes, her lissome figure shown to its best advantage. "Yay. You're here." Her gaze shifted to Granger, and Sidney saw her green eyes brighten with interest.

Granger's neon blues widened minutely, and a smile tugged at his lips.

"Selena, this is Officer Granger Wyatt. Granger, my sister, Selena."

The two clasped hands and peered into each other's eyes for a long moment.

Sidney cleared her throat.

Selena pulled her hand away. "Come on out to the patio.

Lunch is waiting. We already ate, but we saved you some." She led the way through the house.

Granger's gaze swept over her sister's tall figure from top to bottom, which Sidney admitted was pretty spectacular. Sidney was happy to see sparks fly between the two. Her sister had been held hostage to Randy McBride's capricious nature since she was sixteen and they were high school sweethearts.

Married at eighteen, Selena never batted an eye at another man, though it was rumored her rodeo bum husband philandered while he was on the road. Randy drank too much, gambled away paychecks, and offered no support when Selena started her business. But he was drop-dead gorgeous, could charm the venom out of a rattler, and had convinced an intelligent woman like Selena that she'd won the lottery when she married him.

Sidney never gave up hope that Selena would see though Randy's pretty veneer and dump him. As it turned out, the bastard left her after she lost their second baby, just when she needed him most. Thinking about Randy made Sidney's stomach churn.

Her mouth watered when she spotted lunch spread across the wrought iron tabletop. Pasta tossed with tomatoes and fresh herbs, crisp green salad, grilled eggplant, and a plate of rosemary cheddar cheese scones. A perspiring glass pitcher of ice tea reminded Sidney of how hot and thirsty she was.

She and Granger did a double take when they greeted Ann. A giant raven was perched on the back of her chair. Ann offered a treat on her palm, and the glossy black bird scooped it up in its beak, then in a showy flutter of wings, the bird took flight across the garden and disappeared into the gnarled branches of a giant oak.

Sidney turned her gaze to Bailey, sprawling on the flagstones at Ann's feet, snoring loudly, all four paws bandaged.

"He's dead to the world. Pain pills," Ann said.

"What happened to his paws?"

"Not sure. The vet thinks he was dropped off far away from home and had to trot back, ten to twenty miles. He also got whacked on the skull."

"Holy smoke," Granger said.

"Thank God our psycho didn't kill him," Selena mused, placing plates and silverware on the table.

"Yeah, it could've been worse," Ann said, stroking the dog's big sable head, avoiding the lump.

"How are you doing?" Sidney asked.

Ann looked tired, with purple shadows beneath her eyes, and an unmistakable tension in her posture. "Better, now that Bailey's home. Please, officers, sit and eat."

Sidney happily complied. Her stomach somersaulted from the aroma wafting over the table.

Granger needed no further prompting. He loaded his plate and was stuffing his mouth before Sidney even got started. Selena filled Sidney's glass, and she drank thirstily.

"Tea?" Selena asked sweetly, holding the pitcher over Granger's glass.

He nodded, smiling up at her.

"I've seen you patrolling around town," Selena said. "You look vaguely familiar."

"I grew up here, but I was in Afghanistan for four years."

"Ahhh. Welcome home, soldier. So, you went to Garnerville High."

"Class of 2006."

"I was the class of 2007. We were in school together. We never actually met, though."

"I was involved in ranching stuff—4-H, animal husbandry."

"I wasn't." She laughed. "I'll have to get out the yearbook."

Granger was certainly a handsome man, Sidney acknowledged, with his short tousled hair and wind burned cheeks, and he kept in great shape mending fences and lugging hay bales.

Selena always had a weakness for cowboys, and Granger was the real deal. Sidney found herself hoping their mutual attraction would grab hold and stick.

Sidney twirled pasta around her fork and ate without speaking. Everyone was quiet for a minute, the sound of silverware clicking against plates.

"We found something that may be from the crime scene," Selena said, breaking the silence.

Sidney's antennae shot straight up. "What's that?"

"I'll get it." Ann left the table and returned holding the baggie. Sidney felt her heartbeat pick up as she examined the butterfly. She passed it to Granger. "Look at this."

His jaw tensed and he looked back up at Sidney. "Holy heck."

"Looks like a drop of blood," Sidney said.

Ann and Selena watched with rapt attention.

"Where'd you get this?" Sidney asked.

"Arthur brought it. Around midday." Ann peered toward the gnarled oak tree.

"The raven?" Sidney asked.

"He brings me gifts."

"You keep them?"

"Yes."

"I'd like to see what else he's brought."

"I'll get my collection." Ann left, promptly returned, set a fishing tackle box on the table, and opened it.

Sidney poked through two layers of small compartments containing an assortment of brightly colored pieces of paper, polished stones, beads, and buttons. She did a quick inhale when she found a match to the amethyst earring belonging to Mimi, which she held out to Granger on the palm of her hand. His eyes widened, and his amazement mirrored her own. The fastidious raven seemed to have picked up items from both crime scenes. How did her team miss this butterfly last night? Where did Author find it? If only the raven could talk! Was that Samantha's blood? "Can I borrow a couple things in this box, Ann? I'd like to have them analyzed."

"Of course."

Sidney took out her phone and snapped pictures of the butterfly before turning back to Ann. "I understand the perp kept Bailey's collar."

She nodded.

"If you get a threatening call, let us know. We might be able to trace it back to the caller."

Sidney saw fear pass over Ann's face, and she said in a firm voice. "This man is interested in you because he believes you can recognize him."

Ann breathed in and out, carefully. "I can't."

"I know. Matt told me last night. But the man you saw doesn't know that. The news of this murder will be in the morning paper. We could add that you couldn't recognize him because of your facial blindness."

She stiffened. "No. I don't want the whole town to know."

"Ann, it's a good solution. Otherwise, you're vulnerable. I can't protect you. We don't have the manpower to post someone twenty-four-seven here at your farm."

Ann's mouth tightened, and her eyes flashed. "I can take care of myself."

Sidney looked to her sister for help.

"Listen to Sidney, Ann," Selena said, placing a hand on her friend's arm. "Your life may be in danger."

"No." Ann crossed her arms, lips a tight seam on her pale face.

"When will Matt be here?" Sidney asked.

"He won't."

"He told me he'd be staying with you."

"That's not necessary. He needs to work."

"I'm staying nights with her," Selena said. "We'll both be

armed."

Sidney felt her stress level rise a notch, and turned back to Ann. "Have you ever shot a gun?"

"No. But Selena will give me lessons."

"This isn't a *Kill Bill* movie, Ann," Sidney said with an edge. "This is real life. A sadistic killer is loose in your neighborhood."

"No."

Sidney stared hard at Ann, but the woman averted her eyes. She had a stubborn streak as wide as Lake Kalapuya. There was nothing more Sidney could do to persuade her.

"I can stop by every night on my way home and check things out," Granger volunteered, a loaded fork in one hand and a scone in the other. "Our ranch is just a few miles up the highway."

A smile reshaped Selena's beautiful mouth. "That'd be great. We'll feed you."

The two locked eyes and Sidney watched color creep up from Granger's neck into his cheeks. Selena's eyes were shining— sparks of attraction shooting off in the midst of a life-threatening crisis.

The table was quiet as Sidney scraped the last bite of pasta off her plate and chewed. Signaling to Granger with a nod toward the door, she stood to go. "Thanks for the great lunch. We need to go talk to your neighbors."

Granger gulped down his tea, grabbed a scone for the road, and shot Selena a flirtatious smile. "Thanks for lunch."

"See you tonight." She beamed.

CHAPTER THIRTEEN

GRANGER DROVE a few hundred yards north on the highway and turned onto Miko's gravel driveway, and the rich smell of turned earth and manure flowed through the open windows. Sidney spotted a two-story clapboard farmhouse with a big shaded porch, rolling green fields, apple orchards, a sun-bleached barn, and a few utility sheds. Everything tidy and well maintained. Two curious dogs, both gray-muzzled mutts, loped up to the Yukon, tails furiously wagging.

Miko Matsui stepped out of the barn into the sunlight wiping his hands on a rag. He frowned when he saw their police vehicle, but he gestured for them to park next to the barn. He went back inside, limping slightly.

When Sidney and Granger entered the barn from the bright autumn sun, the darkened interior blinded her for a moment. She blinked as her eyes adjusted, then her gaze swept over several big pieces of farm machinery, neatly stacked bales of hay, and a gaggle of Silkie hens pecking the earth and clucking indignantly at their arrival. Miko was leaning under the hood of a big farm truck, only his khaki dungarees and work boots visible, and she heard metal clinking against metal. She smelled the sweet scent of apples before she saw the dozens of boxes stacked on the flatbed, ready for market.

Miko backed out from under the hood, wiped his hands, then lowered the hood with a sharp clang. He turned to face them, scowling. A handsome man about five-foot-eight, of Japanese descent, Miko looked every bit his fifty years. His face and neck were deeply creased, his hands sunburned and calloused, his short hair surprisingly white. His eyes were so dark she could barely delineate the pupil from the iris.

Sidney introduced herself and Granger, but Miko made no move to shake hands. He stood silently waiting.

"I'm sorry to have to deliver some disturbing news," she said.

His eyes narrowed minutely.

"Last night a woman was discovered in the woods just up the road from here. She was murdered."

Miko's face remained expressionless, but Sidney caught a slight twitch at the corner of his eyes.

"And you're here to accuse me?"

"We're not accusing anyone. We're conducting our investigation, which means we want to talk to people who live in the area. See if anyone noticed anything suspicious."

"When was she murdered?"

"Around 11:30 p.m."

His shoulders slouched, and for a moment he looked like he might faint.

"You better sit down, Mr. Matsui." Granger took his arm and guided him to a wooden bench. Miko's body slumped onto it. "Would you like some water?"

He shook his head.

"Are you all right?"

"No, I'm not all right. That's the same time my wife was killed, three years ago." He made a faint gesture towards the woods. "Back in there." He gazed up at Sidney, his dark eyes searching hers. The pain in that look took her breath away. "Was this woman murdered the same way as Mimi?"

"I'm sorry, Mr. Matsui. I can't comment on an on-going investigation."

"Who found her so late?"

"Your neighbor. Ann was walking her dog. Bailey ran off into the woods and she went after him. A terrifying experience. Are you two friendly?"

"I've never met her. She keeps to herself. And since Mimi was killed, I do the same. People in town look at me like I'm a murderer." His voice thickened for a moment, but then he regained control. "I don't sell at the farmers market anymore. All my produce goes out of town."

"I'm sorry to hear that." She meant it. Indiscriminate judgment of people angered her. "I'm sorry to ask, Mr. Matsui, but where were you last night at eleven-thirty?"

"I'm a farmer. Work starts at dawn. I'm dead asleep by eight."

Sidney took out her iPhone and brought up a picture of Samantha. "Do you know this woman?"

He pulled wire-rimmed glasses from his breast pocket, set them on his nose, and studied the picture. "No," he said sadly. "No one should die this young."

They shared a moment of respectful silence.

She brought up the photo of the origami butterfly. "Does this mean anything to you?"

A muscle twitched along his jaw. "No. What is it?"

"Nothing important." Certain he was hiding something Sidney pocketed the phone.

Granger had whipped out his notebook and was scribbling notes. She turned back to Miko. "We're going to give Mimi's case a fresh look. Mind if I ask a few questions?"

"Not if it helps find her killer."

"Did you attend her church?"

"No. I'm a Buddhist. But I went to her concerts."

"I understand two men from her congregation were brought in for questioning during the investigation."

He nodded. "Derek Brent and Tom Sevinski. I can't see either of them as her killer, though."

"Why is that?"

"Tom and Mimi didn't like each other, and everybody knew it. They were on the fundraising committee, and they disagreed on everything. He was a control freak. They got into a yelling match a couple of times. But Tom's old and frail. Has a heart condition. Can't imagine him… doing that to Mimi."

"What about Derek?"

Miko made a face. "He's a piece of work."

"How so?"

"Arrogant. Stuck on himself. He played piano for the choir. Mimi was asked to do a couple solo pieces for the Harvest Concert, and he practiced with her a few nights a week, alone at the church. One night after practice, she came home upset. I asked her what was wrong. She wouldn't tell me." Miko's face tightened. "Something happened between them. I never found out what. But they did the concert together. She was killed a few weeks later."

Silence.

"Turns out, he had an alibi," Miko continued. "Said he was visiting his sister's family. They live in Maple Grove. They vouched for him." Miko gave Sidney a piercing look. "Even without an alibi, it couldn't have been him."

"Why is that?"

"If you think the same man killed both women, it wasn't Derek. He was in a bad car wreck a few weeks after Mimi died. He was mangled. Burned. Last I heard, he was in a wheel chair with no hope of fully recovering. He left town to go to some nursing home. So, he couldn't have killed the woman last night."

Sidney reflected on the two men. Neither sounded like a strong suspect, but both names would stay on the list. "Where was the nursing home?"

Miko shrugged. "Beats me."

"What's his sister's name?"

He thought for a long moment. "Becky... something."

Granger stopped scribbling. "Is your son around? We'd like to talk to him."

"He's at the store." Miko cast Granger a suspicious look.

"Just routine questions."

The sound of tires crunching on gravel came up the driveway and stopped outside the barn. A car door opened and shut, the sound of heavy boots approached, and the silhouette of a muscular man appeared at the door.

"Dad, you okay?"

"Yeah. These officers want to ask you a few questions."

"We'll talk to him outside, Mr. Matsui. Stay put for a few minutes."

Outside, face-to-face, Sidney sized up Noah, committing the details to the memory bank she'd trained herself to develop. He had Miko's dark skin and eyes, full lips, stood about six-feet tall and had shoulder-length black hair. He wore faded jeans, a denim shirt, and thick-soled work boots. Tattoos ran from his hands up his forearms, disappeared under his rolled-up shirtsleeves, and reappeared on his neck. His muscular build boasted of a significant amount of time devoted to weightlifting. He stood next to an old, white Ram pickup, his legs spread apart, hands folded in front, eyes hard, jaw tense. A stance meant to intimidate.

"I'm Police Chief Becker, Noah, and this is Officer Wyatt. Mind if we ask you a few questions?"

"Shoot."

Sidney showed Noah the picture of Samantha. "You know this girl?"

"Never seen her before."

Noah arranged his face into a jailhouse smirk, one she had encountered countless times on felons in Oakland. "That's interesting, since Samantha testified against you in court three years ago. You're the charmer who got her hooked on pain pills, introduced her to heroin, and supplied her habit."

Tightening his lips, Noah's gaze bore into Sidney with such ferocity she felt it like a beam of heat.

"Couldn't have made you too happy that her testimony put you behind bars," Granger said, with a steel edge in his tone. "While she got a light sentence."

Noah smiled, but it was a dark smile.

"Witnesses say you threatened her," Sidney said. "Told her she'd pay for being a snitch."

"That's old history. I did my time. Paid my debt. What're you harassing me for?"

"You been in touch with Samantha since you've been out?" Granger asked.

"Now why would I do that? It's a parole violation to associate with known felons. If she said I did, she's a lying bitch." He pulled a pack of Camels from his pocket, tucked a smoke between his lips, lit it with a Bic lighter. His cheeks hollowed as he sucked in smoke, then he exhaled long tendrils through his nostrils.

"Samantha was killed last night," Sidney said. "Her body was found in the woods behind your property."

Aside from Noah's eyes narrowing, he showed little expression. "Killing woods. Took my stepmom. I stay outta there." He took another drag and blew it out, squinting one eye. "I can't say I'm surprised Sammy's dead. She crossed a lotta lines. Ratted people out." He paused a beat. "Someone was gonna get her sooner or later. But it wasn't me."

Granger's eyes went hard, and he delivered a burning glare. "Where were you last night around 11:30?"

"In town, drinking at Barney's."

"You got a witness?"

"Yeah. The waitress. Tracy."

"Tracy got a last name?" Sidney asked.

He shrugged, said nothing.

Sidney brought up the picture of the origami butterfly and held it out to him. This mean anything to you?"

"Jack shit."

She watched his cold expression closely, looking for a sign of recognition, but got nothing. "Just one last thing. Mind if we swab you for DNA?"

"Yeah, I mind."

"We'd like to rule you out as a suspect."

"Get a warrant." He spat on the ground, grabbed a bag from inside the truck and walked off toward the house. The dogs followed, wagging their tails.

Miko stood in the barn entrance, watching, showing no emotion.

~ ~

Sidney and Granger climbed into the Yukon and sat in the driveway.

"You think Noah's capable of killing his stepmom?" Granger asked.

"He seems hard enough to do just about anything."

"I agree. There's something way off about that dude."

"Look up Derek Brent and Tom Sevinski," Sidney said. "See if either has a record. See if there's an address for Derek."

Granger got busy on the computer. A few minutes later he said, "Both men are clean. No forwarding address for Derek.

She pulled out onto the highway and spotted a white SUV parked on the shoulder. "Jeff Norcross is tailing us," she said.

"He's like a rash."

She pulled alongside the reporter and asked politely. "What are you doing out here, Jeff?"

"My job."

"You'll be briefed about the homicide as we gather facts. I don't want to see any speculation in the paper."

"You trying to squash my first amendment right, Chief?" He

smiled but his tone was deadly serious.

"Little dramatic, don't you think?"

"A woman's been murdered. That's pretty dramatic."

"Let's not scare the holy hell out of the public, Jeff. Stick to the facts, which will be released to you in a daily briefing."

"My job is to snoop. Just like yours. If I uncover facts you don't, I'm willing to share."

An invitation for her to do the same. No way. Use diplomacy. "If you discover anything that helps my investigation, contact me immediately. Please don't make a mad dash to print it. We want to catch a murderer, not forewarn him so he can cover his tracks."

Jeff saluted, face drawn.

Sidney rolled up her window and pulled into the traffic lane.

"What an ass," Granger said. "He thinks he's on a path to a Pulitzer. How did he know we had a murder before we released the briefing this morning?"

"He uses a scanner, I'm sure. Listens in to our radio comm."

"That legal?"

"They now have apps that turn your phone into a scanner. Hard to prove. Hard to stop."

She glanced at him. "Use discretion."

"Righto, gov'nor," he said with a Cockney accent. "Me lips is sealed."

CHAPTER FOURTEEN

IT WAS PULLING toward three in the afternoon. Long day. Sidney rolled her taut shoulders back and forth as she drove. She needed to hit the gym, work the kinks out of her muscles. On the way back to town, she tried calling Matt Howard but got no answer. After leaving a voicemail, she called the station and Winnie updated her on messages.

"You got eleven in all, Chief. None time-sensitive. Four from your mother."

No surprise there. Though Sidney repeatedly told her mom not to call the station, Molly dialed 9-1-1 up to ten times a day. Emergency Response transferred her over to Winnie. Winnie dealt with Molly patiently, explaining that Sidney was out keeping the peace. "Did it sound like an emergency?" Sidney asked.

"Nope. She needs toilet paper and batteries for her clock."

"Duly noted."

"Jeff Norcross from the *Daily Buzz* called twice," Winnie continued. "He wants additional info on the murder. What should I tell him?"

"I just talked to him. He's been tailing me. No info available at this time. I'll update him tomorrow."

"Aye, aye, Chief."

"Pull everyone in for a meeting at the station at five. Order a few large pizzas from Sal's. Veggie, meat combo, pepperoni, and Hawaiian. Grab a few slices yourself."

"Will do. You didn't like those anchovies last time."

"Thanks for the memories." Sidney wrinkled her nose, remembering the indigestion that kept her up half the night. After disconnecting, she discovered Granger was dozing next to her, his head rolling against the headrest with the movement of the car. She took pity on him, knowing when he got home tonight he'd still have ranch chores waiting. On top of that, he'd committed to stopping in at Ann's every evening. Sidney listened to the soft drone of his snores until they reached the outskirts of downtown.

"One last interview, Granger."

His head snapped to attention. "What, Chief?"

She chuckled. "Sorry to interrupt your beauty sleep, but we have one last interview. Tracy, at Barney's. After that, we have a task force meeting at the station, then I'll release you crime slaves for the night."

"Tracy, right." He adjusted his shades and wiped a touch of drool from his mouth.

Sidney pulled into the lot at Barney's Bar and Grill, the town's tourist hotspot and epicenter for petty crime—drunken brawls, small time drug deals, the occasional addict needing to be scraped off the floor and carted to the ER. The lot was full, and a dozen Harleys were lined up in front, reflecting sunlight off polished chrome like sparklers.

Sidney and Granger crossed the deep, recessed porch and stood in the entryway scoping out the interior. Uninspired architecture. A cavernous box with tables scattered across a scarred, wood plank floor in front of a bandstand. Garlic, onions, and grilled meat seasoned the air. The place was doing a brisk business, every table full. Adorned in expensive leather vests and chaps, gray-haired bikers loitered at the bar, their toothpaste smiles and smooth complexions belying their badass appearance. Probably vacationing businessmen trying to recapture their youth.

Slipping into memories of her early twenties, Sidney recalled taking breaks from work in Oakland, returning home, and celebrating here with old friends—bodies writhing on the dance floor to ear-splitting rock bands with sweaty men who reeked of beer. Most of those friends were married now and had the good sense to avoid Barney's.

A hostess rushed up to Sidney carrying plastic coated menus. Early-twenties, busty, dressed in Levi cutoffs and a tight T-shirt that provided a wandering eye a place to focus.

"Hi, I'm Cindy. Two?" She smiled, plum lipstick smeared on her front teeth.

"We're not staying," Sidney said. "Just want to talk to Tracy for a minute."

Cindy cast her gaze around the cave and pointed. "That's her over there."

They weaved around a dozen tables to reach Tracy, who stood at the back of the restaurant facing the smoky kitchen. She wore the standard Barney's uniform—chopped off Levi's and sprayed-on t-shirt. She was medium height with a shapely figure and a long, dark ponytail that brushed her shoulder blades. She turned, carrying a steaming plate of food in each hand.

Sidney and Granger waited until she delivered the meals to two patrons before intercepting her. "Tracy?"

"Yeah?" Tracy's smile faded as her gaze swept over their uniforms. She was mid-twenties, with skillfully applied makeup that enhanced her pretty features. Tracy bore a resemblance to someone whose face teased the corners of Sidney's mind but wouldn't materialize.

"We need to ask you a few questions."

Tracy scanned the room, taking in the heads that turned to watch them. She faked a big smile, flashing perfect teeth. "I'll take my break in five minutes and meet you out back. Please go."

"Sure. Just one thing. What's your last name, Tracy?"

"Matsui."

Granger and Sidney shared a quick look as they walked out of the bar. No wonder Tracy looked familiar. She was Mimi's daughter, and she was the spitting image of her mother.

"Mimi's police report said Tracy lived out of town at the time of the murder," she said. "I'll run a background check." They climbed into the Yukon and Sidney got to work on the laptop. "Tracy comes up squeaky clean. Moved back to town after her mother died. Wonder how she feels about her stepbrother coming home."

"She's going to cover for him," Granger said tersely.

"Count on it," she agreed dryly. "When you've been a cop as long as I have, Granger, you assume everyone you question is lying to you all the time, about everything."

"Even Miko?"

"To protect his son, you bet. He knew something about the origami butterfly but pretended ignorance."

Granger gave her an admiring glance. "You're an ace at noticing things."

"Comes with practice."

Granger's face was brooding, thoughtful, his mouth turned down at the corners. "How do you stay so calm when you're dealing with stone-faced liars, and possibly a sadistic murderer?"

"The same way you took care of wounded soldiers in combat situations. Autopilot. You flip a switch. Build a callus."

"It doesn't always work. You should see my dreams."

"Mine too. A real horror show." She saw a smile twitching at the corner of his mouth. Suddenly, they were both laughing, and she gave him a playful cuff on the arm. "Come on. Let's see what Tracy has to say."

When they reached the narrow alleyway behind Barney's, they found the waitress nervously pacing the oil-stained asphalt, sucking on a cigarette as though trying to draw courage from it. Flies buzzed around an overflowing dumpster that reeked of stale grease and rotting food.

"I only have a minute," Tracy said, blowing out smoke and setting an immediate protective boundary.

Sidney got straight to the point. "Can you confirm your stepbrother's whereabouts last night?"

"Yeah, he was here. He got here around ten and stayed right up until midnight." The words came without hesitation and sounded rehearsed. She swallowed and nervously flicked her cigarette ash.

"You know Samantha Ferguson?"

"Everyone knows Sammy. Knew Sammy," she corrected herself. "This used to be her stomping ground before she went to rehab."

"How'd you know she was dead? Noah tell you in the last half hour?"

Blood rushed to Tracy's face as she realized her mistake. She dropped her cigarette and crushed it with the toe of her shoe, then looked at them brazenly. "No, Dad told me."

"He just had to rush to the phone and call you at work, huh? About a woman he didn't know."

A tough little nugget under the pretty packaging, Tracy gave Sidney the evil eye.

"He tell you how she died?" Granger asked.

"Overdose, my guess."

"You're in for a shock," he said sternly.

Tracy froze and her sable-colored eyes widened with surprise. "She was murdered?"

"Yeah."

For a long moment, the waitress looked stricken. She rubbed her arms as though suddenly chilled, though it was warm in the alley.

"You know anyone who might want to hurt Samantha?" Sidney asked.

"A lot of people. People she snitched on to get herself a lighter sentence." Her lips formed a harsh line, and when she spoke her bottom teeth showed. "She sent my stepbrother to jail for three years. She got two months. Then she was right back here, using and selling again."

"Selling?"

"Yeah. To support her habit."

"Can you give us names? Users, dealers?" Granger asked.

"I'm no snitch." Tracy's tone held a touch of defiance, but the way she tightened her crossed arms suggested fear. "I know better."

"People would get even?" he asked.

She tightened her lips.

Sidney got right up into Tracy's face. "You cover up for a murderer, I'll make sure you see jail time for obstruction."

Tracy's cool thawed several degrees. She stepped back, lowered her gaze.

"What kind of relationship did Noah have with your mom?"

She drew in a breath, blurted, "The normal kind."

Sidney held her gaze, waited for more.

"They had problems, okay? He couldn't hold down a job, so he had to move back home. Couldn't kick drugs."

"When was this?"

"Three years ago, when he was twenty-seven. Mom didn't want him there. She didn't like his drug use or his creepy friends coming around."

"How'd your stepdad feel?"

Tracy fidgeted with her wristwatch, sliding the band back and forth. "He wasn't happy, either. Noah didn't pay for groceries, wouldn't help with chores…" She fell silent.

"What else aren't you telling me?"

"He stole money a few times. Miko was going to kick him out, but… well, Mom was killed, and my stepdad couldn't deal with anything for a while. Then Noah got busted."

"Who were these creepy friends of his?" Granger asked.

Tracy bit her bottom lip, looked longingly toward the restaurant door. "I gotta get back to work."

"We're not done, Tracy," Sidney said sharply, and handed her a business card. "You better think real hard about any names you want to share. You live here in town?"

"Yeah. Moved back after Mom died to help my stepdad. He was a zombie for a while."

"You married?"

"I live with my boyfriend and his two kids. He teaches science at the high school. Look, I have to get back to work." She opened the screen door, peered back at them, seemed to gather some courage, and her dark eyes flashed with anger. "Leave my family alone. They've suffered enough. People treat Miko like he's a murderer. Noah served his time. He's changed. Harass someone else for a change." She let the door bang shut behind her.

"No love lost between her and Samantha," Granger said as they strode out of the alley.

"Nope. She wasn't too broken up about her murder, either."

"You think she knows who did it?"

"She's got her suspicions. Noah and his druggie friends are first in line."

"Yet, she covered for him."

"Covering up for a family member is instinctual."

"Lots of friction between Noah and his stepmom. Goes to motive."

She flashed him a grin. "You're catching on, Granger."

"Trying." He grinned back.

Once seated in the Yukon, Sidney starting typing notes into the laptop while details of Tracy's conversation were fresh in her mind. She enjoyed having Granger as a partner. He was intelligent and observant. A good person for bouncing around ideas. After this homicide was put to rest, she and her officers would go back to their solitary lives, riding solo, rarely seeing one another. The hours of each shift staggered, each patrolling a different segment of town. One day she hoped to have a budget for pairing up her officers. The town was growing. People she didn't know were moving here, and a criminal element was always at work in the moving tide of tourists.

CHAPTER FIFTEEN

WITH SELENA WATCHING the house, Ann felt safe enough to catch up on sleep. She was dead on her feet, and when she stood, she felt a head rush from all the wine she drank in lieu of eating. She snapped the heavy drapes together, blocking out the afternoon sun. Bailey hopped up awkwardly beside her on the big mattress. Sedated by pain pills, he fell asleep instantly. The feel of his body curved against hers triggered tears. She was overwhelmed with relief that her hound made it safely home.

She drifted into a damp world of glistening black trees where little moonlight sifted through the canopy. Branches thrashed in the wind, gnarled roots writhed like snakes over the ground, leaves morphed into scaled insects, bushes clawed her clothing like talons. She ran in slow motion, legs heavy, feet bared and bloodied, terror constricting her throat. Behind her, an assailant smashed through the underbrush with demonic speed.

With a gasp, Ann's eyes opened wide. Her heart hammered her chest. A movement in the corner of the room caught her eye. There a dark figure stood. Motionless. He lifted a finger to his lips. "Shhhh."

Ann sat bolt upright and screamed. Bailey was instantly on his feet on the mattress, his barks matching the elevated pitch of her shrieks.

The door burst open and Selena switched on the light, handgun in hand. "What's wrong?"

Ann pointed to the corner, and panted, "A man. Standing right there."

No one was there.

Selena quietly crossed the room, flipped on the light in the walk-in closet, and entered. Ann heard her ruffling through racks of clothing. She came back in and looked under the bed, then disappeared into the adjoining bathroom. Ann heard her cross the tile floor, sweep the shower curtain aside, and a few seconds later, shut the window.

Selena reemerged, tucked the gun into her waistband, and sat next to Ann. "You were dreaming. No one is here. You're safe."

Ann trembled uncontrollably. "I heard you shut the window."

"It was only open a crack."

From the deep grooves between Selena's brows, Ann knew her friend was deeply concerned.

The cell phone buzzed on the nightstand. Ann reached for it. "Unknown caller. Should I answer?"

"Yes. See if you can get the caller to identify himself."

Ann swiped her finger across the screen. "Hello?" She listened. "Who's calling, please?"

No sound. The line went dead.

"Probably a telemarketer. I get several a day," Selena said evenly.

Ann tried to believe her.

"Should we search the house together?" Selena asked.

Ann nodded and padded after Selena into the living room. After arming herself with a poker iron, she and Selena searched the house; every conceivable place a man could hide, every closet, the pantry, and they tested doors and windows to ensure they were locked. They were safely barricaded. *Against what?*

Selena sat Ann down at the island in the kitchen. "I'm going to make you a nice bowl of soup. Alcohol on an empty stomach is not a good remedy for shredded nerves." Selena continued chatting as she pulled ingredients from the fridge and set to work. Clicking a steady beat on the cutting board with her knife, she chopped potatoes, onions, celery, and carrots, then sautéed them in a cast iron pan with olive oil, garlic, and fresh herbs.

Watching the unruffled motion of her friend, listening to her soothing voice, Ann was calmed, and the heavenly aroma lifting from the pan made her stomach clench with hunger.

After adding salt, pepper, and fresh cream to her pot, Selena transferred the ingredients to the blender, pulverized them, reheated the mixture in the pot, and finally, ladled thick potato soup into two bowls. She set one in front of Ann.

Ann tasted a spoonful. "Hmmm. Smooth and creamy. Perfect."

"Comfort food." Selena poured them both a glass of lavender sage ice tea and straddled the stool next to Ann. She broke off a chunk of crusty bread from a fresh loaf, slathered it with butter, dipped it into her soup, and ate enthusiastically. She reminded Ann of an adoring mother with a sick child, who watched with approval as Ann finished her bowl. "Feel better?"

Ann nodded. "Much."

"Want to talk?"

Ann shrugged. "Yes, but I don't want to pretend I'm okay. I'm not."

"I'm listening," Selena said, pushing her empty bowl aside.

"I feel the same way I did after John died. Anxious. Weighed down by dread. Bad dreams." She paused, not knowing how to untangle her thoughts, each wired with stinging emotion. The episode in the woods last night cracked open a sealed vault and vivid memories of John's violent death were leaking out. How could words frame the terror she felt that evening? How could she describe the residue of sorrow that felt like cancer in her bones?

Selena's eyes darkened with concern. "You've never talked about John's death before. I've never asked. I felt I would be intruding."

"Thank you for that. It's hard to talk about." Ann stared at her hands, tightly clasped in her lap. An uncomfortable sensation reminded her of who she really was behind the mask she assumed every day. "The worst part is that Matt was part of it. I'll never forgive myself for doing that to my son. I should have left John years earlier. Or killed him. Matt would have been better off, even with me in jail." Ann glanced at Selena to gauge her reaction. She saw care and sadness in her friend's eyes, but no judgment.

"John beat me for fifteen years, Selena, and I put up with it. I was emotionally paralyzed." Ann felt the heaviness in her chest, the old wrenching in her stomach. "When he got drunk and violent, I put myself between his rage and my son. I was his punching bag. Matt witnessed years of violence. I know now how that affected him. The feeling of helplessness tore him apart."

Ann swallowed and continued. "One night ten years ago, Matt tried to defend me. He hit John on the back with a baseball bat. It hardly fazed him. John was a big man. Powerful. He punched Matt in the face so hard, our son flew across the floor into the wall. He lay there. Bleeding, unconscious." Ann winced as the old touch of panic set in. "Something inside me snapped. I raced out of the house to a neighbor and called 911. The police came quickly. They dragged John out in handcuffs. He bucked and fought, screaming that he'd come back to kill us. They tased him over and over, and finally subdued him enough to get him into the car. He served eight months in jail, enough time for us to sell the house and escape here to the lake."

"What a nightmare," Selena whispered. She reached over and covered Ann's hand.

"John wasn't out a week when he surprised me in the garden. Beat me nearly unconscious. Then he strangled me." Ann closed her eyes for a moment. Sweat dampened the back of her neck. "Matt came home just in time. He and I killed John." Ann forced herself to meet her friend's gaze, certain she would see horror, but Selena's eyes were soft with compassion.

"I know what happened, Ann. It was in the paper."

Ann shivered, remembering the humiliation she and Matt endured, on top of everything else that happened. "Yeah. The whole town knew. They probably think I'm a murderer."

"They don't. Everyone knew John was a violent drunk."

"A monster." Ann reached for her glass with a trembling hand. "See? I'm a wreck."

"You're strong, Ann. Give it time. This will pass."

Ann's hand tensed on her glass. "No, it gets worse. Back then, it got so bad, I thought about killing myself."

Selena released a little gasp.

"I took my boat out to the middle of the lake. I was going to let myself sink to the bottom like a stone and not come up. But at the last moment, I couldn't do it." Ann felt the sting of tears. "I couldn't abandon Matt."

Selena handed Ann a tissue.

Ann blew her nose and continued in a quivering voice. "To ease the pain, I tried every kind of pharmaceutical cocktail there was. I tried hypnosis, meditation, even a special diet with no grain or sugar. Nothing helped. Until I found therapy."

"What kind of therapy?"

"Grief therapy. I got into a group of women who had also experienced violence. They understood what I was going through. The therapist said we were suffering from PTSD."

Selena looked at her earnestly. "That's something combat veterans get."

Ann sniffed. "PTSD can affect anyone. It could be from a mugging, a rape, even a car accident. Sometimes the symptoms are temporary. Sometimes they last a lifetime, and every day is a challenge."

"Is that how it is for you?"

"Yeah. Lucky me." Ann ran her fingertips under her eyes. "Jude taught me how to manage the pain. Stash it away. Keep it from running my life. But it's back. Full force."

"Jude was your therapist?"

"My lifesaver, more like it."

Selena's head cocked slightly.

Ann met her direct gaze. "I know what you're thinking."

"What am I thinking?"

"I should go back to therapy."

"Doesn't sound like a bad idea."

Ann tightened her jaw, shook her head. "I can't."

"Why not? It helped you before."

"My facial blindness. It's hard for me to meet new people, even on a good day. They'll think I'm a freak."

"You're anything but a freak, Ann. Just the opposite. You're so gifted, it's scary. Look how you transformed this farm from a dry patch of dirt into a paradise. Flowers and herbs and vegetables. Everything thriving. You and I have built a wonderful business together. All of our products started from your ideas." Selena's tone softened. "And you helped me get through the worst year of my life. You listened over and over to all my stuff about Randy."

Selena's kindness made Ann feel even more vulnerable. She despised appearing weak in the eyes of others. She felt a burning in the back of her throat and tears streamed from her eyes. She roughly tried to knuckle them away. They kept coming.

Selena handed her a box of tissue and put a comforting hand on her shoulder. "Have a good cry. Give it all you've got."

Emotion welled up like a geyser and overflowed. Ann wept, shoulders shaking, using tissue after tissue. Selena stayed the distance, rubbing her back, encouraging her to let it all out. Minutes went by. Maybe five. Maybe ten. Finally, Ann wiped her face and honked her nose one last time. She knew she must look a mess, eyes red and puffy, face bloated, but she didn't care, and she knew Selena didn't either.

"Feel better?" her dear friend asked.

Ann nodded, straightening her shoulders. "A little."

Selena made them both a cup of chamomile tea with honey and they sat sipping in quiet companionship. The wind moaned under the eaves of the house and jangled the outdoor chimes in an erratic rhythm, as though expressing Ann's anxiety.

"So, what's your game plan?" Selena asked.

Ann's fingers strummed the counter top. "I'll give Jude a call."

Selena picked up Ann's cell phone and handed it to her.

"Now?" Ann swallowed to steady her voice. "I'm not ready."

"Yes, you are."

Squinting at the screen, Ann went to contacts, brought up Jude's number, and sat staring at it, her mouth dry as cotton.

"You're going to make an appointment," Selena said firmly. "I'm going with you, to make sure you go." She took the phone from Ann's fingers and pressed the call button.

CHAPTER SIXTEEN

WHEN GRANGER AND Chief Becker returned to the station, Darnell, Amanda, and Winnie were crammed into the conference room milling around the white board where Winnie was posting photos of the two crime scenes. Granger noted everyone moved slowly and looked as wiped as he felt. His stomach growled at the smell of pizza, and he smiled at the four large takeout boxes spread across the counter, along with soft drinks and paper plates.

Chief Becker was the first to step up to the counter and pick up a plate. "Let's get this show on the road, people. The sooner we get done here, the sooner your heads can hit your pillows."

No more prompting was needed. Caps twisted off drinks, pizza boxes opened and hot gooey slices slapped paper plates. Granger shoveled three slices onto his plate, piled high with ham, sausage, veggies, and melted cheese. Everyone took their seats and stuffed their mouths for several minutes without interruption. He noticed the chief managed to get through two sizable slices of pepperoni before moving to the whiteboard to add more photos, including Noah Matsui's mug shot.

Granger washed down the flavor of spicy tomato sauce with an ice-cold cola while watching her closely, wanting to learn everything he could from her years of experience. In the military, to do his job well, he had to trust the decisions of his superiors, and Granger implicitly trusted Chief Becker. If she were military, he was certain she'd be a high-ranking officer, maybe a captain or major. In any situation, the chief seemed to know the right thing to do. Toughness when it was needed. Diplomacy when it was the better choice. The center of calm.

She was a tall woman who moved with easy grace, and she gave off an aura of confidence. Not beautiful like her sister, but nice-looking—a pleasant face with a wide mouth—and hazel eyes that could be kind or stand up to the toughest glare. He hoped he'd never be the target of those eyes when she was angry. They could burn holes in your skin.

The chief paced in front of the whiteboard, shrugging her shoulders as though trying to loosen taut muscles. Her eyes had dark smudges underneath. Operating on fumes, like the rest of them. She faced the group. "Let's review the results of Samantha's postmortem examination."

The officers wiped their fingers with napkins; laptops open in front of them.

"An autopsy is not just a clinical procedure. It's the last line of defense for a victim. A way for them to talk to us. We learned from Samantha's autopsy that she was abducted around noon, which means the perp had her for up to twelve hours. Though paralyzed, she was fully conscious. What the perp did to her during that time is unknown. We do know, that during the last minutes of her life, she was terrorized—dragged through the woods, propped against a tree, forced to watch as her wrists were slit and her life drained away. We assume Mimi Matsui encountered the same fate." Sidney paused to let her words sink in. "We are dealing with a cold-blooded, sadistic killer. He's smart. We need to be smarter."

Granger saw tight expressions around the table. This perp worried, even frightened his fellow officers, and troubled Winnie especially, whose face was pinched with worry. Her normal duties took her to administrative meetings, not murder briefings. But she insisted on sitting in, determined to understand this tragic event affecting their community.

The chief lifted her bottled water to her mouth and took a swig. "There's evidence Samantha was sexually active within twenty-four hours of her death. Semen, condom lubricant, and a single pubic hair were sent to the lab. If she was assaulted, hopefully the results will lead us to her killer."

The chief added the picture of the raven and butterflies to the crime board. "We have a new detective on board. Arthur." She proceeded to relay the raven's penchant for delivering gifts to Ann, pointing to the pictures of the amethyst earring and the second butterfly. "Our mischievous crow apparently visited each crime scene and brought back pieces of evidence."

There were surprised chuckles around the table.

"These origami butterflies link the two murders," Sidney said. "The perp wanted us to find them. We need to discover their origin and what they symbolize."

"Is that writing inside the first butterfly?" Amanda asked.

"Yes. Unfortunately, it was washed out by rain. This tiny symbol is legible, but we don't know what it means."

"So, there may be writing inside the second butterfly?" Amanda said.

"Yes. It's at the lab. Want to brief us on Samantha's digs?"

Amanda sat forward in her seat. "Samantha lived in a one-bedroom duplex. To her credit, it was neat as a pin. I combed the place. Took samples from the bathtub drain and bed sheets for body fluids and hair. I ran random fingerprints through AFIS, came up empty. No one with a record." She frowned. "I found it odd Samantha had no diary, journals, or communication of any kind that might incriminate her, or anyone else. It's like she sanitized her life. I questioned her neighbors within two blocks of her duplex. Most of them didn't know her, and those who did saw nothing suspicious. She kept to herself, stayed in at night."

Darnell sat slumped in his seat.

"You here, Darnell, or sleep walking?" Sidney smiled.

"Here. Barely." He sat up straighter in his chair. "I got her phone records and a list of people she'd spoken with over the last few weeks. Dead space for six weeks while at rehab. No phones allowed. Once out, she made calls to a handful of friends and family members, and a few calls to local businesses, mostly restaurants."

"Any to Barney's?"

"No. Mostly take-out food."

"Anything on social media?"

"Nothing raised a flag. Seems she wiped everything clean while in rehab. Like Amanda said, a sanitized version of her life. You'd think she was in line for sainthood."

"Credit card purchases, bank withdrawals?"

He studied his laptop for a moment. "Her last purchases were downtown three days ago, just household supplies and groceries. But she did pay with a credit card for a meal at Katie's Café at 11:35 a.m. yesterday. At fifty dollars, she must have paid for two."

"Bingo," Sidney said. "That's where she had her ham and eggs. Confirms Dr. Linthrope's timeline. I'll stop by Katie's Café after the meeting. See if anyone remembers who she ate with. What else do you have?"

Darnell squinted at his computer, glanced up. "The opposite was true before rehab. Her fellow employees at Hogan's told me she was a party girl. A hell-raiser. Shooting up smack, snorting coke. Sometimes she came to work high, but they covered for her."

"Enablers," Sidney said with an edge. "Think they're helping, but they're making it worse."

Darnell nodded. "She sold and bought drugs from contacts at Barney's. She wasn't living high off the hog, just paying for her habit. No one wanted to cough up names of her druggie friends." He frowned, referring to his notes. "Two months ago, she overdosed at a party in Jackson, hosted by the bartender at

Barney's, Jason Welsh."

The chief straightened her shoulders. "Overdosed?"

"Yeah. She would've died if the paramedics hadn't reached her when they did. They hit her up with naloxone. That near-death experience may have been her wake-up call. The parents stepped in and placed her in the country club of all rehabs. New Life Clinic in Salem. Samantha hadn't made so much as a blip on the radar screen since."

"They must sprinkle fairy dust to cure their addicts," Amanda said dryly.

"Or she got the holy shit scared out of her, and was frightened into going straight," Granger said.

"Samantha's father mentioned Jason Welsh. Any other men in her life?" Sidney asked.

"Matt Howard's name came up," Darnell replied.

The chief stared at him for a second. "Same names keep popping up. Bring Jason Welsh in for questioning tomorrow, Darnell. I'll talk to Matt."

"Roger that."

Chief Becker turned and tapped Mimi's photo on the board. "Mimi's case went cold. We can't let that happen with Samantha. These two victims lived in different worlds, but there's a connection between them. We need to find it. Make sure you show Mimi's photo to everyone you question about Samantha."

Nods around the table.

The chief's shoulders sagged slightly, showing exhaustion was taking its toll.

"Okay, that's it," she said. "Go home. Get some sleep. Be sharp tomorrow."

Everyone helped clean up, and then the room cleared out quickly, but Granger lingered. "You going to Katie's, Chief?"

"Yep." She ran a hand over her forehead, smoothing back wisps of hair that had escaped her ponytail. "I'm also going to pay

Matt Howard a visit. He has some serious questions to answer."

"Want some muscle?"

She shook her head and gave him a tired smile. "Thanks, but I need you to go check on Ann and Selena. Make sure they're okay."

"I'm on my way."

CHAPTER SEVENTEEN

WHEN GRANGER pulled into Ann Howard's driveway, he found the lights blazing in every window, casting long yellow shafts into the yard. He felt a touch of excitement in his gut at the prospect of seeing Selena. The one bright spot in this whole dismal case. He exited the car and climbed the stairs to the porch. The surface of Lake Kalapuya shimmered under schooners of brooding clouds and the air smelled like rain. Another storm barreling in from the coast.

The door opened before he reached it. Selena stepped outside and shut it behind her. She wore tight jeans, a green parka, and a green knit hat pulled low on her forehead. Her hair fell past her shoulders, straight and pale as corn silk. Even in the hard yellow porch light, she looked beautiful. She didn't smile. He sensed her tension. "You going somewhere?" he asked.

"Yeah, with you. We're going to search every inch of this property. Ann's seeing ghosts. Men in the house. Out here."

Granger morphed into cop mode. "Where out here?"

"Over there."

His gaze followed her pointed finger to the border separating Ann's farm from Miko's. A hazy tunnel of light appeared through an opening in the trees. Granger didn't like it one bit that two women were living next door to a hardened felon. "Wait here. I'll check everything out."

"I'm coming with you." She pulled a .38 pistol from her

pocket, held it down at her side.

"Put that gun away. Stay behind me at all times." He thumbed on his flashlight, unsnapped the holster of his sidearm, and rested his hand on the hilt. With Selena shadowing him, he scoured the area surrounding the house, casting his beam between trees and under bushes, looking for footprints. *None.*

"Check under her bathroom window," Selena said.

He pulled back bushes and illuminated the area but saw no tracks.

"What's with those scuff marks in the dirt," she asked. "Looks like someone roughed up the dirt with their shoe."

"Just messy dirt," he said logically. "Could've been like that for days, or weeks."

She set her jaw, looked unconvinced. "Ann thought she saw someone in her bedroom. He may have gotten out through this window."

Granger tried to slide open the widow. It was latched tight.

"It was open a crack when I checked. I locked it. I guess it's farfetched. An intruder would only have had seconds to get out the window before I checked the bathroom."

It did sound far-fetched. "In her current state of mind, Ann could have conjured anything. Little green men. Trolls. There's no evidence someone was here."

"There was a faint smell in the bedroom and bathroom that I've never smelled in the house before."

"What's that?"

She shrugged a slender shoulder. "Cigarette smoke. And pot."

"Does Ann smoke either?"

"No. Neither do I, but I've smelled pot at concerts. I didn't say anything to Ann. She was freaked out enough."

"I'll search the house when we're through out here."

"We already did."

He shook his head. "Not much I can do, Selena. No evidence a crime was committed, just a vague smell. That bothers me, though. Let's check the outbuildings."

Her face relaxed minutely. "Guess you're right. I'm probably imagining things, too."

They circled the shed and the barn. Doors locked, windows locked. As he neared Miko's property, the air smelled of apples. Big wet drops of rain began to fall, splattering leaves, the ground, and his shoulders. Water slid through his hair like icy fingers. His beam scrubbed the ground between the border of trees where Ann saw her ghost. The opening was tall enough for a grown man to stand. There were lots of prints stamped into the earth by the same pair of boots, and a scatter of cigarette butts.

Selena gave him a direct stare. "Here's evidence."

"Noah obviously comes here to smoke." He sucked in a breath. "Nothing illegal about that."

"Most of the footprints face our house. He's watching us."

"Nothing illegal about that, either. He's on his own property." His voice was calm, but it made Granger uneasy that Noah habitually watched their house. "I'd feel better if Matt was staying here."

"Me, too, but she won't ask him."

"Stubborn."

"Yes, she is."

"Look, make sure you keep the house locked up tight. Stay alert."

"I promise." She smiled.

He smiled back.

Granger pulled a latex glove and evidence bag from his duty belt, squatted, and picked up several of the butts.

"Cleaning up after him? My, you *are* civic minded."

"Something like that." He now had a source of Noah's DNA to send to the lab. He straightened up, standing close enough to Selena to smell the sweet scent of her hair. He was six-foot-two, but in her boot-heels, her eyes were level with his. Celadon green in the dim light. Her proximity felt intimate. He respectfully took a step back.

"You've solved the mystery of the ghost." She sounded relieved. Glistening raindrops ran down her cheeks. "Come on in the house. I saved dinner for you."

Granger was full from pizza. "Great," he said, snapping his handgun in place. "I'm starving."

They heard the crunch of gravel, and a body materialized in the opening, limping slightly. It was Miko, carrying a sizable basket of apples. "I saw your flashlight, Officer. Please give this to Ann Howard. Tell her I'm sorry for the bad experience she had last night."

"I'm sure she'll appreciate it."

After Miko shifted the weight of the basket over to Granger, Selena stepped forward, arm outstretched. "I'm Selena, Ann's friend and business partner. I'll be staying here the next few nights."

"I'm Miko. Nice to meet you." He gently held her hand rather than shaking it.

"Does Noah come here to smoke?" Granger asked.

"Yes." Miko looked toward Ann's house. His eyes narrowed, and his mouth turned downward for a moment, but he said nothing more. He bowed slightly and backed away, disappearing through the silvery curtain of rain.

CHAPTER EIGHTEEN

BY THE TIME Sidney parked in the full lot, the rain had lightened to a drizzle, and it was prime dinner hour at Katie's Café. The clean smell of pinesap swept in from the forest, and a dark, brooding sky hung over the lake, threatening more rain.

Normally at this hour, tourists would be seated on the sidewalk patio, but the tables stood empty and slick with rain, the shallow puddles reflecting the overhead strings of twinkly white lights. Inside the café she was met by the tinny drone of voices and the aroma of roasted coffee and grilled seafood. People were lined up at the espresso bar, their gazes fixed on the multi-tasking barista. Two waitresses delivered platters of food to people crammed into the eating area that barely accommodated ten tables. The evening specials were scrawled across a chalkboard: Prime rib with Gouda mashed potatoes. Grilled scallops with coconut rice pilaf.

Out of respect for her sister, Sidney had boycotted Katie's since Randy McBride appeared on the scene two months ago. Selena's ex had abruptly quit rodeo and picked up a new career as prep chef and baker-in-training at the cafe. He had given Selena the courtesy of one visit, updating her on his life transition while packing some of his belongings. In parting, he pulled her close in the driveway and kissed her. A bedroom kiss, Sidney thought, watching from the window. When they came up for air, they were both flushed, and Selena's eyes glistened with emotion. Randy had given her a filament of hope. Cruel to let her think things could be patched up between them. With one foot in her life and the other out the door, he effectively kept Selena in limbo. Thinking about it made Sidney bristle.

The chic little restaurant reminded her of how the blue-collar town was changing. Just three years back, Katie's had been a slipshod coffee shop, catering to farmers and cowboys. Designer coffee drinks had replaced pots of Maxwell House, and eggs Benedict on arugula replaced six-egg omelets, greasy bacon, and pancakes the size of frying pans. Prices doubled, irritating the old-timers who migrated to Jake's Grill, where a hard-working ranch hand could still get massive proportions at affordable prices.

Sidney tugged her thoughts back to her homicide investigation. She was here with a purpose. She searched for Katie and spotted her behind the cashier's counter. The swinging door to the kitchen opened behind Katie and Randy stepped out carrying a huge sheet of cookies in both hands. Tall, lanky, strikingly handsome, his sandy hair netted, he bent over to slide the sheet onto a shelf in the display case. Sidney sidled up to the glass. Randy glanced at her and dropped the tray onto the shelf with a thunk. The cookies bounced, a few breaking apart.

Katie jerked her head toward Randy and followed his gaze to Sidney. She was a red-haired, fleshy, matronly woman with loose jowls, who wore sensible shoes and a flowered dress covered by a white apron. Randy nodded a greeting at Sidney, snatched up the handful of broken cookies, and hurried back into the kitchen. The door swung shut behind him, but not before she saw Gus, Katie's husband, standing over the smoky grill. Randy was framed in the rectangular window in the door, head down, back to work chopping vegetables.

"Chief Becker," Katie's smile wavered. "Haven't seen you for a while. What can I do you for?"

Sidney smiled back. Katie and Gus Carter were good people,

hard workers, stalwart supporters of the community. "Got a minute?"

"Just. We're busy."

"I need to ask about Samantha Ferguson."

Katie's brow deeply creased. "I heard. Terrible. Can't believe Sammy's dead."

Sidney wasn't surprised Katie knew. News circulated fast in a small town, and people moving in and out all day made the cafe a prime center for the transmission of gossip. "Are many people talking?"

She shrugged. "Mostly locals. No one knows any details, so rumors are flying. Was she really raped and murdered?"

"Murdered, yes. Raped, we don't know."

Katie visibly shivered. "Are you making headway with her case?"

"Working on it."

"Poor Sammy. She came in all the time."

"She ate here yesterday?"

Katie nodded.

"Who waited on her?"

"I did."

"Do you remember who she ate with?"

"Of course. Matt Howard."

Matt Howard. Again. His name just kept cropping up.

"How was the mood between them?"

Katie tucked a strand of hair behind her ear and half smiled. "They were having fun. Laughing. Seemed to be very taken with each other. Pecking each other on the lips in between bites. She was such a lovely girl. So friendly." Her expression sobered, and she locked eyes with Sidney. "Is Matt a suspect?"

"No. Just routine questions. I'm trying to establish a timeline."

"They were here for an hour. They left around 11:30."

"Do you remember what she ordered?"

"Let's see." Katie put a finger to her lips, eyes narrowing. "She had ham and eggs. He had Pepper Jack Quiche."

"Thanks, Katie. You've been very helpful."

Katie corroborated Dr. Linthrope's findings of Samantha's stomach contents and the time of her last meal. The window was narrowing on the last hours of her life, and Matt Howard was one of the last people to see her alive.

Sidney noticed movement in her periphery, and Katie's teenage daughter, Allison, stepped into view. The pretty teenager with a busty figure had been helping in the shop since she was knee high. Raindrops were spattered on the shoulders of her raincoat and glistened in the locks of her long red hair.

"Hi, Mom. Hi, Chief Becker."

"Hi, Allison."

"You're late," Katie said.

"Sorry, Mom." Allison removed her wet raincoat and hung it on a coat rack. "Just moving slower these days."

Sheathed in a tight knit dress, Allison was very pregnant. In the two months since Sidney had seen her, her abdomen had swollen considerably, and judging from the size and position, she was nearing her delivery date. Though the family wasn't talking, most folks in town assumed the father was her high school boyfriend, Doug Ratcher, linebacker and small-town celebrity. No word of marriage in the works, but that was the family's business, not Sidney's.

"Better get to work, Allison," Katie said. "We're swamped."

"Okay. Just want to say hi to Dad and Randy first." Allison shot Sidney a peculiar look before waddling through the swinging door. She made a beeline for Randy, who lifted his head as she approached. He grinned his big, sexy cowboy grin that Selena found irresistible, and Sidney found repugnant.

"Should she be working?" Sidney said. "She looks ready to deliver."

"She's fine. Still a month away." Katie's face flushed with pleasure. "She's carrying that child like a champ. Allison was built to have babies. And plenty of them."

"Spoken like a proud grandma."

"I am. It's a boy." She beamed. "Allison is only here a couple hours each night. Makes salads and desserts. Easy. Gives her something to do."

A waitress barreled through the door, a platter in each hand. Behind her, Sidney spotted Allison and Randy wrapped in a body lock so tight, oxygen couldn't fit between them. The door shut, and through the window Sidney watched Randy tilt the teen's chin up. Sidney felt a jolt of surprise when he kissed her, open-mouthed, steamy. *Christ.* Her brother-in-law was cavorting with a teenager.

What Allison did next surprised Sidney more. She glanced back over her shoulder and met Sidney's stare. A little triumphant smile curled her lips. Realization sunk in. The sensual display had been staged for Sidney's benefit. Allison wanted Sidney to know Randy had a new woman in his life. She wanted Sidney to relay the message to Selena.

When Katie cleared her throat, Sidney pulled her attention away from the window and realized her expression still showed surprise. "What's going on between those two?"

Before Katie could comment, Allison came back through the door tying an apron over her bulbous belly, a snarky look on her face. The sweet girl Sidney had watched grow up was displaying terrible judgment. Messing around with an older, married man, and taunting Sidney, the police chief, who could cause her a world of grief in so many ways. Must be hormones out of whack. Sidney would have relished taking the girl aside and laying a harsh lecture on her, but that was her mother's job, and Katie was taking Allison's behavior in stride.

"Take over this counter for me, Allison, so I can take a break. Follow me, Chief. We need to talk."

Sidney rounded the counter and followed Katie's wide derriere into a kitchen filled with pastry racks, huge pots and pans, and myriad food smells. Chopping vegetables, his knife a blur, Randy kept his head down. They turned down a narrow hallway and entered a break room furnished with a coffee nook and small Formica table.

"Have a seat, Chief," Katie said. "Coffee?"

"No, thanks." Impatient to get the conversation over with, Sidney sank into a chair.

Katie sat across from her and got straight to the point. "You looked shocked when you saw Allison and Randy kissing."

"I was."

Katie looked flustered. "Selena didn't tell you?"

"Tell me what? That Randy's seducing your daughter?"

Katie flinched. "That sounds sordid."

"Sordid describes it pretty well."

"They're in a relationship."

Sidney paused. "I don't want to go all morality police on you, Katie, but he's a married man. Allison's just a kid. What, sixteen?"

"Eighteen. A grown woman. Fully capable of handling Randy." She swallowed. "I thought Selena knew. He and Allison are living together in our guesthouse."

Another surprise. "That was fast. He's only been back two months."

She tilted up her chin. "They've been dating for nine months. He stayed with her when he came to town between rodeo gigs."

"Nine months?" Sidney sat motionless, processing. "You're not going to tell me Randy's the baby's father, are you?"

"That's exactly what I'm telling you."

The air left Sidney's lungs. Allison, who Katie said was built to have babies, was about to present Randy with the one thing Selena was unable to give him. The news would devastate her.

Katie crossed her arms and looked defensive. "Randy told us

he and Selena are getting divorced."

"He's never mentioned divorce. Trust me." Sidney exhaled, long and slow, calming herself. "Selena hoped they'd get back together."

Katie's expression softened, and her blue eyes darkened with sympathy. "I'm sorry for Selena. I really am. But it's been a year. When was the last time she even saw Randy?"

Sidney sighed. "Weeks ago. He stopped by to pick up some belongings."

"The fact that he doesn't spend time with her should have told her it's over."

The goodbye kiss he gave her told her otherwise. "Randy should have come clean about Allison months ago. He owed Selena that much. They were together eleven years."

Katie frowned, a confused expression on her face. "I agree. He should have told her. He hasn't been completely honest with you, or us."

Honesty was never Randy's strong suit.

"Well, I guess I understand why he didn't tell Selena," Katie said, casting her eyes downward, perhaps casting around for a reasonable explanation. "He didn't want to hurt her."

Or he's being his usual callous self.

"Well, Randy's part of our family, now. For better or worse."

For worse.

"He's doing our baking every night. Helps Gus with dinner. A hard worker. And smart. He's taking over some of the management responsibilities so that I can cut back on my hours." She gave Sidney a direct stare. "Once the divorce is final, we're going to plan a wedding. Maybe in the spring. Selena needs to know. Randy and Allison have kept a low profile, but they want to come out of hiding. Go out in public together."

"When are the papers being served?"

"Good question."

The two women looked at each other, probably thinking the same thing. Something was keeping Randy from making the final move. Probably a glimmer of realization in his Neanderthal brain that he still loved Selena. But he slept with Allison and got her pregnant. He was going to be a father. That decision would dictate his actions for the rest of his life.

"Tell him to get moving with those papers. I'll break the news to Selena." Sidney said her goodbye and left the café through the back door. She felt sickened, but she also felt relief. They were finally done with Randy. He'd been living a double life right under her sister's nose, and Selena never caught a whiff of his deceit. In time, her sister would recognize this terrible episode in her life was a blessing—gift wrapped and tied with a big red bow. The Carters were now assuming responsibility for Randy and his conniving ways. His silky-smooth charm had won them over, but the sheen would wear off. His true nature would seep out of hiding and stain their lives for the worse.

CHAPTER NINETEEN

"HI, OFFICER WYATT," Ann said warmly when Granger and Selena entered the house with the big basket of apples. "Thank you for coming."

Bailey limped to the door, wagging his tail and sniffing Granger with interest.

"Call me Granger," he said, affectionately petting the dog.

"You did see someone out there, Ann," Selena said, pulling off her cap and shaking her hair free. "Noah. He stands out there and smokes."

Ann looked relieved. "I'm not going crazy after all."

"No, you're not."

Granger followed Selena across the living room and hoisted the laundry-sized basket onto the kitchen counter. "This is from Miko. He just dropped it off."

"Miko?" Ann could not have looked more surprised if he had said the Easter Bunny bounded over.

"There's a card," Selena said.

The three gathered around the basket as though a baby had been delivered. Granger recognized Granny Smith, Gala, and Fuji apples, but the other varieties stumped him. The two women started exclaiming as though the basket was laden with gems.

"A Pink Pearl!" Selena held a medium-sized, conical shaped, yellow-green apple on the palm of her hand like a trophy.

All smiles, Ann picked out a lopsided russet apple. "Here's a

Hudson's Golden Gem!"

"What's so special about them?" Granger asked, removing his wet jacket and hanging it on the back of a barstool.

"I'll show you." Ann washed the two different types of apples and sliced them into quarter pieces on a cutting board. They all helped themselves to a sample.

The flesh inside the Pink Pearl was bright purple-red. Granger took a bite and a sweet-tart flavor filled his mouth. "That's different. And tasty."

"Try the Golden Gem," Selena said.

This apple had an intensely sweet, nutty flavor, and was juicy and crisp, similar to a pear. "Really good. Never been to an apple-tasting before."

"Wait 'til you see what we make with them." Selena's eyes sparkled. "These Granny Smith apples will make a great molasses-upside-down cake."

"I'll make down home, honest apple pie," Ann said. "Using several varieties in a pie makes the flavor richer." She opened the envelope from Miko, unfolded the notepaper inside, and moved her lips silently as she read. She smiled, and color appeared on her pale cheeks.

Granger and Selena shared a glance. This token from the stranger next door meant something special to Ann.

"I'm going to bake him the best apple pie he's ever eaten." Ann put the note down and sprang into motion, crisscrossing the room, pulling out bowls, a rolling pin, flour, sugar, moving to some internal compulsion.

"Let me get you dinner," Selena said sweetly to Granger. She removed her damp jacket and blended into Ann's choreography, pulling items from the fridge, pantry, and cabinets.

Settled on the barstool, Granger watched the organized chaos with amusement, obviously rehearsed many times, for neither bumped into the other. A cold beer appeared in front of him with a plate of warm cheddar cheese scones and pats of butter, followed by a bowl of creamy potato soup. Suddenly he was starving. The soup was delicious. "What kind of business do you two have?" he asked between bites.

"We make organic products, right out there in the barn." Selena straddled the stool next to his and sipped a Corona from the bottle. "Scented candles and flavored honeys and vinegars."

"What got you started?" He brushed crumbs off his trousers.

"We met at the farmers market seven years ago. I was selling homemade scented candles and soaps." She glanced at Ann, who was vigorously rolling out pie dough on the counter. "Ann was selling flavored honey, vinegars, herbs, and flowers. We started talking and realized if we combined our labor and ideas, we could double our output and increase our product line. Long story short, after a lot of experimentation, we now have fourteen products we sell on-line, in gift shops, and grocery stores. I also teach five yoga classes a week."

"So, for fun, you work some more."

"Yoga isn't work. It's pleasure. And it helps pay the bills."

Granger wanted to know if anyone was helping Selena pay those bills. She wore a wedding ring on her right hand. What did that mean? Was she widowed? Divorced?

Selena's warm gaze met his and she gave him a radiant smile. His insides tingled.

"What about you, Granger? What do you do when you're not working?" Ann asked.

He wiped his mouth with his napkin. "Seems I'm always working, too. My parents are getting older. Dad's got Parkinson's. It's gotten worse the last few years. When I got out of the Marine Corps, I moved into the bunkhouse at home so I could help out. My brother and I keep the ranch going, for now, until they decide it's time to sell."

"Sorry to hear about your dad," Selena said softly. "Your

parents are lucky to have you and your brother."

"You are a good son," Ann added emphatically.

Blushing, he waved away their compliments. "That's what families do. Support each other. Good times and bad."

The two women looked at him like he walked on water. His chest swelled a little. Being in the company of two attractive women was a pleasant change from his usual routine; slouched on the couch in his sweats, eating a frozen dinner while watching ESPN.

"You always work nights?" Selena asked.

He nodded. "Your sister and I volunteered for the night shift so Darnell and Amanda could be home with their families. Darnell has two toddlers. Amanda has a three-year-old."

"Noble of you both. Kids are a handful. It's hard, though, to meet people when you work nights. I've told Sidney to rotate shifts so she can have a social life. She's not getting any younger."

"Me neither. I'm twenty-nine. Always thought I'd be married by now."

"You want kids?" Ann asked.

"Yes, ma'am. I love kids. My parents married for life. Going on thirty-five years. I expect to do the same."

Again, the two women gave him admiring glances. He appreciated the attention, but heck, he wasn't special. Just doing what normal people do.

"You grew up on the ranch?" Selena asked.

"Born and raised. Just a few miles down the highway. Wrangling cattle. We also have chickens, goats, four dogs, and five cats."

"A regular menagerie," Selena said. "I love animals. I have four cats. Bet you've got some nice horses, too."

He grinned. "That we do. Six quarter horses, a couple paints, two palominos, a Morgan."

Selena smiled. "I love to ride."

"Spent half my life in the saddle. Use to team rope with my brother in high school rodeo."

Both women stared at him like he was dense as wood. Realization set in. He cleared his throat. "Would you like to come out and ride sometime? We have great trails leading off the property down to the lake."

Selena grinned. "I'd love to."

"Don't know when, though. We're putting in long hours at work right now."

"Guess you won't have time to cook."

"No problem. Freezer's stocked. TV dinners."

"Ugh." She gave him an exaggerated expression of sympathy, bottom lip jutting out. "Since you've volunteered to stop by every night, the least we can do is feed you. What do you like to eat?"

"Everything."

"Chicken stew and buttermilk biscuits tomorrow?"

"Sounds great. Look forward to it." Granger found it hard to tug his attention away from her expressive green eyes, and he felt color creep into his cheeks. When he was attracted to a woman, he had no defense. His emotions were transparent. Growing up, his mom knew right off when he was lying, while his poker-faced brother got away with everything. "Well, that was a delicious dinner, Ladies. I better be shoving off. Chores are waiting."

He shrugged into his jacket and Selena walked him to the door. The sound of rain pelting the earth pulled his attention out into the world again, to his responsibilities. As he crossed the porch, he glanced back at her tall, willowy frame in the doorway. She gave a little wave, the warmth of the house behind her, the lure of home-cooked food inviting him to come again. He walked to his truck wondering how Selena could possibly be single. If he had a woman like her, he'd bend over backwards to give her everything she wanted. He'd treat her like a queen.

Something made him glance toward the opening in the trees.

No one there. Granger did a rudimentary check of the whole area, skimming the tree line further east to an area where the shadows seemed especially dark. There the figure of a man stood. In less time than it took to blink, he disappeared. Christ. Had someone been there, or was he, too, imagining ghosts?

Granger pulled his flashlight from his duty belt and took a quick jog along the border of trees to the back of the property, the beam casting a wobbly tunnel through the night. When he reached the area where he thought he saw the silhouette, he searched for footprints. Branches swayed and creaked in the wind. Rain slanted toward the earth, pattering his jacket, running through his hair and down his face. He discovered a spot where the grass looked matted, and he shoved his way through the tangle of wet pine branches, emerging onto Miko's property. He cast his light back and forth over the furrows. No sign of anyone.

Soaked through and chilled, he was about to turn back when his beam found a trail of footprints in the mud leading toward the lake. He followed. Somewhere up ahead along the lakeshore, an engine revved. Granger sprinted toward the sound and sidled through a copse of aspens. He reached the dirt road that ran parallel to the shoreline as the taillights of a truck disappeared around a thicket of trees, leaving a cloud of exhaust in the air. *Shit. Just missed him.* His beam scoured the deep grooves left in the mud but the earth was too wet to hold the tire pattern. No way to identify the truck. Probably Noah.

Granger pulled out his phone, searched for a number, and dialed.

After three rings, a sleepy voice answered. "Miko here."

"This is Officer Granger Wyatt. I need to talk to Noah."

"Not here."

"Know where he is?"

"He's at Barney's most nights."

"Sorry to wake you."

Miko clicked off.

Granger slogged back to his truck, rain dripping from his nose and chin. *Christ. Was that even Noah? Or was someone else watching Ann's farm?* The thought chilled him.

CHAPTER TWENTY

SIDNEY CLIMBED into the Yukon and followed her GPS to Matt Howard's home on the north end of town. Five minutes later, she turned right on Blue Spruce road, drove a few hundred feet, made a hard left, and bounced into his gravel driveway. Through the rain, the headlights revealed a tidy gray house with white trim, surrounded on every side by forest. If someone wanted total privacy, this was the place. His white landscaping truck and trailer were parked on the side of the house, while an array of outdoor toys took up space in the carport: snowmobile, kayak, dirt bike, motorcycle. It appeared Matt Howard played as hard as he worked.

The lights were out, but nonetheless, she climbed the porch and rang the doorbell. Raindrops pattered her cap and jacket and pinged on the metal roof. The forest smelled of cedar. She rang again, waited. A light appeared in the front window and she heard footsteps approaching. The curtain was yanked back, the door swung open, and Matt stood behind the screen door knotting the belt to his flannel bathrobe. His hair was sticking straight out, and his eyelids looked puffy.

"Hello, Chief. Sorry, I got home too late to return your call."

"It's raining out here, Matt."

He jerked open the screen door. "Sorry. Come in."

She shook the rain off her hat, stepped inside, and surveyed the living room, always interested in the domestic lifestyle of bachelors. From all the homey touches, she would have guessed a woman lived here. Nice furniture, framed art on the walls, big plasma TV, clean carpeting, smelled of home cooking. It didn't look like the house of a killer. But then, it never did.

"Have a seat." He gestured to a chair and sat across from her on the couch, leaning forward with his elbows on his knees.

"Sorry to wake you." She wasn't. "I've just got a few questions, and I'll be on my way." She pulled out her phone and brought up a photo of Samantha. "You know this woman?"

His eyebrows arched in surprise. "Yeah, I know Sammy."

"How well?"

"We've dated on and off. Why? What's going on?"

"Samantha was found dead last night, Matt."

Matt recoiled as though kicked in the gut by a mule, face frozen in shock. It took a moment for him to find his voice. "The woman in the woods?"

"Yes. I'm sorry."

Matt sat perfectly still, then he leapt to his feet and paced over the carpet like a restless cat, the news apparently too difficult to process by inaction. "Oh my God!" His face contorted into a mask of agony. "Oh my God!"

If Matt was acting, it was one of the best performances she'd ever witnessed. She gave him a minute to work off the agitation and settle back down on the couch.

His eyes welled with tears, and there was a quiver to his voice. "How did she die?"

"I'm sorry. I can't tell you that."

"Please tell me she didn't suffer."

"All the facts will be revealed after we close the investigation."

"Do you know who did it?"

"I was hoping you could help me figure that out. Okay if I tape this?"

He nodded.

Sidney took out her iPhone and put on the recorder, laid it on the table between them. "Let's start by you telling me about your relationship with Samantha."

Matt put his head in his hands and didn't look up for several seconds. He swiped tears from his eyes and said in a hoarse voice, "I met Sammy at Barney's back in April. I stopped in for a beer after work. I sat at the bar. She was there with a bunch of people I didn't know. They were all laughing, having a good time. Sammy caught my eye a couple times and smiled. She was really pretty. I smiled back. She came over. We hung out for a couple hours, had a few drinks. We both got a little wild and crazy, I guess, and ended up back here." He looked down at his hands and heaved out a ragged breath. "I can't believe she's dead."

"Matt, please continue."

"I don't bring girls home like that. Honest, I don't. But there was something about Sammy. She was smart and funny as hell. I've never laughed as much as I did when I was with her. I guess I fell for her pretty hard right from the start. She liked me too, at first." He sniffed, and she saw new tears glisten in his eyes. He wiped them with his sleeve.

"It didn't last?"

He shook his head.

"What happened?"

He shrugged and looked at Sidney with a hollow expression, as though a light had left his body. "I guess I wasn't wild enough for her—or rich enough. Her folks have a lot of money. Gave her a BMW, paid for her apartment. They probably didn't think I was good catch."

"Why weren't you wild enough?"

"The crowd she hung out with did drugs. I didn't. I have a business to run. I don't stay up late. She wanted me to do coke, party all night. We were from different worlds. I wanted her to straighten out her life. She wanted me to loosen up."

"Her mother said you wouldn't leave her alone after she broke it off with you."

"I did call her a lot." He sniffed. "I showed up at Hogan's a few times after work. I just wanted to talk to her. She told me she was going to call the cops if I didn't leave her alone. I finally got the message. I didn't see her for months, then out of the blue, she showed up here the night before last. Clean and sober. Fresh out of rehab. She said she just wanted to talk. Part of her recovery was apologizing for her past bad behavior. I said she didn't need to apologize. We ended up talking all night."

"I'm sorry to have to ask you this, but did you have sex?"

"We made love."

Silence.

"So yesterday, the morning of her death, she was in your bed."

He nodded, looked away. She saw his chin quiver.

"Take your time."

He met her eyes again, a bit more composed. "I took the morning off, and we went out to eat."

"Katie's. She paid."

"She wanted to pay." He looked puzzled. "How'd you know that?"

"Then what did you do?"

"I had to go to work. She dropped me off back here."

"What time?"

"Around noon."

"Can anyone confirm you were working the whole day?"

"I had to check up on my three crews, so I was in transit most of the day, going from one job to the other."

"Matt, listen to me very carefully. You need to account for your movements the entire day, every minute." Sidney spoke firmly. "I want names and numbers, in writing, tomorrow at the station. Can you do that for me?"

"Yeah, I can do that."

"Something else. I need a DNA sample. That okay?"

"You already know it'll come back to me."

"You didn't use a condom?"

"No. She's on... was on the pill."

"It's procedure." She took a plastic tube from her duty belt, pushed up the foam tipped stem and swabbed the inside of Matt's cheek, then secured the sample back in the plastic tube. "Thank you."

Sidney pulled up the picture of the butterfly and held her phone out to him. "Does this mean anything to you?"

"It's an origami butterfly. I've seen similar ones in town at the Art Studio. I think one of the local artists makes them. He's a paper sculptor."

"Know his name?"

"No, sorry."

She brought up the photo of Mimi. "Know this woman?"

"No."

Sidney turned off her recorder. "You've been very helpful, Matt."

Sidney yanked on her hat, let Matt walk her to the door, stepped out into the rain, and heard it lock behind her. She darted through the downpour, scrambled into the Yukon, put on the wipers, and drove back to the highway, her mind systematically fitting pieces of information together. It wasn't looking good for Matt.

He was the last known person to see Samantha alive. He had time and opportunity to inject her with a neurotoxin when they returned to his house after breakfast. It's possible she could have laid in his bed all day, paralyzed, a prisoner in her own body, while he made appearances at his job sites. And he was in the vicinity of the crime scene last night. He easily could have transported her to the woods, killed her, and showed up at his mother's house in record time. Tomorrow, Matt's alibi had to be one hundred percent bullet proof, or she *would* arrest him.

Only she didn't believe he did it. No question, Matt loved Samantha. Sidney had uncovered no motive for him to kill her. In fact, he had every reason to want her alive. Looked like their relationship might have developed further. Matt said he didn't use protection when they had sex, but a trace of condom lubricant was found inside her. Did Samantha have consensual sex with someone else before she showed up at Matt's house? Or did the condom lubricant come from her killer? Who did the single pubic hair belong to?

Sidney's impatience welled up like a wave. While waiting for lab results, which might identify the killer, she and her team were putting in long hours, chasing an array of leads, possibly spinning their wheels. Her job was to follow the evidence wherever it might lead, and there were still several pathways tunneling away from the epicenter of the crime. She intended to burrow down each one, until there were no more doors left to open. Hopefully, something would materialize before she had to arrest Matt.

~ ~

The door was unlocked again. Sidney needed to impress upon Selena that she was putting their security at risk. A murderer was out there somewhere, and the house was hidden behind the yoga studio, veiled by trees. Easy pickings for a burglar. She locked and bolted the door. Instead of placing her holstered Glock in the gun safe as usual, Sidney decided to keep it close at hand. Her homicide investigation was stirring up the old feeling of anxiety that haunted her in Oakland—a cold, relentless companion.

With her sister absent, the house was quiet and dark. Sidney's attitude softened when she thought of the gut-wrenching conversation she would have to have with Selena tomorrow—Randy's infidelity, a pregnant teenager, the reality of divorce. Poor Selena. Sucked into a sleazy, real-life soap opera by a man who had no moral decency.

Sidney flicked on the light and watched four cats waddle toward her from various parts of the house. Chili and Smokey paused halfway through the room to stretch extravagantly, while Basil and Curry wasted no time twining between her legs. She smiled when she heard their motors running.

"Miao," Smokey mewed, big gold eyes pinned on hers.

"Meow to you, too."

They padded after her, necks craned upwards, watching like starving wild beasts for any sign of a treat. Sidney ignored them. They were too fat as it was.

Selena normally left her a healthy dinner under foil in the fridge, ready to nuke. What she found tonight was a plate of the rosemary cheddar scones her sister had baked that morning. She grabbed one in a napkin and ate it in big bites while climbing the stairs to the second floor, the caravan of cats bounding up behind her.

Sidney switched on a lamp and light spilled across her childhood bedroom. Basil, Chili, and Curry leapt upon the single bed that was covered with a faded handmade quilt from the eighties. The furniture was mismatched: a knotty pine headboard, a walnut chest of drawers, an oak desk shoved under the window that held her computer and printer. Mystery novels, her weakness, were crammed like Chinese puzzle pieces into the shelves of a sagging bookcase, painted cranberry red. All these furnishings had been pulled from the parade of furniture flowing through the house from her mother's thrift store.

Smokey jumped up on the desk and stretched lazily across her keyboard, his furry gray image reflected in the computer screen, big gold eyes unblinking. Sidney scratched him behind the ears and he promptly rolled over on his back, displaying his stomach for her to stroke. She surveyed the room with an objective eye while running her fingers through his fur.

When she'd returned home two years ago, she had stripped the walls of high school pennants and rock star posters, leaving them completely bare. After a hard day's work, to clear her mind, she needed to rest her eyes on empty space. A thirty-five-year-old woman should not be living this way, holed up in her childhood bedroom with her sister as a roommate, her social life scoring a big zero.

Sidney performed her nightly beauty routine, slipped into a cotton nightgown, and burrowed under the covers in the darkened room. Chili, Curry, and Basil filled in the niches of her body while Smokey draped himself around the crown of her head like a wooly hat.

The muffled patter of rain on the roof made her feel insulated and isolated. She remembered lying in Detective Gable Ryan's arms on nights like this in Oakland, pleasantly exhausted and sweaty from making love. Feeling her aloneness like an ache, she pressed her face into her pillow and punished herself with futile thoughts. Maybe she should have been more patient. Maybe she shouldn't have pressed him so hard for marriage. Eventually, he might have come around.

Who was she kidding? Gable told her repeatedly he'd never marry or bring kids into the brutal world they witnessed every day in homicide. He moved out after four years, citing glaring differences in their future objectives. He told her he could no longer deal with the guilt of holding her back from the life she truly wanted. In hindsight, she saw that she should have been the one to leave, instead of putting that terrible burden on him.

After taking the job as police chief in Garnerville, Sidney made another miscalculation. She thought working the night shift would fill her lonely evenings and distract her from thoughts of Gable. But the grueling schedule prevented her from meeting anyone else, and trapped memories of the handsome detective inside her head. Sidney needed to let him go. Move on. Accept that some things break and just stay broken.

Lying in the dark, the wasted years she invested in Gable haunted her. Aware that female fertility declined with advancing age, and the likelihood of losing a pregnancy increased, her fear of missing out on having children loomed large. Her biological clock bleeped like a smoke alarm on a low battery. Like Selena, she craved the soft, silky feel of a baby in her arms. The empty nursery down the hall mocked her. While Selena's uterus swelled with her second baby, Sidney had shared her sister's excited anticipation. They spent many happy hours together painting the walls lilac, placing little stuffed animals and velvety blankets in the crib, layering the drawers with tiny clothes and knitted booties. Selena carried Alissa for six months before losing her. The loss hit Sidney as hard as it did her sister. A dark depression settled over the household, so dense they could feel it like a coating on their skin.

~ ~

The buzz of Sidney's phone stirred her into consciousness. She swam through a murky dream inhabited by bloodless corpses with wide-eyed stares. Her hand shot out from under the covers and located her phone on the nightstand. Bracing for bad news, she pulled herself into a sitting position. A call at seven in the morning had to be an emergency. "Chief Becker."

"Morning, Chief." The chipper tone of her dispatcher flooded her ear. "Just got a call from the mayor's office. He wants to meet with you at eight."

"Thanks, Jesse." No emergency. Just politics.

Stifling a yawn, she threw the covers aside and headed for the shower. While the hot water soothed her muscles, she speculated on what Mayor Burke had to say. Acting as mayor of a small town wasn't a full-time job. The pay was abysmal, but Fletcher Burke didn't need the money. A partner in one of the best law firms in the county, Burke & Snyder, he took on the duty six years ago mostly as a social responsibility. From the start, the well-connected lawyer attracted a flurry of business investments, helped local businesses get low-interest loans, and formed committees that substantially increased tourism. On a small-town scale, the trickle-down-theory worked astonishingly well. All of Garnerville benefitted. Sidney marveled at how one individual could make a difference in the lives of so many. She and Fletcher shared a good working relationship, one of mutual respect, and they were careful to stay out of each other's way.

Sidney stepped out of the shower, toweled dry, wrapped her body in her terry cloth robe, and opened the door to clear out the steam. While pulling her hair into a ponytail, she heard a soft thumping noise coming from down the hall. She peeked into the hallway and saw the closed door to Selena's room. *Odd.* She could have sworn it was open last night when she turned in. Did her sister come home while she was in the shower?

The rhythmic thumping stopped for a few seconds, then started again. Feeling tension in her chest, Sidney made a detour to her bedroom, grabbed her Glock, and advanced to Selena's room holding the handgun at her side. She felt a thin stream of cool air flowing under the door over her toes.

"Selena?"

No answer.

Sidney stood to one side, twisted the handle, and opened the door with enough force to slam it against the inner wall. She listened. No sound of an intruder. She peeked into the room, pulled her head back. It appeared empty. She brought the gun up to eye level with both hands, stepped into the doorway, and scanned the room.

A stream of cold air drew her gaze to the window, open several inches, the blinds pulled almost all the way up. The base of the blinds bumped steadily against the window frame in the wind. *Simple explanation.* Her sister left the window open and a current of wind shut the door. Then Sidney imagined a different scenario.

The back door was unlocked when she arrived home last night. Had someone been in the house? Heard her come in? Retreated to the bedroom and exited from this window during the night? The thought chilled her.

Sidney crossed the room to the window. The sill was wet, and so was the carpet beneath her feet. Last night's rain. She scanned the sunlit yard below in slices, studying the shadows closely. Yellowing flowers. Withering vegetable garden. The remaining rust and ochre leaves on the trees fluttering in the breeze. Peaceful. No human movement.

She gazed directly below. A long drop. Rose bushes undisturbed. Not likely someone would choose this way to leave the house. Nor would he leave by unbolting the front or back door if he wanted his presence to remain undetected. An intruder would go through a downstairs window, pull it shut it behind him, and no one would be the wiser.

Sidney closed the window and blinds, then turned and viewed her sister's room as she would a crime scene. Like her own bedroom, it was furnished simply with charming gems rescued from Molly's Thrift Shop—botanical prints on the wall, worn Persian rugs, a celadon vase from China, mismatched antique lamps. Nothing looked out of place in the array of practical items lining the surface of the desk, nightstand, and dresser. One side of the chenille spread that covered the bed was smooth. The other side had an imprint on the pillow, and the spread was ruffled, as if someone had taken a nap on top of the covers. One of three brightly colored throw pillows lay on the floor.

Chili loped into the room, leapt onto the bed, and immediately formed a cozy nest in the center of the pillow. Again. Simple explanation. It would be logical to assume the cat was the mystery culprit who ruffled the spread. But Sidney took a moment to think illogically. She put herself into the head of a psychopath who might surreptitiously enter a woman's home and invade her most private space—her bed. Sidney pictured a stranger lying there, quickly rising, unknowingly pushing the pillow to the floor.

Unease settled into Sidney's gut as she searched under beds and closets throughout the house and checked all the doors and windows. All locked except for the window in the laundry room. How long had it been unlocked? Days? Weeks? Or just since last night? The tension in Sidney's stomach tightened as she asked herself a hard question. Was she emotionally capable of handling these Garnerville murders? Was her anxiety warranted, or was she allowing the old stress of investigating homicides play havoc with her imagination? Pushing her worries aside, she hurriedly dressed for her morning meeting.

CHAPTER TWENTY-ONE

SIDNEY PARKED THE YUKON at the curb and sprinted up the stairs of City Hall, a domed two-story brick building with an extended portico and four imposing columns, circa 1889. The brass plaque posted by the entrance stated the design was inspired by classical Greek architecture, but a step into the interior quickly dashed that ill-conceived notion. Remodeled numerous times, it languished in the purgatory of the bland and unimaginative, featuring boxy rooms, utilitarian furniture, humming fluorescent lights, and a musty smell that breathed through the ancient heating system.

A red-haired twenty-something woman sat guard in the reception area, blue fingernails tapping her keyboard. "Morning, Chief." She beamed a high-wattage smile that was a bit blinding first thing in the morning. Somehow, she looked familiar. No doubt, they'd met at some civic function that Sidney could not remember.

Sidney read from the nameplate on her desk. "Morning, Sara."

"Mayor Burke's waiting in the conference room. Can I bring you coffee?"

"That'd be great. Cream, one sugar."

Sara smiled. Another flash of impossibly white teeth.

The spacious conference room retained some of the building's original elegance: coffered ceilings, marble-tiled floor, walls lined with sepia-tone photos of prominent historical figures. The ornately carved, highly polished display case, sideboard, and conference table looked like relics predating the First World War.

The mayor stood talking to Jeff Norcross in front of the bay window, their figures striped by sunlight slanting through the blinds. Gray-haired and attractive, despite his over-sized nose and slightly jutting chin, Mayor Burke was one of the few people in town who wore a suit to work. This morning he looked distinguished in tailored gray flannel, a white oxford shirt, and red striped tie.

Sidney attempted not to frown as she assessed Jeff Norcross. The owner and sole employee of the *Daily Buzz* sported a lacquered blonde comb-over, gaunt face, and pale blue eyes behind wire-rimmed glasses. He wore his standard khaki Dockers and long-sleeved polo shirt.

Grave expressions transformed into smiles as the three greeted each other, then tightened again as they took seats at the end of the table.

Sara strolled in, placed a steaming mug of coffee in front of Sidney, and quietly left. Sidney took a grateful sip.

"Have you seen the morning paper, Chief?" Jeff pushed his glasses higher on his nose with an index finger.

"No. Haven't had time."

Jeff passed the paper to her and both men remained silent as she focused her attention on the lead story. Above a photo of Samantha Ferguson appeared the bold headline:

Local Woman Murdered

The body of local resident Samantha Ferguson was discovered in the Siuslaw Forest Wednesday evening around midnight. As of yet, no details have been released. Police Chief Becker stated the case is under investigation, and they are pursuing several strong leads.

The article went on to highlight the young woman's interests, future dreams of a career in art, and her surviving family members.

No mention of her struggle with drug addiction or her less than exemplary lifestyle. Her father, a retired surgeon, traveled abroad annually with Doctors Without Borders, and the Fergusons often sponsored charitable events here in town. Sidney realized she needed to brush up on her social awareness. She shouldn't be learning who the leading citizens of Garnerville were from the newspaper.

Mayor Burke cleared his throat when she looked up. "So, Chief Becker, we're facing a grim situation here. A beautiful young woman from a high-profile family was murdered, her killer is at large, and only a dribble of information has been released to Jeff and me."

"I've extended the courtesy of printing just the bare facts," Jeff said with a hint of indignation. "But now the complete story needs to be told. Rumors are flying. Scaring people."

Sidney turned her attention to the reporter with whom she had a congenial, if indifferent, relationship. Working out of a cubbyhole here at City Hall, Jeff mostly covered rotary events, weddings, and obits. Details of minor crimes were fed to him through briefings from Winnie. Sidney knew he was salivating to fully cover Samantha's homicide. "I appreciate your concern, Jeff, but we don't reveal details of ongoing investigations. This case needs to be handled with sensitivity. We have to carefully evaluate what we release to the public."

"The public needs to know a serial killer's on the loose," he said sharply.

Mayor Burke sat upright. "What?"

Sidney blinked, stunned. How did Jeff know about a serial killer? Was he grasping at straws, or had someone leaked classified information? "Where'd you hear that?"

"I have my sources." With a tight smirk of satisfaction, Jeff turned his laptop around to face her and the mayor.

Sidney's stomach twisted. On the screen was the photo of an

origami butterfly, identical to the one found on Mimi's body before it got rain-washed.

"Chief Becker, want to tell me what's going on?" Mayor Burke asked, the muscles tightening around his mouth.

"Similar butterflies were found on the bodies of Mimi Matsui and Samantha," Jeff interjected. "Which ties both crimes to one killer."

"That true?" Burke asked. "We're dealing with a serial killer?"

Sidney drew in a slow, careful breath, and said evenly, "We're still processing information, but that seems to be the case."

The mayor's face paled.

Sidney turned to Jeff. "I was going to give you full disclosure after the lab results come in. How'd you get this information?"

"Sources." Cocky grin.

"If you're covering for someone who hacked into police files, that's a felony. Who's your source?"

The cocky grin was replaced by thinly veiled hostility. "Confidential."

"This isn't Deep Throat, Jeff," she said coldly. "National security isn't at stake. We're trying to catch a dangerous killer, and you're impeding my investigation."

Jeff pressed his lips together so hard they turned white.

She leaned forward in her seat. "Only a few people have access to this information. I know you didn't get it from my deputies or the M.E. You must be colluding with the killer."

Jeff's face flushed beet red.

"Who sent it, Jeff?" Mayor Burke asked sharply.

Silence.

He shot Jeff a warning look, and repeated sternly, "Answer the question."

The reporter raised his hands in a gesture of surrender. "Christ. Okay, okay. An anonymous email."

"Show me the email," Sidney said.

Jeff's fingers worked his keyboard, and an email opened that contained one line of type and an attachment. The topic line read: *Newsflash!* The type read: *Beautiful butterflies found on the bodies of Mimi Matsui and Samantha Ferguson.* Jeff clicked on the attachment and revealed the butterfly.

"Coldblooded bastard," Burke said.

"Is this the only email you got from him?" Sidney asked.

"Yes." Jeff's expression looked determined. "I won't mention the butterflies, but people need to know a serial killer is targeting women in Garnerville."

"That's not entirely true." Sidney kept her voice steady. "These aren't spontaneous, random murders. These two women were selected well in advance. Their deaths were carefully planned. A determined killer with time on his hands is going to get his victim. No one can protect her. To scare the hell out of all the women in town, and everyone else for that matter, including tourists, would be a huge mistake." Sidney could not allow the story to be driven by Jeff's desire to sell papers and make a name for himself. "Don't rush this story, Jeff," Sidney said. "You go big, you'll draw news teams from across the state. They'll turn our town into reality TV. Reporters from every network will be parked on Main Street, harassing people, following my officers, blowing every nuance out of proportion. They'll push you off the story. That what you want?"

"She's right," Burke said. "The town would turn into a media circus."

"I need a few more days to investigate this case," Sidney said. "My department and the county deputies can get more done working quietly. Before folks put up their guard."

Jeff pursed his lips, glared.

"Work with us, Jeff. You'll get first crack at breaking the story," Sidney said. "Every detail."

"Keep the story small, for now," Mayor Burke agreed. "People are freaked out enough by Samantha's murder."

Sidney was relieved the mayor was letting her take the lead. Smart move. If her decision blew up in their faces, she would take the heat, not him. "Jeff, you can help by advising people to use caution. Stay in groups at night. Lock their doors. Be alert. If anyone saw anything suspicious Wednesday night, they need to come forward and share that information." She paused and waited while he took notes, fingers clicking on his keyboard. "No details about the crime scenes. Agreed?"

Jeff puffed out a breath of frustration. "Agreed."

Sidney didn't like his lack of conviction.

"Can you trace that email to its source, Chief?" Mayor Burke asked.

"I'll have Darnell take a look, but from my experience in Oakland, I'd say it's virtually impossible. No telling how many servers the message traveled through before it got to Jeff. It would be like trying to catch a minnow in the ocean." She turned to Jeff. "If you get contacted again, notify me immediately. You could be instrumental in breaking this case."

Jeff's eyes brightened at the prospect.

"Thank you for working with us, Jeff," Mayor Burke said in an appeasing tone. "Now I need to speak with Chief Becker alone."

The reporter nodded, grabbed his computer, and left the room.

"I'm sorry you had to learn about the killer this way," Sidney said when the door closed behind the reporter. "I know it's a shock."

"Understatement." He ran a tanned hand through his thick crop of hair. "What else can you tell me?"

She exhaled, thinking, but there was no way to make the words less blunt. "Both victims were abducted, held hostage for several hours, then killed and staged the same way."

His eyes widened. "Holy hell. He abducted them? Held them hostage?"

"Yes."

"Sick bastard." His face was marked momentarily by a shadow of disgust. "Where the hell did he take them? What did he do to them?"

"I can't answer that."

"How were they killed?"

"Their wrists were cut. They bled out."

"Gruesome." He was silent for a long moment. "Are we dealing with a sexual predator?"

"We're not sure. Lab reports should let us know on Monday."

"So, these aren't random killings?"

"No, sir. I believe the killer knew his victims. This perp is methodical and careful. He stalked each woman and waited for the perfect opportunity to abduct her."

Mayor Burke looked a little dazed. "Never thought anything like this could happen here. It's frightening to think a vicious killer's out there. Watching. Perhaps waiting to strike again."

Sidney shifted her weight in her chair. "People tend to think of these killers as blurry figures lurking in the shadows. In reality, he could be someone we know. Many psychopaths have families, go to church, are active in their communities, appear quite normal."

"Comforting thought." His forehead creased. "Why is the killer contacting the press after three years of anonymity? Why disclose evidence now? He suddenly wants attention?"

"My guess? In his own eyes, Mayor, the perp is successful at what he does. He's the best. He's stumped the cops for three years. He deserves recognition. He wants more of a challenge, so now he's leaving clues."

"He's thumbing his nose at us?"

"So it seems. We have some strong leads and several persons of interest. Hopefully the lab results will give us enough evidence to make an arrest."

"You're that close?"

"I believe so." Sidney prayed she wasn't making a false promise.

"I know you're understaffed, Chief. Putting in long hours. You have my full support and appreciation." They stood and shook hands, and he gave her a resigned smile. "Keep me posted."

She nodded silently, and left City Hall, her mind darting between thoughts, trying to connect random dots. She didn't have enough evidence to form a coherent picture of the killer and his perverted motivation. Jeff's urge to break the story was unsettling. Gagging him was a short-term solution. If the killer wanted details of his crimes to be made public, he'd find a way to make that happen. Sweat dampened the back of her neck. She didn't have much time.

CHAPTER TWENTY-TWO

AT NOON, Ann stood and stretched. She'd been working in the loft all morning, staying too busy to allow extraneous thoughts to derail her. Bailey was stretched full length on the Navajo rug in front of the portable heater, snoring, his bandaged paws occasionally twitching.

Before Selena left for town to teach her yoga class, she made sure her holstered .22 pistol was clipped to Ann's belt. The two had practiced shooting in the pasture for two hours. Ann could now load and safely fire the handgun. The holster felt cumbersome, but being caught unarmed in a life-threatening situation would be worse.

Ann wandered to the window, picked up her binoculars, and scanned Miko's covered porch to see if he discovered the apple pie she'd left that morning in a cooler on his porch. Her lips curved into a smile. The cooler was gone.

Miko was nowhere in sight, but she spied Noah seated on a green John Deere tractor plowing through a sea of yellowed corn stalks, his dark hair blowing in the wind. A flock of blackbirds flitted behind the tractor like a shifting cloud of smoke, darting from sky to earth to peck at the crushed, uprooted husks. Three ravens suddenly lifted from the highest cedar boughs and glided gracefully on eddies of wind. They jetted into the cloud of blackbirds, dispersing them like so many bits of soot streaming from a chimney. Ann smiled at their mischievous antics. The blackbirds regrouped, only to be waylaid again by the larger ebony birds. An opera of nature playing out in the sky. Ann wondered if Arthur was one of the ravens.

Abruptly, her gaze was pulled to Noah, who'd brought the tractor to a halt and was standing over the steering wheel, waving at the ravens in an aggressive manner. The cawing ravens responded by dive-bombing his head, missing by feet. Noah's anger spilled into the morning like an errant storm, dulling the brightness of the day. He reached down and brought up a shotgun, and to her horror, he aimed it at the ravens.

Dear God!

The gun exploded. Two ravens spiraled to the ground. The other shot like a missile to the safety of the trees.

Ann tore down the stairs, out of the barn and across her fields; her boots crushing basil, tomatoes, lettuce. She burst like a big ox through the bordering tree branches and stumbled onto Miko's cornfield, blood pounding like a war drum in her ears. Two ravens hobbled in the dirt on each side of the tractor, each dragging a wing. Noah stalked one poor raven like a demon, gun aimed at its back, stomping the ground, tormenting the creature.

"Stop it!" Ann shrieked.

Noah fired the weapon at the same time her scream pierced the crystalline air.

The raven exploded into a mass of shredded feathers, some shooting into the air and others gracefully turning and tossing and fluttering on the breeze.

Noah turned his sight on the other raven, now desperately struggling to take flight, lifting a foot or two before plummeting back to the ground. The creature hobbled frantically toward the safety of the trees, dragging its useless wing across the rich, black earth.

Cawww! Cawww! Cah. Cah.

Arthur!

"Stop!" Ann shrieked. She stumbled through tangled sleeves of dried stalks, willing herself to reach Arthur before Noah unleashed a new round of buckshot. Something moved in her peripheral vision.

"Don't shoot!" she screamed.

Noah bestowed Ann with a long assessing stare. She read fierce determination and malice in his posture. Turning away, he closed the space between himself and Arthur in a few long strides, lifted his shotgun, and aimed it at the distressed raven.

"No! Don't!"

She heard the explosion, felt it reverberate through her body like a cannon blast. The earth seemed to wobble beneath her feet. Then realization set in. The shot didn't come from Noah's weapon. The blur at the edge of her vision turned into Miko, aiming a pistol at the sky.

"Put it down!" Miko yelled.

Noah locked eyes with his father, and the two engaged in an interminable battle of wills. Ann's pulse raced. The landscape became a photograph. Silent. Motionless. Finally, Noah shrugged, strode back to the tractor, lowered the shotgun on the floor of the John Deere and resumed work on the field as though there had been no interruption.

Miko and Ann reached Arthur at the same moment. She fell to her knees and the raven hopped onto her lap with a pitiable squawk, his right wing as bent and useless as a broken kite, his side too bloody for Ann to discern his injuries. "Hello," Arthur croaked weakly.

"My God, it talks," Miko said.

"Yes. I taught him. Hurry. We need to get him to the vet."

Miko nodded, shrugged off his fleece sweatshirt, and gently wrapped Arthur like a baby in a papoose. "I'll drive. You call ahead."

He carried Arthur carefully, and they hurried to an old white pickup truck parked by the barn. Miko transferred Arthur to Ann's lap, gunned the engine and peeled out of the driveway, wheels spewing dust and gravel. He handed her his cell phone, she stabbed the digits on the pad, and hurriedly related the emergency to the assistant who answered.

Miko frowned when she handed back the phone. "Please, Ann, leave your gun in the glove compartment."

Ann forgot she was armed. If she had remembered, would she have threatened Noah with it? With shaking hands, she unclipped the holster and placed it in the glove box.

The ride to town was surreal. Ann alternately cooed to Arthur and swiped her tears. The raven's black eyes shone like obsidian beads, twitching occasionally, signaling he was alive. Ann stole blurry glances at Miko, his gaze trained on the highway, the muscles set stiffly along his jaw, his dry, callused hands gripping the wheel. Their bodies leaned to the left, then to the right. The white lines of the highway rushed up to meet them and vanished beneath the hood. Forest swept by on both sides.

Miko braked in the veterinarian's lot and he rounded the truck to open her door.

Dr. Jacobs met them in the waiting room and gently took Arthur from her arms, then disappeared with his assistant through a swinging door.

"Evermore! Evermore!" Arthur's pitiable squawks echoed down the hall.

Ann stood dazed, Arthur's blood staining her sweatshirt and jeans. Her perception of the world seemed a bit off kilter; the relationship of physical objects to space out of alignment.

In this tilted universe, Miko stood next to her as steadfast as a pillar. They had not exchanged a word during the drive, both focused intently on their mission. Odd she thought. He always looked so imposing in his fields, body strong and straight, but standing beside her he was a smaller version of the man anchored in her binoculars, matching her height of five-foot-eight. She peered at his anonymous face, trying to memorize a feature she could use in the future to identify him. His eyebrows were thick and black with a beautiful arch, and his mouth was framed on each side by a deep groove. But what she would remember was his hair—short and stiff and white, with threads of black woven through.

"Ann, please sit." Miko gestured toward a row of chairs lining the wall and she sank into the nearest one. "Can I get you coffee?"

In the corner stood a table stocked with carafes of coffee, teabags, packets of sugar, tiny creamers, disposable cups. This offering of refreshment provided a sense of order, of normalcy, to a room where people waited anxiously for news of injured animals. Would the verdict induce heartbreak, or infinite gratitude, as it did with Bailey only yesterday.

"Coffee?" he asked again.

She nodded. "Yes. Thank you."

"Milk and sugar?"

"Please. One each." The logical part of her mind told her she was perfectly capable of getting her own coffee, while the intuitive side told her she was in a state of shock and needed to be treated gently. She had just witnessed a second act of brutality in as many days, and her mind was reeling. It would take time to find her way back to normal.

Ann watched Miko cross the room. Despite his slight limp, she sensed strength in the bunched muscles of his compact body. She also sensed his calm. He wore soiled denim overalls over a red plaid shirt, sleeves rolled up to the elbows, forearms ropy, work boots crusted with dirt—yet he exuded an air of dignity. Ann worked at reconciling the man who lived as an image in her binoculars with the life-sized version occupying space in the small room.

Miko returned with two Styrofoam cups and handed her one.

His chair creaked as he settled himself beside her. Stretching out his legs, he crossed one boot over the other. She inhaled his smell—a mix of soil and sweet hay and a hint of motor oil. His fingertips were etched with engine grease and she pictured him working on his farm truck.

They both sipped coffee.

"I'm sorry about the bird," he said in a grave tone.

"He's not just a bird. His name is Arthur. And he's my friend."

He held her gaze but she couldn't discern his expression. Did he think her crazy?

"Teaching an animal takes time and patience. You must be close," he said.

"Very," she said softly. "He's visited me daily. For four years."

"He's loyal."

"Yes."

"I apologize for Noah. He doesn't appreciate that the life of every creature is sacred. He's a hunter. He enjoys killing for sport."

"What he did today wasn't sport. It was savage."

She heard him slowly inhale.

"To a gentle soul, it would seem so." He took a gulp of coffee and his Adam's apple bobbed in his throat like a marble. "Growing up on a farm, you get used to seeing where your food comes from. We buy our beef and pork from neighbors who raise animals for slaughter. Many farmers and ranchers kill animals they consider pests. Moles, gophers, mice, rats, and yes, unfortunately, sometimes birds. I will talk to Noah to make sure he leaves the ravens alone."

Ann sifted through his words, looking for threads of truth. She bought venison from local hunters, beef and chickens from local ranchers. Animals killed humanely. But what she witnessed in the cornfield today was vengeful. Sadistic.

"You've been through a lot in the last two days," he continued. "Chief Becker told me what you saw in the woods."

Ann's stomach tightened as her mind shifted to the night of terror.

"It was a shock to learn there'd been another murder," he continued. "That young woman was killed in the same area, at the same time of night as my wife. You were there. Did she die the same way as Mimi?"

"I don't know. I didn't see the crime scene." She shuddered, not wanting to know. "The way the cops acted, I'm sure they believe it's the same man."

"Three years I've lived with this," he said with a touch of bitterness. "No justice for Mimi. No justice for my family. All the while, knowing a killer's still out there. Free to kill again. Maybe now they'll put out more effort to find him, and people will stop pointing the finger at me."

"I never believed you did it," she said, her voice barely above a whisper, offered as a benediction.

His dark eyes met hers. "I appreciate hearing that."

"Chief Becker is a skilled detective from a big city. She'll get you the justice you deserve."

"We all deserve." He clenched his jaw, eyes glistening, and looked away.

Ann was afraid of men, and had not deliberately touched a man in years, other than her son. A quality of decency in her neighbor filtered through her fear. She sensed the rawness of his suffering. His weathered hand rested on his knee, close to hers. Ann found the courage to take his hand in her hands, to cradle it as she would a baby bird before restoring it to its nest. His fingers were rough and callused and foreign.

Miko didn't pull away.

They didn't look at each other but sat taking comfort in the warmth of touch.

When she withdrew her hands, Miko spoke, and the tone of his voice sounded lighter. "I had your apple pie for breakfast. It was so good, I ate half of it."

Ann flushed with pleasure. "Your beautiful apples inspired me. Such a variety. Pink Pearl. Rustic Gold. You're a gifted farmer."

"You are, too. I can smell your herbs when the wind blows from your farm to mine."

Ann saw a movement around his mouth and his lips pulled back to reveal his teeth, even and white, with three crooked incisors on the bottom, and she knew he was smiling. She had always been able to sense emotion through some unconscious mechanism and resonate with it. She smiled back.

"Sometime you should come over and see my farm. Get more apples. Some vegetables. I have jeweled yams and Yukon Gold ready to harvest."

"I would love to. I'll make scalloped potatoes and sweet potato pie and save some for you."

"Wonderful." His smile widened.

"Do you grow tomatoes?"

"No."

"I'm at the end of the season. I need to strip my vines before the frost comes. I'll bring you some heirlooms. Herbs, too. Do you like basil?"

"I love basil. I make Caprese salad. Tomato sauce."

"You cook?"

His smile withered. "I used to. Not anymore since Mimi died. It's not worth the time it takes to cook for one."

"I know. I'm alone, too, but I always cook extra for my son. I send Matt home with meals a few times a week."

"Lucky man. Noah eats out most nights."

She searched her mind for something more to say but the

thought of Noah filled her with dread. She despised Miko's son for watching her house, for shooting her ravens, for touching her inappropriately in her stand at the farmers market. There was something terribly off about him. Hiding her loathing, she asked, "Is your son home for good?"

Miko shrugged. "That's up to Noah. How long he wants to do farm work. If he stays, he has to earn his keep and stay out of trouble. I won't have it any other way. So far, he's been a big help. He works hard." He turned his empty cup in his hands, gazing at it as though it were a crystal ball forewarning the future. "I'm not a young man anymore. I don't want to work this hard forever. The farm's been in my family for three generations. My daughter doesn't want to farm, and if Noah doesn't take over, I'll be forced to sell."

"That would be a shame," she said sadly. Ann didn't like change. The thought of her neighbor being replaced by strangers frightened her. But that would be preferable to Noah taking up permanent residence. "I'll continue with my business for another twenty years," she said. "It's not a big enterprise, like yours. My partner, Selena, helps a lot. I don't know what I'd do without work. I'm not very social."

"Me neither. My dogs and chickens are good company." He chuckled. "They don't complain as long as they're fed. It's been nice to have my son home. With Mimi gone, the house gets too quiet. Too big."

Ann heard the warmth in Miko's voice and recognized his love for his son. She sensed his loneliness, something she also experienced, especially at night. Soon after Mimi's murder, Noah went to prison. How did Miko cope? Ann recalled his black hair turned white almost overnight. She wished she'd reached out to him back then.

The door swung open, and the vet's assistant stepped into the waiting room. Patricia was a stocky woman who dressed like a man, had spiky pink hair, and an amiable personality. "Good news, Ann. Arthur's gonna pull through. The buckshot only hit his wing. It was broken, but Dr. Jacobs set it. Whether he'll be able to fly again, time will tell. We'll keep him here for a few days until he's well enough to hop around. You'll have to keep him caged for a while so he doesn't bang his wing."

Ann felt the tension in her shoulders ease up. "No problem. I can do that."

"Let me take care of the bill." Miko rose to his feet and walked with Patricia to the counter, pulling his wallet from a back pocket.

Ann said nothing. It was only right that Miko should be held accountable for the sins of his son. Her neighbor's handling of the crisis had been admirable from start to finish. He took control. He knew what to do. Her estimation of him surpassed her imaginings.

CHAPTER TWENTY-THREE

IT WAS 9:00 A.M.

For the first time since Samantha's murder, Sidney had gotten a decent night's sleep and felt reasonably rested. Still, anxiety hummed just below the surface, and would continue to do so until Samantha's killer was put behind bars. Sidney hadn't had time to grab breakfast before her meeting with the mayor, and her stomach loudly protested. She drove to Burger Shack, placed her order, parked in the lot, and indelicately wolfed down a hot flaky biscuit stuffed with bacon, eggs, and cheese. Sometimes, nothing hit the spot like greasy fast food.

It was a cool autumn day with erratic gusts of wind and quick-scudding clouds. Leaves of every shape and color spiraled from the trees and carpeted the earth with vibrant tapestries. Gold and red leaves tumbled onto the hood of the Yukon.

Sidney pulled out of the lot, drove three blocks down Main Street, and parked in front of the Art Studio. Matt Howard had seen paper sculptures exhibited here, and she hoped to find the source of the origami butterflies. She paused on the sidewalk to admire the paintings and ceramic pots displayed in the window, gratified the studio brought local artists into the public eye. So much talent in the area she'd known nothing about.

She entered the large room that smelled faintly of oil paint and turpentine. Art of every kind hung on the walls; charcoals, pastels, watercolors, oils—some excellent, some amateurish.

A man stood facing a canvas on a tall wooden easel, apparently too consumed by his work to notice her. He added vivid color in bold brush strokes to a landscape of Lake Kalapuya and the surrounding mountains. Post-impressionist style, she remembered from her high school art class. From the back, the artist looked like a young man, lean build, broad shoulders, light on his feet. He wore beige linen pants, a blue cotton shirt with the tails out, and boat shoes with no socks. His dark hair curled around his collar, lightly salted with gray.

"That's beautiful," she said. "Reminds me of Van Gogh."

He turned, startled, brown eyes wide, and then he smiled warmly. "High praise. Van Gogh is one of my gods." His features were pleasantly arranged in a tanned face, and the lines radiating from the corners of his eyes told her he was around forty. His gaze darted to her shield and gun and back to her face. He laid his brush on his palette and extended a hand. "Chief Becker, I presume?"

"Yes. Are you the owner?"

"David Kane, at your service."

His fingers were strong and stained with specks of paint. She glanced at his other hand. No wedding band.

"Haven't seen you at a Chamber meeting, Chief."

"I work evenings. I've meant to stop by and introduce myself, but you know, been busy fighting crime." She glanced around at canvases on other easels, all in various stages of completion. "You certainly bring out the best in your students."

"I do my humble best. I can only mine the gold that's in the shaft." David raised his brows questioningly. "Are you here to talk art? I can't help but wonder about the timing. Sammy's murder, I mean."

"You knew her?"

"Certainly. She took classes here this summer." He thrust his hands deep into his pockets, his tone and expression somber. "A tragedy. Beautiful young woman. Frightening to think she was murdered. One of the attractions of Garnerville is low crime. That's why I moved here from San Francisco."

"Garnerville is a safe community. Our murder rate is nominal. Only four in the last decade." She didn't want to defend her town by citing statistics. No murder was defensible. "Low crime is why I took the job of police chief. I moved back here from Oakland two years ago."

"Oakland?" He whistled. "High murder rate."

"Don't I know it. I was lead investigator of a homicide unit."

"Whew. Tough job. We're lucky to have someone with your experience." He rocked back and forth on the balls of his feet. "Garnerville is your home town, then?"

"Born and raised."

"A true Oregonian." His serious demeanor dropped away and his eyes became a warmer shade of brown, appraising her in a complimentary fashion. "Where are my manners? Can I offer you a cappuccino?"

"Sure." She smiled. "I live for my next java jolt."

"Come with me." He led her into a back room equipped with an updated kitchen. Modern-style chairs were arranged around a rustic wood table, tasteful art crowded the original red brick walls, and the cement floor was stained wine red and polished.

David pulled two white porcelain cups from a cabinet and turned to a commercial-size coffee machine that took up half of one counter.

"That's a serious coffee maker," she said. "You've got your priorities straight."

A flicker of amusement touched the corner of his mouth. "I think I was a Barista in a former life."

"In this life, have you always been an artist?"

"Yeah, but I didn't get serious until eight years ago. I was a real estate developer. When the market went soft, I took a break. Turned to what I really love. Painting. It took hold of me and didn't let go. Seems I'm still taking that break."

The smell of strong coffee filled the room. The machine hissed as he crowned each cup with a cloud of steamed milk. He sprinkled chocolate on top, set one cup in front of Sidney, and settled next to her.

She sipped and let out a sigh of satisfaction. "You make a mean cup of java."

He grinned. "Life is short. I take joy in simple pleasures."

"Good policy. Your studio is great for the community. Nice to be able to make a living doing what you love."

He laughed. "I never said I was making a living. I don't have to work. I'm secure financially. I do this for purely selfish reasons. I enjoy people. I enjoy teaching. Sharing my passion with others." He cocked his head, a glint of interest in his eyes. "You like being a civil servant?"

"I do. My dad was police chief here for eighteen years. Guess it got passed in my DNA. Keeping our community safe is my way of helping people."

"You like solving mysteries?"

"Yeah. I like the challenge." She cleared her throat. "Which brings me to my purpose for being here." Sidney pulled out her phone and swiped through her photos until she found the origami butterfly. "Can you identify this?"

David studied it with genuine interest. "It's beautiful." He glanced up at her. "I don't know its source, but it's by a very skilled artist. Those intricate folds were done with jeweler's tools, under magnification."

"Really?" Sidney looked at the butterfly with new appreciation. "So, this is valuable?"

"Relatively. No Van Gogh, but certainly a collector's item."

Sidney rubbed her chin. Why would her suspect leave a valuable piece of art with his victims? What did it symbolize to his psychopathic mind? She glanced back at David. "I was told there's a paper sculptor who shows here at your studio. Could you give me his contact info?"

"Sloane Pickett. But this isn't his work. Way too intricate." He sipped his coffee. "Does this have something to do with Sammy's death?"

"Possibly."

"Hmmm. Tell you what. Text me a copy of that photo, and I'll see if I can find the artist. I'm connected to artists internationally through social media."

"That would be great."

"Happy to help." The words were sincere, and he held her gaze steadily. David recited his number and Sidney sent him the photo. It popped up on his screen seconds later.

"When was Samantha a student here?"

He squinted at the ceiling for a moment. "Most of July."

"What was her specialty?"

"Pastels. Landscapes. She'd taken art classes in high school. Naturally gifted. She could have gone places."

"Did she have any disputes with other students?"

"No. She was very friendly. A wicked sense of humor."

"Any boyfriends?"

"Hmmm, I don't know about boyfriends, but a guy walked in here one night and stood just inside the door." David strummed the tabletop with his fingers. "Big. All muscle. Covered in tattoos. When Sammy saw him, she looked surprised, then upset. She turned back to her work and ignored him, and he split." His brow furrowed. "Now that I think about it, right after, she packed up her gear and left. She looked really tense. That was the last time she came to class."

Sidney brought up a picture of Noah on her phone. "This him?"

"Oh yeah, that's him. Not someone you forget."

"You've been very helpful, David." Sidney drained her cup

and rose to go. "Thanks for the great coffee, and for being my investigative assistant."

"Anytime, Chief. I enjoyed your company." He smiled clear to his brown eyes and held her gaze longer than necessary. Her face warmed. He placed a hand on the small of her back as they returned to the studio.

"We're having an exhibition here tomorrow night," he said. "Maybe you'd like to stop by. Meet some of the local artists. Have some Champagne."

"Sounds like fun." She meant it sincerely. She couldn't remember the last time she spent an evening enjoying something cultural. She'd make a point of juggling her schedule to attend for a couple of hours. "If your Champagne is as good as your coffee, I'm in."

"I'll put a special bottle on reserve," He said, a touch of flirtiness in his tone. "Just for you, Chief."

"My friends call me Sidney."

"Sidney," David said, his smile crinkling the corners of his eyes.

His good humor was infectious, and she smiled back. "I better scoot."

"Yeah, you better go take a bite out of crime. Be safe." He opened the door, and she felt his gaze follow her as she crossed the sidewalk and slid into the driver's seat of the Yukon. Her stomach did a little flutter as she revved up the engine and pulled out into the traffic lane. She still felt the warmth of David's hand on her back. It had felt good to be touched by a charming, confident man.

Sidney caught her reflection in the mirror. She deliberately downplayed her looks while on the job, which meant no makeup or jewelry, and her crisply starched uniform hardly said sexy. Yet a lot of nonverbal communication had fired between her and David, and he'd made it crystal clear he was attracted to her. For a long while, she hadn't put much thought into her appearance, other than being well-groomed and professional, but now she found herself wondering what dress she should wear to the art show. What jewelry? Should she wear her hair up or down?

Maybe her love life was about to come out of hibernation. Or not. *Down girl.* She warned herself not to invest too much hope in the evening. She'd been let down by romance too many times to place a Cinderella-filter on reality.

CHAPTER TWENTY-FOUR

SIDNEY'S PHONE hummed as she drove away from the art studio and pulled to a halt at the traffic light. "What's up, Darnell?"

"Two things. First, a deputy from county found Samantha's car. It was parked at the Gas n' Go on the highway. The manager said it had been parked off to the side for two days, and he was about to have it towed, but instead, he decided to call the sheriff. A deputy ran plates and got a hit on Samantha. He's having it towed to Salem for processing."

"Could be the point of her abduction. Lab probably won't find anything. The perp would have avoided touching her car. Were her purse and phone there?"

"No. They're missing."

Sidney processed her thoughts out loud. "If the perp was trailing her, that location would be the perfect opportunity to make his move. He could have pulled his truck, or van, beside her BMW, blocking the view of her car from the store. Then when she came out, he would have walked up behind her, jabbed her with the needle, and put her in his vehicle.

"Chief, the gas station is just a mile down the road from Matt Howard's house. She probably just left his place after they had lunch at Katie's. If he followed her, she wouldn't have been alarmed to see him. He could have injected her easily."

Darnell sounded like a prosecuting attorney building a case, pounding another nail into the coffin of Matt's wobbly defense.

"Or it could be some random psycho who followed her from Matt's house," she said. "Think about it. Matt had time and opportunity to inject her at his house. Isolated. Private. Why would he risk abducting her in a public parking lot?"

"So it looked like she left his place alive," Darnell said. "Got abducted by someone else."

"You make a good point," Sidney said. "But let's see what the evidence shows before we rush to make an arrest. Anyone remember seeing her?"

"No. And there were no charges on her credit card. She paid cash."

"Any video footage?"

"Nada. Machine's been down for months. They just use the camera as a deterrent."

Sidney hit the steering wheel with the palm of her hand. In a town with low crime, people got sloppy with their security. She was going to have a firm discussion with the gas station owner. "What's the second thing you wanted to tell me?"

"I've got Jason Welsh waiting in the sweat box."

"I'm two minutes away." Sidney clicked off as the traffic signal changed. She drove down Main Street, pulled into the station lot, entered the building through the back entrance, and met Darnell outside the viewing room.

The young officer looked like a renewed version of the crumpled, depleted man slumped in his chair at the briefing the night before—clean-shaven, uniform crisp, exuding energy.

Sidney rarely saw Darnell, whose shift ended as hers began. She realized it had been a while since they had spoken about anything but police work, and it had been weeks since she'd had more than a passing conversation with his wife and kids. That social oversight needed to change. "How's the family, Darnell?"

"All good," he said, his dark eyes lively. "The little one slept through the night. Gave Mariah and me some needed rest."

"Two kids are a handful. Into everything, I bet."

"You have no idea. It's a holiday to come to work."

"And I thought you just loved your job."

He flashed a smile, teeth white against his dark skin.

"After we put this murder case to rest, we're going to throw an office picnic," Sidney said. "Lots of barbecue. The works. All family members invited."

"Great, Chief. Barbecue is a magic word around our house." Darnell handed over Samantha's file and nodded toward the interview room. "Jason's ready to go."

They entered a space barely larger than a broom closet that featured a two-way mirror and controls for the video and audio in the interview room.

Sidney studied Jason Welsh through the one-way glass. The bartender from Barney's, who had been linked to Samantha as a romantic interest, wore a bored expression. He leaned back in his chair, legs outstretched beneath the scarred metal table, hands clasped behind his head, dressed in faded jeans, a long-sleeved blue shirt, and Converse sneakers.

"He have a record?"

"Nope. Clean."

"He's not what I expected."

Darnell chuckled. "Ain't playgirl material, that's for sure."

"Not even close."

Jason appeared to be around thirty years older than Samantha, and he hadn't aged well. His thin, weathered face had a long jutting chin, a slash for a mouth, and big ears protruding from limp gray hair. She thought he bore a strong resemblance to Laurel from the fifties comedy team, *Laurel and Hardy*.

Darnell thumbed a few buttons. "Audio and video are on."

"Let's go in. Take notes."

Darnell pulled a notepad and pen from his breast pocket and

followed her into the windowless room with a concrete floor and dull white cinderblock walls. They pulled out metal chairs and seated themselves. Sidney sat across from Jason under the glare of florescent lights. "Thanks for coming in, Jason."

"No problem." He sat straighter in his chair, hands folded on the table, expression wary.

"You're not under suspicion. We just have a few questions about Samantha Ferguson. This conversation is being taped. That okay with you?"

"Sure." His eyes darted across the ceiling and located the video camera.

"We know you were working the night Samantha was killed. We also know you two were tight."

"Tight? You mean like a couple?"

"Yeah."

He laughed.

"Why's that funny?"

"Where do you people get your information? Sammy and I weren't an item. Do I look like her type?" He proceeded to tick three points off his fingers. "I ain't rich, young, or good-looking. She was all three. Drop-dead fucking gorgeous."

"You two never dated?" Sidney asked, hearing Darnell click his pen and scribble.

"Dated? Nah. Samantha didn't date." He looked from Darnell to Sidney, giving each an equally assessing stare. "She thought of herself as a free spirit. Didn't want to be tied down with one dude. Basically, she slept with anyone who could get her high."

"Including you?"

He shrugged.

"Is that a yes?"

"On a rare occasion. I don't have anywhere near the deep pockets she needed to feed her appetite."

"Appetite?"

"For drugs, the high life."

"What's the high life?"

"Trips to the city. The coast. Concerts. Partying all night on blow. Expensive gifts."

"Specifically, what gifts?"

"Clothes. Diamond earrings, a fancy watch. Shit like that."

"Know the brand of the watch?"

He gave her the ghost of a grin, pushing his limp gray hair back from his forehead. "A Rolex. Gold and silver, with little diamonds around the face."

Darnell scribbled.

"Who bought her those gifts, Jason?"

"Couldn't tell you."

"You can't, or won't?"

"Don't know anything."

Silence.

She let him relax a moment before dropping the bomb. "Want to tell us about the night Samantha OD'd at your house?"

His eyebrows arched, and he nervously wet his lips. "Nothing to tell."

Sidney's voice toughened. "You have drugs at your party?"

"No," he said too quickly, glancing up at the camera and then leveling a direct stare at Sidney, challenging her to back off.

She held his gaze.

His eyes dropped to his hands and looked back up. Sweat gleamed on his upper lip. "Sammy was high when she got there. Slurring her words, staggering. She passed out within minutes. I called 9-1-1. The EMTs arrived right away and shot her up with naloxone." Jason swiped the sweat with his index finger. "Brought her back from the brink. Literally. It's in the police report."

The report, which Sidney had read, disclosed little more than Jason stated. He lived out of town, so the incident had been written up by an officer on call from the Jackson station. She imagined the scenario. Cop gets the call at 3:00 a.m. Drags himself out of bed, arrives at Jason's after the EMTs left with the patient. The partygoers, by that time, had removed all trace of drugs, and very likely planted evidence in Samantha's car. The officer smelled pot in the house, did a superficial search, saw no evidence of drugs. He found drug paraphernalia in her BMW, determined she was responsible for her own OD, wrote up the report. He went home and tried to catch a few more winks before his workday started. Case closed.

Sidney tried a different tack. "You ever see Noah Matsui hanging around Samantha?"

A look of fear tightened Jason's face for a split second and then was gone. He spoke slowly, as though pulling his words together as he thought of them. "Yeah, but that was years ago. He was her supplier. But he's been out of the picture lately."

She knew he was lying. "Now he's back."

Jason shrugged. "He's keeping his nose clean, far as I know."

"Who got Samantha high after Noah was out of the picture?"

"Don't know."

"You watch over the bar at Barney's. You hear things. See things." Her voice tightened. "You know who the suppliers are."

"Don't see nothing. Don't know nothing."

Sidney narrowed her eyes, gave him another piercing stare.

"Look Chief. I wanna keep my job. I get paid for minding my own business."

She glanced at Darnell, his dark eyes hard, taking it all in.

"You see Noah around since he's been out?" she asked.

"He comes in sometimes."

"When was the last time?"

"Couldn't tell you."

Sidney held his gaze, watched him squirm in his seat.

"You see how busy the place gets? Noah stays away from the bar. Sits in his sister's section."

"He ever have company at his table?"

Jason crossed his arms and clenched his jaw. "Don't know. Ask Tracy."

"You ever see him with Samantha since she got out of rehab?"

"Nope."

"See her with anyone else?"

He shrugged.

"Samantha stayed clean the last two months of her life. She was starting college in two weeks. Trying hard to get her life on track. A ruthless killer robbed her of that chance." Sidney softened her voice and leaned forward in her seat. "Samantha was your friend, Jason. She trusted you." She opened the file and slipped a picture of the crime scene in front of him, taken far enough away that he couldn't see her slit wrists. "You think she deserved to die like this?"

Jason's face went white, and his mouth gaped as he stared at the picture. His eyes squeezed shut, and tears spilled out. He knuckled them away, and after a long silence, asked hoarsely, "How did she die?"

"Viciously. Alone in the woods. Terrorized."

"Bastard…" Jason seethed through clenched teeth.

"Who's the bastard?"

Jason wiped his nose with the back of his sleeve. His fingers trembled.

"Talk to me, Jason."

He struggled to restrain himself, but anger vibrated off him. A vein swelled on his forehead.

"You cared about her, Jason. She deserves justice. Give me a name."

The vein on his forehead pulsed.

Silence.

"Here's what I think." Sidney met his moist eyes. "You and Samantha spent a lot of time together. Enough to make her parents and friends think you were her boyfriend. You did drugs together. When people get high, they babble. I think you had a private window into Samantha's life. You know who gave her those expensive gifts, supplied her habit. Someone with big drug connections."

"Chief, you're dead wrong." His voice cracked, and he paused to compose himself. "There's no big drug trafficker in Garnerville. If there was, I'd know. Dealers here are small-time. They get their dope from out of town. Mostly opioids and smack. They sell to a handful of faithful users."

"Who is he?"

Jason sat still. Not a word, an expression, a twitch.

Sidney wanted to shake him. She balled her hands into fists under the table.

Darnell's shoulders lifted and tightened. His eyes sparked. He looked as though he, too, wanted to grab Jason by the shirt.

"Give me a name," Sidney said, forcing her hands to unclench. "For Sammy."

Jason sat back with his arms crossed, his jaw set in determination. "Don't you get it? What happened to Sammy was payback. A warning. Snitch, you die. Nobody in town's gonna talk to you."

"Someone will, Jason. Someone always does. Just pray it happens before there's another murder. That will be on you."

His lip curled up in a sneer. "I told you all I know. I'm outta here." He scraped back his chair and rose to his feet.

Sidney rounded the table and stood inches from him, their eyes level. She smelled coffee on his breath, felt his body heat. "If I find you've obstructed this investigation by holding back evidence, I'll make it my personal mission to put you behind bars."

He flinched.

"You on drugs, Jason?" she asked in a threatening tone. "Maybe we should investigate you more closely."

A muscle twitched in his cheek. He shook his head instead of answering. Afraid his tone would give him away?

"Do some hard thinking, Jason. See if you have a conscience somewhere in that thick skull of yours." She handed him her card and backed away. "Call me with that name."

Clutching the card, Jason lurched out of the room.

Wrestling to control her temper, Sidney returned to the table and tucked Samantha's photo back in the folder.

"What an ass-wipe." Darnell said, his eyes bright and angry. "He and Samantha were tight. Yet, he's protecting a murder suspect. You scared him shitless, Chief."

"Yeah, but is he more afraid of me, or the man he's protecting?" She rubbed the tight muscles in the back of her neck. "Who the hell is this mystery man?"

"Jason looked terrified when you mentioned Noah."

"He's scared all right. But Noah's hardly a high roller."

"I'll get on the computer. Bore through convicted drug dealers in the tri-city area."

"Specifically, any with money."

"Most are meth cookers. Brains fried, toothless. Hardly suave guys who give away Rolex watches."

The young officer's earnestness impressed her. She forced a smile. "You never know what will slither out from under a rock. See if any other women in Oregon have been killed in a similar fashion to our two victims."

Darnell left to work on the computer. Sidney entered her small office and made a call to Officer Amanda Cruz.

Amanda picked up on the second ring. "What's up, Chief?"

"When you searched Samantha's duplex, did you come across expensive jewelry? A Rolex watch with diamonds, or diamond earrings?"

"No. I'd remember that."

"Thanks, Amanda." She clicked off and sat back in her chair, brushing an eyebrow with an index finger and staring out the window. The sky was beginning to cloud over and the wind sent leaves swirling over the parking lot.

Winnie buzzed her. "Matt Howard's here."

"Send him in."

Sidney swiveled her chair to face the young man as he shuffled through the door. Dressed in dirty work clothes, eyes red-rimmed under his ball cap, Matt looked grief-stricken. Hardly the kind of man who would instill fear in Jason, or the headstrong waitress, Tracy.

"I'm on my lunch break but I wanted to drop this off." He handed Sidney a file folder.

"Accounts for my whereabouts the day of Sammy's death. Names and numbers of everyone on my work crews."

Inside was a single sheet of paper with a list of names and numbers. Thorough. "Thanks, Matt. We'll check this out."

He lingered, shifting from one foot to the other. "Know when those lab tests will be back?"

"Should be Monday."

"So, I have three days of freedom before you arrest me?"

She hated to admit he might be right. His testimonies wouldn't be worth the paper they were printed on, unless lab results pointed to another suspect. She repeated one of her father's time worn adages. "Justice will prevail."

"Even if the pope vouched for me, I'd still be arrested."

"Or the lab results will prove your innocence."

Looking unconvinced, he turned to leave.

"Quick question, Matt. Did you ever see Samantha wearing expensive jewelry?"

He scratched the back of his neck. "Is a watch considered jewelry?"

"Yep."

"The last time I saw her she was wearing a Rolex. It had a

circle of diamonds around the face."

"Any earrings?"

He thought for moment. "Yeah. Diamond studs."

"Know where she got them?"

He shrugged. "I assumed her parents bought them for her. A reward for getting clean. Why?"

"Not important."

After Matt left, Sidney updated her case file. Samantha's jewelry wasn't found on her body, and likely had been taken by her killer, along with her purse and phone. Why did the killer keep them? Again, no pattern between the two victims. Mimi's purse and phone were still in her car.

Sidney gave a description of the jewelry to Winnie and told her to notify pawnshops in the tri-city area to watch out for them. Then she called Samantha's parents. Jack Ferguson answered and Sidney gently asked about the jewelry. He knew nothing about it, and put her on hold while he asked his wife. When he got back on the line, he assured her they knew nothing of the watch and earrings. Jason had been telling the truth, at least about this. Gifts from her anonymous boyfriend.

CHAPTER TWENTY-FIVE

SIDNEY PULLED into the driveway as Selena's Jeep disappeared behind the descending garage door. She met her sister in the kitchen where Selena was squatting on the tiled floor over a shattered picture frame, pulling out the bigger fragments of glass and dropping them into the trashcan.

"Did you break this?" she asked, looking up.

"No." The photo was a close-up shot of Selena and Randy grinning at the camera, taken years ago, before calamity ruptured their marriage. To Sidney, the smashed frame seemed oddly prophetic. "One of the cats must have knocked it off the counter. Probably Chili. He makes it his life's mission to get into trouble."

"Chili the rabble rouser. It was set back close to the wall. Don't know how he managed it."

"Mischief is an art. If he were human, he'd be one of the Three Stooges."

"Yeah. Curly."

Sidney set the frame safely on the counter. She crouched and helped her sister pick up pieces of glass, then she got out the dustpan and broom and swept up the smallest shards.

"So, what did you want to talk to me about?" Selena scooped a few almonds into her hand from a glass container, leaned against the counter, popped them in her mouth, and crunched while studying Sidney's face.

"I stopped by Katie's Café last night to ask questions about Samantha." Sidney drew in a long breath and released it. Delivering this bad news to her sister was harder than she anticipated. "We talked about Randy."

Selena frowned, and waited expectantly.

"He's going to serve you divorce papers."

Selena's eyes widened, and her mouth fell open. It took a few moments for her to respond. "Wow. That just knocked the wind out of me."

"There's more. He's living with Allison in the family guesthouse."

"Allison who?"

"Katie's daughter."

"You mean, like roommates?"

"Yeah. Roommates who sleep together."

Sidney had seen shock portrayed on many faces in her profession, and her sister showed all the symptoms. She stared, blinking, seemingly unable to comprehend the words.

"I don't believe any of it," Selena finally said. She paced the length of the kitchen, turned and paced back to Sidney. "Randy told you this?"

"No. He was busy cooking. Katie told me."

"She's mistaken. He wouldn't cheat on me. Certainly not with Allison. She's just a kid. What, sixteen?"

"She's eighteen. And very pregnant."

Selena's eyebrows pinched and Sidney could practically see her mind churning, trying to make sense of it.

"I heard the rumors," Selena said. "Doug Ratcher knocked her up. The high school linebacker, right?" She didn't wait for an answer. "So that's what's going on. Doug won't take responsibility. Somehow, Katie got Randy to take on the burden. In exchange for a job."

"Randy and Allison made the decision on their own," Sidney

said quietly. "He's the father of her baby."

"Impossible." Selena's breathing grew rapid. Sidney could see the pulse pounding in her neck. "He's only been back two months."

"He's been staying with her between rodeo gigs for the last nine months."

Selena looked as though she'd been punched in the gut. She gagged, and barely made it to the trashcan before she retched everything in her stomach. Then she dry-heaved, holding her hair back with one hand, the side of the bin with the other.

"Take a breath." Sidney came up behind her, handed her some paper towels, rubbed her back.

Selena lifted her head slowly, as though it weighed twenty pounds. She straightened her posture and wobbled.

Sidney steadied her with a firm hand to her elbow.

Selena tried to speak, but all that came out was a soul-wrenching sob, and she fell into Sidney's arms.

Sidney held her tight and felt Selena's tears seep into the fabric of her uniform. When she pulled away, her mascara was smeared across her cheeks, and bits of vomit were clumped in her hair. In between choking sobs she mumbled something incoherent about Randy.

"We better sit down." Sidney guided her sister into the living room.

Selena sank like a heavy weight into the pile of throw pillows on the sofa. Sidney settled next to her, along with the four cats, one draped across each lap, two draped on the back of the sofa. Selena looked like the tear streaked little girl in sneakers and pigtails Sidney consoled and protected when they were kids. Only back then it was scraped elbows and knees, not a pummeled heart. Selena was just eleven when Sidney left for the police academy at age eighteen.

"I'm sorry… (hiccup)… to keep you away from work."

"It's okay," she said gently. "I'm on a break." She wasn't. But her sister was in crisis. Her heavy workload could wait.

"I can't believe Randy cheated. He wants a divorce?" Pain etched Selena's face. "I've been so stupid. Thinking we'd get back together. And all this time he's been sleeping with someone else." Selena dissolved into a new chain of sobs.

Sidney handed her sister tissues from her duty belt and felt a hot prickle of rage sweep up to her hairline. For years, she had watched her brother-in-law inflict emotional damage on Selena. She imagined herself storming into Katie's and arresting Randy on some trumped-up charge, slamming him into a cell, and leaving him there to rot—or at least breaking a tray of gooey pastries over his head. Jelly donuts would do the trick, or chocolate éclairs.

Selena blew her nose, wiped her eyes, smeared more mascara. New tears filled her eyes. At this rate, she'd need a beach towel. Sidney brought a box of tissue from the bathroom and patiently waited for another break in the flood of sobs and wilted tissue.

"What else did Katie tell you?" Selena finally asked, voice hoarse.

Sidney sorted through all the information Katie had dumped on her, pulling out enough details to be honest without being brutal. "Randy told Katie and Gus you had agreed to a divorce. Katie thought it was in the works."

"He's a liar."

"He did a con job on them, Selena. They think he's a stand-up guy. A great match for Allison. They brought him into the family like a long-lost son. Into the business. They're grooming him for management." For now, Selena didn't need to know about the upcoming wedding.

"I can't believe it." Selena's eyes squeezed shut but tears still leaked out. "He traded me for a teenager. Got her pregnant." She sniffed, blotted her eyes. "I feel so old and useless. If only I could have had a baby, none of this would have happened. He never would have left me."

"It's not your fault." Sidney locked eyes with her sister. "Don't take responsibility for Randy's shitty behavior. He abandoned you. He sexually manipulated Allison."

Selena hung on every word, chin quivering.

"Adults are supposed to guide and educate young people, not lure them into the bedroom."

"You're right. He's despicable. Lowdown and sleazy," Selena sputtered. Then her voice grew stronger, angrier. "Cheating! Lying! Sleeping with a teenager! A grown man!"

"Now you're catching on. A decent man would never have taken advantage of Allison. Never have left you." Sidney paused a few beats. "One day you'll be thankful he's out of your life. He doesn't come anywhere near to being good enough for you."

Selena slowly nodded. It appeared she had reached a plateau where the sharpest sting had worn off. The weeping, for the moment, had ebbed. More would come. Lots more.

"You've created a life apart from Randy," Sidney reminded her in a calm, soothing tone. "Your business is thriving. You pay all your own bills. It's clear to me, you've been happy."

"You're right," she sniffed. "I've been fine."

"Better than fine. You're smart, kind, and beautiful."

"I'm also fucked up, insecure, and neurotic." She gave Sidney a lopsided smile.

Sidney smiled back. "Runs in the family."

"Right now, I'm disgusting. My mouth tastes awful. I need to shower." Selena licked her dry lips and picked a bit of vomit from her hair with her fingernails.

"I need to get back to work. It's been a hell of a week."

"You look exhausted. Why don't you come to Ann's for dinner? I'm making chicken stew and buttermilk biscuits."

"Yum. What time?"

"Seven o'clock. That's when Granger stops by."

"I'll try." Sidney rose from the couch.

Wiping her nose, Selena shook off Chili and got to her feet. The orange tabby meowed and settled into the warm spot she left on the sofa. They walked across the worn Asian rug to the front door.

"I'm going to pack up all of Randy's clothes and pile them in the yard," Selena declared. "I want every single thing of his out of here this afternoon."

"Time well spent."

"I'll leave a message for him with Katie. He's never stepping foot in this house again."

"Great." Positive action. Good sign. Sidney put her hand on the doorknob, hesitated, and turned back to her sister. "Look, I want you to pull yourself together tomorrow night. Get beautiful. We're going out."

"Where?"

"The Art Studio. They're having an event. Great art. Champagne. It'll be fun."

Selena frowned, and her shoulders slumped. "I'm really not up for it."

"Yes. You are. Do it for me?" Sidney bit her bottom lip. "There's a guy I'm interested in."

"A guy?" Selena's light green eyes brightened with interest.

"It may not go anywhere, but I'd like to get your opinion."

"Before you take the plunge?"

"Yeah."

"Be careful. You can't put toothpaste back in the tube."

"I know. I'll go slow."

"Of course, I'll go with you, but I won't stay long."

"Great." Sidney hugged her sister tight and left the house.

She was grateful Selena had Ann, and they provided support for one another. Both were so wounded. So fucked up. Sidney's fingers tightened on the steering wheel as she settled into the driver's seat of the Yukon. There were so many lost people in the world, slogging through the shit fields of life, wearing painted masks of happiness. Something Sidney understood too well. *Master of illusion.*

CHAPTER TWENTY-SIX

THE GRIEF GROUP met in a small upstairs room at the Episcopal Church. The pitched roof gave it the appearance of an attic, closed in and musty, with dust motes swirling in the light from three dormer windows. Shelves along two walls spilled over with yellowed books, and five folding chairs were grouped in a circle in the center of the wood-planked floor. To Selena, it looked like a forgotten room, where distressed people came to hide and turn their souls inside out.

Someone had volunteered to bring a carafe of coffee and cookies. Gripping a warm Styrofoam cup, Selena huddled in the circle next to Ann, watching other women wander in. Glancing at Ann, she fought an impulse to run. Her friend sat hunched in her seat, hands clasped in her lap, face a stone mask. Hell, if Ann could do this, so could she.

A slender teenager, dark-haired and pale-skinned, took the chair next to Ann. Her features were almost too strong to be pretty, though her expressive hazel eyes softened her brooding appearance. She wore a man's motorcycle jacket, baggy jeans, and ankle high Nikes. A cigarette was tucked behind one ear and a letter was tattooed on each knuckle of her hands in blue ink, spelling GUYS SUCK. There was something tragic and vulnerable in her posture—one arm looped over the back of the chair next to her, her legs sprawled out in front. Maybe this was an attempt at toughness, but instead, she came across like a little girl dressed in her big brother's clothing. Catching Selena's gaze, she leered back. Selena glanced away.

A pretty black woman, dressed in an oversized orange sweater and faded jeans, with close-cropped bleached hair, approached Ann with her hand outstretched. "Hi, Ann. It's so nice to see you again."

"Hi, Jude." Ann's lips formed a stiff smile and she allowed Jude to clasp her hand briefly before pulling it back into a nest of interlocking fingers. "This is my friend, Selena, who I told you about."

Jude's inquisitive brown eyes turned to Selena, her manner amiable and confident. Selena sensed in her an innate strength that reminded her of Sidney.

"Nice to have you join us, Selena." Jude smiled, showing a gap between her front teeth.

Selena nodded, noncommittal.

Jude seated herself next to Motorcycle Jacket.

The last straggler, who had been nervously hugging the coffee corner, slouched across the floor with darting eyes, as though the planks might open up and swallow her. She completed the circle by taking the remaining seat between Jude and Selena.

"Hello, Ladies," Jude said. "So nice to have you here today. We have two new faces, so let's open the meeting by going around the circle and introducing yourselves. Share whatever is most pressing in your life. Everything we say here is confidential, which means it never leaves this room. Agreed?"

Everyone nodded.

"Becky, want to start?"

With grave concern, Selena studied the woman sitting next to her. Becky was so thin she gave the impression of wasting away. She could be forty or fifty, hard to tell by her gaunt face. Her gray pallor, ice-blue eyes, and limp blonde hair gave her a faded look, like a photograph not fully developed. Gray slacks and matching sweater added to her colorless appearance. In contrast, a Rolex with diamonds around the face sparkled with her slightest move, catching light from the windows.

"Becky?" Jude repeated.

Becky blinked, cleared her throat, and began to speak in a hesitant voice. "Hi, I'm Becky. I've been seeing Jude since my son died of a drug overdose, nine weeks and two days ago. Joey was only eighteen. Just graduated with honors and a basketball scholarship to OSU." She stared at her hands for a long moment.

"Becky?" Jude said. "Anything else?"

Lifting her drawn face, Becky cleared her throat again. "A part of me died with Joey. Since the funeral, I've lived in purgatory. I can't concentrate, can't eat." Her eyes glistened with tears. Jude passed her a box of tissue. Becky blotted her eyes and continued in a voice so soft, Selena had to strain to hear. "My husband died two years ago. Now I'm alone. I'm not a mother anymore. I'm not a wife. I don't know who I am. I feel invisible. This is the only place I don't feel so alone, so useless."

The room was dead quiet.

As Becky spoke, Selena's pain returned, crawling out of the silence. A wave of grief washed through her so sharply it brought tears to her eyes.

"Selena," Jude said gently. "I notice your strong reaction to Becky's words. Would you like to share what you're feeling?"

All heads turned to Selena.

Selena wanted to bolt, but running away would never get her closer to healing. "Becky just described my feelings exactly after my miscarriage last year. My second in four years."

Selena met Jude's dark eyes, which seemed an anchor in a stormy sea, and continued. "I understand how it feels to be invisible. After I lost Alissa, I went about my normal life; shopping and cooking, teaching my yoga class, but it felt meaningless." She chewed her bottom lip. "All around me, people were taking pleasure in life, enjoying their families, making plans for the future, but my world was collapsing. My husband and I shared the same house, the same bed, but emotionally, we were a million miles apart. We couldn't connect. Randy blamed me for the death of our babies. He looked at me like I was defective." Selena closed her eyes, pressed the heel of her palm against her forehead, and felt more tears burn to the surface. "When I really needed him, he left me."

"It's okay," Jude said softly. "Let the tears come."

Selena let go of her reticence and cried in front of these strangers. She felt a gentle hand rubbing her back. Becky. On her other side, Ann took her hand and held it tight. The box of tissue appeared. More tears. Selena said in a husky voice, "I just found out my husband's living with an eighteen-year-old. She's pregnant."

Becky gasped.

"Bastard," Motorcycle Jacket hissed between clenched teeth.

Selena felt raw. She had opened an ugly wound for others to see. But the faces around her were soft with compassion and understanding. Their empathy felt like a soothing balm, dulling the sharpest stings of grief.

"Thank you, Selena," Jude said quietly.

A respectful silence enveloped the room.

"Want to go next, Ann?" Jude asked.

Ann sat straighter in her chair and her interwoven fingers tightened. She said bluntly, "I have prosopagnosia."

"Want to explain what that is?" Jude said.

"It's facial blindness. I can't distinguish one person's face from another's."

Looks of surprise from Becky and Motorcycle Jacket.

"I can't tell any of you apart," Ann continued, words nervously running together. "My disorder makes me anxious about going out in public, so I stay home most of the time. It's a struggle to find a connection with people. I try to memorize a unique feature about them, a limp, slouched posture, so I can remember who they are. I know Jude and Selena by their hair. But when Selena wears a ponytail, I no longer know who she is." Ann spoke as though the words were lodged in her throat, fighting to come out. "So if you see me in town, don't think I'm a snob. Tell me who you are, and I'll say hello." She lapsed into an awkward silence.

"Anything more you'd like to say about that, Ann?" Jude asked.

Ann coughed, shook her head. "That's all for now."

"Thank you." Jude allowed silence to settle into the room. These pauses seemed to cleanse the air between people sharing. She turned to Motorcycle Jacket. "Nicole?"

The teenager impatiently brushed a lock of unruly hair from her forehead. "I'm Nicole. Thanks for inviting me into this fucking crazy group. Looks like I fit right in."

Selena smiled. Nervous laughter from Becky.

"I'm a survivor of incest." Nicole's mouth twisted into a scowl. "Thanks to dear old Dad, the sleazy pervert. I was his main squeeze after my mom died when I was twelve."

Selena's gut twisted at the pain embedded in Nicole's sardonic humor.

The only sound in the room was the wind pushing tree branches against the outside wall—a scraping, haunted sound

"I don't want to dredge up all that crap today," Nicole continued. "What I will say is that I finally got the strength to tell someone. The nurse at school. She became my advocate. She stood by me through the whole nightmare of reporting him and testifying." Nicole exhaled sharply, as though eliminating a nasty odor. "Now he's rotting in a tiny cement cell. Hopefully, with a jail mate named Predator, who's giving him a taste of what he did to me." With a rueful smile, she sagged in her chair, depleted, and something tender entered her voice. "Now I live with a foster family. Decent people. They make me come here. Fucking therapy with all you fucking nut jobs." A shiver passed over her, something dark and ethereal that revealed her fragility. "What I want to talk about, what I need to talk about, is Sammy Ferguson's murder."

A chill touched Selena's spine. She met Ann's gaze and saw her shudder.

"I knew Sammy," Nicole said. "I ate at Hogan's all the time. She and I use to joke around. She was beautiful and smart and really funny. Sometimes she gave me a free Coke or dessert. I'm having a hard time accepting her murder. And knowing her killer is still out there." Fear tinged her voice and was mirrored on the faces of the other women.

"I knew her from Hogan's, too," Jude said sadly. "Her death came as a shock. Very scary the killer hasn't been caught."

Bright spots of color now burned in Becky's cheeks.

"Becky? Want to add something?"

The thin woman's lips tightened minutely.

"We're listening."

"I don't want to speak ill of the dead," Becky huffed. "But Sammy brought this upon herself."

"What? You're blaming the victim?" Nicole asked, indignant.

"I knew Sammy, too. She grew up in my neighborhood. Maple Grove. I know her parents." Becky paused, swallowed. "She wasn't Miss Perfect as you all seem to think. She was strung out on drugs, and she was in and out of treatment for years. The hurt she caused her parents…" She shook her head as her voice trailed off.

"I don't believe it. That's gossip," Nicole said angrily. "She never seemed stoned to me."

"Hold on, Nicole," Jude intervened. "Let Becky talk. She has a right to speak her mind. Is there a point to this, Becky?

"Yeah, there's a point. Sammy got my son high. I found pills in his room. I had to press him hard, but he finally confessed he got them from Sammy." Becky inhaled sharply, exhaled. "I told her parents. Years of friendship went straight out the window. Jack accused Joey of lying. He said if I brought charges against Sammy, their lawyers would ruin Joey's life. Have him locked up for years."

"What did you do?" Ann asked, brow furrowed.

"I had no proof the pills came from Sammy. Joey was eighteen. An adult. About to leave for college. I only had him for one last summer. I couldn't control him, but I did take away his car privileges. Drove him everywhere. Talked to him endlessly about the risk of doing drugs. I quoted statistics. Told him thousands of people are dying all across the country from overdosing. 'Yeah, Mom, I know,' he told me. 'Don't worry. I won't do anything to jeopardize my scholarship.' But he got hold of heroin laced with Fentanyl. Probably from Samantha. He shot it up. Died alone in his bedroom. I found him the next morning." Tears welled in Becky's eyes and she clenched and unclenched her jaw, trying to compose herself. "I torture myself with the thought that if only I found him sooner..." She swallowed and said with chilling bitterness, "I blame Sammy for his death. For introducing him to drugs."

A solemn mood settled over the room. Selena was almost overwhelmed with pity for her.

A haunted look fell across Jude's face. "So terribly sorry for your loss."

Becky bent her head low and made a strangled noise, trying not to cry. "Will this pain ever go away?"

"The answer to that is yes," Jude said in a tone that was calm and believable. Selena needed desperately to believe it too.

"Sadly, grief never completely fades," Jude continued. "Right now, your world feels closed in, and there's a dark, sad place in your heart. But in time, your world will expand again, and there will be more parts to it. You will learn to hold your pain in a private, sacred place."

Becky sniffed and nodded.

Jude looked at the circle of women with soft, sad eyes. "Anything else we need to say about Samantha's murder?"

"Is her killer going to kill someone else?" Nicole asked, her body stiff with fear.

Selena felt the tension in the room.

Ann suddenly blurted, "I stumbled upon her killer in the woods Thursday night. Dragging her body."

Stunned silence.

"Oh my God. Did he see you?" Jude's eyes were wide, the white's showing.

"Yes. He chased me."

Several women gasped.

"I outran him," Ann said hurriedly. "I hid. He couldn't find me."

"Thank God," Becky said. "He would've killed you, too."

"Did you see who it was?" Nicole asked.

Ann frowned. "I saw him. But I don't recognize faces."

Murmurs of comprehension.

"But he thinks you saw him," Nicole said.

She nodded, face drawn.

"Let's slow down, here," Jude said. "Take it from the beginning. Tell us the whole story, Ann. Step by step."

Ann started reciting her story in a dull monotone, and then her voice picked up speed and vibrated with emotion and she brought her experience into the room in sharp, vivid detail. Selena broke out in goose bumps.

No one interrupted, just listened, faces mobile and open. Unguarded. Expressions shifting from shock to stark fright. When Ann finished, the room erupted with questions. It was clear to Selena that Sammy's murder had haunted these women, the horror locked in their imaginations, magnified by the rumors of rape and torture floating around town. Ann patiently answered each question and sketched in missing details. For the remainder of the session, emotions gushed, peaked, and eventually tapered off. Airing their feelings communally gave the women some relief, but no one would feel safe until the killer was caught.

"Sammy's death was a traumatic event for our whole community," Jude summarized. "This brutal tragedy can make us feel helpless. But we can take steps to protect ourselves. As the newspaper article this morning recommended, we need to stay alert. Don't go out alone. If we notice anything unusual, report it immediately to the police." She turned to Ann. "You had a terrifying experience, but you outsmarted a killer. You have strong instincts for survival."

"Not so sure about that. I'm a wreck," Ann said. "I'm glad Selena persuaded me to come back to therapy."

All eyes turned to Selena.

"This your first time in therapy?" Jude asked.

Selena nodded. "I confess, I didn't come willingly. I guess I was expecting to be dissected like a bug under a microscope."

"Not today." Jude gave her a teasing grin. "Maybe next time. Therapy can be summed up in one word. Healing. People come because they are suffering. Sorrow can feel like a heavy balloon lodged in your chest, weighing you down. Here, we support each other, share the burden, deflate its power." Jude's gaze swept the room, settling momentarily on each woman. "Therapy is not a panacea. It's not something you complete or recover from, like the flu. You just keep pushing through the pain until you reach the other side."

Selena glanced at Ann, her friend's soft eyes trained on Jude, filled with hope and trust.

"Okay, ladies, that's it for today," Jude said. "Continue to show up and support each other. Next week, same time, same station."

The women rose to their feet and folded their chairs, placed them against the wall, and quietly filed out. As they descended the stairs, Selena said to Ann, "That was extremely painful. But I'm glad I came. It was a relief to talk about my feelings without being judged."

"It was a relief to talk about Sammy's murder," Ann said.

~ ~

They emerged into a windswept autumn day. Tops of trees swayed against a clear cerulean sky. Rounded aspen leaves vibrated in the wind, sounding like flowing water. Leaves the color of apples and persimmons cartwheeled across the lawn and collected like snowdrift against the side of the church. Passersby strolled along the sidewalk wearing complacent expressions. A man walked a dog. A woman pushed a baby carriage. A young couple jogged by in colorful athletic wear. All oblivious to the world of pain exposed in the attic of the church.

Becky stood on the sidewalk, wind blowing her sallow hair, her clothes hugging her spare frame.

"Need a ride?" Selena asked as they approached.

"No, thanks. My brother's picking me up." She glanced up the street. "Here he comes now."

A silver Mercedes sedan eased to the curb and parked. The windows were down, and a familiar piano concerto drifted into the street before dying with the engine. Chopin. Recognizing the car and the driver, Selena turned to Becky with a touch of surprise. "Derek's your brother?"

"Yes. You know him?"

"He comes to my yoga class."

She blinked. "You're his yoga teacher? He's mentioned you many times. You've really helped him."

Derek got out of the car and joined them on the sidewalk. Normally, he wore baggy yoga clothes, but today his khaki shorts and white cotton shirt emphasized his lean frame and muscular build. He was over six feet tall with broad, perfectly square shoulders and slim hips. Derek must hit the gym in addition to practicing yoga. Selena saw there were no burn scars on his arms or legs. The fire had affected only the left side of his face and throat and his left hand.

Derek smiled, the scarred tissue on his face masklike, offering little movement beyond his mouth, the one blue eye frozen in its tight seam. "Didn't expect to see you here, Selena."

She smiled back. "Small town."

"So, you're all in the same group."

"Yes. I just met your sister." Selena's throat tightened, and she suddenly felt self-conscious. She'd been found out. Caught attending a therapy group. Soon the whole town would know that Randy ditched her for Allison. She didn't need rumors flying that she was so devastated she had to seek professional help. She was determined to get through the divorce with dignity and grace.

Derek gazed at them with a steady, unruffled expression. He didn't strike her as the type of person who would gossip or judge her. She forced barbed thoughts of Randy back into submission and introduced Derek to Ann.

He politely shook her hand, and they chatted about trivialities; the beautiful fall colors, the inexorable approach of winter, how unready they were for the cold. The sun highlighted the golden hair on Derek's tanned forearms, and the wind tousled his dark hair. Outside of the yoga studio and in this more neutral environment, Selena viewed him in a different light. Non-threatening, and appealing.

"How'd your session go?" he asked his sister, wrapping an arm around her shoulder.

"Painful." Becky leaned into him, seeming to take comfort in his presence. "I talked about Joey. We all talked about Sammy."

For a moment, a long moment, he stood utterly still. The

muscles tightened around his mouth, then relaxed. Selena was certain he felt a surge of anger and had suppressed it.

"You knew her?" Selena asked.

"Yeah, I knew Sammy. Like you said, small town." His cool tone warned Selena not to pursue the topic.

"Personal friend?" she asked, her curiosity getting the better of her.

"Family friend. Becky and I used to play tennis with her parents. Doubles."

Before the topic of Sammy could be probed further, Becky changed the subject in an awkward segue. "I'm starved. How about we grab some lunch. I'm craving curry. We could try the new Thai place that just opened."

"We can do that." Derek smiled down at Becky. His expression relaxed, and Selena saw the exchange of genuine affection between the two.

"What are you ladies up to?" His gaze traveled to Ann and came to rest on Selena. "Care to join us? My treat. Spicy food. Cold beer."

"I love Thai food," Ann said.

"Me, too. That's a tempting offer, but we need to get back to the farm," Selena said, speaking for Ann as well. "We have a lot of bookkeeping to do."

Derek regarded her with a serious, searching gaze, and then said graciously, "Well, another time then."

"Sure thing. Let us know how you like their curry."

Derek flashed a smile that gave Selena a little pleasurable twinge in her belly. He opened the door for Becky, and with a little wave, she sank into the passenger seat. Derek pulled out into the traffic lane, the stirring concerto filling the air and fading down Lake Street.

"Why didn't you want to go to lunch?" Sounding annoyed, Ann pushed her hands deep into her jacket pockets. "He was treating."

"I don't want to encourage him. He's getting a little personal in yoga class. I think he wants to ask me out."

Ann stiffened, her typical reflex when imagining intimacy with a man. "You don't need that right now."

"No, I don't." Selena steered Ann toward her green Jeep, the last vehicle in the parking lot, now covered in mottled orange leaves drifting from the giant oaks. The wind carried the fresh scent of the forest and felt cool on her skin.

"He certainly has a nice build," Ann said.

"His face isn't bad, either. One side of it, anyway." Selena pressed the remote button and the door locks clicked open.

"Are those burn scars?" Ann asked, strapping herself in.

"Yeah. He was in a car accident a few years back. He recently moved back to town."

Ann put a finger to her mouth. "Hmmm. Is his last name Brent?"

"Uh huh."

"I remember that accident. Horrible. He lost control of his car. It hit a tree and caught fire. He was trapped inside. A truck driver dragged him out just before the car exploded. Derek was severely mangled and burned." She glanced at Selena. "Happened just down the highway from my place."

"He lives near you?"

"About two miles north. Strange. That truck driver never should have been there, but he happened to leave work ten minutes late that day. No one else was on the road."

"Wow. Pulled from the jaws of death. That could make a nonbeliever see Jesus."

"Amen. He used to be the pianist at the Episcopal church."

"I remember seeing a few of their concerts."

"Heck of a musician. Could play anything. Now that I think about it, his singing partner was Mimi Matsui."

Selena mulled this over. "He must've been devastated when she was killed."

"I'm sure he was. He was in the accident three weeks later. Terrible time in his life." She paused. "He sure made a miraculous recovery."

"He's a very motivated guy. He pushes himself hard in my yoga class." Selena sat for a minute, contemplating the steering wheel and thinking about Derek. "Don't you think it's odd, Ann, that Derek knew both murdered women?"

"Lots of people knew both women."

"You're right. Probably nothing to it." She started the engine, pulled out of the lot, and headed down the highway. "I have to get going after lunch. I'm sorry to leave you alone, but I promised Sidney I'd go to a function at the Art Studio. I won't stay long."

"I'm a big girl, Selena. I can stay home alone." Her mouth tilted upwards. "Besides, now I have some muscle."

"Bailey?" Selena asked dubiously. "He's knocked out on pain pills most of the time."

"I mean the .22 you left me."

"Don't let a gun give you a false sense of security. Keep the doors and windows locked. Don't wander around outside. Especially after dark."

"Yes, ma'am." Ann laughed, deep and throaty. "I know the drill."

It was like music to hear Ann laugh again. "How's Arthur?"

"Fine. He'll come home in a couple days."

"That was awesome that Miko rushed over to help you and drove you to the vet. I'm glad you have a connection with your neighbors." She swallowed, thinking of Noah shooting Arthur. Cold-hearted bastard. "One neighbor, anyway."

"I'm not worried about Noah. I have a gun. I'll be fine."

CHAPTER TWENTY-SEVEN

SELENA SHOWERED, PUT ON her makeup, and tried to psych herself up for the night's social event. Maybe it was time to practice mating strategies. Single for the first time in eighteen years, she didn't have a clue how to flirt with men or date.

The art happening called for dressy casual. Selena decided on a wine-red halter dress that Randy used to call her "let's have sex dress." The silky fabric hugged her frame, and bared her back and shoulders, and was short enough to show off her toned legs. Studying herself in the mirror, she tried different facial gestures, smiles, and head tilts. She reminded herself to keep her shoulders back, chest out, stomach in.

She looked good on the outside. On the inside, she cringed. She preferred to stay home, stretched out on the couch with the four cats piled on top of her, eating popcorn and watching sappy romances, nursing her heartache. But she'd promised Sidney. She could hear her sister's blow dryer in the other bathroom. Sidney needed this. Her first romantic venture since she came home two years ago, heartbroken over Gable.

Suck it up. I'm doing this.

Selena crossed the room to her dresser and saw that her three-tiered jewelry box was open. She always left it closed. Sidney must have been looking for something. A thin stream of cold air touched her back. The window was open. She shut it, latched it tight, and gazed at the yard below, nostalgic for her mother.

Over the years, she and her mother had planted maple and apple trees, myriad flowerbeds, and carved straight, clean furrows for the large, productive vegetable garden. They spent many happy hours together kneeling in fertile soil, gloved hands weeding, planting, harvesting. This was Molly's favorite time of year. The colors of autumn were stunning. In her mother's absence, Nature continued to perform her seasonal duties, irrespective of humans and their unceasing problems. If it weren't for Ann's dilemma, Selena would have visited her mother today at the memory center and taken her homemade cookies. Hopefully, she would find time tomorrow.

"Ready?"

Selena turned to see Sidney standing in the doorway. She wore a formfitting black dress that highlighted her shapely figure, and was accented with a freshwater pearl necklace and sparkly drop earrings. Perfect. Sexy, and elegant. Released from its perpetual ponytail, her thick auburn hair fell in lustrous waves around her shoulders. "Wow, you look amazing. This poor mystery man won't know what hit him."

"Thanks. I needed to hear that." Sidney beamed. "You're wearing your killer dress. Men are going to be drooling over you all night. Ready for that kind of attention?"

"Nope." She meant it. "But I'll grin and bear it." Selena checked her makeup, hung a tiny beaded handbag from her shoulder, just big enough for a lipstick and comb, and followed Sidney out to the Yukon.

~ ~

The Art Studio was crowded by the time Sidney and Selena arrived. The large classroom had been divided into spacious corridors by movable walls, and people stood in small groups holding drinks, talking in soft tones, and admiring the displayed art. Gentle cello music drifted behind the drone of voices, and in one corner two men in white shirts and bowties busily poured drinks behind a bar.

Sidney recognized many of the top-tier citizens, including Mayor Burke and his wife, Cecille, a few council members, and many business owners. Jeff Norcross from the *Daily Buzz* snapped pictures of VIPs for the society page. Men were dressed in slacks and shirts with open collars. Most of the women wore stylish dresses and heels, a few wore pantsuits, and one lady looked very artsy in a brightly flowered kimono and silk leggings.

"Let's get a drink," Selena said a little stiffly and hurriedly. "I need stamina to get through this gauntlet."

Sidney rarely drank. Even during off hours, she was on call and needed to be clearheaded to face an emergency. She was an ace at making one glass of wine last a whole evening.

After the bartender splashed Chardonnay into their plastic glasses, Selena gulped down half and had it refilled. Though her sister had insisted she was fine, Sidney sensed her underlying melancholy and recognized her attempt to take the edge off the ache in her heart. They migrated to the buffet table.

"Classy," Selena said, eyes brightening, examining the hors d'oeuvres like a scientist over petri dishes. "Caviar and crème fraiche on brioche, asparagus quiche, and what's this?" She picked up a slender cracker, spread it with chunky mystery dip, and took a bite. "Hmmm. Fresh lobster salad… with just a touch of tarragon." She nibbled as delicately as a rabbit. "Try some. You don't get hors d'oeuvres like this every day."

"Nope. Not eating. It took me too long to get my lipstick this perfect." Plus, Sidney didn't want food between her teeth when she saw David.

"Worth it," Selena said. "You look sensational."

"I agree," a man's voice murmured behind Sidney's right shoulder. "You clean up nice, Chief."

Sidney turned to find David standing next to her, his smile

spreading to his warm brown eyes. He wore dark slacks, a blue Oxford shirt, and Italian loafers. His expertly tousled hair and shadow of a beard gave him the look of a man who lived well and would be at home anywhere in the world. At the same time, his manner was approachable, even playful.

"I've been watching for you all evening," he said with a lazy smile. "You like to keep a man waiting."

She smiled back. "Fashionably late. It's an art."

That seemed to amuse him, and he regarded her quite openly, looking at her shoulders and throat with admiration. She introduced him to Selena who was taking a sip from her glass, her cool green eyes peering over the rim, sharp and evaluating.

David arched a single brow. "Selena as in 'Selena's Kitchen?'"

"One and the same."

"I buy your products," he said with enthusiasm. "Your chili honey has a real kick. I blend it in my cocktails, and I use your pear and pomegranate vinegar in my salad dressing. Haven't tried your lavender honey yet. Any suggestions?"

Selena brightened like a beaten dog lured out of the doghouse with the promise of sirloin. "I use it to make rosemary lavender crumb cake and shortbread cookies. It's also great in lemonade."

"I'd love those recipes."

"They're on my website, which is posted on the labels."

Sidney listened, amused. David seemed to know his way around a kitchen. Always a plus in a man.

Their attention was abruptly drawn to a noisy fuss at the front door as several prominent citizens, including Mayor Burke and his wife, crowded around two new arrivals. Sidney recognized them immediately. James and Reese Abbott, a power couple from Portland, frequently featured in the *Daily Buzz*. The Abbott's had bought a vacation home in Maple Grove last year, in addition to a half-dozen lake view properties that were in the planning phase of development. Sidney didn't like the sound of that, but whether she liked it or not, the small-town culture of Garnerville was irrevocably changing.

The Abbotts sponsored elegant fundraisers to help disadvantaged children and animals and donated tidy sums of money to their causes. But James Abbott's altruism didn't extend to his business dealings. As CEO of NetStorm Electronics, he had a reputation for ruthlessly seizing or steamrolling smaller companies to eliminate competition, destroying careers and marketplace diversity in the process. The way he and Reese were being received tonight, like royalty, illustrated how the intoxicating power of money could give the shadiest individuals an alluring appeal.

Reese Abbott glanced around, caught David's eye, and waved with an expectant smile.

"Old business friends," David said, waving back.

"Go play host," Sidney said. "Selena and I will browse."

His eyes lingered on hers for a moment, a quiet smile offered silently before he leaned in close to her ear. "Can I take you for a drink later?"

Sidney's stomach did a little somersault. "Yes."

He reached down and squeezed her hand before navigating his way through the crowd.

Selena locked eyes with Sidney and mouthed the word WOW. "He's steaming hot, Sid. Definitely not from around here."

"Moved here from San Francisco."

"Sophisticated. He's sure not shy about letting you know he's interested. Refreshing to see a guy who doesn't play games."

"He wants to take me out later."

Selena gave her a knowing smile. "Hope your drought's over."

"Let's not get ahead of ourselves. It's just a drink." David was smooth and charming, but as far as Sidney knew, he could be a player. And she'd had her fill of men who were allergic to settling down. "Let's actually look at art."

They turned to a camera flash in their faces. Through dots of light, Sidney saw Jeff Norcross facing them with his Nikon camera poised at his eye. "A couple more, ladies. You look gorgeous. And a few of you alone, Chief Becker."

Not displeased to have her image immortalized when she looked this good, Sidney posed graciously.

"Look in the paper tomorrow." He grinned and melted into the crowd.

The evening unfolded pleasantly. Sidney and Selena split up, each running into their own friends, and the wine eased the stress Sidney had been carting around the last few days. She found it enjoyable to meet the townsfolk on a social level rather than as an authority figure. She realized, as chief of police, she needed to do this more often—rub elbows with the power players, get a full scope of how the town was changing, and how law enforcement should be administered in the future. David mentioned never seeing her at chamber meetings. She made a pledge to herself to adjust her schedule and start attending.

Groupings of people shifted throughout the evening and she and David crossed paths several times. They introduced each other to friends, and she admired his social ease discussing politics, art, world affairs, even cooking, for which he appeared to be especially fond.

While standing before one of David's stunning landscapes, a lavish interpretation of the Cascade Range, he introduced her to James and Reese Abbott. Sidney found them a little full of themselves, and standoffish when she didn't offer the genuflection they seemed to expect from a civil servant. Tall and silver-haired, James was more distinguished than handsome, with a Roman nose and intelligent gray eyes that never warmed.

Reese, nearing sixty and a decade older than her husband, kept age at bay with nips, tucks, and injections. Her wrinkle-free skin was stretched over sharp cheekbones and she was painfully thin with disproportionately large breasts swelling above the bodice of her slinky green dress. Sidney felt sympathy for her. The Abbotts ignored Sidney and talked business with David, apparently interested in several art pieces for their Maple Grove home. As Sidney quietly wandered away, David cast her an apologetic smile.

Sometime later, Sidney's back stiffened when she left the restroom and came upon James Abbott standing alone in a corner of the studio, seemingly mesmerized by a pastel drawing. She was about to cough to announce her presence when his eyes watered and his expression crumpled in misery. He pinched the bridge of his nose, a shudder passed over his shoulders, and he made an abrupt pivot and almost collided with her as he brushed past.

Curiosity drew Sidney to the pastel like a magnet. A beautiful piece. The sun sinking over Lake Kalapuya, rendered with bold, vibrant slashes of color. The skillfully applied hues captured a deeply mysterious, moody quality to the lake. She read the name card posted underneath.

Title: Setting Sun
Artist: Samantha Ferguson.

Sidney felt a jolt of surprise. Samantha! As David had told her, the young woman had been a gifted artist. Tragic, such a promising career cut short. Sidney's thoughts darted back to Abbott. Why did the tough-minded CEO have such an intensely emotional response to Samantha's work? Clearly, he knew her well enough to have formed a strong attachment. What social sphere brought these two people together? Samantha's parents also lived in Maple Grove. Did the families play golf or tennis together? Socialize at the exclusive country club?

Was Abbott the mysterious high roller who gave Samantha an expensive Rolex and diamond earrings? Seemed unlikely. She couldn't picture the drug-riddled hell raiser having an affair with the cold, calculated CEO of an international company.

Sidney intended to find out the exact nature of their relationship, discreetly. She didn't need to become an annoying blip on Abbott's radar screen. The man was ruthless and powerful, and he thought nothing of squashing his adversaries like insects.

By nine o'clock, the studio had emptied to a dozen people, mostly tourists, lingering near the entryway and bar. Sidney was surprised Selena had lasted the entire evening, taking a break from the excruciating changes in her life. Then Sidney's heart skipped a beat.

Randy and Allison casually sauntered through the door. Selena's fair-haired husband was tall, lanky, and handsome in a roguish sort of way, though underdressed in a plaid western shirt, faded Wranglers, and scuffed cowboy boots. In contrast, the petite teen at his side was a classic study in spherical shapes. Her gray knit dress stretched tightly across her globe-shaped stomach and grapefruit-size breasts, and her face was as round as a cherub's. Plodding ponderously, leaning back a little to negotiate her disproportionate weight, Allison looked ready to drop a baby at any moment. Sidney's only thought was to get them out of the studio before Selena spotted them.

Too late.

Frozen at the bar, Selena peered at Randy over the heads of the remaining stragglers.

As if by radar, Randy's head swiveled, and his gaze locked onto Selena.

A slow ache tightened Sidney's throat as her sister's face drained of color.

Sidney approached the couple, placing her body between them and Selena. "It would be a good idea if you two left."

"Nice to see you, too, Sidney," Randy said.

"Nothing nice about it. You've done enough damage, Randy." Her gaze lowered to Allison's. "You, too. Go."

Allison lifted her chin defiantly. "We're not leaving. We just got here."

Sidney leveled them both with her withering stare that melted hardened criminals.

"Let's go." Randy grabbed Allison's arm and turned toward the door.

"Stop it, Randy," Allison said, voice shrill, loud enough to attract attention. "I'm staying."

Her hormones had to be way out of whack, overriding her sensibility.

Sidney didn't like the look on her sister's face as she joined them—hard, as though chiseled from granite, capable of anything. Selena got into Randy's face, searching his eyes as if trying to read his soul, but finding nothing there.

"Selena, let's go outside," Randy said in a low, desperate tone. "Let's talk."

"You cheating, lying prick," Selena said so quietly only the small group of four could hear.

Randy winced.

"Leave him alone," Allison snarled, voice raised like a sideshow barker. "You dried-up old cunt."

Sidney was shocked. Sweet little Allison wasn't so sweet anymore.

"You've been screwing my husband!" Selena was seething, but still quiet.

"He's not yours anymore. Maybe you haven't noticed. We're having a baby."

"That's enough," Sidney said sharply. "Turn around, Allison. Leave."

"Or what? You gonna arrest me?" The skin tightened across Allison's nose and cheekbones. She turned back to Selena. "He's divorcing you. The papers are ready. You're the gone girl."

The two women stared each other down, Selena's hands balling into fists.

"You wanna hit me?" A glimmer of violence sparked in Allison's eyes. "Go ahead. Try me."

Selena looked like she was seriously considering it.

The remaining guests had gathered, casting disapproving glances at Selena, who towered over the pregnant teen by a foot.

"Cut Allie some slack, Selena," Randy said. "For Christ's sake, she's pregnant. Let's talk." His hand encircled her arm.

She yanked away and slapped him so hard across the cheek, his face snapped to the left.

A collective gasp erupted from the spectators.

Allison's hand shot into Selena's hair and yanked hard, pulling her forward like a dog on a leash. With a shriek, Selena roughly shoved the teen away. Allison teetered backward for a long-suspended moment, arms swimming in air, then she regained her balance, legs spread wide apart, strands of Selena's hair clutched in her fist.

Sidney imposed herself between the two women at the same moment Allison launched a loaded blow meant for Selena, and her fist caught Sidney square in the jaw. Explosive pain shuddered up the side of Sidney's face and rang like a church bell in her ear. Little bursts of light clouded her vision and she tasted warm blood in her mouth. She shook her head to clear it.

Everyone stood still as a photograph, as though the air had been vacuum-pumped from the room.

Sidney wiped blood from her lip with her fingertips and gritted her teeth to control her temper. Somehow her voice sounded commanding as she made sweeping gestures toward the door. "Everyone out. Party's over. Time to go. Now!" Her voice, low and dangerous, cleared the room of spectators. She turned to Randy and Allison and nodded at a row of chairs against the wall. "Sit. Don't even think about moving."

Randy lurched toward the seats, arm firmly linked through Allison's, pulling her along. As their butts met the chairs, David stepped into the room from a door marked OFFICE. His gaze darted from Allison and Randy to Selena, who stood hollow-eyed next to Sidney, hugging her chest. His eyes landed last on Sidney, wiping blood from her mouth.

"Holy hell. Who hit you?"

Feeling her bottom lip swelling, Sidney nodded at the couple.

Randy slumped in his chair like a man facing the gallows. Allison had lost her bluster and nervously chewed a fingernail, her stomach resembling a helium balloon trying to launch into air.

"You hit a woman?" David asked Randy, eyes flashing with anger. "The police chief?"

Before Randy replied, the front door opened and Granger entered the studio, dressed in uniform, face ruddy from the cold, collar turned up on his jacket. He appraised the scene, eyes resting on Selena a bit longer than necessary, then he turned to Sidney and gasped. "Who hit you?" His gaze followed David's to Randy.

Selena pointed to Allison. "It was her."

A veneer of toughness crept back over Allison's face as all eyes turned to her.

"Get the hell out of here," Sidney said to the couple. "I'll deal with you in the morning."

They wasted no time crossing the cement floor, their heels tapping out a beat to the mournful strains of the cello sonata pouring from the speakers.

"Why'd you let them go?" Selena asked indignantly when the door shut behind them. "She assaulted you!"

"That blow was meant for you, after you belted Randy," Sidney said. "You shoved a pregnant woman. What if she'd fallen? Hurt the baby?"

Selena's shoulders slouched, and a fixed sadness settled over her features. "I don't know what came over me."

"You were defending yourself." Considering the circumstances, Sidney thought her sister acted with admirable restraint. Sidney may not have been so nice to Randy. And little Allison—a hellcat on steroids—ratcheted up the tension from zero to sixty in seconds. Sidney turned to Granger. "Obviously, you got a complaint."

"Several. Apparently, there was a helluva slugfest going on over here."

"A regular Ali versus Foreman," Sidney said. "Can you get Selena back to Ann's?" Sidney didn't want her sister driving. She had spotted Selena getting refills at the bar the whole evening.

"I was about to head over there anyway." His baby blues softened when he turned to Selena. "Did you bring a coat?"

She shook her head, her face so tense it looked like marble.

Granger shrugged off his jacket and draped it around Selena's shoulders. Sidney heard him speaking to her in a gentle tone as he escorted her outside.

David locked the door behind them and turned to her with curious eyes, but he remained silent, no doubt sensing she needed a little cooling down time.

She blew out a breath and sighed. "Glad that's over."

David put a hand under her chin, tilting her face toward the light. "That little pregnant girl is a piece of work. Packs a whammer. You okay?"

"I'll live." His proximity and his musky scent of sandalwood were doing an excellent job of shifting her focus away from the evening's drama.

"Let's get you an ice pack." With a warm hand to her back, David guided her into his office, a handsome room furnished with a leather couch, matching chairs, and an ornately carved walnut desk. Glass shelves running along one wall displayed art pieces illuminated by soft spotlights in the ceiling. Inviting, cultured, masculine. Sidney sank onto the chestnut-colored couch.

David disappeared and returned with crushed ice in a baggie. "This will reduce the swelling. That's gotta hurt."

"Doesn't tickle." Sidney's lip felt as big as a doughnut. She winced when she pressed the bag to her mouth.

He sat next her, his knee brushing hers.

"Sorry that drama took place in your studio."

"Want to tell me what happened?"

"The abbreviated version, the cowboy with the pregnant girlfriend is Selena's husband."

David's eyes widened. "As in present tense?"

Sidney nodded. "Randy's a former rodeo star. They separated a year ago." She gave him a quick version of their story.

"Poor Selena." David made a low whistle. "A lot to swallow. Selena's lucky to be rid of him."

"Agreed." Sidney's fingers were getting numb from holding the ice pack. She switched to the other hand. "Selena's strong. She's been doing just fine without him."

"I don't understand why people resort to cheating and lying. Honesty is easier, in the long run. I was married twenty-one years. My wife and I had problems like everyone else, but we were committed to working them out. Some things you just accept for the greater good, for the kids."

"Married, as in past tense?"

Sadness darkened his face. "Kelly died eighteen months ago. Cancer. That's why I moved from San Francisco. Too many memories."

"I'm so sorry," she said softly.

David picked up a framed photo from the side table and handed it to her. "Here's Kelly and my three kids. Erica, Lacey, and Dillon."

Sidney stared into the face of a pretty woman with dark hair and a bright smile. Grouped around her, arms slung across shoulders, were two young women and a teenage boy. An affectionate family portrayal. Erica and Lacey resembled Kelly. Dillon was the spitting image of David. "Beautiful family."

A smile lifted the grief from his face. "I've been blessed. The girls are away at college. Dillon lives with me. He's fourteen." David's arm and leg pressed lightly against hers. He seemed completely comfortable with close physical contact. Sidney was rusty at being touched by a man and was hyper conscious of his presence. The warmth of his body and musky scent were intoxicating.

"Ever been married, Sidney?"

"No, haven't been lucky enough to find the right guy."

David's lingering gaze seemed to see her soul, and she read compassion and tenderness in his eyes. The moment felt so intimate, she lowered her eyes back to the photo. In contrast to the richness of David's life, shored up by a loving family and fond memories, Sidney's life seemed barren. At thirty-five, her greatest accomplishment was her career, which she had wrapped around herself like armor for the last two years. She reflected on all the moments she missed by not having a family, all the lost joy.

Seeming to sense her discomfort, David pushed himself up from the couch and crossed the room to his desk. "Well, Chief Sidney Becker, I have some great news for you that should put a smile on your face." He grabbed his laptop and reseated himself with one ankle crossed over a knee, this time not touching her. "I found the source of your butterfly."

A spurt of excitement dissolved her somber mood. Work. Something she could relate to.

David brought up a website featuring dozens of photos of origami art. Horses, frogs, swans, dragons. Each as intricate as the butterflies found at the two crime scenes. "These are stunning." She studied a photo of the Japanese artist, Satoshi Akira, thirty-eight years old, who had luminous dark eyes, strong cheekbones, and a sensual mouth. Sidney read her bio out loud, "A biologist by training, Akira skillfully uses her own specially made paper to create representations of the natural world. She avoids cutting and gluing, using only paper folding to create her pieces. One side of her paper is always blank, the other side is printed in vivid colors of her own design." Sidney glanced at David. "That's why we couldn't trace the paper."

He nodded. "There's nothing else like it."

"It says here a buyer can have a spiritual verse inscribed on the blank side, locked inside forever once it's folded."

"Did you find something inside your butterfly?"

"Yes, but the ink was washed out by rain." She didn't tell him there was another butterfly at the lab. "Satoshi lives on the coast in Sand Hill. Maybe she can tell me what was inscribed in the butterfly. The number of her agent is listed here."

"Afraid that's impossible."

"Why?"

"I called this morning. Satoshi's dead. She killed herself two months ago."

"How?"

"Slit her wrists."

"Slit wrists?" The hair stood on Sidney's arms. Satoshi's suicide resembled her two Garnerville homicides, and one of the artist's butterflies was found at each crime scene. Commonalities too strong to be coincidence. A strange energy surrounded Sidney. She wondered how closely Satoshi's suicide had been investigated. *Was it possible she, too, was murdered?*

"I don't know how the butterfly is connected to Samantha's death," David said, "But there may be a way of finding out. Her agent told me that Miguel Angel, a gallery owner in Sand Hill, collected Satoshi's work. He knew her personally."

Her gaze rested upon David for a moment before she withdrew, her thoughts turning inward. "Maybe he'd recognize our butterfly. That could give us an important lead. Sand Hill is only an hour away. I could drive over in the morning."

"Her agent gave me Miguel's contact info. I took the liberty of calling. He said he'd be in the gallery in the afternoon. I didn't mention the butterfly."

Feeling a flush of gratitude, Sidney smiled her appreciation. It had been a long while since a man had gone out of his way to do something special for her. "Good work, David. You just got promoted to junior detective."

"Do I get a badge?"

"Sure. I'll pick one up at the toy store tomorrow."

He laughed.

"There's something else you can help me with," she said.

"Shoot."

"Tell me about James Abbott."

"James?" He reflected for a moment, scratching the perfectly trimmed stubble on his chin. "Not much to tell. I don't really know him outside of business."

"You don't know if he's a ladies' man?"

"Hmmm." David frowned. "I don't like gossip, so I'm telling you this in strict confidence."

"Mum." She raised her hand in the three-finger Girl Scout salute. "Scout's honor."

"James and Reese have a rocky history. He's an alley cat. Always has been. He takes up with a woman, and Reese looks the other way—for a while. Then they have a volcanic blow up, and she leaves him. James dumps the other woman, they reunite, and it scabs over. Until the next time."

"Poor woman."

"Agreed. She's made a hard choice to stay with him. Is he a suspect?"

"I need to ask him routine questions."

"James won't be available until Monday. Right about now, he's on his private jet flying to New York City."

"And Reese?"

"She's with him."

Hiding her disappointment, Sidney said, "I'll contact him on Monday."

David looked at her with boyish enthusiasm. "Since you're officially off duty tomorrow, maybe you'd let me tag along to Sand Hill. I'd love to see Satoshi's work. Wouldn't mind taking in some ocean air, either."

Not keen on mixing business with pleasure, Sidney's instinct was to dissuade him. "I'm going to try to meet with the detective who worked Satoshi's case. That could take some time."

He shrugged. "I don't mind waiting. I'll bring a book."

On impulse, she planted a light kiss on his mouth.

He smiled. "Is that a yes?"

She smiled back. "I'd love your company."

His smile widened, and there was the comfort of friendship in his lingering glance. She admired David's honesty and confidence. Her romantic instincts had been muddled by a history of disappointment, but she was certain he wanted to kiss her. How should she respond? If she did what her body wanted, they might never get off the couch. A little overwhelmed by the strength of her feelings, Sidney crossed the room to admire a sculpture on one of the shelves. Graceful spires of glass swirled upwards like exotic petals, and a spectrum of colors fluidly melded within the crystalline forms. "This looks like a Chihuly."

David joined her, standing close, his hand finding the small of her back. "I'm impressed. You know your art. I bought it twenty years ago when he was still affordable."

The heat from his touch radiated through her dress to her skin. Sidney found her voice. "How does he fuse these vibrant bursts of color?"

"He rolls the molten glass in small shards of colored glass during the blowing process."

"Genius."

"Are you talking about Chihuly or me?"

"Your genius has yet to be revealed."

"That can be remedied."

Sidney stood perfectly still, barely breathing.

David swept her hair back and kissed the cove of her neck.

A whisper of pleasure.

"Couldn't help myself," he murmured. "I've wanted to kiss you since the moment I met you. Your mouth looks off-limit at the moment."

"No pain, no gain."

David pulled her close and kissed her gently. It hurt more than she expected. Sweet, piercing pain. When he lifted his mouth, the world began to move again. He looked relaxed and composed, sure of himself, while her knees trembled slightly. A little flag of warning popped up in her mind. *He's so much like Gable. Be careful.*

"You're a beautiful woman, Sidney."

His warm brown eyes were level with hers and she saw tiny flecks of amber in the irises. She didn't trust herself to speak, or to stay in the room alone with him. "Maybe we should go have that drink you promised me."

He blinked and gently pulled away. "Of course. Actually, let's have dinner. I was too busy to eat tonight. I'm starving."

"Me, too." She hoped her smile hid her nervousness.

"Is the Black Rabbit okay?" he asked.

"Best restaurant in town." Small and cozy, two blocks down the street. They could walk. "I have a soft spot for their Chicken Marsala."

"I love everything on the menu. Just had their stewed lamb shank. So tender, the meat just fell off the bones. I think rabbit with fig sauce is next on the list."

"Hmmm. I may have to get more adventurous."

David gave her a flirtatious smile. "I hope you do."

Her stomach fluttered.

He glanced at his watch. "If we hurry, we can squeak in before they close."

David locked up the gallery, and they stepped out into the chilled night air. Storm clouds scudded across the moon. Venus twinkled above the lake and a damp breeze blew inland off the water.

"A good storm's coming in," he said.

"A slammer." Sidney stopped at her Yukon parked at the curb and grabbed her coat and handbag, which held her gun. Even off duty, she was a cop, and she felt more prepared for trouble with her Glock close at hand.

David helped her into her coat and then he reached for her hand. Though he looked worldly and playboy handsome on the outside, his values appeared to be pleasantly old-fashioned. Sidney appreciated that his hands were strong and larger than hers.

Fingers interlocked, she and David strolled down the sidewalk through the soft light cast from the storefronts. He picked up their conversation about cuisine where he'd left off. Sidney loved listening to him. His voice was smooth and deep, and he had a gift for making ordinary gab sound charming and consequential.

"They have a wonderful Merlot here," he said. "Cakebread from Napa Valley. Rich, with dark cherry and plum flavors, and a hint of sage."

"You know your wine."

"Nah, I memorized it off the label last time I was here. But it is like drinking velvet." He squeezed her hand. "A glass will make you forget you got slugged in the mouth."

His touch, his scent, his closeness was doing a very good job of making her forget. "Wine is always good medicine."

"Gets better the more you drink."

The first drops of rain plopped in her hair as David ushered her through the door into the Black Rabbit. A couple left as they entered, and though late in the evening, a few tables were still occupied by couples speaking softly. Candlelight reflected off crystal glasses and silverware, and Sidney's stomach clenched when luscious smells reached her nostrils.

The smiling host stepped forward with menus, and said a bit formally, "Nice to see you, Chief Becker." His tone lightened when he turned to David. "Hey, David."

"Hey, Carson. Could we get that table by the window?"

"You bet. Great view of the lake. Right this way."

As was her habit, Sidney positioned herself at the table so she could view the whole room, the doorway, and the sidewalk. David's eyes sparkled in the wavering candlelight as he studied the menu. She bowed her head to do the same. Minutes later, a red-haired, smiling waitress dressed all in black approached and stood poised to take their order.

CHAPTER TWENTY-EIGHT

GRANGER STOLE A GLANCE at Selena, who sat stiffly in the passenger seat, her gaze focused straight ahead, eyes glistening in the glow from the dash. Rain drummed the roof and the wipers worked furiously to clear the cords of water coursing down the windshield. The highway unfurled like an iron-gray ribbon and the forest streaked past in a dark blur. She hadn't said a word since getting into the truck. Just sat there in stony silence.

When Granger spotted her in the gallery in that red dress, she took his breath away. Willowy figure, bared shoulders and back, skin smooth as ivory, hair a soft sheet of gold. Then he saw the misery etched on her face, the rigid way she held her body, and he understood something terrible had just gone down. Then he saw Chief Becker's face.

He cleared his throat. "What exactly happened at the gallery tonight?"

She looked at him with level green eyes and said coolly, "Is this official business? Are you interrogating me?"

"Heck no, I'm not interrogating you. I'm off duty."

"Sorry. That was rude." She sighed. "It's been a rough night."

"Who were those people? The cowboy and the pregnant girl?"

"The cowboy is my husband, Randy. The pregnant teenager is his girlfriend."

Granger frowned, trying to understand. "You're his wife? She's his girlfriend? I take it you and Randy are no longer together?"

"Good deduction, Sherlock." Her voice was cool again. "Soon to be divorced."

Granger shifted in his seat, uncomfortable. He didn't want her to think he was grilling her. He'd leave it be. Still, she was a strong presence in the car. He was conscious of her slightest move and the faint scent of her perfume, which reminded him of his mother's flower garden.

The headlights of a cargo truck momentarily blinded him. A wall of water flooded the windshield as it roared past.

Selena gasped.

The windows cleared and Granger could see the road again, a pale gray snake in the darkness. "We're okay," he said firmly, watching the taillights disappear behind him in the mirror.

She fidgeted with her bracelet and then started talking in a rambling monotone. "Randy and I have been separated for a year. He used to be a big rodeo star. Wasn't too successful the last couple years. I paid the bills. But it wasn't finances that broke us up." She swallowed. "I had two miscarriages in the last four years. After the last one, he went crazy. Moody and angry all the time. He blamed me. Made living together total hell." She lowered her head and hid her face behind a veil of corn silk hair. "A year ago, he just up and left."

Granger felt a rush of sympathy for her. Losing two babies had to be tough, without her husband rubbing salt in the wounds, and then abandoning her. "I'm sorry, Selena. Randy sounds like an insensitive ass."

"Yeah, it's finally sinking in. I'm tired of making excuses for him. Anyway, long story short, Randy's with Allison now." She sniffed, took a tissue from her purse and wiped her nose. "He's done well for himself. Got a new career and the baby he always wanted. I just wish I had some warning they were going to show up tonight. I made a total ass of myself. I slapped him pretty hard."

"Can't say I blame you. What happened to the chief?"

"Allison tried to slug me. She got Sidney instead." Selena's voice choked a little. "Seems all Sidney does is pick up the pieces of my life."

"Hey, she's your sister. You would have done the same for her."

"In a heartbeat." She wiped tears from her eyes with trembling fingers, her face quiet and luminous. Their eyes met in the dim light. A smile lifted one corner of her beautiful mouth. "You're a really decent guy, aren't you?"

He shrugged. "I try to be. My parents brought me up right."

New tears welled in her eyes.

Granger regarded her with concern and tenderness, searching for words of comfort, but he came up short. Instead, he did what came naturally, and offered his hand. In Afghanistan, he had clasped the hand of many a Marine who was injured or dying, lending support to someone in a world of pain.

Selena accepted, cradling his hand gently between her long, slender fingers—a fragile connection that he hoped would strengthen and grow.

The storm increased in tempo, loudly pelting the roof and exploding off the hood of the truck. The wipers squeaked against the windshield. Reluctantly, he pulled his hand away, holding the wheel steady against the hard-driving pummels of wind.

~ ~

"Hey, Bailey." Toweling her hair, Ann entered the kitchen fresh from a shower, the holstered .22 attached to the belt of her jeans. The hound whimpered by the front door, looking over his shoulder, and she knew he was itching to get out for a hike. Tired of her self-imposed exile, Ann also longed to walk in the forest, get wet leaves beneath her shoes, feel the damp breeze on her face. But that wasn't going to happen.

She stepped out on the porch and watched Bailey carve a

pathway through the drizzle, furrowing the grass with his nose, looking for the perfect spot to pee. The rain played a soft percussion on the roof, and she smelled the sweet scent of apples coming from Miko's farm. Always alert, Ann studied the periphery of her property. To the south, the forest gave off a blue-black chill. She studied the opening in the trees between the two farms and saw the red glow of a cigarette through the leaves. Hunched over the glow was the barely discernible shape of a man. Noah. Then he was gone.

Feeling a chill, Ann called to Bailey, and they barricaded themselves in the house, all doors and windows locked. She rubbed the hound dry with a towel and poured kibble into his bowl. While Bailey crunched, she poked the stew on the stove and took a little broth in a wooden spoon, blowing on it to taste. She forced herself to concentrate on cooking, not the man outside who watched her house. Chicken, peas, potatoes, carrots, onions, in a white wine broth perfectly seasoned with garlic, thyme, and bay leaves.

She ladled a bowlful and ate the stew seated at the island, dipping in buttered bread, sipping a luscious Pinot Noir. The handgun felt bulky on her hip so she pulled it from the holster and laid it next to her bowl.

The storm increased dramatically. The roar of the rain on the roof put up a mask of white noise that drowned out everything. She didn't hear footsteps on the porch and was surprised when the doorbell rang. She glanced at the clock. Eight-thirty. Had Selena forgotten her key? Was it Granger?

She crossed the great room, lifted a slat in the blinds and peered out at the porch. Her heart skipped a beat. Miko stood there holding a large basket of vegetables, his hood pulled up to keep out the rain.

Thrilled, she swung the door open wide. The man straightened, and at once, she knew he wasn't Miko. Too tall. Shoulders too broad. An alarm wailed in her brain.

"Hello, Ann."

Her pulse began to accelerate. *Noah!*

He shifted the weight of the basket. "I'm dropping this off for dad. And I wanted to say I'm sorry for hurting those ravens."

Caught by surprise, Ann stared blankly.

"How's the bird?" he asked.

"Arthur will need a lot of recuperating," she said angrily. "You broke his wing."

"Like I said, I'm sorry. I didn't know he was your pet."

Ann pictured Noah in the cornfield stalking the raven, shotgun trained on his back. If it wasn't for Miko, he would have killed Arthur.

"You forgive me?"

He was vile. Repugnant. But she nodded because she was frightened. "Yes."

"All better between us?"

She couldn't read his face. Was he smiling? "Yes."

Noah advanced a step. "I'll put this in the kitchen for you."

"Please, leave it on the porch." Instinctively, she started closing the door.

"It's too heavy for you." He inserted a foot and pressed against the door with the basket.

"Leave it." She tried to keep her voice neutral, but she felt the strain, felt a touch of panic. "Please go!" She shoved the door hard, knocking the basket from his hands. It lodged in the entryway, potatoes and yams skidding every which way across the floor.

Noah didn't move. He was absolutely still. His face and body betrayed nothing, but his eyes burned with a kind of cruel energy, and she sensed malice in his stance.

"Now look what you've done, Ann." He spoke with a frightening stillness. "That wasn't nice. I came as a friend."

The strong smell of alcohol wafted off him, and she had a sharp déjà vu of her husband, moments of calm before an outburst of violence. Her only thought was to get to the gun on the counter. She made a dash for the kitchen.

Dropping all pretense of a polite visit, Noah bolted into the room and encircled her from behind in his powerful arms. Ann struggled, but his strength was immense. It was like fighting a grisly. The sour sweetness of his breath sickened her.

"Calm down, Ann. I'm not going to hurt you."

"Let me go!"

"Relax. Let me show you what a nice guy I am. That's all I ask."

Feigning consent, she stood immobile.

"That's better. Just a friendly visit." He held her for a long time. An eternity. Neither moved. Ann barely breathed.

"You smell good."

Silence.

"It's not good for a woman to be alone all the time. Without a man." She felt his face in her hair, his voice low and husky. "It doesn't have to be that way." His nose rubbed against her scalp. "I'm right next door. I can come over any time you want. Help you around the place. Too much work for a woman." He bit the outer edge of her ear. "We can have a little fun. I know how to make a woman feel good." He breathed deeply into her hair. "What do you say, Ann?"

She released a long careful breath. "Okay."

His sloppy tongue dove into her ear and his hands moved up to cup her breasts.

Ann head-butted his chin, kicked his shin hard with the heel of her shoe.

He gasped, loosened his hold.

She wrenched away and made a break for the kitchen. As her fingers skimmed the butt of the handgun, Noah yanked her back into a vise-like grip. "Jesus, Ann! Why'd you hit me?"

"Let me go!"

"A minute ago, you wanted it." He started dragging her to the couch. "Guess you like it rough."

Ann screamed.

Bailey started barking, jumping on Noah's legs, growling, teeth clenching tight on his sweatshirt. Noah released an arm to shove the hound away. Ann grabbed the heavy brass candlestick from the end table and swung it over her head. She heard it thwack Noah's skull.

He let out a shrill cry and released her. Then his fist slammed into her face. Ann's knees seemed to liquefy and she slumped on the couch. Noah's massive weight fell on top of her, squeezing the breath from her lungs.

"Crazy fucking bitch," he rasped.

Ann shut her eyes, breathing through the exquisite pain. There was light in her eyes, pain in her head, warm blood in her nostrils. She couldn't move. Noah had her legs pinned beneath him. He shackled her wrists above her head with one huge hand. Through the pain, she felt the release of her zipper, then he started yanking down her jeans.

Ann struggled to breathe. Bile surged up her throat. Noah's hand fumbled with her clothing. The wind pushed against the house, its timber frame groaning. The rage of the storm almost drowned out a pair of voices yelling sharply, getting louder, closer, and then Noah's body was yanked away from hers. With the dead weight off her chest, Ann gulped in oxygen and tried to focus, but double vision shot through in nauseating flashes. She heard Selena's muffled voice, saw a blurred face looming over hers.

"Ann, are you okay?" Her friend's voice sounded anxious as she helped Ann into a sitting position. Shaking with adrenaline, Ann took big gulps of air, and the fog in her head started to lift.

"Ann, are you okay?" Selena repeated.

"I don't know." Ann shook her head, blinking hard, willing herself to focus. She saw a blurry man in uniform roughly handcuffing another blurry man. "Is that Granger?"

"Yes. You're safe now."

Her vision was clearing. Noah didn't look so big any more. Granger was just as tall, just as strong. She saw blood running down Noah's face from a gash on his forehead. Had Granger hit him? No, she remembered now. She had.

"Why are you arresting me?" Noah said. "I didn't do nothing." The house seemed to swallow his voice, but Ann recognized the arrogance in his tone. "She let me in. She came on to me. Started kissing me. Then she went nuts. Fucking hit me."

"He's lying!" Ann said. "He attacked me!"

"Yeah, I punched her. Self-defense. She's a crazy bitch."

"Shut up!" Granger snapped.

"See this blood on my face? I was holding her down to keep her from hitting me again."

"Liar!" Ann was on her feet, ready to pounce. Selena held her back.

"See? She's fucking nuts. She killed her husband. You know that, right?"

"Shut the fuck up. Get on the floor." The intensity in Granger voice was so fierce it was frightening.

Noah didn't budge.

Granger leaned toward him in a threatening manner. "Want to add resisting arrest to assault?"

Noah obeyed, sinking to his knees, and then he lay prone on the floor, hands cuffed behind him, motionless, as quiet as Bailey when he was sleeping.

Granger crouched in front of Ann and asked very gently, "Are you okay?" She nodded yes.

"Is it okay if Selena takes a few pictures of you? We'll need it for evidence."

Ann realized her jeans were unzipped and halfway down her hips. Blood stained her white t-shirt. She touched her face, felt sticky blood around her nose.

"So sorry, Ann. Hold still for a second." Selena held up her cell phone, and a few flashes went off. "Okay. All done."

Feeling her face burn hot and red, Ann adjusted her clothing and slumped back on the couch.

Selena moved the basket out of the entryway and shut the front door, and the ruckus of the storm faded to a background noise. She disappeared and returned with a warm washcloth and gently washed Ann's face. "You're going to be okay."

"Is my nose broken?"

"No. It's bloody, is all. Your cheek is swelling."

"I want him out of here," Ann hissed. "Get him out."

Selena turned a pleading eye to Granger.

"Can you hold on a few minutes, Ann?" he said kindly. "I've called for backup."

Ann understood. Noah was dangerous. Granger needed help getting him into the police vehicle, getting him to jail. She didn't want Granger hurt.

There was the distant moan of an ambulance or police siren, or both. It grew piercingly loud. She heard vehicles brake outside, and more people stormed into her living room. She recognized two more police uniforms gathering around Granger, lifting Noah to his feet, escorting him toward the door. The female officer spoke sharply, "You have the *right* to remain silent. If you do *say* anything, it *can* be used against you in a court of law..."

Another man in a different uniform crouched in front of Ann, introduced himself as Thomas, an EMT, and proceeded to shine a penlight in her eyes, asking her to follow it while he moved it from side to side. Thomas asked her questions, including what year it was, and who was the current president. She answered with clarity, and he appeared to be satisfied. "You're going to be okay, Ms. Howard. No concussion. Do you want to ride with us to the ER? We'd like to check you out completely."

"No. I'm fine."

"You sure, Ann?" Selena asked. "I'll go with you."

"I'm okay."

"Your face is going to hurt for a few days. Keep icing it. Give her Tylenol." The EMT looked at Selena. "You staying with her?"

"Yes."

"Keep her awake for a couple hours. Bring her in if she shows any sign of disorientation."

"Will do."

The worst of the storm had passed. When the EMT opened the door to leave, Ann heard a soft pattering of rain, and only Selena and Granger remained in the room. She noticed for the first time that Selena was dressed up, wearing a wine-colored dress and heels, and she remembered she had told her she was going to the art show. Selena stepped out of her heels, padded into the kitchen, and returned with a bag of frozen peas from the freezer. "Here, Ann, press this to your face."

Ann obeyed, winced, but soon the cold numbed the pain.

"This is all my fault," Selena said mournfully, sinking next to her on the couch. "I never should have left you alone. We knew he was out there, watching. Apparently waiting to find you alone."

Ann heard the torment in her friend's voice. "It's not your fault. This is all on me. I let him in. I didn't have the gun with me. So stupid."

Wheels crunched on the gravel driveway, footsteps crossed the porch, and a woman wearing a tight black dress and sparkly jewelry strode briskly into the room.

Granger nodded, said in a professional tone, "Chief."

"Hi, Sidney." Selena's calm voice didn't conceal an edge of anxiety.

Chief Becker sat in the chair closest to the couch. "How are you doing, Ann?"

"Better, now that he's gone."

"An EMT checked her out, said she's okay," Selena said.

"Is Noah in jail?" Ann asked.

"On his way," Chief Becker said.

Ann sighed her relief. "Thank God he's off the street. Now the town will be safe again, like it was when he was in prison. He's the killer, isn't he?"

A long pause. "Let's take the investigation one step at a time. He's a suspect, for sure."

"It has to be him! He attacked me! He's violent."

"He'll be locked away, Ann. You're safe." A pause. "Do you want me to call Matt? Let him know what happened?"

"I'll call. It'll be best coming from me. He's going to feel guilty he wasn't staying here. It's not his fault. It's no one's fault but mine. I was so stupid."

"You did nothing wrong," Selena said. "You opened the door to your own home. You should expect to be safe."

"Granger, Selena, can you let me talk to Ann in private?" Chief Becker asked softly.

"Sure," Granger said. He put a hand on Selena's elbow and guided her outside to the porch. When the door clicked behind them, Chief Becker pulled her cell phone from her purse. "Let's start at the beginning, Ann. I'm going to record this. Take your time. Go slow. Tell me everything."

Ann clasped her hands tightly, took a deep breath, and began reciting details. "I was home alone, finishing dinner. The doorbell chimed at eight thirty. When I looked out the window, I thought it was Miko, holding a basket of vegetables." Overcome with emotion, she had to bite her bottom lip to keep it from trembling. "As soon as I opened the door, I knew it was Noah. He reeked of alcohol. I asked him to set the basket on the porch and go, but he forced his way in and grabbed me." Ann trembled, and her voice quivered. She proceeded to describe, moment by moment, the course of events, the violence, right up to the moment Granger pulled Noah off of her. She breathed in deeply, trying to quell the shaking. "If he and Selena hadn't gotten here when they did, Noah would have raped me."

Chief Becker sat quietly, absorbing the shock of her words. "Is there anything else you want to add? Any small detail?"

Ann shook her head. "Not right now."

"Thank you. I know that wasn't easy." Sidney turned off her phone's recorder and put her hand on Ann's arm. "Let me know if I can help in any way."

Ann nodded.

"In the meantime, you're in good hands with Selena. I'll let her know we're done."

Not wanting to be alone, Ann got to her feet and followed Sidney out to the porch.

Selena and Granger stood quietly talking at the end of the porch, beyond the glare of light. Crossing her arms against the chill, Ann couldn't help but glance into the distance, her eyes excavating the shadows along the border of trees, darting to any small movement, almost expecting to capture the silhouette of a man.

"I have to go to the station to question Noah," Sidney said to Granger. "I'll take your statement in the car. Then you need to help Amanda next door."

"Next door? Who's Amanda?" Ann asked.

"Officer Amanda Cruz," Sidney said. "We have a warrant to search Noah's room."

"Poor Miko," Ann said, almost to herself. "His family's coming apart again."

"I'll be right in, Ann," Selena said gently.

Ann walked back into the living room, leaving the door wide open.

~ ~

The rain had let up and gauzy veils of mist hung in the trees.

Sidney climbed into the driver's seat of the Yukon and glanced back toward the house where Granger and Selena stood together on the darkened end of the porch. Selena leaned forward and kissed Granger on the cheek. He pulled her into his arms and held her close. Comforting her. A solid guy. Sidney prayed their relationship would deepen and grow. Selena deserved to have a decent man in her life, one who understood commitment, one who knew how to fully love and support a woman.

Granger came down the stairs and scrambled into the passenger side of the Yukon, his face flushed with color.

Sidney wanted to hug him. "Good job, tonight," she said in a professional tone, turning on her recording app. "Let's get your statement before Amanda arrives."

Granger recited the facts concisely: when he and Selena arrived, the front door was open, and vegetables were scattered across the porch—immediate cause for alarm. He bolted inside and saw that Noah had Ann pinned to the couch and was trying to pull down her jeans. When Granger yanked him off, he saw that her face was bloody, and she appeared to be only half conscious. Noah's jeans were unzipped, and he was exposed. "I cuffed him, called for backup. Called you."

"Clear as day." Satisfied, Sidney turned off the recorder. "Your testimony corroborates Ann's. Noah's assault charge and attempted rape is ironclad."

Headlights brightened the interior of the SUV as Amanda pulled into the driveway next to the Yukon. The three convened behind her Jeep. "How'd it go with Noah?" Sidney asked.

"He's booked. In the drunk tank," Amanda said. "Darnell's waiting at the station."

"You didn't let him make a call, did you?"

"No."

"Good. We don't need him telling his dad to hide evidence before you two get over there." Sidney handed Amanda the warrant. "Do a thorough search. Look for diamond jewelry, women's clothing, a pair of men's work boots, size twelve, and anything else connecting Noah to our homicides. Call me if you find anything."

"Will do, Chief." The two deputies piled into Amanda's Jeep and pulled out of the driveway.

~ ~

The tires of the Yukon hissed over the soaked tarmac as Sidney drove to town, her mind backtracking over details of the night's events. She and David had been enjoying a quiet, intimate dinner at the Black Rabbit. She had been beguiled by David's charm and the superb food and wine, which she barely touched before receiving Granger's alarming call.

Sidney wasted no time calling Judge Whitman and requesting a warrant. She apologized to David, left the restaurant, and stopped by the judge's house to pick up the document, ever thankful for small town efficiency. Sidney was on good terms with everyone connected to law enforcement in the three-town area. They trusted her, and knew she always went by the book. With Noah in lockup, she could finally get into the arrogant felon's face.

Thank God Granger arrived on the scene when he did and prevented Ann from becoming a rape victim. Though Selena could handle guns, and was a decent shot, she'd been drinking all evening and wasn't in a clear state of mind after her encounter with Randy. Sidney shivered, thinking what might have happened if Selena stumbled upon the scene alone.

CHAPTER TWENTY-NINE

GRANGER AND AMANDA rapped on Miko's front door, armed with the warrant. Miko appeared in the entryway in wrinkled pajamas, his sleepy expression morphing into one of alarm. Seeing police officers on his doorstep at midnight probably jolted him back to his wife's murder, Granger thought.

Looking like a man bracing for a blow, Miko asked, "Is Noah okay?"

"He's been arrested," Granger said. "He's at the station."

Miko's shoulders sagged. "Drugs?"

"Maybe you should take a seat, Mr. Matsui."

"What did he do?"

"He forced his way into Ann's home, about an hour ago, and assaulted her."

The blood drained from Miko's face. "He didn't…"

"No. Selena and I got there in time."

"Is Ann okay?"

"She's pretty banged up. He slugged her in the face."

Miko shook his head, stared at the ground and muttered in a hoarse tone, "What is wrong with that boy?"

"We need to search Noah's room," Amanda said gently. "Here's the warrant."

Miko blinked at them, dazed, like a drowning victim roused back to consciousness. "His room is upstairs." Clutching the warrant, he padded down the hallway and led them up a narrow, creaking staircase. After passing two bedrooms and a bath, they reached Noah's room at the end of the hall. Miko switched on the light and stepped aside to let them enter.

The room reeked of pot and was in a state of chaos, with dirty clothes strewn across the floor, the desktop, and the unmade bed. A cabinet holding a TV and DVD player stood in one corner, and a bookcase sagged beneath a burden of tools, hand weights, stacks of DVDs, and porn magazines.

Granger and Amanda donned latex gloves and began going through the pockets of his discarded clothing, some dusty and smelling of sweat. A pale ghost in the dim hallway, Miko tentatively asked questions about Ann and Noah.

"Sir, it would be best if you left us alone to do our job," Amanda said.

"Can I go see Noah?"

"Sorry. Not tonight."

He retreated into the darkness.

~ ~

Sidney pulled into the station lot at midnight, used her key card to enter, and hurriedly changed into the spare uniform she kept at the office. After pulling her hair into a ponytail, with her cop persona soundly in place, she buzzed Darnell to come to her office.

After a quick greeting, Darnell updated her. "I got an EMT over here to sew up Noah's head. He noticed fresh tracks on Noah's arm and asked what drugs he was on. Noah said zip. He's high, drunk, totally out of it."

"Breath test?"

"Alcohol level 0.15 percent."

"Jeeze, he's a tank. Let's get him in the sweat box, see if we can squeeze anything out of him." Sidney clapped Darnell on the shoulder as they left her office, thankful for his crisp professionalism. He and Amanda had been roused from bed to deal with tonight's emergency. No one was getting much sleep.

The station had two holding cells, which housed suspects until they were transported to Jackson. The Jackson station had six cells, a police force twice the size of Garnerville, a courthouse, four criminal attorneys, and two public defenders. Garnerville utilized Jackson's bare-bones legal apparatus when needed, and the system bumped along with relative efficiency.

The drunk tank was comprised of tiled walls and a cement floor with a drain in the middle designed to wash away piss and vomit. Noah lay spread-eagle on his back, mouth gaping, his gurgling snores rumbling off the walls.

Darnell and Sidney each grabbed a massive arm and elevated Noah to his feet. Blubbering incoherently, he stumbled between them like a sleepwalker into the interview room and slumped heavily into a plastic chair. Beneath the hard glare of the florescent lights, hands cuffed to the steel tabletop, he blinked at his surroundings as though in a dream.

"I made coffee. I'll get him a cup," Darnell volunteered.

"Hope it's strong."

"A spoon can stand in it." He left, reappeared, and parked a sixteen-ounce disposable cup in front of Noah. Then he took his seat, clicked his pen, and opened his spiral notepad.

Noah didn't look good. Eyes dull and glazed, skin sallow. A square of gauze with a spot of blood in the center was taped to his forehead, and his bruised left brow was puffed up like a marshmallow.

"Drink. It's free," Sidney said.

Noah picked up the cup and took a big gulp. Then another. When the cup sat empty, he shuddered to life. His face hardened, hostility glinted in his dark eyes, and his lips twisted into a snarl. "I want out of here. You had no right to arrest me."

"You're in serious shit," Sidney said.

"False arrest."

"You viciously attacked Ann. Tried to rape her."

"Bullshit."

"You can't worm out of this, Noah. I have the testimony of two people who caught you in the act. One was my officer. Ironclad."

"She agreed to have sex. She wanted it."

"You slugged her. She was bleeding. Half conscious. Hardly sounds consensual. You're going back to jail. Plain and simple."

He jerked his wrist, rattling the chain on his cuffs. "I ain't saying shit."

"Your alcohol level is off the charts," Sidney said. "And you're using again. The EMT saw your tracks. How many illegal drugs are we going to find in your tox screen?"

"Fuck you."

"You could help yourself here. Talk."

Silence.

Sidney opened Noah's file and read in silence, taking her time. Minutes passed.

Noah fidgeted, slumped in his chair, sat bolt upright, crossed and uncrossed his legs. Anxiety peeled off him in waves.

Finally, she looked up. Noah's face was shiny with sweat. She lowered her eyes to the file again. "Hmmm. Parole violation on top of assault. It's looking bad, Noah. Real bad." Her eyes locked on his. "Work with us. Maybe get yourself some amenities in jail."

Noah glared.

Sidney felt the intense heat of his animosity. She didn't flinch.

He redirected his focus to his hands, tightly clasped.

The phone vibrated in her pocket. She pulled it out and scanned a text from Amanda with two attached photos. Sidney felt a spurt of adrenalin. After sending back a thumb's up emoji, she showed the photos to Darnell. His eyes widened.

Watching, Noah squirmed in his seat.

"My deputies are searching your bedroom," Sidney said.

"They hit the jackpot."

Beads of sweat sprouted on his upper lip.

Sidney enlarged the first photo and held it up to Noah. "Want to tell us why you have Bailey's collar?"

He blinked. "Found it."

"Where?"

"On the dirt road at the end of our property, by the lake."

"When was this?"

"Two days ago."

"Which day?"

"Thursday."

The day after Samantha's murder. Sidney stared at him, waiting.

"So I kept her freaking dog collar. So what?"

"It has her phone number on it. You been calling her, Noah? And hanging up?"

The muscles tightened around his mouth.

"We have your phone. We'll find out."

"Maybe I called a couple times. Didn't mean nothing by it."

"Here in Oregon, harassment is a crime."

Stony silence.

"Tell me about this." Sidney showed him a photo of an origami butterfly in a glass box, a perfect match to the two found at the murder scenes.

His jaw clenched tight.

"When I showed you and your father a similar photo, you both said you had no idea what it was. Yet, here you have a duplicate sitting on the bookcase in your bedroom."

"So what?"

"Impeding a murder investigation is a crime. Where'd you get this?"

"None of your fucking business."

"You aren't helping yourself, Noah."

"What the fuck is this? So I have a fucking dog collar and butterfly. So what?"

"We can now link you to the homicide of Samantha Ferguson."

"Bullshit!"

"The collar and butterfly are tied to her killer."

"Fuck that! You ain't pinning no murder on me!" Noah yanked hard on the cuffs. The cords in his neck stood out like rope. His biceps bulged. The heavy metal table lurched towards him, screeching on the cement floor.

"Settle down, Noah," Sidney said evenly. "I don't want to leave you shackled in here all night in the dark with no cigarette or bathroom breaks. Which I'm about ready to do."

"I didn't kill no one!" Spittle shot from his mouth like missiles.

"I want to help you. So, let's figure this out." She gave him a minute to get himself under control, though his knee bobbed like a jackhammer. "Tell me where you got this butterfly."

Sweat dripped down the sides of his face and collected along his jaw line.

"Talk to me, Noah. Then we'll let you take a break. Use the head. Have a smoke."

He swallowed. "If I talk, I'll look guilty."

"You look more guilty by not talking."

He lifted his hands as high as the cuffs would allow and wiped his jaw with the back of his hand, then he met her hard stare. "Sammy gave it to me."

Sidney and Darnell exchanged a look.

"When?"

"A week before she went to rehab."

"This is a valuable piece of art. Why would she give it to you?"

"She wanted to get high." He swallowed again, his Adam's

apple traveling up and down his neck.

"So you gave her drugs."

"Yeah. But that's all I'm guilty of. I didn't kill her!"

"Where did she get the butterfly?"

Noah tightened his jaw.

"Was it the same man who took her on trips, bought her jewelry?"

Silence.

"You think he'd protect you if he was sitting in your place? You want to take a murder rap for him? Give us his name, Noah."

Noah sat motionless, staring at his tattooed hands. A bead of sweat dripped off his jaw and plopped unto the tabletop.

Another drip.

They sat in silence for several minutes, Darnell lazily doodling in his notebook, Sidney checking messages on her phone and texting back replies.

"I want protection," Noah said hoarsely. "I'm a dead man if this gets back to him."

Sidney noticed about a dozen drops of sweat had collected on the table. She tucked her phone into her pocket and gave Noah her full attention. "We'll protect you. You have my word. I'll make sure you do your time in another state, under another name." Far-fetched, but cops could weave any damn fantasy they wanted if it meant getting a suspect to talk.

Noah's jaw sawed back and forth. Another drop of sweat plopped on the table.

Sidney searched his face for clues, for signs of the cold-blooded psychopath who planned two murders with meticulous care. A man with a precise M.O. that involved incapacitating and abducting a woman, holding her hostage for up to twelve hours, and for his grand finale, slicing open her wrists with surgical precision. A man with discipline. In Noah, Sidney saw a vicious brute filled with hostility, capable of spontaneous rape and violence, a man who craved immediate gratification and succumbed to impulse. Noah was not her killer.

"Give me his name, Noah."

Noah looked at her long and hard and hissed between clenched teeth, "James Abbott."

Adrenalin charged Sidney's system. *James Abbott.* Long seconds passed while she digested the information. The ruthless CEO who dressed with impeccable taste and ran a multi-billion-dollar company could certainly intimidate a hardened criminal like Noah, and Jason, Barney's tough-talking bartender. But these men existed in different hemispheres, subject to different laws of gravity. In what scenario would their worlds collide? She studied Noah with narrowed eyes. Was he blowing smoke? "Why do you think you're a dead man if Abbott found out you talked to me?"

"Why do you think?" he sneered.

"Don't play me."

"He's a killer. He killed Sammy."

"Why do you think he killed Sammy?"

"Because of the way he treated her. He threatened her. Roughed her up."

"Slow down, Noah. Start at the beginning. Were Abbott and Samantha involved?"

"Yeah."

"For how long?"

"All summer."

"How did they meet?"

"Fundraiser at the country club. It's no secret. Everyone at Barney's knew. Sammy couldn't keep a lid on anything. When she was high, she shot off her mouth to anyone who would listen." Noah's lips twisted. "She bragged about how she had him on a leash, slobbering all over her, getting her high, buying her all kinds of crap. Whatever Sammy wanted, Mr. Big Shot got her."

"You say he roughed her up?"

"Yeah. He found out she slept around. Wasn't his personal property like he thought. Got his balls twisted in a knot."

"You sleep with her?"

Noah wiped the sweat from his jaw. "Nah. I knew to leave her alone. Abbott got in my face in the parking lot at Barney's. Told me to back off, or…"

"Or what?"

"He didn't say. But I knew what he meant." Noah shot himself in the temple with an imaginary gun.

"Why would he kill Sammy?"

"Revenge."

"For what?"

"She didn't like to be controlled. She told him to go screw himself. They were done. He went psycho on her. Slapped her around. Scared the crap out of her."

"Samantha tell you this?"

"Yeah, one night when we got high at Jason's crib. She bitched all night. On and on. Said Abbott wouldn't leave her alone."

"When?"

"Couple days before she went to rehab. She was hiding out at Jason's. But Abbott found her. She saw him sitting in his car, watching the house."

"Abbott stalked Sammy?"

"She thought so. She went into rehab partly to get away from him. The place had security. She thought she'd be safe. But Jason told me Abbott showed up there, too."

"He went to the rehab facility?"

"Yeah." Noah scowled. "He's got money. Power. He can do whatever he wants. They let him see her. Sammy told him if he didn't leave her alone, she'd tell his old lady."

"How'd Abbott take that?"

"Bad. Told her if she went anywhere near his old lady, she'd prefer death to what he'd do to her."

The hair rose on Sidney's arms.

"He's a psycho, man." Noah sat back and crossed his arms. A look of defiance crept over his face. "I ain't saying another word 'til I use the head. I gotta piss, bad. And I wanna call my dad."

Sidney nodded at Darnell.

Darnell unlocked Noah's cuffs from the table, allowing his hands to hang loose in front of his body. Darnell accompanied him to the restroom with Sidney right behind, her hand on the hilt of her sidearm.

Sidney stood in the doorway as Noah emptied his bladder with his back to her, her thoughts racing through her brain. How much of Noah's babble was rooted in fact? One thing was certain, Abbott needed a close look. His polished exterior might be concealing a deeply troubled man; one who enjoyed dominating a woman and who threatened a terrifying revenge if she didn't submit. But was Abbott a killer? Sidney wanted nothing more than to get in his face, put him in the hot seat, grill him. But the powerful CEO was on his private jet flying to the east coast, untouchable.

She exhaled a tense breath. In the meantime, she hoped her trip to Sand Hill tomorrow would not be futile, and that she'd uncover evidence that would help break her case. Lab results would be in on Monday. One way or another, she intended to make an arrest in the very near future.

~ ~

After an intense search of Noah's bedroom, Granger and Amanda had found Bailey's collar, the origami butterfly, and Noah's cell phone, but no boots, women's jewelry, or anything else related to the homicides.

They returned to Ann's farm and Granger was relieved to see Matt's van parked next to his truck in the driveway. The porch lights burned bright holes into the darkness, but the interior lights were out. The farmhouse looked quiet, as though silently watching over its residents. Granger figured everyone inside must be passed out from sheer exhaustion.

Though Noah was in custody, he and Amanda did a thorough search of the grounds. No footprints. No sign that the earth had recently been disturbed.

They drove back to the station with their evidence and found Darnell and Chief Becker studying the crime board in the conference room. The four officers gathered round the table for a quick briefing. Granger listened intently. The chief put into words the theory that Granger had been developing.

She was convinced Noah was not Samantha's killer. She pointed to the new photo of the origami artist, Satoshi Akira, and informed them that her death in Sand Hill looked suspicious and had similarities to their Garnerville murders. She informed them she had an interview lined up that morning in Sand Hill with the officer who worked Satoshi's case.

Granger had shared at the last meeting that he spotted a shadowy figure at Ann's farm, and had followed the footprints to the dirt road by the lake in time to see the disappearing taillights of a truck.

Chief Becker now made special reference to the incident. "The killer is still out there, a real and dangerous threat to our community, specifically to Ann and Selena. Those footprints could very well be those of our perp, still waiting for his chance to silence Ann. I want one of you posted at her house at all times. Advise the two women to stay alert and keep doors and windows locked.

"Matt's over there right now," Granger said.

"Good. I still want a cool-headed professional present. We have two armed women who are frightened enough to shoot at anything. Even the mailman."

"I'll head out there," Darnell volunteered.

She gave him a tired smile of appreciation. "Catch some sleep over there. Her couch is rent free."

"I could sleep standing up right now." Darnell pushed himself to his feet and shuffled out of the room.

"I'll relieve him at noon," Granger said.

"I'll take the evening shift," Amanda said.

"Let's head home, get some shut eye." Chief Becker stifled a yawn. "Stay alert out there and keep in touch." The chief walked out of the staffroom ahead of them, went straight to the parking lot and got into her car. Granger had never seen her look so whipped. He drove straight home, peeled off his uniform, and did a face plant in bed at 4:00 a.m.

CHAPTER THIRTY

AS SIDNEY and David drove down the six blocks that comprised the business district of Sand Hill, she was relieved to find not much had changed during her ten-year absence. In her early twenties, she had often escaped to the small fishing town with her boyfriend du jour, mixing a little steamy romance with hiking and relaxation. Tucked into an inlet where the Suskany River emptied into the sea, the area was known for its scenic harbor and miles of rolling sand dunes. Because of its remote location, Sand Hill had escaped the stampede of tourists that turned other coastal towns into pits of commercialism. Instead, the town mostly attracted art and nature lovers.

Sidney passed coffee houses, bohemian boutiques, and art galleries operating out of bleached, wood-shingled houses, some dating back decades. She scanned the larger buildings looking for the Police Department and would have missed it entirely if David hadn't pointed it out with a note of surprise. "That's it."

Sidney backed up twenty feet and turned into the parking lot, equally surprised that law enforcement had taken up residence in the historic Baptist church. The white clapboard building on the tidy green lawn featured a graceful bell tower and a row of arched stained-glass windows. Sidney would have expected to see seniors pouring out the door after a lively game of Bingo, rather than uniformed officers racing off to fight crime. An annex with barred windows in the rear of the building added the appearance of a functioning police station. Two patrol cars and an unmarked white Tahoe were parked in the lot.

"Blessed are the peacemakers, for they shall be called sons of God," Sidney said as she parked next to the Tahoe.

"Come again?" David said. "Churches inspire you to spout Bible quotes?"

She grinned. "Just something my dad used to say."

"A zealot or a philosopher?"

"A bit of both."

The drive from Garnerville had passed quickly. Sidney discovered she and David shared much in common, including a love for rhythm and blues, and they drummed up a lot of nostalgia for sixties bands like John Mayall and the Allman Brothers. They reflected on how electronic gadgets impacted every nuance of their lives and laughed about their addictions to their smart phones. David took a few time-outs to respond to texts from his kids, his thumbs a blur on the keypad. She found that David was easy to talk to, and by the end of the drive, he had coaxed out private details of her life that she had shared with no one but Selena.

Sidney released her seat belt, feeling reluctant to end their pleasant visit and shift from social mode to cop mode. "Time to part ways, David."

He looked relaxed sitting in the passenger seat, eyes hidden behind aviator glasses, his beard a shade darker than it was last night. "Sure you don't want me to tag along?"

"Sorry. Business."

They climbed out of the Yukon and stood together on the sidewalk. David looked fit and handsome in jeans and a light parka over a dark blue t-shirt, his hair perfectly tousled. A khaki backpack was slung over one shoulder.

"Good luck in there. Hope you make headway on your case."

"Thanks. What're you going to do to amuse yourself?"

"Explore the town, the beach." He gazed down the street with interest. "Test out the coffee. Find a good restaurant so I can treat you to a wholesome lunch."

"Concerned about my health?"

"You didn't eat dinner last night."

"Yeah, dinner was a bust." She ruefully recalled the one bite of Chilean sea bass with citrus sauce she managed before getting the call from Granger.

"Sorry you had a rough night," he said.

"Goes with the territory."

He pulled her close and she lingered in his arms, enjoying the feel of his hard body pressed to hers. Their lips met and they softly kissed. Her bottom lip was still tender, but her stomach did little flip-flops. When he pulled away, she resisted the urge to bring him back into the embrace. It took a moment to regain her bearing.

Tossing Sidney a wicked grin, David ambled away down the sidewalk, the wind blowing back his jacket and riffling through his hair.

Sidney watched until he disappeared around the corner, feeling a little dazed. *How had this happened?* A charming man had swept into her life like an errant storm. David had all the right components. He was smart, funny, financially sound, and a committed family man with a realistic take on a marriage. If Kelly hadn't passed away, Sidney was certain his marriage would have endured.

With a sigh, she switched her thoughts from David to business. Officially it was her day off, but she looked reasonably professional in a navy blazer over a white cotton blouse, black stone washed jeans, and comfortable but stylish Italian loafers. Her hair hung loose; a good decision since David had reached over and fingered a lock and mentioned the loveliness of the color.

Again, she tugged her thoughts away from David and stepped into the church's interior. Filtered light streamed through the stained-glass windows, highlighting six cubicles that had replaced the rows of wooden pews in the nave. Two glass-fronted rooms were built in the sanctuary. One had a large desk and appeared to belong to the police chief. The other had tables, chairs, and a whiteboard, obviously the conference room. Like Garnerville, the small department consisted of four officers, three reserve officers, and a few volunteers, reflecting the town's small population.

Seated behind the administration desk in the vestibule, a matronly receptionist typed on her computer while speaking into a headset. Her fingers paused, and she smiled up at Sidney. "Can I help you?"

"I have an appointment with Officer McKowski."

"And you are?"

"Police Chief Becker, from Garnerville."

"One moment." The woman spoke into her mic and then glanced at Sidney. "He'll be right with you."

A portly man left a cubicle with a file folder in hand and strode briskly up the aisle to greet her. Thinning gray hair crowned a round, deeply tanned face, and he wore emerald green seersucker pants and a bright yellow sports shirt. If his intention was to stand out on the golf course this morning, he would easily win the prize.

"Nice to meet you, Chief Becker. I'm Officer McKowski," he said, mashing her fingers in his pudgy hand. "Come this way."

McKowski's brusque tone, hurried manner, and outlandish attire suggested he had a tee time to meet, and he was doing her a favor by making a detour to the station.

Sidney followed his scent of Aqua Velva into the sparsely furnished conference room. McKowski shut the door behind them and motioned to the table, where two bottles of water had been placed to designate seating. They sat opposite one another and scooted closer to the table.

Sidney had made the appointment through the answering service, stating only that she wanted to discuss the Akira case.

The officer folded his hands over the file as though reluctant to open it. "So what exactly do you want to know about Satoshi Akira's suicide, Chief Becker?"

Sidney got straight to the point. "I want to propose that her death was not a suicide."

McKowski's face took on a puzzled expression. "You think she was murdered?"

"It's very possible."

"We haven't had a homicide in Sand Hill in a decade. And that was a bar fight between two out-of-towners." He rubbed the back of his neck in an agitated manner, perhaps realizing Sidney would not be dismissed in a hurry. "Her case was cut and dry. No evidence pointed to foul play."

"May I see her file, Officer?"

"Call me Dan." He pushed the file toward her with his index finger and sat back in his chair with his arms crossed.

Sidney opened the file and read the report. Then she sorted through the crime scene photos and studied them one by one, memorizing every horrific detail. The photos were not easy to look at. Despite her years of experience, Sidney felt a queasy flutter in her stomach.

Discovered approximately five days after the time of death, Satoshi's body was in an advanced stage of putrefaction—bloated, discolored, with insect and rodent activity present. Releasing a slow breath, Sidney placed the photos back in the file, twisted the cap off her water bottle, and took a long, cool sip.

She turned back to McKowski. "Have you ever investigated a murder, Dan?"

"No... but if you're suggesting we did sloppy police work..."

He straightened his shoulders and sat taller in his chair, a posture of machismo that didn't disguise his nervousness, and possibly, his resentment at being questioned by a woman. Sidney had noted from her research online that only one woman was employed with the Sand Hill police force, a rookie, and the first hired in the entire history of the department. Nearing retirement age, McKowski most likely was entrenched in the 'old boys club' mentality, where the concept that women were the weaker sex was pervasive, and men seldom looked at women as peers.

"I'm not suggesting anything, Dan. Just trying to gather facts. Satoshi's death was brought to my attention because it resembles two murders we've had in Garnerville, and we have evidence linking her to both crimes."

He blinked several times. "Two murders? You think you have a serial killer in your area?"

"I'm convinced we do."

"What connects your homicides to Satoshi?"

"The women were carefully staged. Propped against a tree in a seated position. One ankle crossed over the other. Barefoot. Wrists slit."

McKowski's face paled. The photos in Satoshi's report showed the same body positioning.

"I'm investigating quietly. Please keep this under wraps."

"Of course."

"It says in your file, Dan, that high school boys found the body in the old historic lighthouse."

"Correct. They broke in around midnight. They wanted to drink beer and smoke pot up on the top story, see the great views. If they hadn't been blasted out of their minds, they would have been warned off by the smell. But they went in. Got the shock of their lives."

"It says no autopsy was performed. No tox screen. No pathology test of any kind."

"Her body was melting in its own juices, Chief. The whole lighthouse stank to high heaven. We needed to dispose of the body quickly. She was cremated."

"A pathologist should have been notified," Sidney said coolly.

"The M.E. made the final decision."

"If you had deemed the death suspicious, Dan, the M.E. would have performed an autopsy. Now vital evidence has been destroyed."

His face flushed red, and he blustered, "The death wasn't suspicious. She lived like a hermit, holed up in her little house up on the bluff. Loneliness and isolation lead to depression," he argued with an air of authority. "Depression can lead to suicide."

His convenient theory based on pop psychology angered Sidney. She stared at her hand, gripping her water bottle, and slowly counted to three before she said in a controlled voice, "It says a blade was found at the scene. I don't see a picture of it in the report."

His face colored. "You're sure?"

"Yes, I'm sure. Do you have the blade in the case file?"

"We don't store unnecessary evidence. Everything we have regarding her case is in that folder you're holding."

"No photo. No blade." Sidney gave him her deadly stare. "Do you remember the make, the brand of the blade?"

McKowski picked at the paper on his water bottle. "I believe it was a barber's straight edge razor."

Sidney resisted the urge to throw the folder at him and handed back the file. "Was anything found with the body? Jewelry? Any of her origami pieces?"

"No. Only the skirt, blouse, and underwear she had on."

Sidney was disappointed there was no butterfly, but every other aspect of the crime matched her two homicides. Except the blade. Why did the killer leave the blade? To avert suspicion of a murder? If so, he succeeded. But that begged the question, why was he now contacting the *Daily Buzz*, seeking attention, taunting law enforcement over his latest victim in Garnerville?

Sidney was certain the perp felt threatened by women—the likely reason he injected the neurotoxin—so he could exert full control over each victim for hours before the deadly finale. Was he taunting Sidney because she was the first female police chief in Garnerville's history? Did he need to show her a man had the upper hand?

McKowski's voice interrupted her thoughts. "Why Satoshi? Why here?"

She met the officer's eyes. "That's what I'm trying to find out. Did you talk to her friends? See if anyone was threatening her?"

"We spoke to a few people. Mostly to inform them of her death. No one mentioned anyone suspicious. She didn't have a boyfriend."

"I'd like to see the crime scene."

"I can arrange that." He hesitated for a moment, watching his fingers drum the table before meeting her gaze again. "Do you mind if another officer takes you? It's my day off. I have an appointment."

"No problem." Preferable.

Looking relieved, McKowski slapped his armrests and heaved himself out of his chair. "I'll send in Officer Megan Conner. She was with me the night we found the body." He stretched his arm across the table and shook her hand. His was damp. "Please keep me notified of any updates."

"Will do."

He hurried from the room, and Sidney wiped his sweat from her hand on her jeans. A few minutes passed before the door opened, and Officer Megan Conner walked in. She was a slender black woman with striking hazel eyes, and a crisp, professional manner. Dressed in the standard blue uniform of the Sand Hill department, she wore her hair slicked back into a bun at the nape of her neck.

She reached out her hand to Sidney. "I'm Officer Conner. I hear you want to go up to the lighthouse, Chief Becker."

CHAPTER THIRTY-ONE

PERCHED ON THE FURTHERMOST tip of a rugged peninsula, the historic lighthouse could be seen from almost anywhere in town. Sidney remembered once viewing it from a sailboat, miles out in the open sea. The design was unique; a cylindrical tower that housed the fog signal equipment, attached at the base to one side of an octagonal room.

"I remember taking a tour of the lighthouse when I was a teenager," Sidney said, making mild conversation, sitting next to Conner in her cruiser. "Quite an engineering feat for the 1890's. Is it still open to tourists?"

"It was condemned ten years ago," Officer Conner said. "The historical society was gearing up to restore it, but Satoshi's death put a damper on their plans. They're only now getting back to the project. In another few weeks, you wouldn't have been able to see it…" She glanced at Sidney and returned her focus to the road. "As it was that night."

Sidney heard a catch in Conner's voice and glanced over at her. "You knew her?"

Conner's hands tensed on the steering wheel. "It's a small town, Chief Becker. Everyone knows everyone." She parked on the paved road and she and Sidney trudged along the shoulder following the contour of the cliff. The asphalt was riddled with cracks and cheat grass burst through the openings in verdant green tufts. The tall yellow grass in the surrounding fields shimmied and tossed in the brisk morning wind and voluminous clouds blossomed in a deep blue sky. Even behind sunglasses, Sidney's eyes narrowed against the glaring sunlight.

The structure loomed in front of them. Peeling paint and chipped stucco told of more than a century of punishment from gale force winds, brutal sun, and torrential storms, yet it stood solidly erect on a cliff of scoured granite. The waves below rushed to shore in great hunched mounds and crashed against boulders in showy explosions of spray and foam. The area around the dwelling was wood-planked, and a long walkway connected the lighthouse to the keeper's home, some six hundred and fifty feet away. A brick cistern and a dilapidated barn also stood on the barren property.

Officer Conner pulled a jangling ring of keys from her jacket pocket and inserted one into the rusty lock. They heard it click, but the door resisted when she pushed against it. Both women leaned in hard with their shoulders, and finally, it groaned open.

"How did the kids get in?" Sidney asked.

"They climbed through a back window. All the windows are now boarded up." Sidney noticed Conner's face had paled. The young officer stripped a flashlight from her duty belt and handed it to Sidney, then stepped aside to let her enter. "Watch your step."

Sidney thumbed the switch and followed the beam inside. She noticed the smell immediately. Though faint, the stench of putrefaction still lingered in these close quarters deprived of sunlight and fresh air. The circle of light darted from floor to walls, illuminating scraps of wood and rusted debris strewn across the floor. Layers of peeling paint exposed the original stonework, and veils of spider webs hung like garlands from the ceiling.

"She was found on the second floor," Conner said behind her in a thin voice, her silhouette framed in the doorway. "If it's all right with you, Chief, I'll wait out here."

"No problem." For most, viewing a crime scene once was

enough to imprint grisly details in their minds for life. In Oakland, Sidney returned to the epicenter of violence several times, to get a greater understanding of the full scope of what took place, to try to understand a sick mind capable of conducting acts of depravity.

Dark memories threatened to surface as she climbed the steel mesh spiral stairway. She forced them down and focused on the crime scene at hand. A man with above average strength carried Satoshi up these stairs, and if Sidney's assumption was correct, the woman was trapped in an unresponsive body, but fully conscious. What had Satoshi been thinking those last minutes of her life? What was her killer thinking? Was he delirious with anticipation of some kind of emotional climax, just seconds away?

She stepped off the stairway that spiraled upwards and flashed her beam around the circular room until she found the crime scene. The smell was stronger up here. Remembering the photos, Sidney's pulse quickened, and a wave of nausea rolled in her gut.

An attempt had been made to wash away the blood, but even under a dull coat of dust, Sidney could see a wide stain from each wrist embedded in the rotting floorboards. The arterial spray that fanned the wall was a fading ghost. Sidney envisioned the killer posing his victim with care, neatly arranging her clothing, crossing one bare ankle over the other, placing each arm at her side, and when all was perfect, slicing through each fragile wrist.

Had the killer stood in this very spot watching his methodical planning come to fruition? Had he fixed Satoshi's head in such a position that her wide-eyed stare was trained on his while her life ebbed away? Sidney felt herself sinking into the old familiar dread, with an awful gnawing in her gut. What had this poor woman done to warrant such a grisly death?

A movement to her left spiked her adrenalin. She backed up quickly, and something brushed against her cheek. She gasped when her beam revealed a huge gray rat across the room, frozen in the light, eyes luminous red. It hissed and scurried into a hole in the floorboards, its tail slithering behind like a snake.

Heart pounding, Sidney caught her breath and found she had backed into a thick strand of cobweb, which stuck to her face and hair like cotton candy. With impatience, she brushed it off and forced herself to move about the room slowly, examining every square foot of space. Aside from rodent droppings and numerous spiders disturbed in their webs, she saw nothing out of the ordinary, no further clues. She descended the stairs, her spirit stained with residual horror.

Out in the open air, she inhaled a deep cleansing breath and heard Conner lock the door behind her. Their eyes met, and they shared a moment of understanding. "You never get used to it," Sidney said. "That's why I left homicide in the big city."

"Even in a small town, death follows you."

"True. But at least now I don't have it served up with my meals three times a day."

They both smiled. Gallows humor.

Sidney stood gazing at the stunning view, letting the warm sunshine dilute the crime scene images. Billowing clouds drifted in a deep blue sky that merged with the blue of the sea. "How well did you know Satoshi?"

Conner's posture stiffened, and her lips tightened into a seam. Almost immediately, her eyes turned glassy, and her tough expression collapsed. She jammed her hands into her pockets and stared out to sea. "We were close."

Sidney said gently, "Anything you tell me, Megan, is off the record. If you want her killer found, talk to me."

Officer Conner blushed with the realization her secret was exposed. "We better head back." She turned abruptly and headed for the cruiser.

Sidney followed several feet behind to give the officer space and time to think. When they were both strapped inside the vehicle, Conner sat for a minute, contemplating the steering wheel with her dark brows drawn together.

"You know it wasn't suicide, don't you?" Sidney said.

Silence.

"Confidential," Sidney said. "I promise."

"Satoshi didn't kill herself," Conner blurted, and faced Sidney. "She was happy. She loved her life."

Sidney took a chance. "Satoshi loved you."

Conner nodded, said in a shaky voice. "We were going to move in together."

"I'm so sorry for your loss," Sidney said quietly.

A strained look tightened the officer's face. "It's been tough. Not being able to talk about it. I've been openly gay for years, but Satoshi was ashamed of being a lesbian. We saw each other in secret. I was slowly easing her out of the closet."

"She was a beautiful woman."

"And a beautiful person. Gentle and kind."

"Her work is stunning."

"She was totally committed to her art." Conner half smiled, and pulled onto the road, tires bouncing over ruts and potholes. The smell of brine and sweet grass filtered in through the open windows.

"Tell me about Satoshi."

"Where do I start?" She paused. "She lived a very sheltered life in Japan. Upper middle class. She came to Oregon seventeen years ago on an art grant, and stayed. After she bought her cottage ten years ago, she focused obsessively on her art. Her agent conducted all her business transactions. That isolation made her incredibly naïve, and oblivious to the dangers of the world."

"Did she ever mention anyone taking an unhealthy interest in her?"

"She wouldn't have noticed. Satoshi didn't have a clue how pretty she was, or the interest she stirred in men. They flirted shamelessly, but she ignored them."

"That must have pissed off some men."

"Yeah. I witnessed it a few times when we were out together."

"Did anyone show signs of stalking her?"

"It's a small town. I think I would've known." She lowered her voice and added in a conspiratorial tone, "After she died, I did find something."

Sidney's antennae shot up.

"When it became clear her case was going to be dismissed as a suicide, I started investigating on my own. I have a key to her cottage. I went up there one night and copied all the business files from her computer." Conner swallowed, her eyes trained on the road. "I spent days combing through her records. Two men flagged my attention. Both had sent her several emails. Both were collectors who owned several of her pricier pieces. There had never been any problems with their payments. That's why she didn't direct the business through her agent. To reward their loyalty, Satoshi dealt with them personally. Gave them the red-carpet treatment."

"Why did you find them suspicious?"

They had reached the edge of downtown. Conner pulled up at a traffic stop where children on a field trip, walking two-by-two, were ushered across the intersection by three adults. Conner met Sidney's gaze. "They wanted to meet Satoshi in person. And both picked dates close to the time of her murder."

"Did she meet with them?"

"Yes.

"Here in town?"

"Yes. In her studio." Conner blew out a ragged breath. "I wish to God I'd been with her for those meetings. Maybe I would've picked up on something she couldn't. But she wouldn't let me. She was fiercely private. She insisted on keeping her business separate from our personal time."

"Do you know the names of these men?"

The last of the children scampered to the sidewalk, and Conner carefully crossed the intersection. "One man always signed his first name. James."

"James Abbott?"

"I don't know his last name, but he was from Portland."

Sidney began pushing bits of information together. The Abbotts were from Portland. James worked in Portland. He had an intimate relationship with Samantha, and he had given her one of Satoshi's butterflies. He also was a highly disciplined man who appeared to have an addiction to extramarital affairs, a desire to control women, and an animosity if they didn't bend to his will. A lot of puzzle pieces fitting together. "Who was the other man?"

A look of fear flitted across the officer's face. "He called himself 'The Collector.'"

Sidney's scalp prickled. In light of what happened to Satoshi and the other women, a man calling himself "The Collector" had a sinister ring. "Where is he from?"

"I don't know. It wasn't in the files, but I instinctively didn't like him."

"Why is that?"

"His fussiness. Calling all the shots, insisting she bend her schedule to accommodate his. His payments had to be in cash instead of PayPal, which made her feel like a bank clerk."

"He didn't want a paper trail."

"Yeah, like he was already planning her murder."

Sidney nodded. "Where were you the night of the abduction?"

"Out of town. Visiting my mom in Ashland for the weekend."

"Why did it take so long for you to know Satoshi was missing?"

"She sent me a text saying she was going out of town."

"Unusual?"

"Not unusual, but abrupt. Usually, she notified me in advance. She worked hard, compulsively, and on occasion she needed to recharge. She enjoyed taking off and having a solitary adventure. When I didn't hear from her after three days, I thought she went somewhere off the grid. Also not unusual." Conner blinked away tears, struggling to compose herself. "But actually, she was being murdered. The killer had access to her phone. He must have read her texts and discovered we were planning to get together. He must have sent me that text about her leaving town."

Sidney concurred. The killer had the foresight to clear Satoshi's schedule. He wanted no interruption. "And her car was gone?"

"They found her Honda parked at the lighthouse behind the barn." Conner swallowed. "He thought of every angle."

Sidney agreed. "Can you take me up to her cottage?"

"Yeah. I still have a key, but the house has been emptied of her belongings."

Sidney felt a surge of anger, thinking of the wealth of forensic material that was never processed. "Let's go."

CHAPTER THIRTY-TWO

OFFICER CONNER TURNED down a side street and drove steadily toward the bluffs above the bay opposite the lighthouse, about a ten-minute drive. The cottage was isolated, the front facing the sea, the back surrounded by trees that obscured the small house from the road. No one would know the bungalow existed if not deliberately looking for it.

Conner parked in the driveway and the two got out and walked around the entire house, a small clapboard affair with a covered veranda encircling three sides. The studio was on the west side and appeared to be a recent addition. Constructed with large windows to take advantage of natural light and dramatic sunsets, the location was perfect for some voyeur to observe Satoshi from the cover of trees. An exterior door on the veranda was used to admit clients without taking them through her private living quarters.

The cottage had seen a few rainstorms since the crime took place two months ago. Nonetheless, Sidney carefully examined the yard close to the house. Weeds had invaded a bonsai garden in the backyard, and the stunted trees and ornamental shrubs were in need of care, but nothing looked disturbed other than by the hand of nature.

They mounted the wood planked veranda, and Sidney discovered a trail of boot prints leading to the studio door. The right boot must have stepped in mud, for the tread pattern was stamped clearly, as though stenciled. The prints did not retreat from the door. Sidney's pulse quickened. The visitor entered the dwelling. "Someone has been here recently. Watch where you step." She gestured to the prints.

Conner's eyes widened, and she nodded.

"When did it rain last?"

"A few days ago. Friday."

"Who else had a key?"

"No one. Unless the killer took Satoshi's key off her ring." Conner sidestepped the footprints, pulled her keys from a pocket, opened the door and stood aside.

"Wait here." Sidney wanted no distractions. No contamination. She removed her shoes, entered barefoot. The muddy footsteps continued inside on the hardwood floor.

The empty room was sunny, inviting, with stunning views of the bay. Sidney pictured Satoshi here, consumed by the work she loved, bowed head occasionally lifting to view the changing sky and sea. Tempting to be a recluse here, Sidney thought, far from the madding crowd. A link between the three victims suddenly clicked into place. All three women were gifted artists. She recalled Samantha's tumultuous pastel, Satoshi's butterflies, Mimi's exceptional singing voice. The killer picked creative women. Why? A piercing sadness overwhelmed her. The lives of three talented women, who had so much to contribute, had been cut short by a narcissistic madman.

The footprints led to the far end of the room and became muddled, as though the intruder spent time there, perhaps contemplating memories of past visits. Another set of prints, more faint, led through the studio door into the interior of the house. Sidney followed them though the living room to a back room. The adjoining bath and impressions in the carpet made by the frame of a bed told Sidney this was Satoshi's bedroom. The pattern of the last vacuuming was undisturbed, except for the flatter shapes made by the intruder. He went to the spot where the bed had stood and again spent time there, the indentation in the carpet long and thin, as though he lay on his side.

Sidney closed her eyes, trying to understand the man's compulsion to visit this room. She could feel his presence—dark and malignant. Had he lain here with Satoshi? He could have come to the studio under the pretense of business, injected her, and carried her into this room. Whatever he did with her, hidden from the world, he was able to accomplish in a leisurely manner. Later, he could easily have transported her to the isolated lighthouse in the dark of night.

She opened her eyes and studied the room. When the man roused himself, he made a last set of prints leading to the window. There, they disappeared. Feeling a touch of nervous excitement, Sidney backtracked through the house to the porch. She fished her phone from her handbag and pulled up a photo of the cast made from the boot prints found at Samantha's crime scene. She compared it to the prints on the porch. They appeared to be a perfect match. She turned to Conner. "Can we get a forensics expert up here? ASAP."

"Yes, ma'am." Conner walked out to the yard and spoke into her phone for a few minutes in clipped notes. Sidney joined her as she ended her call.

"A specialist is on his way."

"Good. Got any latex?"

Conner hurriedly pulled a pair of latex gloves from a pocket on her duty belt.

With Conner trailing her, Sidney returned to the back of the house and searched the ground more carefully under the bedroom window. No prints, but upon close inspection, she saw someone had scuffed the ground with a branch or the heel of a boot. Sidney tried the window. It gave. Her scalp tingled. "My guess, the killer came back here to relive his crime, and wished to do so again in the future. He left the window open in the event the door locks were changed."

Conner released a deep breath. The officer was quiet and Sidney could feel her tension, though she was trying to hide it. "What is it you're not telling me, Chief Becker?"

Sidney met the officer's expectant gaze as she stripped off her latex gloves. "Satoshi's murder is similar to two we've had in Garnerville."

"He's killed before?"

She nodded. "One just four nights ago. Those boot prints on the porch appear to match our Garnerville killer."

Conner's expression was grave as Sidney filled in the details of Samantha's murder. "He thought Satoshi's case was put to rest," Sidney said. "A suicide. He felt safe enough to come back here. He got sloppy, left his boot prints."

"Maybe he left something else. Hair, fiber, prints."

"We can only hope."

Conner blew out her breath in frustration. "If Satoshi's death was investigated more thoroughly, maybe they would have caught the killer. It might have prevented Samantha's death."

"Never second guess yourself in this business," Sidney said. "We're dealing with a highly intelligent killer."

"Yeah. And he's in control," Conner said with bitterness. "Moving cops around like chess pieces."

"Not for long. We'll get him. We're on a collision course." Sidney spoke with a confidence she didn't completely feel. An ominous mood descended on her that she was unable to shake. When a psychopathic killer felt cornered, unpredictable behavior could be triggered. To gain some measure of control, he might kill again, or flee, or strike out at law enforcement, escalating the danger to Sidney and her officers. She met Conner's gaze. "Tell me more about the two men who came to Satoshi's studio. What origami pieces did they order?"

"James ordered an octopus. Complicated design. She worked

on it for weeks. The other customer ordered a winged horse. Also complicated."

"Could anything have been stolen?"

She shrugged. "Like what?"

"Butterflies."

"Her butterflies were popular." She was lost in thought for a moment. "Come to think of it, her exhibit case was open, and the top shelf was empty. She had a few butterflies displayed there. I wondered about that, but I wasn't supposed to be in the house. I certainly never reported it."

"I need a copy of Satoshi's files. I won't reveal they came from you."

Conner nodded. "I'll get you a flash drive before you leave town."

"Did Satoshi write messages inside her creations?"

"Always. She inscribed sayings from the *I Ching*."

"What's I Ching?"

"An ancient Chinese book of wisdom, dating back to the fourth century. I don't really understand it, but for her, it was a form of spiritual practice."

"Do you have the book?"

"I'm sorry. I don't. She kept meticulous records of her work, with a photo of every origami piece and its hidden message, but all her belongings were shipped to relatives in Japan."

"Damn."

"The Miguel Angel Gallery here in town has photos of her collection. The owner worked closely with Satoshi. They were good friends. He sold her work internationally, and she trusted him. Maybe he documented the messages, too." She bit her bottom lip. "After she died, he wouldn't talk to me. He thought I was just a cop nosing around in Satoshi's business."

"Talking to Miguel is my second reason for coming to Sand Hill."

Conner raised her brow. "I hope you have better luck than I did."

Not wanting to disturb whatever evidence existed on the premises, they waited outside for a half-hour until a forensic expert from the County Sheriff department arrived. Middle-aged and balding, Tom Briggs wore field clothes and carried a forensic kit. After conferring with him for a few minutes, the man's extensive knowledge won Sidney's complete confidence.

"No point waiting around, Chief Becker," Briggs said. "This will take time. If any fingerprints are found, I'll be able to share that info by the end of the day. Most people have their prints in the database for one reason or another, so we might get a match. My other findings will be sent to the lab."

"You're going to find Officer Conner's prints in the house. For the record, she's not a suspect. I'm mostly interested in prints found on the bedroom window."

"Got it."

Sidney thanked him, gave him her card, and she and Conner headed back to the station. The clock on the dash read eleven forty-five. "The gallery doesn't open until one," Sidney said. "I'll go grab lunch. What's good to eat around here?"

Conner smiled with a touch of amusement. "You're in a fishing town, Chief. Eat fish. Try the Octopus Café on the pier. It's a nice day to sit outside."

"Sounds good."

Conner disappeared into the station. Sidney called David, thinking it had been a mistake to invite him. She would be bad company.

He answered on the first ring, cheerful as usual. "David Kane, at your service."

"Ready for lunch?"

"Been ready. I'm starving. The whole town smells like grilled fish."

The heaviness in her chest would not allow her to match his light tone. "Good. Meet me at the Octopus Café."

"On the pier. Good call. I have the town memorized. Especially the eateries."

"See you in a few."

CHAPTER THIRTY-THREE

SELENA STRUGGLED to contain her thoughts as she guided her students through the meditation at the end of her class. Random thoughts kept carrying her back to the public brawl with Randy, and Noah's horrific assault on Ann.

She tugged her attention back to her students. "Open your eyes. Smile. Go out into the world and have a beautiful day. Be kind to all you meet."

The students got to their feet, stretching and rolling up mats. After everyone left, Derek remained, as usual, browsing the gift shelves. Anxious to get back to Ann, Selena hoped he would make his selection quickly, and go.

"I heard you had a showdown with your ex and Allison Carter last night."

The accusatory male voice made her flinch and was loud enough to make Derek turn and take notice. Jeff from the *Daily Buzz* had entered the studio so quietly, he caught her off guard.

The reporter acknowledged Derek with a friendly nod and turned back to Selena. "Sorry I left early and missed the show. It got ugly, I hear. Wrangling with a pregnant woman is never a good idea."

Derek's one good brow arched in surprise.

Selena's mouth went dry. "It wasn't a show, Jeff, and I don't want to talk about it."

"It's public news."

She crossed her arms, hugging her elbows. "It's not news. It's gossip."

"The Garnerville Chief of Police got slugged at a public

function. How is that not news?"

"You're not planning on printing that trash, are you?" Anger edged into her tone.

"Yes, I am." He held out his phone and showed her a horrible moment frozen in time—Selena looming aggressively over a petite and very pregnant Allison. She looked like a monster.

"This comes courtesy of one of your spectators," Jeff said with a smirk. "He thought it was relevant news."

Selena glanced at Derek, who was watching with a confused expression on his face.

"You don't know what we're talking about, do you, Derek?" Jeff said.

"Not a clue."

"Selena's husband got little Allison Carter pregnant. Last night, all three had it out at the art gallery. Hair pulling. Name calling. I hear it was riveting. For the grand finale, Allison slugged Chief Becker in the mouth." Jeff smiled with smug satisfaction. "That about sum it up, Selena?"

"It wasn't like that," Selena said. "Don't you dare print those photos, Jeff."

"Or what? You gonna have your sister arrest me? I don't owe you any favors, Selena. You and the chief haven't exactly been helpful to this struggling journalist. You're withholding information about Sammy's murder. The public deserves to be informed."

"I don't know anything."

"Oh yes, you do. I know your sister talks to you."

"Hold on, Jeff," Derek interjected in a reasonable tone, approaching. "I agree with Selena. That story isn't the high standard of reporting we expect from the *Daily Buzz*. And there could be blowback. Chief Becker is highly respected here in town. Show her in a bad light, and folks could get angry. Maybe suspend advertising dollars. That what you want?"

Jeff's expression didn't waver. His eyes locked on Selena. "I would reconsider, in exchange for information about Noah Matsui. He was booked last night for assaulting Ann Howard, your business partner. They transferred him to Jackson this morning, got him lawyered up. He won't talk to me. Tell me about Noah, and

I'll stay mum about Ann."

She could feel the slow burn of anger rising from the pit of her stomach. Jeff's threat of using Ann's attack as fodder for morning entertainment made her even more determined not to help him.

"Is Noah a suspect in the homicide investigation?" Jeff asked. "Did they find evidence when they searched his house?"

Selena's mouth dropped open. "How did you know that?"

"I'm a reporter. I have my ways."

"How about giving Selena some slack, Jeff?" Derek said in an assertive tone, inching closer to Selena and standing next to her like a bodyguard. "This is a lot to throw at her after everything she went through last night."

Jeff studied Derek for a long moment and then he turned off his phone and stuffed it into his pocket. "Sure. I'll grab breakfast and give her some breathing room. But I'll be back." With a sharp snort of breath, he turned and left.

"He can be such a bastard." Tears pricked in Selena's eyes. She bit down on the inside of her cheek and several moments of silence passed while she struggled with herself.

"Take a minute," Derek said gently, guiding her to a row of chairs lining one wall.

Selena lowered her head and traced a design on the knee of her yoga pants, trying to pull herself together. It seemed all she did these days was cry. She was sick of herself. And sick of letting Randy control her life. Enough.

She pushed her back against the chair and said firmly, "Thank you for stepping in, Derek. You seem to have some sway with Jeff."

"Jeff's rough around the edges, but overall, he's a decent guy. He wants to break this homicide story, badly. Guess he thinks it'll put him on the map. He's not going about it diplomatically, I agree." He half smiled. "Reporters are a different breed of animal."

"He certainly is." Selena viewed the side of Derek's face that was free of scars, admiring his handsome profile. "You two are friends?"

"Yeah, we're friends. We don't get tattoos and drink beer together, but we do respect each other. He's been renting my guesthouse for the last four years. While I was rehabilitating in

Sand Hill, he took care of my property. Fed my fish. I'm grateful for that."

"You have pet fish?"

A glint of humor appeared in his eye. "Not exactly. I have several two-hundred-gallon marine aquariums."

"Holy Hannah. They must take up your whole house."

"They're in my lab."

"Lab?"

"A facility behind my house. Let me back up a little. I'm a marine biologist." He ran his hand through his thick, dark hair, spiking it on top. "Before I moved to Garnerville, I worked for a research company in San Diego. Spent a lot of my free time diving, collecting specimens, doing studies on my own projects."

She blinked, realizing she had never bothered to ask Derek about his life before Garnerville. "You study the ocean?"

"Understatement. Oceanography is my life's work."

"So, you're a scientist?

"Yeah, I admit it. I'm a science geek and environmentalist. Humans are having a catastrophic impact on our oceans. I'm working on finding solutions for living in harmony with the natural ecology. I also explore treatments for chronic diseases using the venom of sea creatures."

"Venom as medicine? That sounds counterintuitive."

He chuckled. "Actually, it's not. For decades, scientists have been studying the venom of spiders, snakes, and sea creatures for medical purposes."

"So, you're saying poisonous creatures that can kill us in an instant could also save our lives?"

"Exactly. Snake venom is already being used to treat ailments like heart attacks, Alzheimer's, and brain injuries." Derek's eyes brightened, and his voice became animated. "My special interest is sea creatures. Biotech companies are finding that toxins found in anemones and cone snails have the potential to treat autoimmune diseases. Research like mine could take off in the next decade and could provide natural therapies that don't have the serious side effects of prescription drugs."

She met his eyes with all sincerity. "That's commendable,

Derek, that you're working to save the planet and help people who are suffering. I had no idea you even worked. I thought…"

He gave her the ghost of a grin. "I just drive around in a nice car and do yoga?"

She managed a tired smile in return. "Pretty much. I'm sorry I never asked about your work. I didn't want to pry."

"You've been a little preoccupied."

"A little."

"If you're interested, come out to my lab. I'll show you what I do. Introduce you to my pet fish."

Selena's hands tensed in her lap. Another invitation. Even though Derek was being light-hearted, she sensed his keen attraction to her, and there was an underlying intensity to his character that both frightened and intrigued her. She looked off to one side to avoid his penetrating stare. Her instinct told her to keep him at arm's length, but on the other hand, Derek was an interesting guy—intelligent, and strong-willed. He'd lived through a terrible catastrophe and beaten the odds, and now he was in better shape than most of the men she knew.

"Just a friendly visit," he said in a soothing voice, a voice that conveyed confidence and control. He flashed that quick smile again, his teeth even and white. "I think you'll love my sea creatures and coral reefs. They're pretty cool."

With the emphasis on friendly visit, Selena had a change of heart. She felt her tension ease a notch. She could use a break. Ann's farm felt ominous these days. "I'll stop by this afternoon for a bit. Where do you live?"

"Not far from Ann's. I know you're staying there."

She frowned. "Seems everyone knows my business."

"It's a small town, Selena. People talk."

"And judge."

"If you want to avoid judgment, live under a rock. These days, simply breathing opens you up to criticism. What Jeff is threatening to reveal about you and Randy is probably already circulating through town. Tomorrow it will be old news. Then it'll fade away."

Feeling drained, Selena rubbed her tired eyes. Derek was right. She couldn't keep people from talking, and eventually her blip on the radar screen would disappear altogether. "Just so you know, Randy and I are getting divorced. I'm moving forward with my life."

"That's good to hear." Sadness touched his face, warming his brown eye. "I'm sorry for everything you've been through. If there's anything I can do to help…"

"Thanks. Just talking helped." She straightened her shoulders. "I better get going before Jeff comes back."

Derek fished out his wallet and handed her a card. "Here's my address. See you this afternoon."

CHAPTER THIRTY-FOUR

SITTING ON THE PIER in the warm sun with the sound of waves washing against the pilings, Sidney and David indulged in fresh seafood. He ate heartily; halibut tacos with cilantro slaw. She pushed grilled salmon and rice pilaf around on her plate and tried hard to focus on David's cheerful musings. Between bites, he spoke of his morning adventure exploring gift shops, getting a surprisingly good espresso at a food truck, walking barefoot on the beach. "It was good to feel sand between my toes again. Didn't realize how much I missed the California coast."

She pulled her thoughts away from murder and psychopaths and allowed his enthusiasm to gently lift her spirits.

Looking a little windblown, hair finger-combed, David picked up his backpack, which had been empty when he left her at the station, and now was bulging.

"How'd you manage to stuff it to the gills?" she asked.

"Easy. Gifts for the kids. Starfish, seashells." He showed her a piece of driftwood sanded smooth by the ocean, and a perfectly symmetrical sand dollar. He traced the petal-like pattern on its surface with his finger. "Look at the perfection of the design."

"Nature is amazing," she said, admiring his ability to find beauty in simple things.

He opened a side flap on his pack and pulled out a small white box tied with a red ribbon. "Something for you."

Sidney opened it, a smile teasing her lips. On a bed of cotton lay a black freshwater pearl on a gold chain. A rainbow of color shimmered beneath the pearl's surface, similar to rainbows reflecting on soap bubbles. "This is beautiful, David, but..."

"Uh uh. Don't say it."

"Say what?"

"That I'm trying to bribe a public official, and you can't accept it."

She laughed. Actually, she was thinking it was too soon for David to be giving her such nice gifts. Jewelry was personal, symbolizing something not yet communicated between them.

"Okay, I admit it. It is a bribe." David's easy smile reached his chestnut brown eyes, crinkling the edges. "A down payment for a kiss, redeemable at my choosing."

Remembering the sweetness of his kisses, she realized she was looking forward to the next one. "It's a deal." She lifted the chain to her neck and struggled with the clasp.

David brushed her hair aside and fastened the clasp, his warm fingers grazing her skin. She held her breath until he pulled away.

"Now that you've interrogated me about my morning, care to share yours?" he said.

"It wasn't pretty. Talking about it will ruin your appetite."

"Don't worry about me. I have an iron stomach. I pretty much connected the dots anyway."

"That so?" Her eyes challenged him.

David swallowed a bite of food, wiped his mouth with a napkin, and said, "You didn't come out here in the middle of a homicide investigation just to talk to a gallery owner about Satoshi's butterfly. You obviously saw a connection between her death and Sammy's."

She was impressed. Good analysis.

"I spoke to a few folks in town about Satoshi's work," he continued. "People opened up, filled me in. I found out she died in the lighthouse, and rumors are flying that it wasn't suicide."

She could see how people would open up to David. He was friendly, unguarded, and genuinely interested in what they had to say. "So people are talking."

"Yeah, they are. Back to your objective for coming here. I'm thinking you wanted to confirm that the same nut job murdered both women. My guess, Sammy's wrists were also cut, and you found the butterfly with her body. Am I right?"

David had a logical mind. He'd make a great detective. "I can say neither yay or nay. What else you got?"

"That's it. Your turn."

Sidney related a few details about Satoshi and Samantha that weren't privileged. He listened attentively. As she spoke, she realized getting her jumbled thoughts out in the open helped her view the evidence with more clarity.

David's expression turned somber. She wondered if sharing details of her work would push him away. He wouldn't be the first. Murder didn't make good dinner conversation. One man she dated asked her how she could consider having children with such a high-risk job. Another suggested that if she liked police work so much, she should marry a cop and get herself a safer career. Sidney felt a thud of apprehension when David mimicked her thoughts in a grave tone.

"This guy sounds extremely dangerous, Sidney. He scares me, and I'm not even the gender he chooses to murder."

"My team and I can handle him. And we can handle ourselves. I'm more worried about the next vulnerable woman who crosses his path and catches his attention."

His eyes narrowed. "You care deeply about others. To the extent of putting your own life at risk."

"Yes. I care."

"I admire that." He took her hand and held it, running his thumb over the back. His voice was low and unexpectedly tender. "I know you're good at your job. Please be extra careful."

They regarded each other in silence and much was unspoken. David wasn't pulling away. He was showing concern. It softened her heart. David's touch felt nurturing and sent tingles up her arm. A young waitress brought their coffee and Sidney reluctantly pulled her hand away.

"I have a confession," he said, stirring cream into his coffee. "I'm carrying. A .380 Beretta Pico in an ankle holster. A habit I've carried over from the military."

"When was this?"

"When I was in my twenties. Army. First Lieutenant."

So David had been an officer in the military, responsible for men and women under his command. That explained his ease around her uniform. "You always carry?"

He nodded. "It's an increasingly dangerous world."

"Yeah, it is. You ever use your weapon as a civilian?"

"Fortunately, no. But if I have to, I'm a decent shot. I practice weekly at the range."

"Commendable."

"We could practice together sometime."

She smiled. "Is that your idea of a dream date?"

He smiled back, and then got serious again. "I want to support you and know you're as safe as possible."

Again, his words hit the soft spot in her heart. "Sure. Let's practice together. I'm getting rusty."

They lingered at the table, sharing a slice of chocolate ganache cake, nursing coffee, watching seagulls squawk for scraps of fish from a handful of fishermen. Shoals of clouds swam through the sky and sharpening gusts of wind stirred whitecaps on the water. A good storm was brewing on the horizon.

Officer Conner appeared and walked along the pier until she reached Sidney's table, the wind pulling wisps of hair from the tight coil at the back of her neck. She nodded politely at David and handed Sidney a manila envelope. "Here's the info I promised."

Sidney thanked her and did a quick check of the contents—a flash drive and a few pages of printed emails. "Great work."

"Let me know if I can do anything else to help, Chief Becker."

"I'll be in touch."

Sidney watched Officer Conner walk back to her patrol car, reflecting on the officer's good instincts and bold initiative. If she ever got a budget to hire another officer, Conner would be at the top of her list.

~ ~

The art gallery stood out in sharp contrast to the rustic, sun-bleached shops surrounding it. The white stucco façade had clean, modern lines, as did the sign that read Miguel Angel Gallery. An elegantly pruned tree in a big red pot stood sentry on each side of the door. The stylish gallery could have been a transplant from a fashionable art district in any big city.

Sidney and David stepped from the sun baked beach town into a calm, cool, pristine environment. The interior of the gallery was a long, spacious room where every object had been positioned with tasteful discernment. The walls, the sparse furnishings, and all of the art frames were soft white, which made the colorful canvases immediate points of interest.

"Very Zen," David said.

A slender figure dressed in flowing black pants and a black silk shirt stepped from an office and approached them with athletic grace. "I'm Miguel. Can I help you?"

Miguel had expressive dark eyes, a full mouth, and a single lustrous ebony braid that fell nearly to his waist. If Officer Conner hadn't referred to Miguel as male, Sidney would have been hard pressed to determine his gender.

"I'm David Kane. I called yesterday regarding Satoshi Akira. This is Police Chief Becker."

Miguel's genial expression disappeared and his eyes darkened. "Thank you for looking into Satoshi's case. Dismissing her death as a suicide was a terrible injustice to her memory and to her family."

"You two were close?" Sidney said.

"As close as business colleagues could be. Satoshi was a quiet, private person, but we had great respect for one another." A touch of bitterness edged into his tone. "She would never have killed herself."

"You believe she was murdered?"

"I'm certain of it. She had everything to live for. She was excited about her new project, a series of origami sea creatures with large proportions, several feet in diameter. She had already created a magnificent sea horse and an octopus. Both sold before they were finished."

"Did Satoshi ever speak of anyone stalking or threatening her?"

"Never. She was so gentle I can't imagine anyone hurting her."

"I understand you collect her work."

He nodded. "I'm an avid fan. Would you like to see my collection?"

"Yes," she and David said simultaneously.

"Come with me."

David placed a hand on Sidney's back and they followed Miguel to the rear of the gallery. He pulled a set of keys from his pocket and unlocked an unmarked door. They entered another pristine room where dozens of framed origami pieces adorned the walls.

"They aren't for sale. I come in here just to enjoy them. Satoshi's spirit lives and breathes in this room."

David and Sidney drifted through the room, admiring the small masterpieces. She stopped abruptly at a display of colorful butterflies encased in glass boxes.

"You like her butterflies," Miguel said, joining them.

"Very much. I'm hoping you can help me identify a couple we found in Garnerville." Sidney fished her phone from her handbag and brought up the photos of the two butterflies found at the crime scenes, and the one found in Noah's bedroom.

"Why is this one so faded?" Miguel asked in a disapproving tone.

"It got rained on."

"Shame." Miguel rubbed his chin. "Hmmm. They're identical to the ones in my collection, except for the paper on the faded one. Satoshi was doing these small floral prints about three years back."

The timeline fit Mimi's death exactly.

"She switched to bigger motifs with lotus blossoms this year, like these newer ones." He pointed to the photos of the other two butterflies.

Next, Sidney swiped to the photo of Mimi's butterfly after it had been unfolded at the lab, with only the mysterious symbol legible. "Recognize this?"

His face twitched with irritation. "Someone took it apart? That's sacrilege. It can never be refolded."

"This is evidence in a murder case, Miguel. The crime lab was focused on catching a killer. They had no idea it was valuable art." Sidney paused for effect, and Miguel's expression sobered appropriately.

"Was someone else murdered like Satoshi?" he asked.

"That's under investigation. I was hoping you could tell me who bought these butterflies and what was written inside."

"I don't know her private business contacts, so I can't tell you who the buyers were."

"Does the name James Abbott ring a bell?"

"No. Sorry." Miguel pointed to the mysterious symbol on the unfolded butterfly. "But I can tell you about this hexagram. It's from the *I Ching*."

"The Chinese book of wisdom?" Sidney remembered Officer

Conner referring to the same book.

"Yes. For each of her pieces, Satoshi did an *I Ching* reading, and before folding it, she wrote the verse on the blank side of the paper."

"What is the *I Ching*?" David asked. "Fortune telling?"

Miguel smiled. "Not exactly. Seeking predictions about the future implies the future is already written, and we have no power to affect the outcome. The *I Ching* is more about getting guidance in the present, to help us make decisions that create the future we would choose. It's more a book of divination. Like consulting an oracle."

"An oracle?" David's eyes brightened with interest.

"Along with the Bible and the Koran, the *I Ching* is one of the most translated and studied books in the world. It teaches morals and ethics, and how to live in harmony with everything in the universe."

"Where can we find this book?" Sidney asked.

Miguel met Sidney's gaze. "My copy is in my office. I'd be happy to look up the hexagram in your photo."

"I'd appreciate that," Sidney said, a little chill racing along her spine. She wanted desperately to understand why three women were brutally murdered. Perhaps a clue to the killer's motivation lay within the book of wisdom.

Miguel's office was painted a soothing moss green and was minimally furnished with a glass-topped desk, a bookshelf, and three modern-style chairs. Two beautifully sculpted bonsai trees were strategically placed to please the eye. The gentle sound of falling water drew her attention to a stone and slate water feature in one corner.

Miguel pulled a thick book from the shelf, settled himself behind his desk, and motioned for them to sit. "There are sixty-four hexagrams, representing sixty-four virtues and situations," he explained. "Each hexagram is made up of six lines. The lines are stacked one upon the other, and each line is either solid or divided in the center. The order in which they are stacked gives each line a special meaning." He glanced at Sidney. "May I see that hexagram again, Chief Becker?"

Sidney pulled up the photo and passed over her phone.

He slipped on a pair of frameless reading glasses and continued speaking as he studied the small screen. "Hexagrams, like architecture, are built from the bottom up, one line at a time. This one has two broken lines on the bottom, two solid lines, one broken line, and one solid line on top." He bowed his head over the book and thumbed through the pages until he found what he was looking for. "This is hexagram fifty-six. The Traveler. It's a metaphor for a man traveling through a transition in his life." He read silently for a minute. "Let me read you the part I believe Satoshi would have inscribed in the butterfly. '*The superior man applies punishment with understanding and prudence and does not keep people imprisoned. Trifling with unimportant matters, the traveler draws upon himself calamity. Like a bird burning its own nest, the traveler first laughs with joy and then howls in sorrow.*'"

Sidney looked from Miguel to David. "Sounds like a warning."

"Ominous," David agreed.

"Did the buyer get a copy of the inscription?" she asked.

"Yes, of course."

"So, he would interpret its meaning in a very personal way," she spoke slowly, feeling her way through her thoughts.

"Naturally. It's the hexagram he attracted."

"How so?"

"When you consult the *I Ching*, you don't choose the outcome. The hexagram chooses you. It responds to the question you need to have answered at the time." He paused, peering at her over his glasses. "I can demonstrate by giving you a reading. Would you like to cast a hexagram?"

Deeply curious, Sidney nodded.

Miguel opened a carved wooden box on his desk and pulled out a purple drawstring bag and a folded cloth of gold brocade. He spread the cloth on the surface of the desk, opened the velvet bag, and three tarnished brass coins slipped out. Each coin was embossed with worn Chinese characters and had a square hole in the center. "These coins have passed through many hands over the years. Please hold them for a minute to make them your own."

Sidney picked up the coins and warmed them in her closed hand.

"Think about a question you want answered," Miguel instructed.

Wanting to lighten her tense mood, she responded with a chuckle. "Will I be getting a substantial bonus at the end of the year?"

Miguel cast her a sobering glance. "I see you don't take the *I Ching* seriously, Chief Becker. I suggest you suspend your disbelief. Otherwise the answer you get back will reflect your disbelief."

Sidney put up her hands. "Sorry."

"This reading can enable you to see the truth through surface appearances and restore your connection to a deeper meaning within your experience."

Feeling chastened, Sidney realized she could use a good dose of enlightenment.

"Close your eyes. Open yourself and listen. Find your question and hold it in your awareness."

With eyes closed, Sidney took a few moments to quiet her thoughts, to block out the art gallery and the two men seated in the room. As she shifted her consciousness from the exterior world to her interior self, her shoulders relaxed, and soon her single most pressing question surfaced and burned brightly in her mind. *Will I identity a ruthless killer in the near future, and make an arrest?*

Sidney imagined the question going out into the great unknown, to whatever existed beyond her mind's feeble ability to understand. She opened her eyes and murmured. "My question is out there."

"Very good." Miguel said, his face quiet and luminous. "Now toss the three coins."

Sidney willed the coins to give her guidance as she tossed them onto the cloth.

After studying the coins, Miguel drew an unbroken line on a blank sheet of paper. "Toss them five more times."

Each time Sidney dropped the coins on the golden cloth, Miguel added a broken, or an unbroken line, until the stack of six was completed. He thumbed through the book of *I Ching* until he found the desired page. "Here it is. You cast hexagram sixty-three. Aftermath. One who stands above things, brings them to completion."

Aftermath. Completion. Good omens, implying success.

Miguel handed Sidney the book and she read out loud:

"Water over Fire: the condition after completion. There is an obvious threat that the Water can extinguish the Fire, or that the flame can cause the water to evaporate. Water always moves downward, fire always burns upward. Beware of becoming overly confident or too complacent."

An interpretation of each line was written beneath the reading by a Chinese scholar. She retreated into silence as she continued to read. A warning murmured in a distant region of her mind.

"What is it?" David asked.

She cleared her throat. "Lines four and six hold warnings. Line four says:

"Appearances can be deceiving, and the situation shows signs of decay. While everything appears stable, remain on guard because it can deteriorate very rapidly."

"And line six?" David asked.

"The head gets wet. Danger. Getting the head wet is the idea

of patting yourself on the back or getting too emotional when clear thinking and action is required."

"You look troubled, Chief Becker," Miguel said, pushing his glasses to the top of his head. "Don't make quick assumptions about this reading. The *I Ching* is not a simple book to understand. When you use it to peer into your future, it's like unfolding and discovering yourself. This can take place over a period of hours, days, even weeks. If you listen closely, it will tell you when to accept your circumstances, when you need to change, when to fight, when to retreat, or when to step around the obstacle that stops you."

"I understand, Miguel. Is it possible to get a photocopy of my hexagram and the one on the butterfly?"

"Sure. My copier is in the other room. I'll be right back." He took the book and left.

Sidney lowered her head and massaged the space between her eyebrows with the pad of her middle finger. The weight of the burden she carried, her lack of sleep, and the grueling pace she had set for herself since Samantha's murder seemed to hit her all at once. She felt mentally and physically exhausted.

"Hey, don't look so dejected," David said. "The world didn't just come to an end. It's just a book. You could cast another hexagram and get something entirely different."

"I'm not superstitious, David, and I don't believe in omens, but this hexagram hits close to home. It warns of danger and my case deteriorating."

"The prophecy also says completion. That's a good thing." David placed a hand on hers in her lap. "This time tomorrow, your perp could be behind bars."

"I hope you're right."

"You'll be fine." David exuded strength and wellbeing and a kind of calmly contained energy. "Just be careful."

She forced a smile. "I'm always careful."

He smiled back, but Sidney read concern in his eyes.

Miguel walked in and handed her the photocopies.

"Just to be clear, Miguel, the *I Ching* does not forecast your fate, correct?" David asked. Sidney knew the question had been for her benefit.

"There's no such thing as fate," Miguel said with confidence. "We each decide the course of our own life journey. Free will is a universal law. The Oracle will never tell you what to do, much less bind you to a predetermined outcome beyond your control."

"Thank you, Miguel," David said.

"You've been a big help," Sidney said with warm appreciation.

He shook their hands. His was firm, smooth, soft. "Just catch this killer, Chief Becker."

Sidney and David stepped out of the gallery to discover the wind had picked up its intensity and brooding storm clouds were racing inland, threatening a torrential downpour. Her hair whipped across her face and she pulled her jacket tighter around her. They walked in silence the two blocks to the Yukon, still parked in the lot at the station.

"Give me your keys," David said. "I'm driving. You need a break."

Sidney gratefully fished her keys from her handbag. "Thank you."

Any attempt to beat the looming storm was futile. When David left the narrow streets of the beach community and turned onto the highway, Sidney's feeling of foreboding deepened. The gray asphalt ribbon snaked through towering walls of dense forest, and a ceiling of black clouds clung to the treetops, darkening the day. Less than halfway home, the sky opened up. Their headlights burrowed through sheets of hard driving rain that bounced off the hood in little explosions. The wipers slashed the windshield, and the wind pushed against the Yukon with muscular force. David tightly gripped the wheel as he concentrated on keeping the vehicle within the margins of the road. Sidney was relieved to be in the passenger seat.

CHAPTER THIRTY-FIVE

SELENA DROVE TWO MILES north up the highway from Ann's farm, then made a right turn down a long, well-paved driveway to the edge of the lake. Surrounded on three sides by forest, Derek's large home had clean lines and lots of windows facing the water. The front lawn rolled down to the glittering shoreline where a sailboat and motorboat bobbed at the dock. The Asian-style landscaping was simple yet beautiful, with Japanese maples, bamboo, and statuary placed as focal points, and a graceful wooden bridge arching over a pond stocked with koi. Rain came down softly and hung like glass beads on leaves and branches. The air smelled of wet earth. Selena parked on the dirt road that ran parallel to the shoreline. Using the more direct route on her return to Ann's would shave off half a mile.

Attached to the north side of the garage was a guesthouse, likely the place Jeff rented, barely visible through a copse of golden aspens. She hoped the bulldog reporter wasn't home. She didn't need another round with him today.

One of the garage doors was open. A red pickup truck faced outward, its left bumper and headlight smashed in, the kind of damage she had seen on vehicles that collided with large animals. Derek may have recently hit a buck or bull elk.

The walkway to the front door led through a rock garden with white gravel raked into intricate spirals. Holding a box of cookies in one hand, she pushed the hood of her parka back from her face, tucked her cell phone and keys into her pocket, and rang the doorbell.

Derek appeared within seconds, looking fit and handsome in faded jeans, a long-sleeved rugby shirt, and well-worn boat shoes. "You made it. Come in."

The Asian influence of the garden flowed into the interior of the house. She stepped into a spacious room with vaulted ceilings and a panoramic view of the lake. The sparse furnishings were simple and elegant, with plush carpets, polished hardwood floors, and Asian relics displayed on shelves on each side of the fireplace. No clutter. Not a speck of dust. Yet the room felt inviting and warm. "These are for you. Pecan chocolate chip cookies with quinoa and kale. Just baked."

He lifted the box to his nose, inhaled, and his good eye brightened. "Smells delicious." His gaze flickered over her. "You're wet."

"No biggie," she said, though she felt the chill dampness through to her skin.

"Let me take your jacket." Derek slipped her parka off her shoulders and draped it over the back of a chair. Rain dripped to the floor, but he didn't appear to be bothered in the least. She was happy to see his furnishings weren't just beautiful objects to admire. "Your garden is gorgeous. You must have an army of gardeners."

"That would actually be me. I do everything myself. I love working outside."

"Did you study Asian landscaping?"

He laughed. "Nothing that prescribed. I just do what feels right, though I did live in China and Japan while growing up. Guess Asian sensibility stayed with me."

"Was your dad in the military?"

"Government work. He was a diplomat."

"Ah, Foreign Service." No wonder Derek was so well

mannered, so polished. "Pretty high up there in the food chain."

"Wielding power over others."

"Something tells me you're not complimenting politicians."

"You guessed right. I grew up around them. When you live in a bubble of wealth and privilege, and everyone kowtows to you, it's hard not to have an inflated sense of your own importance. Self-interests tend to overshadow public service."

"There are some good ones."

"Agreed. And they get plenty of my campaign dollars."

The more she learned about Derek, the more mysterious he seemed. Something about him made her uneasy, even a little afraid. His life experience was vast. In contrast, hers seemed meager and insufficient. Since she was sixteen, Randy had been her one true love, a country hick who showed little interest in the world beyond ranching and rodeo. She had never slept with another man, and her inexperience gave her no tools to deal with a man as sophisticated as Derek. Why he was attracted to her, she didn't understand.

They stood in awkward silence for a moment.

"How's Ann doing, by the way?" he asked.

"Better. Her son Matt is there, and my sister stationed an officer at her house, just to calm everyone's nerves. Ann was moody this morning, but we talked her into playing cards. After she won a few games of hearts, her mood lightened, and she even helped me bake cookies."

"Acting out normal behavior can be healing."

"Yep. Good therapy."

"Can I get you something to drink? Wine? Iced tea?"

"No, thanks. I can't stay long." Setting a time limit felt like a necessary precaution. "I need to get back to work."

"Of course." He stared directly into her eyes, and she could tell he found it unsettling that she was uncomfortable. "Well, you came to see the aquariums. Let's go out back to my lab."

As he guided her down a hallway, she glanced into the beautiful kitchen and dining room, and several bedrooms, everything straight out of *Architectural Digest*. At the end of the hallway, they came to a substantial stainless-steel door. He punched numbers into the code box, opened the door, and they stepped into a large, windowless room brightly lit by florescent lights. The door clanged shut behind them.

CHAPTER THIRTY-SIX

THE RAIN HAD TAPERED to a drizzle by the time Sidney and David got back to Garnerville. Sidney had sat quietly the whole trip, head pressed against the backrest, eyes closed, the soft patter of rain calming her nerves. She felt the car slow and turn into a gravel driveway, and ease to a stop.

"Hey, Sleeping Beauty," David said softly. "Home sweet home."

David had parked in her driveway next to his Lexus SUV where he'd parked it that morning. They left the Yukon and she felt light rain on her face. "I have to change into my uniform and get to the office," she said hurriedly, her mind suddenly buzzing with thoughts of work. "My gut tells me we're on the verge of a breakthrough in this case."

"Hey, slow down. Don't go charging off." David put his foot up on the bumper, unstrapped his ankle holster, and handed it to her. "Wear this. I'll feel better knowing you have a backup. Do that for me?"

"Yes. I promise."

David's face glistened with rain. His beautiful brown eyes held her gaze and his mouth tipped into a sensuous smile. "Time to redeem my kiss."

He pulled her into his arms, their bodies melding together, and he kissed her slowly and deliberately. Blissful. She was a little lightheaded when he released her.

"Call me when you have some free time," he murmured. "I want to finish that kiss." He pecked the tip of her nose, squeezed her hands, and headed to his car.

Sidney wanted to call him back, invite him into the house to finish what they'd started. Instead, she ran up the porch stairs and entered the laundry room through the back door. The four cats rushed to meet her before the door shut, mewing loudly, rubbing against her legs. Sidney entered the kitchen with the cats clinging to her like Velcro. Odd behavior. Were they missing Selena? Upset about being left alone so much?

No, something else was troubling them. Something felt wrong, yet the house looked as it normally did, neat and clean, nothing out of place. Remembering the laundry room window, unlocked yesterday, she rechecked it. Still locked. She started second guessing herself. Was she getting paranoid? Imagining things?

Mewing, still clingy, the cats bounded after her as she went up to her room. She changed into her uniform, added her duty belt and badge, and checked her Beretta 9mm semiautomatic, making sure the magazine contained a full load before holstering the weapon. She lifted her pant leg and strapped on David's ankle holster holding the .380 Beretta Pico.

Before she left the house, she made a detour down the hall to Selena's room, her senses on high alert, listening intently for any unusual sound. The room looked tidy, bed smooth. Still, her anxiety increased, though she couldn't pinpoint the origin of the sensation.

Her phone pinged, a new text, reminding her that she had not checked in with the station since morning. She called in to get her messages and slowly walked around Selena's room, half-listening as the recordings played on speaker.

Nearing the bookcase, on the wall opposite the bed, she got signal interference. As she walked away, the messages came in clearly again.

A stab of something deep in her belly made her stop, mute her phone, and return to the bookcase. Hoping her suspicion was wrong, Sidney waved her phone up and down in front of the shelves. A strange buzz emanated from an AC adaptor in the electrical outlet.

Sidney's adrenalin spiked; her skin tingled all over. Years of watching forensic teams work a room told her exactly what it was. The small circle on the phony adapter was a tiny camera lens. A couple of days ago, when she'd sensed someone in the house, she'd been right.

The lens had a view of the entire room. Some pervert was spying on Selena, maybe watching Sidney at that moment. She turned away and adjusted the blinds as if she hadn't seen the camera. She'd have to get a forensics tech to check it out, but first she needed to find her sister.

Sidney left the room and called Selena's cell in the hallway. She counted seven rings before voicemail picked up, each second seeming like ten.

"You've reached Selena McBride. Please leave a message, and I'll return your call promptly."

"Selena, call me. You're in danger," she practically shouted. She clicked off and punched out a quick text: "Selena, call me as soon as you get this!" Then she called Granger.

"Hey, Chief."

"Where's Selena?"

"She went out."

"Where?"

"She said she was running a quick errand. Hold on, maybe Ann knows."

Sidney heard voices in the background, and Granger came back on. "She's dropping off cookies to a friend down the road."

"What friend?"

She heard mumbled voices again.

"Derek Brent. Why does that name sound familiar?" Granger paused a beat. "Christ. He's on our suspect list. He was Mimi Matsui's keyboardist."

"I thought he was in a wheel chair, living out of town," Sidney said, voice rising, fighting a touch of panic.

"So did I. That's why he missed our dragnet. Hold on." She heard him direct another question at Ann.

Long mumbled answer.

"Ann says he's fully recovered, and he's in Selena's yoga class. He moved back to town two months ago and lives just down the road from here." She heard him cuss under his breath. "I remember Miko saying Derek and Mimi had some kind of beef a couple weeks before she died."

"If he's doing yoga, he's probably strong enough to drag a woman through the woods. Let's get over there."

"I'm leaving right now."

Sidney ran out of the house, screeched out of the driveway, and headed north on the highway. The hiss of the Yukon's tires on the wet asphalt played in the background while images from the past few days flashed through her mind: the impression of a body on her sister's bed, the unlocked window, the framed photo of Selena and Randy smashed on the kitchen floor—and now the phony AC adapter. All this painted a sinister picture of a stranger stealing into the house who was obsessed with her sister. She recalled Granger's tale of a dark figure lurking in the woods behind Ann's house. Sidney now theorized that it wasn't Ann he was watching, but Selena. The stranger might be her serial killer, stalking her sister as his next victim. Her hands tightened on the steering wheel.

Her phone buzzed and she saw it was the forensic tech working in Sand Hill on Satoshi's house. She pushed the button on her dashboard. "Chief Becker."

"Tom Briggs, here."

"Whatcha got, Tom?"

"I just finished up at Satoshi's place. Lifted prints from about a dozen individuals. Ruling out the moving men, whose prints are on file, two men should be of interest to you—James Abbott and Derek Brent."

Sidney gasped. "Tell me about Derek."

"You know him?"

"I'm headed to his house right now. What do you have?"

"His prints are in the kitchen, studio, and bathroom. My guess, he'd been a frequent visitor. And, he owns homes in both Sand Hill and Garnerville."

Sidney's thoughts raced. "No prints on the bedroom window?"

"Didn't say that. We got a nice palm print on the glass. Clear as day. Can't ID it, though. No palm prints in the system. But someone recently ejaculated on the floor of the bedroom where the bed used to be."

Sidney felt a spike of adrenalin. The killer had revisited Satoshi's bedroom, laid on the floor, relived his crime to get his rocks off, and left forensics a gift of DNA, which would seal his conviction.

"Early Christmas present, Chief. You've got the bastard. I'll rush this sample through the lab. By tomorrow, we'll know his identity. See if we get a match to Abbott or Brent."

"Good job, Tom." Her heightened expectation of closing in on her suspect was layered with a sense of dread. Sidney clicked off and tried Selena's number again. No answer.

"Stay cool," Sidney told herself aloud in the car. She called Judge Seymore Whitman, summed up the evidence and requested a search warrant for Derek Brent's property. Then she got on the radio to Darnell, told him to swing by the judge's house, pick up the warrant, and get to Brent's house with Amanda.

Switching on the pulsing lights, Sidney stepped on the gas and took the curves on the slick highway as fast as she dared.

CHAPTER THIRTY-SEVEN

HALF A DOZEN large marine aquariums burbled in Derek's lab, and the work counters were covered with scientific equipment. A mini reef of vibrant coral grew inside each tank, and a colorful variety of cone-shaped shells were half buried in white sand.

"You were right, Derek. These are spectacular," Selena said, awestruck. "Where are these mysterious sea snails you're so excited about?"

"You're looking at them." He pointed to the sand at the base of a tank. "Inside those beautiful shells are some of the most venomous creatures on Earth."

"Really? Snails?"

"You bet. The sting of a small snail is no worse than a bee sting, but a sting from the larger species, nicknamed the 'cigarette snail,' is lethal."

"Why are they called cigarette snails?"

"If stung by one of these babies, you're dead in the time it takes to smoke a cigarette. About three minutes."

"Aren't they dangerous to work with?"

"Sure, if you don't know what you're doing. But I know how to milk their venom and collect samples safely. Then comes the fun part. Research. Breaking down the molecular structure of the toxins."

Didn't sound like fun to Selena. "Can you make one come out of its shell?"

"They're nocturnal and shy. But I'll make one of the bigger ones appear for you." Derek fished around with a net in a tank of darting fish until he captured a squirming orange and white striped fish about five inches long. "This is my food tank. Live meals for the snails." He slipped the fish into a tank that appeared to hold no life other than coral. "The animal's vibrations through the water will alert the snail. Watch and learn."

As the fish fluttered, the sand at the bottom of the tank started shifting. The tapered end of a cone shell emerged with a protruding rubbery hose-like mouth. The snail froze. The fish drew near. With lightning speed, a thin line shot out from the snail's mouth and impaled the fish. The fish instantly became immobile and the snail reeled it in. To Selena's astonishment the tiny mouth expanded like a balloon and swallowed the entire fish, two times its size. Bloated, like a snake after a meal, the snail buried itself back in the sand and disappeared. The hair stood on Selena arms. It was grotesque.

"Fascinating, isn't it?" Derek's eyes were bright with enthusiasm, like a kid sharing a new Christmas toy. "They're one of the slowest creatures on Earth, yet they've evolved to skillfully hunt far speedier animals. There's a harpoon on the end of the lasso that's no bigger than an eyelash. The venom stuns the fish, then the snail swallows it and digests it whole."

"An efficient killing machine. The snail doesn't even have to move. Can a human survive a sting?"

"Depends on how much toxin gets absorbed. You could survive a light dose, but you'd be paralyzed for weeks, even months. I've seen patients in hospitals in Viet Nam who were fully conscious but couldn't twitch a muscle. Not even an eyelid."

Selena's body went rigid. She recalled Sidney saying that before Samantha Ferguson was murdered she had been injected with a neurotoxin that had the same effect. The coincidence frightened her.

Derek went on talking. "These patients were prisoners in their own bodies, fed by IV tubes, yet their minds were alert and active."

"That's horrifying." Selena forced her voice to remain calm, her face expressionless, though her hands had gotten clammy.

"It's scary stuff, but that power can also be used for good. The venom has the potential of being a pain reliever a thousand times stronger than morphine." He nodded at a stainless steel refrigerator door. "I have multiple samples in there from different species."

"It's like storing nuclear waste."

He chuckled. "Nothing that dangerous. And my lab is safe and secure."

Selena shifted from one foot to the other. "Thank you for showing me your snails. Your work is fascinating."

His gaze met hers, and she realized he was standing uncomfortably close, emanating his strange intensity. She suddenly felt smothered by the locked room and his presence and the emotional connection he wanted from her that she was unable to give. She looked away, breaking eye contact.

A long moment passed, then he said in a dull tone, "Ah, I know you need to get going." He led the way back to the thick metal door and plugged in a code. She felt relieved when she stepped back into the house and heard the loud clink of the door locking behind them.

Her fear abated as she followed Derek down the hallway, closer to the great room and the front door where she could escape. Wary, she peered into open doorways; a bedroom, a home gym— expecting what? A dungeon with chains? She paused in the doorway of a dimly lit room. "What do you do in here? Is that a shrine?"

He stopped beside her. "Nothing that pretentious. Just a quiet room where I meditate. Do a little yoga."

The serene peacefulness drew her inside. The walls were bare except for a gold and red silk tapestry of a dragon in the sky.

"That's beautiful. Chinese?"

"Yes. I love what dragons personify. Strength, courage, prosperity."

"And yin and yang. The two forces in nature."

"True," he said with appreciation. "Male and female, darkness and light, negative and positive. One can't exist without the other. According to Chinese theory, wise people detect these forces in all things—the seasons, even their food—and they regulate their lives accordingly."

"Do these forces guide your life?"

He thought for a moment. "Yes. I like to be plugged into what's happening around me. Even to what's invisible."

Vibrations. Energy. She understood. She too listened to the invisible communication coming from all things, especially those found in nature. But those forces were open to interpretation—not always user friendly. Beneath the dragon was a black lacquered table that held a single candle, an incense burner, a framed photo, and a thick book that looked decades old. "What's this book?"

"The *I Ching*."

"Oh, I've heard of it. It tells your fortune."

"Something like that."

She nodded at the photo, a portrait of a beautiful Japanese woman with lustrous ebony hair, a sensuous mouth, and dark, luminous eyes. "Is that your guru?"

"Never thought of her that way, but yes, in a sense, she was my guru. We were very close."

"*Were* close?"

His expression darkened with grief, and the hint of stress tightened the corners of his mouth. "Satoshi died two months ago."

"I'm so sorry." Selena regretted intruding into his sacred room, and a deeply personal part of his life. A second female friend of his had died within a period of three years—first his singing partner, now this woman. "Was it sudden?"

His face darkened with a look that frightened her. "They say she killed herself."

"But you don't believe that."

"No."

Murder loomed large in her imagination, and a chill prickled her scalp.

It seemed a full minute before he spoke again. "Satoshi was a kind, gentle person. A gifted artist. I met her while I was recovering in Sand Hill. We spent a fair amount of time together." He turned away, revealing the scarred side of his face, a rigid mask, as though he was hiding behind it. "She helped me find my way back from a very dark place, and unbearable pain."

"It must have been terrible."

"You have no idea." He swallowed. "I'm indebted to her... but now she's gone."

Clearly, he revered Satoshi. She couldn't help but wonder if the beautiful woman had been his lover. "What kind of artist was she?"

"An origami master. Each of her creations was a feat of remarkable engineering. All made from scratch, even the paper. She designed the more complicated ones on a CAD system before undertaking the physical task of folding them. She made birds, dragons, horses. Anything you can imagine."

"Butterflies?" Selena asked with growing pressure in her chest.

"Stunning butterflies."

Selena felt a cold chill as she connected origami butterflies to Samantha Ferguson's murder. Yet another dead woman Derek knew.

His voice filtered into her thoughts. "I have some of Satoshi's pieces. Would you like to see them?"

She felt a strong need to separate herself from his company, to flee the house, but a macabre curiosity enticed her to stay. She needed to secure information that might help her sister's investigation. "I'd love to."

He led her through the living room, the patter of their footsteps the only noise in the house until they entered his office, where the musical sound of running water came from a stone fountain with a bamboo spout. At the same time her eyes fell upon two framed origami pieces on the wall above his desk—a winged horse and a dragon, intricately folded, graceful and fluid in design.

She noticed two colorful butterflies in glass boxes on his desk. Selena picked one up and examined it closely. It appeared to be a match to the one recovered from Samantha's crime scene by the raven. She broke out in goose flesh. Last week when Derek picked up his sister after their therapy session, he momentarily unveiled a surge of anger when Selena mentioned Samantha.

His voice broke into her thoughts. "You okay?"

She realized her mouth had turned down. "I was just thinking how sad it is that Satoshi died."

His brown eye narrowed. The other, fixed in its seam of scarred skin, looked flat and lifeless. "Why do I get the feeling you've seen her butterflies before?"

Selena heard her phone buzz in her jacket pocket in the living room, and she was grateful for the interruption, knowing she would have had to lie to Derek, and she wasn't good at deception. "I better get that. It could be Ann."

She hurried from the room, fished her phone from her pocket, and answered on the fourth ring. Sidney's voice spoke before she even said hello. "Where are you? I've left several messages."

"I'm at Derek's."

"Get out of there. Now. I'm on my way to arrest him."

"Just leaving." Selena hung up, rattled by Sidney's urgent tone. She brought up her text messages and read: *You are in danger. Keep your gun with you.* Her gun was in her purse on the front seat of her car. She felt the heat of Derek's body and realized he was standing right next to her. A shock of adrenalin shot up her arms and made her fingers tingle. She blackened her screen. "Sorry, I have to go."

Derek was gazing at her with a hard look to his eye. His breathing changed almost imperceptibly. "There's something you aren't telling me."

She brushed past him, but his hand lashed out, and his fingers wrapped around her arm. She could feel the pressure of his fingertips. Any attraction she might have felt toward Derek was erased by his aggressive touch. It wasn't rough, but he was trying to restrain her, to make her stay against her will.

She yanked her arm away and hurried across the room, opened the door, and sprinted from the house. She didn't stop or look back until she reached her car, expecting to see him right behind her. Through the drizzle of rain, he was walking slowly toward her across the long rolling lawn and was about twenty feet away.

She got in the car and locked the door before she realized her keys weren't in her pocket. They must have dropped in his living room when she pulled out her phone. Selena grabbed her gun from her purse and held it loosely on her lap, finger light on the trigger. Through the rain on the windshield, Derek looked distorted, like a being from another world. He held out his hand and dangled her keys, then slowly laid them on the hood of her car, gave her a last fleeting look, dark and moody, and turned back toward his house.

Selena waited until he was a good distance away before she snatched her keys, started the engine and the wipers, and fumbled with her phone to call Sidney.

"I'm almost there," Sidney clipped.

"Derek's the killer," Selena stammered, her words rushing together. "He has a neurotoxin in his lab behind the house that comes from snails, and he has a picture of a dead woman who was killed in Sand Hill, and he has two of her origami butterflies, and he knew Samantha and Mimi."

"Slow down, Selena. Take a breath. What do you mean a neurotoxin from snails?"

"He's a marine biologist. He has sea snails in tanks in his lab that are some of the most venomous creatures on earth. He said their toxin could paralyze people while leaving them completely alert. Sound familiar?"

Sidney sucked in a breath. "Too familiar. What about the butterflies?"

"They're in his office in little glass boxes, and they look exactly like the one Arthur found."

As Selena spoke, Granger's truck pulled into the driveway in front of the house and parked. Selena felt an enormous rush of relief. A normal person had arrived. Someone tough. A protector. "Granger's here, thank God."

"Let us take care of this, Selena. Go back to Ann's and stay put. Matt's with her now, but he has to leave. DO NOT go home."

"I'll wait at Ann's until I hear from you. Sid, please be careful."

"Careful is my middle name."

Selena clicked off, admiring Sidney's fearlessness. Her sister was so strong, so capable. She would lock up Derek for good, and the women of Garnerville would be safe again.

Eager to get out of there, Selena waved a trembling hand at Granger, turned the car around, and started driving south, following the dirt road that ran parallel to the lake.

CHAPTER THIRTY-EIGHT

THE JEEP BOUNCED and shuddered down the lane, hitting ruts and puddles. Selena forced herself to take her mind off Derek, to pay attention to the road, to drive around the deepest pits. The lake appeared and disappeared through the trees, the rough water the color of pewter, the low hanging clouds indistinguishable from the lake's surface. The colors and shadows of the woods appeared deeper and more intense than usual.

When the road began a gradual descent, she knew she was halfway to Miko's farm. Ann's farm lay just beyond that, with a short stretch of dense forest in between.

She braked into a sharp turn, but the pedal gave no resistance. Her foot pushed all the way to the floor. The Jeep quickly picked up speed. Panicked, she pumped the brake furiously.

An enormous Douglas fir loomed ahead. She swerved sharply to the left but her right bumper clipped the trunk, then the Jeep dove into a tangle of bushes and came to a startling halt with an earsplitting crack against the mottled trunk of an aspen.

Selena's seat belt thrust her back against the seat. The air bag deployed with an explosive charge that struck her face like a punch. White powder and hot gas fumes filled the air, the limp bag crumpled on her lap. Her face stung, and a sharp pain throbbed in her shoulder from the seat belt. She sat stunned.

Before she could think straight, she caught movement in the rearview mirror. Through the branches she saw a white car come to a halt on the road and then a man in dark clothing was climbing through the bushes moving swiftly toward her. Her door was yanked open. The man thrust out his hand, and she grabbed it. With his other hand at her back, he carefully pulled her from the driver's seat. Upright, she stood there a few moments waiting for the ground to quit moving. She blinked at the rain and turned to see who had come to her aid.

CHAPTER THIRTY-NINE

GRANGER WAS WAITING in Derek's driveway when Sidney pulled up in the Yukon. After a quick greeting, they strode to the front door and rang the bell. Sidney kept her expression neutral, though the man who opened the door startled her. She wasn't expecting half of his face to be disfigured, while the other half was movie star handsome. And she wasn't expecting a man recovering from a brutal accident to exude vitality. He looked like he hit the gym every day. "Derek Brent?"

One eye, flat and blue in color, didn't move. The other eye, sable-brown, flicked over their uniforms with a look of surprise. Then his gaze met hers, and a moment passed as they sized each other up.

"Yeah, I'm Derek."

"I'm Chief Becker. This is Officer Wyatt. We'd like to ask you a few questions about Samantha Ferguson."

He frowned. "I'd be happy to help with your investigation, Chief Becker, but I know absolutely nothing about her death."

"Perhaps you'd humor us. May we come in?"

His frown deepened, but he stepped aside to let them enter. They stood in the foyer of a beautiful home, furnished simply and elegantly, furniture in neutral tones, accented with plush rugs and Asian antiques. Outside the large windows, the rain came down softly and gray mist rose from the water, blending with low hanging clouds. Derek gestured toward the living room, and they took seats facing each other, he on an easy chair, she and Granger on the smooth gray couch.

"May I record this?"

He shrugged and said with reluctance, "If you must."

"Where were you Friday of last week?"

He thought for a moment. "In Sand Hill. Went to pick up some work-related papers I left at my beach house."

"Where were you the night of Samantha's murder?"

The question caught him by surprise. "That's the kind of question you'd ask a suspect. Are you suggesting I'm a suspect?"

"Routine questions. We're making a round of the neighbors on this side of the lake."

"I drove to Jackson and back. Went to a movie."

"What time did you return?"

He hesitated. "Around eleven. I read for a while and went to bed."

"Can anyone verify you were home between eleven and midnight?"

A muscle twitched slightly along his jaw. "No."

Sidney felt a pulse of excitement. This was more than she hoped for. Derek's visit to Sand Hill coincided with the time someone entered Satoshi's house and left boot prints, and he was in the vicinity of Samantha's murder around the time of her death. "Tell me about your relationship with Satoshi Akira."

The question, coming out of left field, again caught him by surprise. "How do you know about Satoshi?"

"Just a rumor we're following up on."

"Did this rumor happen to come from your sister, who was just here? She acted strangely after I mentioned Satoshi."

"Please answer the question."

After a long moment, he answered. "We met when I was recovering from a car accident in a rehab facility in Sand Hill. I was in terrible shape. Satoshi came to the home every Tuesday and

Friday, and made the rounds, offering spiritual solace to the patients. She always stayed in my room for a few minutes. She started visiting longer. By the time I was able to leave, live on my own, we had become good friends."

"Good friends as in an intimate relationship?"

He was silent, his face almost expressionless except for his brown eye, which watched her with unnerving intensity. "How is that any business of yours?"

Sidney did not balk at his disdain, nor did she move to arrest him, which might make him refuse to talk. Right now she needed his cooperation. She forced herself to be polite. "It's my business, Derek, because there is evidence linking Satoshi to the murder of Samantha and Mimi. You knew all three women."

His eyebrow arched. "Satoshi linked to the murders here in Garnerville? That's ridiculous." His face tightened as he reflected for a moment. "You think Sammy and Mimi were murdered by the same man?"

"That's a possibility."

"Are you saying the same man killed Satoshi?"

Before she could answer, the doorbell sounded, the chime seeming to echo in the silence of the room.

"Get that, Granger," Sidney said. "Should be Darnell with the search warrant."

Granger crossed the floor to the front door, then he led Darnell and Amanda back into the room. Amanda gripped the handle of her forensic kit. Darnell handed the warrant to Sidney. She unfolded and scanned the document.

Derek had risen to his feet, a look of alarm on his face. "What the hell is going on? You have no right to search my home."

"This warrant says we do." Sidney passed it to him, which he also scanned. His eye widened. "You think I played a part in these murders? You've made a grave mistake, Chief Becker. Whatever flimsy excuse you have for barging in here won't hold up for a second in court."

"If you have nothing to hide, you don't have to worry. Let us do our job." She instructed the two male officers to go in opposite directions and gestured to Amanda to accompany her. Sidney walked toward an open doorway. "This your office?" Clearly, it was. Computer equipment covered the desk, shelves were full of books, two stunning origami sculptures hung on the walls, and two origami butterflies in glass boxes sat on the desk. Had she found The Collector? "Photograph and bag these," she said to Amanda, pointing to the butterflies.

Derek hovered behind her. "You can't take those. They're valuable works of art."

"We'll treat them carefully. Have a seat in the living room, Derek. Amanda, why don't you wait in there with him."

CHAPTER FORTY

THE MAN WORE a black knitted ski mask. In addition, he had a hoodie pulled over his head, shadowing his face.

Still, Selena knew instantly who he was. Those eyes…

In a heartbeat, it all made sense, and the startling realization kicked in that she was facing the psycho who killed three women. He must have tampered with her brakes, planned this accident so he could meet her alone in the woods.

Her gun was in the car.

She felt the hot hum of adrenaline in her veins, telling her to take flight. It took every ounce of discipline she had to not react, not show a hint of emotion, but instead let her body go completely limp, fall toward him, as though in a faint.

He acted on impulse, his arms encircling her, breaking her fall, holding her dead weight against his strong body. He smelled of forest and earth from barreling through the brush.

Before he could free his hands, Selena jerked up her knee and slammed him in the groin.

With a strangled cry, the man stumbled backwards, grabbing his crotch, and then he doubled over, groaning in agony.

Selena exploded into movement, tearing through the dense brush, twigs scratching her face and hands. She hit the road at a sprint, her senses in overdrive, feet stumbling over ruts and puddles, rain spattering her face. She didn't have much time. A minute head start at the most.

A few hundred feet down the muddy road, she hit a patch of slick rocks and her foot slid out from under her. The ground came up fast and slammed into her skull. She lay dazed, daylight fading in and out.

Drawing in a whistling breath, she sat up slowly, head pounding, vision blurred. Slipping and sliding like a drunkard, she struggled to her feet, the ground shifting, the forest spinning. Was she blacking out? Please, no! Fear held her immobile, then her father's words blasted through her mind. *Fear will keep you alive. Lack of fear will kill you.*

Gathering strength from his words, Selena stepped into the spinning vortex, each foot a heavy weight hitting the earth like an anvil, moving her forward in slow motion.

The steady drip of rain seemed like a roar, covering everything. Was the psycho following her? She turned. The road was clear. Was he moving through the woods, camouflaged by trees? Would he attack her any second and drag her back into his domain? She wiped a trembling hand across her forehead, lurched forward.

The distant sound of a car engine was unmistakable. Selena staggered off the road, stumbled, fell, picked herself up, fell again, and rolled into an irrigation ditch. She held her breath, lying prone in the shallow water. Tires crackled on the dirt road above her, an engine cut out, a car door shut. She saw the beam of a flashlight bouncing through the dark forest, illuminating one area at a time. Then the gray of day faded to black.

CHAPTER FORTY-ONE

SIDNEY SPENT the next thirty minutes searching through Derek's office looking for records identifying him as The Collector, but found nothing. She proceeded to search two bedrooms, looking for women's clothing, jewelry, or Sammy's purse, but found nothing. She hit pay dirt in a room that appeared to be a shrine to Satoshi, with both a photo of the dead women and a book of the *I Ching* on a table. Sidney theorized the killer took the book of wisdom seriously, construing hidden meaning in the verse that instructed him to kill. The room suggested Derek had an unhealthy obsession with the murdered artist.

Sidney returned to the living room where Amanda was keeping a vigilant eye on Derek. He sat rigidly on the couch, coiled tension, ready to pounce.

"Now I want to see your lab," Sidney announced.

"You can't go in there."

Her tone sharpened. "Open that steel door for us, Derek. Now."

"You have no right." His tone matched hers. "My research is classified."

"Let's get something straight between us. We can go anywhere on your property we choose."

His gaze bored into her. "What do you want from my lab?"

"A sample of the neurotoxin you mentioned to Selena. The one that paralyzes people."

"Why the hell do you want that?" His eye lit up with sudden understanding. "The murdered women were injected with a neurotoxin?"

"I'm asking the questions, Derek."

He swallowed and looked genuinely distressed. "Holy hell." He nervously stroked his chin and paced, paused, met her direct stare. "It didn't come from here. None of my toxins have ever left my lab. It's safely locked. They're too dangerous for a novice to handle."

"Give me specifically what I want and we won't have to tear your lab apart."

With a scowl, he led the way. Sidney caught Amanda's eye, nodded for her to follow.

Derek punched numbers into a code box and they entered the brightly lit, windowless room. It looked as well equipped as any lab Sidney had ever seen, and it took her a moment to pull her attention away from the stunning coral reefs and shells in the burbling tanks.

Amanda approached the stainless-steel refrigerator door and pulled it open. Icy mist steamed into the room, revealing neatly stored racks of sample tubes.

"Don't touch anything," Derek said sternly. "Some of those toxins can kill you. They're priceless. It's taken me years to collect that much venom."

"Give me the sample I want," Sidney said. "Our tech will use it judiciously. If it doesn't match what we're seeking, it'll be returned."

"I can't believe Selena got you over here on some trumped-up murder theory," he said, his tone more disappointed than angry.

"Point to the correct sample, Derek. Don't touch anything." Sidney unsnapped her holster and put her hand on the hilt of her firearm. She didn't need him trying to destroy evidence or attacking them with some killer venom.

His gaze darted from her face to her hand and back to her face. He scowled. "It's the third shelf up from the bottom. The tube marked with five Xs. That signifies how potent it is." He gestured to small coolers stacked on a shelf. "Please store it in one of those refrigerated boxes with a couple of ice packs."

After Amanda followed his instructions to a tee, he turned back to Sidney. "You got what you want, now gather up your renegade posse and get off my property."

"I'm leaving all right, but you're coming with me. Derek Brent, I'm placing you under arrest for the murders of Mimi Matsui, Samantha Ferguson, and Satoshi Akira."

His expression of vexation turned to one of astonishment. "You're out of your fucking mind. I'm a scientist, not a killer."

"You're a man who's going to spend a long time in prison."

"You're looking at a career-ending lawsuit, Chief Becker," Derek said, his face flushed with anger. "For harassment and false arrest."

"Save it for your defense attorney," Amanda snapped. "Turn around and put your hands behind your back."

As her officer recited Miranda rights and cuffed Derek, Sidney proceeded to do a thorough job of patting down his outer clothing. Something dark and brooding radiated from his being, and Sidney wasn't convinced he posed no threat. She kept her hand near her sidearm as they led him into the living room.

They were interrupted by the sound the front door bursting open and Jeff Norcross strode into the room, his Nikon camera rising to his face. Before Sidney could speak, he snapped a few photos of her and Derek, the flash blinding her.

"Get the hell outta here, Jeff," Amanda said, advancing toward him.

"Derek, why are they arresting you?" Jeff asked.

"Get the hell outta here!" Amanda grabbed his arm and pulled him toward the door.

"Is Derek a suspect in the murders?" he yelled as she shut the door in his face.

"How does he manage to show up at every step of our investigation?" Sidney asked.

"He lives here," Derek said sourly. "He saw your cars and knew something was up."

"What do you mean he lives here?"

"He rents my guest house."

"Lucky you," Amanda said.

Out the window Sidney saw Jeff in the driveway peering into the windows of the patrol vehicles, shoulders hunched against the rain. A scavenger. But she had to admire his determination.

"Call Dr. Linthrope," Sidney told Amanda. "Tell him to come pick up that toxin and get it analyzed ASAP. You need to dust this house for prints, and search for forensic material confirming one or more of the dead women have been in this house."

"Got it, Chief."

"I want to call my lawyer," Derek said.

"You'll get your chance after you're booked." Sidney motioned a hand toward the door. "Let's go."

Outside, Jeff trailed them like a hungry hyena, his camera flashing, documenting their journey to the Yukon.

"What are they arresting you for, Derek?" he asked.

"They think I killed three women."

Jeff lowered his camera. "Three women? Who's the third?"

"Shut up, Derek," Amanda said.

"Satoshi Akira."

Jeff lifted the camera quickly, hiding a peculiar expression, and continued snapping photos. Sidney did not find it surprising that Jeff knew who Satoshi was. He'd been in Derek's house, seen her work, no doubt heard Derek talk about her. Still, his fleeting look struck her as a JDLR. *Just Didn't Look Right.* Jeff knew something. She made a mental note to grill him later.

Before Derek climbed into the caged back seat, he said to Jeff. "Call my lawyer. Tell him to meet us at the station."

"Count on it," Jeff said.

Sidney got into the Yukon and met Derek's gaze in the rear-view mirror. His face was expressionless except for his brown eye, which watched her with unnerving intensity. "Tell me how Satoshi died," he said.

"You know that better than I."

His jawed clenched and unclenched, and he continued in a low, morose tone, "You're wrong about me, Chief Becker. I would never have hurt her. I loved Satoshi. Not in the way you think, but as a friend. She helped me when I was lost, in acute pain, suicidal. I wouldn't be sitting here today if not for her intervention."

Sidney was trained to pick up signals from people; every blink, every nuance of expression and tone, every subtle body gesture. Her single-minded focus made her a good detective, but she could not read Derek Brent. Still, she could feel his emotion radiating off of him in waves. Dark. Tormented.

She sensed he was a man who had traveled to the depths of hell, lingered there in agony, and chose to claw his way back to walk among the living. Now she threatened to take away that hard-earned privilege. There was enough evidence against Derek to build a solid case, and to clinch the deal, lab results tomorrow would irrefutably conclude he was the killer. She looked away from the single, haunted eye.

Two of the three garage doors were open, and she saw Granger and Darnell searching the garage and Derek's two vehicles; a black Ram 1500 pickup, and a silver Mercedes sedan. She read the license plate on the sedan and a vague memory tried to ignite in her brain. She started the engine and drove, the memory teasing the edge of her consciousness, refusing to emerge. What did surface was the warning that had been intrinsic in her *I Ching* reading.

Water always moves downward: fire always burns upward. Beware of becoming overly confident, or too complacent.

CHAPTER FORTY-TWO

A FEELING of unrest plagued Sidney as she drove down Derek's long paved driveway toward the highway. Something like a splinter kept digging at her, wanting her attention, and would not be ignored. She pulled over to the side of the road, turned in her seat, and critically observed her prisoner.

He glowered, stared out the window.

She would try the good cop approach, see if she could coax anything out of him, confirm beyond question that she had her man. "Look Derek, I want to give you the benefit of the doubt, but how do you account for your fingerprints being all over Satoshi's house?"

"I told you." His good eye found hers, locked onto her gaze. "We were friends. She often invited me over, cooked for me, let me hang out and watch her work, which I found fascinating, and healing. She liked having a quiet, unobtrusive presence in the house. I liked being with someone who cared whether I lived or died. We respected each other. I never tried to move into her private world."

"Did you know her girlfriend?"

"We never met. But Satoshi talked about her. It was obvious she was in love. They were going to move in together. I was happy for her."

"Where were you the night she died?"

"At my house in Sand Hill, packing some belongings for my

move back here."

"Can anyone verify that?"

"No."

That did not bode well for Derek. No alibi. It just put him in the right geographical location at the time of the murder. "What brought you back to Garnerville?"

"Several things. Satoshi's death haunted me. I had to get away from Sand Hill." The corners of his mouth turned downwards in a convincing display of grief. "In addition to that, my nephew died of a drug overdose a week before Satoshi died. I came back to help my sister, who was near emotional collapse."

It was a surprise to Sidney that Derek had a relative in town. She realized she knew very little about him, except that death followed him. "Your sister is Becky Jamison, and your nephew was Joey?"

"Yes."

"I'm sorry for your loss," Sidney said gently, remembering how the teen's tragic death sent shock waves through the community. "It's a shame he got hooked on drugs."

"He wasn't a lowlife," Derek said defensively. "The system got him hooked."

"How so?"

"Becky told me he was prescribed pain pills to relieve a football injury. After a few months, he was addicted, but the doctor cut him off. He was a wreck, going through a terrible withdrawal. Sammy Ferguson came to his rescue, started feeding his habit."

"Samantha? You're sure about that?"

"Yes. Joey told Becky." He snorted his contempt. "The nice girl next door was a drug addled pusher. I confronted her in the parking lot at Barney's. We had a big blowup. She lied, said she wasn't responsible."

Tread carefully, Sidney thought. Keep him talking. "That must have made you angry."

"I *was* angry. Furious." He inhaled, long and deep. Exhaled. "But not enough to kill her. I wanted to see her punished, not gruesomely murdered. I have too much to live for to throw my life away. I'm back to work. My research is three years old, but I'm picking up my old zeal."

Sidney sifted through the emotion in Derek's voice. She heard grief, anger, and his determination to find meaning once again in his work. "You say you left your lab under lock and key. Who took care of your aquariums while you were gone?"

"Jeff."

"Did he understand the work you were doing?"

"No, of course not. Too scientific. I warned him not to touch anything. Just feed the fish and snails."

"You never mentioned what your toxins could do?"

"Not extensively. He showed little interest."

Silence while Sidney mulled this over. Every which way she approached the evidence, guilt and opportunity pointed to Derek. "You can see how this looks bad for you, right Derek? You knew all three victims. You cultivate a rare neurotoxin in your lab. You were in Sand Hill the night Satoshi died, no alibi. Last Wednesday night, you said you were home, within a mile of Samantha's crime scene. No alibi." Sidney paused, studying Derek for any exposed emotion, a hint of guilt, or the narcissistic arrogance that a psychopath can't keep hidden for long.

He sat motionless, a worried expression on his face.

"Perhaps it would be easier in the long run if you just admitted your guilt, and didn't drag your sister through a long, painful trial."

"I didn't do it!"

His sharp tone dislodged the obscure memory of the silver Mercedes lurking in her subconscious, and it clicked open like data on a computer screen. Sidney recited her thoughts out loud. "A truck hit an elk on the highway near your place Wednesday night around 11:15. A man in a silver Mercedes stopped and called it in.

Put flares around the animal, helped the county worker drag it off the road." She swallowed. "Was that you?"

Silence.

"We have the license plate number."

He heaved out a sigh. "Yes."

"Why didn't you mention that?"

"That's admitting I'm guilty," he said solemnly. "Puts me right smack in the area of Sammy's murder."

"You didn't see the red truck that hit the elk?"

His eye widened. "You're sure it was a red truck?"

"Yeah. I found paint chips on the road."

"Jeff owns a red truck. The front bumper is smashed in. He told me someone hit his car in the parking lot at city hall."

Sidney blinked. "Jeff owns a red truck with a smashed bumper?" Her mind went into instant analysis, pushing puzzle pieces around, rearranging them into a new scenario. Her thoughts crystallized around a sudden realization.

If Jeff hit the elk at 11:15 p.m., that put him on the highway near Samantha's crime scene at the correct time. If Jeff was her killer, he would have had Samantha in his truck, incapacitated. That would explain why he hastily fled the scene. Ann saw a tall man with long arms dragging Samantha in the woods around 11:25 p.m., which aptly described Jeff. He would have had ten minutes to drive half a mile and transport Samantha to the spot where Ann observed the killer. Jeff was the only other person who had access to Derek's neurotoxin.

Jeff could have studied Derek's notes, discovered how to administer a small enough dosage to render the desired effect on his victims. He also knew about Satoshi and her butterflies. Had Jeff contacted the artist? Was he The Collector? Officer Conner believed someone stole butterflies from the artist's studio. Did Jeff meet with Satoshi, kill her, steal the butterflies, and later place one at Samantha's crime scene? Did Jeff mastermind the series of events surrounding the murders to point the finger at Derek? Feeling a cold watery feeling in her stomach, Sidney revved up the engine, made a hard U-turn with a screech of tires, and headed back to Derek's house.

"What are you doing? You aren't taking me to jail?"

"No. You have an ironclad alibi. Samantha was killed during the period you were hanging out with that elk."

He gasped.

Sidney parked in front of the house and hurriedly helped Derek out of the Yukon.

With startled expressions, her two male officers paused in their search of the garage and stared at Derek, who stood rubbing his uncuffed wrists, and Sidney, who's expression was so tense it felt like it could crack. The third garage door was up, revealing Jeff's red pickup truck with the smashed bumper. "Where's Jeff?" she asked with urgency.

"He left right after you did," Granger said. "Headed down the dirt road over there by the lake. What's going on?"

"We need to find him and arrest him. Now!"

Both men sprinted into action, heading toward their vehicles.

"Stay alert. He's dangerous."

Heart pounding, Sidney dialed Selena's number. Listened to it ring. "Come on. Come on. Pick up, damn it." She got her sister's voicemail. She clicked off and called Ann, barked into her receiver as soon as Ann said hello, "Where's Selena?"

"I don't know. She never came back from Derek's." Ann sucked in a breath. "Is she okay?"

"Sit tight." Sidney hung up, got into her Yukon, and swerved toward the muddy, pockmarked road. About a mile down, she spotted the two police vehicles parked on the side of the road, and both men wading into the forest through the snarled undergrowth. She immediately saw deep tire tracks gauged into the earth where a vehicle careened off the road and clipped the trunk of a massive

Douglas fir. Beyond that, through the thicket of shrubs, she made out part of a dark green vehicle, same color as Selena's Jeep.

Sidney didn't remember parking, or trekking through the brush, but she reached the empty Jeep in seconds. The officers had all four doors open, and Granger was bending over the passenger seat. He backed out holding Selena's handbag, and passed it to Sidney.

A quick check confirmed her worst fear. Her sister's handgun and phone were still inside. Sidney viewed the scene with an exquisite hyper focus of details. No movement anywhere around them, as though the forest were holding its breath. Her voice sounded clear yet far away. "Selena would never have left her phone and gun behind unless she was panicked, or she was carried out by someone else."

As though in a photograph, Granger and Darnell stood motionless, their faces drained of color. Granger asked, "Is Jeff our killer?"

"Looks that way. Let's search for footprints and car tracks. Hurry. Every second counts."

They hit the road and scoured the area.

"Tire tracks over here, Chief," Darnell said. "And a few large boot prints. Looks like Jeff parked here and headed into the woods where Selena's car crashed. He went after her."

"The prints are nearly washed out," Sidney said. "It's been a while since this happened. Probably right after she left Derek's house, and before Jeff barged into the house flashing his camera."

"Setting up an alibi for himself," Darnell said.

"Exactly." Sidney flagged a trail of Selena's prints, melting back into the mud, leading south. "The distance between these prints indicate Selena was running. She got away from him. But she didn't make it to Ann's."

"Now's he's back, looking for her," Darnell said. "Thinking we're preoccupied with Derek."

"She could be hurt, hiding in the woods somewhere," Granger said.

Sidney prayed that was the case. "You two walk along each side of the road. Look for any sign of Selena, or Jeff's white Toyota Highlander. Stay alert. I'll head down the road in the Yukon."

Sidney drove slowly, peering into the forest on both sides. She rounded several bends before she spotted Jeff's Toyota parked off the road. The headlights cut through burrows of trees, highlighting Jeff, who was crouched over something in an irrigation ditch.

"I found him," she said into her shoulder mic. "A half-mile south. Get here quickly."

Concealed by foliage, Sidney quietly exited the Yukon. She pulled the Pico from the ankle holster and shoved it into the back of her belt. The small gun felt awkward in her hand and she was unfamiliar with its accuracy. She hoped she wouldn't be forced to rely on it. She pulled out her sidearm, a Glock 9mm, a handgun she trusted, and slowly advanced into the woods.

Unaware he had a spectator, Jeff was walking backwards, his arms encircling Selena's torso, dragging her unresponsive body toward his Highlander. Had he injected her with the venom?

For a moment, Sidney had a sensation of being under water, life moving at quarter speed, then it sped up again when Jeff reached the hatch of his Toyota. Sidney stood twenty feet away. She raised her sidearm to eye level, but Selena's body shielded Jeff and she couldn't get a clear shot.

The reporter suddenly jerked his head and locked eyes with Sidney, his emotions shifting from wide-eyed surprise to a cold deadly calm within seconds. She had never seen him like this: unmasked. Controlled. Evil.

"Put her down, Jeff."

Holding Selena's weight against his chest with one arm, Jeff raised his free hand and held a hypodermic needle an inch from

Selena's neck. Selena picked that moment to shudder into consciousness with a dazed expression, eyeballs rolling upwards, teeth chattering, body shivering. She tried to stand, but Jeff restrained her.

Thank God. She had not been injected, but her hair and clothes were soaked. How long had she been in that wet ditch? She appeared hypothermic. "Put her down, Jeff. Selena needs to get to the ER. Now!"

For a long hideous second, he didn't speak. Just the deadly stare.

"Put her down, Jeff."

He sneered. "You think you're in control? You've never been in control. Here's how this is going to play out. You're going to place that gun on the roof on my Toyota. Slowly. Then you're going to back the hell away." He moved the needle closer to Selena's neck.

Sweat dampening her face, Sidney approached his vehicle and did as she was told. He made no move to touch the gun, which meant he would have to release Selena, or the hypodermic, to free a hand.

"Back away," he growled. "Hands up."

She obeyed, moving back about twenty feet.

Letting Selena slide to the ground, Jeff reached for the handgun, his eyes trained on Sidney.

Sidney tasted copper on her tongue and felt a deep sinking sensation in the pit of her stomach. She went for the Pico.

Jeff grabbed the Glock.

They fired simultaneously.

Sidney grunted as a slug slammed into her armored vest.

One of her rounds hit Jeff's left shoulder. Another caught him in the pelvis. With a piercing cry, he dropped the Glock and sank to his knees, fingers pressed to the bleeding wound.

Sidney reeled, trying to get her balance, feeling like she got hit in the chest by a baseball bat. She heard a commotion behind her as her two officers braked, slammed car doors, and charged onto the scene. "Cuff him," she gasped. "Get that gun and hypodermic away from him."

Jeff was moaning in agony. Though he sounded like he was dying, she knew his injuries were not life-threatening. No organs had been hit, but a traumatic injury to the pelvis area, loaded with pain receptors, was intensely punishing. Sidney felt no sympathy.

Ignoring Jeff's groans, Granger pushed him face down on the ground, cuffed his hands behind his back, then turned him over to examine his wounds.

Sidney and Darnell carried Selena to the passenger seat of the Yukon. She was shivering and mumbling incoherently.

"We need to get her warm," Sidney said. "Grab the two blankets in the back." She cranked up the heat full blast and peeled off her sister's drenched parka and shirt. Working fast, Sidney zipped Selena into her own heavy work jacket, wrapped a blanket around her shoulders, and tucked the other one over her lap. "No point calling the paramedics. Granger can get Jeff to the ER faster than they could arrive. I'll be right behind him with Selena."

Darnell and Granger half-walked, half-dragged Jeff, who whimpered like a dying animal, into the caged back seat of Granger's truck.

"Darnell, get back to Jeff's guesthouse," Sidney said. "You and Amanda need to search every inch of it."

"Copy that."

Sidney got into the Yukon and turned to Selena, who was propped up with her head resting against the headrest. Color was coming back to her pale cheeks and she was breathing more evenly. Sidney reached over, brushed her sister's hair back from her forehead.

Selena opened her eyes and asked weakly. "Where am I?"

"In my Yukon. On the road by the lake. You okay?"

Selena squinted. "My head hurts."

"Did Jeff hit you?"

"No, I fell on the road, trying to get away from him. Where is he?" she asked with a touch of panic.

"Shot up and cuffed, in the back of Granger's truck. You're safe now."

"He's a monster." Selena closed her eyes, swallowed. "Never suspected him, even for a second."

Sidney heard the real pain under the surface, but all her professional skills didn't seem adequate to comfort her sister. "It's a shock. He definitely fell under the radar."

"But you got him. The town's savior."

"Don't feel much like a savior. Just a very tired woman who needs a week's worth of sleep." She placed a hand on her sister's shoulder. "How'd you get away from him?"

Selena half smiled. "The age-old retaliation. A hard knee to the nuts. Just like dear old Dad coached us."

Relieved her sister could conjure a touch of humor, Sidney smiled back. "Used it myself a few times. Hang tight. We're going to the ER." As Sidney pulled onto the mucky road behind Granger's truck she heard him notify the ER that they were on their way.

When Granger's tires left the pitted dirt road and hit the smooth surface of the highway, he put on his lights and siren and gunned the engine. Sidney followed suit. With the crisis under control, she flipped a mental switch, and reverted from automatic protocol and survival response to a human being with thoughts and feelings. The aftermath of violence hit her so hard in the gut she tasted bile in the back of her throat. Her heartbeat was still racing, and pain radiated throughout her chest from the bullet's point of impact with her vest.

It had all happened so fast. She knew she would relive the experience for days, processing through every gruesome detail until it lost its power. The whole day seemed surreal—an encapsulated period of time that warped reality and wrenched from her every kind of emotion. First, the trip to Sand Hill, and the grisly visits to the lighthouse and Satoshi's cottage—followed by the ominous *I Ching* reading. Then she returned home to discover an intruder had invaded her home and was spying on Selena. The last two hours were a blur—the race to collect evidence and arrest Derek, followed by the realization she had the wrong man. Jeff Norcross was the killer, and her sister was missing and in grave danger.

Sidney felt a new wave of nausea when she thought of how close Selena had come to being Jeff's next victim. If she'd taken Derek to the station, or arrived on the scene just minutes later, Jeff would have gotten Selena in his car and injected her with the neurotoxin. He'd be heading to his secret lair, where he had kept Sammy for hours before killing her in the woods.

Sidney had forged into a danger zone, confronted a cold-blooded killer, and engaged in a shooting match straight out of *High Noon*. Only one thing had mattered. Saving Selena.

CHAPTER FORTY-THREE

SIDNEY ENTERED THE SMALL community hospital in Jackson at 10:00 a.m., strode down the hall, and greeted Officer Brett Carson, who was stationed outside of Jeff's room. "Thanks for contacting me, Officer. How's he doing?"

"Showing signs of life this morning. Hasn't said zip, but he ate his breakfast."

"Go ahead and take a break. I'll be here for a while."

"Will do."

After the young officer left, Sidney paused at the door of the dark, cramped room, and viewed the monster in human form. She gave herself a stern warning to be on guard. She was dealing with a psychopath. Cunning. Ace actor.

Jeff lay against the pillows in the half-elevated hospital bed with his eyes closed—left arm in a sling, an IV tube snaking from the back of his right hand, his wrist cuffed to the bed, and his long, gangly body hidden beneath the covers. His disheveled blonde hair hung longer on one side where he normally combed it over his balding crown and lacquered it in place. The misplaced hair gave his face a slightly misshapen appearance. On anyone else, it would have looked comical. On Jeff, it accentuated the deformity of his character and mind.

He opened his eyes as she entered, met her gaze, didn't flinch, just stared with a calm stillness. Cuffed, deprived of the use of either hand, and immobile due to the gunshot wound to his pelvis, he probably felt exposed and damned uncomfortable. *Good.*

His face altered in an instant, eyes narrowing, mouth twisting into a smirk.

She wanted to rush him, slap the condescension from his face, punish him for the misery he'd inflicted on so many people. Recalling his hold on Selena in the forest with the needle held to her throat and the cold-blooded look in his eyes as he shot Sidney, she experienced a flash of white-hot rage. She forced down her fury, pushed a chair right up to his bed, seated herself, and waited for Jeff to make the first move.

"What do you want? Come to gloat?"

"Just came to talk. Thought you might want to get some weight off your chest."

"Talk to my public defender." He stared at her with open contempt, then turned his face to the wall.

Officer Carson had updated her on Jeff's condition throughout the day yesterday. Jeff had been groggy, in and out of sleep, and she knew she wouldn't get much out of him, which suited her fine. She'd been preoccupied processing details of the homicides, reviewing lab results, dealing with the news teams that swept into town like a flash flood in a dry gulch.

"You won't have a public defender assigned to you until after your first appearance in court, at which time you'll be able to apply for one. Until then, it's just you and me."

For some time, Jeff didn't move. She sat in silence, except for the sounds filtering in from the corridor—the soft voices of nurses navigating their mobile workstations in and out of neighboring rooms. Realizing it could be a long wait, Sidney pulled her phone from her duty belt and occupied herself checking messages and texting replies.

Snores. Jeff had fallen asleep. He woke twenty minutes later and blinked when he saw Sidney still rooted to the chair. He pressed the call button, closed his eyes. When a male nurse appeared, Jeff asked for coffee.

"May I have a cup, too, please?" Sidney said.

The nurse took in her uniform and nametag and gave her a respectful nod. "I'll grab some from the break room, Chief Becker."

She and Jeff ignored each other. The coffee arrived. His was in a tall plastic cup with a straw, which the nurse positioned on his food tray close enough for him to sip.

Minutes later, his cup was empty. So was hers. She slouched a little in her seat to make her posture nonthreatening, and he could look down at her, giving him the advantage in their power play.

"Get this tray out of my face," Jeff demanded. "And open those fucking curtains."

She knew he felt vulnerable and needed to assert his power. Sidney moved the tray against the wall, snapped open the curtains to let the morning light fall into the room, and reseated herself.

"Thanks." His expression revealed a mixture of relief and wariness. He'd been alone in the dark room. No TV. No newspapers. She certainly wasn't his first choice for company, but still, she disrupted what must have been mind-numbing boredom. His curiosity about what the world was saying about him had to be burning him alive. She could play off that. "I'm not going away, Jeff. You may as well talk to me."

"I'm not confessing anything."

"We don't need a confession. We have you on three counts of murder. Ironclad." She pulled her phone from her breast pocket, set it to record.

"No way you can pin three murders on me." He stared at the phone, his tone defiant.

"I didn't even mention two counts of attempted murder. Selena, and me. One murder, or three, doesn't make much difference. You can only serve one lifetime in prison."

He glared.

"You were careful, Jeff. I'll give you that." She controlled her tone to sound nonjudgmental. "You did a lot of things right. You had us stumped for three years."

"You've got nothing on me."

"Bear with me. Let's start with Sammy."

A sharp alertness tightened his features.

"We can place you within the immediate vicinity of her murder at the time of her death. Too bad you hit that elk."

"Don't know what you're talking about."

"Your truck left red paint chips on the highway and pieces of a broken headlight. They match your truck perfectly, like puzzle pieces."

Nervous laugh. "So, I hit an elk. Proves nothing."

She could feel the tension emanating from him, although he tried to hide it. "You should be looking at Derek," he said.

"Ah, yes. It was skillful the way you pointed all the arrows at Derek. But thanks to you, he has an alibi for the time of Samantha's death. He stopped to help the county worker move that elk you hit off the road. Meanwhile, you were chasing Ann, then killing Samantha. We found the sweatshirt you wore that night. Bailey's saliva is on it—you know, where he tore that hole in it."

A muscle twitched near his jaw.

"Let's move on to Satoshi. Clever the way you set it up to look like a suicide. Leaving the blade behind, stashing her car at the scene." Sidney half-smiled. "Good move. Except you staged her body the exact same way you staged Mimi and Sammy. Only the killer knew how to do that. You were so certain you had the suicide ruling all wrapped up, you felt comfortable enough to return to Satoshi's cottage last week. A palm print we found on her bedroom window, is yours. The footprints on her porch match your boots perfectly. The semen we found on her bedroom carpet matches your DNA."

Almost imperceptibly, he flinched.

"The neurotoxin you were going to inject into Selena was the same as that found in Mimi and Samantha. You're the only one who had access to Derek's lab. Any way you look at it, we have you nailed for three murders." She paused a few beats to let her words sink in. "We know you watched the three women. Planned everything. Left nothing to chance. But fate stepped in. 'The best laid plans of mice and men,' right Jeff?"

Silence.

"The story is all over the press. It went national."

Jeff couldn't hide the sudden gleam of interest in his eyes.

She paused, making him wait, recalling the press conference yesterday, where she and Mayor Burke confronted a rowdy herd of reporters from all over the country. Sidney appreciated that Mayor Burke took the blunt force of the questions, expressing in equal measure his sympathy to the victims of the families and his pride in the outstanding work of his police department. When it was her turn to step into the limelight, Sidney did her best to close off her emotions and answer the questions with objectivity. Her experience with the media in Oakland had taught her to relate only the bare facts. After being pummeled for ten minutes, she smiled and moved away, ignoring the microphones being thrust in front of her, while Granger and Amanda helped her shove through the reporters trying to block her path back into the station.

"What are they saying?" Jeff's voice cut into her thoughts.

"Any damn thing about you they want. Reporters are having a field day at your expense. They say you raped and tortured those women. That sex was your primary motivation."

His eyes narrowed, and he watched her like a reptile. Still. Emotionless.

"They're saying you're a monster. Just another run-of-the-mill serial murderer. Is that how you want to be remembered?"

He was quiet for a long moment, staring at his wrist cuffed to the bedrail. His hand clenched into a fist, then slowly relaxed. She caught a glimpse of fury in his eyes, then it was gone.

"I'm different from ordinary people," Jeff said, meeting her eyes. His expression and tone had shifted. The defiant, nerdy journalist was suddenly back. "But I'm no monster. Someday the world will know the truth. I intend to write a book about every detail."

She imagined him as she had always known him, dressed in his standard khaki Dockers and polo shirt, his Nikon camera held high, flashing pictures of people around town for his innocuous stories. A brilliant role to hide behind all these years, while the beast inside calmly contemplated murder and rape. Sidney was sickened, but she kept her voice calm, firm. "Even if you win a Pulitzer, Jeff, it won't save you from a lethal injection."

She watched the muscles tighten and loosen on his face, like he was grinding his teeth. She continued. "However, if you cooperate, talk to me, I could take the death sentence off the table. You could roost in a cozy cell. Write your book. Let the world know the inner workings of your mind. Maybe Hollywood will come calling to turn your story into a movie. You could get active on social media. Build a huge fan base."

His eyes widened minutely, glimmered with interest.

"Let me help you out. If you fill in a few blanks for me, I can hold a press conference, set the news media straight. Let you watch it on TV."

She endured a long silence. He became calm and still, calculation in his eyes, until finally, he nodded.

Her adrenalin hummed. She had his cooperation. He agreed to confess. "Is it true what the reporters are saying? That sex was your motivation for abducting the women?"

"I didn't touch them… in that way."

"We found evidence on Sammy's body that says you did. You were kind enough to leave a pubic hair behind."

His pale blue eyes watched her, the intensity of the emotion behind them powerful.

Then he looked away, gazed out the window for a long moment. A smile tugged at his mouth.

She guessed he was remembering what he did to Samantha. *Sick bastard.* Watching his lewd expression made Sidney's skin crawl.

He pulled himself from his distraction and glanced her way. Noting her disgust, the smile was extinguished. "I'm no run-of-the-mill killer, Chief Becker. They're missing the nuances. The finesse. The sheer beauty of the ritual."

"Your murders were beautifully orchestrated, I'll give you that."

"Yes, they were. Clean. Elegant. Simple. The ladies died with dignity. Remember Sammy's face? She looked peaceful in death. Even amused. So did Mimi and Satoshi."

Sammy's wide-eyed stare haunted Sidney. She still had nightmares depicting the last few minutes of the young woman's life. The terror. The horror. The coldness in Sidney's stomach moved up to her chest, felt like a hand squeezing her heart. She swallowed, concealing her feelings, and focused on her job. She needed to find out where Jeff took the women after injecting them. His lair. "Help me paint the complete picture. What did you do with Sammy before you killed her? You spent considerable time with her. Twelve hours."

He gave her a cold stare. "We ate pizza. Watched reruns of *Father Knows Best* and *Leave it to Beaver.*"

"That's amusing, Jeff." She gave him a tight smile. "You mentioned some kind of ritual. The butterflies, the *I Ching* readings. Was it spiritual?"

He thought for a moment. "Yes. Spiritual."

Sidney knew he was lying. The butterflies were merely clues he planted to direct the investigation to Derek. She humored him.

"Ordained by the oracle?"

"Yes. I was advised how to proceed. Step by step. I was gentle with Sammy. Caring. She was in a safe place."

"You had a romantic evening with her?"

"Romantic? No. Sacred. Don't misrepresent my intention. Where one may see beauty, others see ugliness. What is death, Chief Becker, but a doorway to paradise."

What a crock. She saw only sadism in the way Jeff dragged Sammy through the forest, her bare feet scratched and bleeding, and in the way he glued her eyelids open so she could watch him torture her.

Another rapid transformation in Jeff's demeanor took place. His mouth turned downward and something like sorrow darkened his eyes. He made a small strangling sound that might have been a whimper, and he squeezed his eyes shut.

A victim now. Misunderstood.

"You think it was easy to kill them?" Tears spilled over, ran unchecked down his cheeks, and his voice quivered. "This is hard to talk about."

Burying her disgust, Sidney touched his hand and said gently. "I understand. We'll take it slow."

Seconds passed. Once he got himself under control, he zeroed back in on her as though gauging her reaction.

She tried to look sympathetic.

"Please include this quote from Lao Tzu." He stared at the phone as though it were a transmitter going out to an audience of millions and said with careful enunciation, "Being deeply loved by someone gives you strength, while loving someone gives you courage."

"Please explain how that applies to your ritual."

"I loved Sammy deeply, which gave her the strength to face eternity."

Though he looked as serious as a choirboy at the confessional, she found the sexual connotation repugnant. Was Jeff playing her? "Let's start at the beginning. Why did you choose Mimi Matsui?"

He sniffed. "Derek picked her."

"Derek?"

"He was sleeping with her."

Her eyebrows arched.

"I see that surprises you," he said. "Derek isn't what he seems. A lot going on behind his polished, upper class façade. Those practice sessions he had with Mimi weren't just about music."

"How do you know this?"

"I watch. I listen. Derek also had close relationships with Sammy and Satoshi."

"One at a time, Jeff. Back to Mimi. How long was she involved with Derek?"

He shrugged a shoulder. "Couple months. Mimi was crazy about him. I could see it in the way she looked at him. My guess, she was going to leave Miko. That's when Derek bowed out. He doesn't like anything messy. He's compulsive that way. See his house? Neat as a pin."

"Back to Mimi."

"Ah, Mimi." His eyes took on a dreamy look. "She was beautiful and tempestuous. Normally, I don't go for the unattainable type. I know my place. But after she lost Derek, I figured she was lonely and could use some comfort. I stepped into the void. Befriended her. Interviewed her. Wrote a great article publicizing her concert with Derek. That night, the church was packed. Practically the whole fucking town showed up. Afterward, when everyone left, and we were alone, I figured she'd show some gratitude. I was wrong." His expression changed, eyes igniting with anger. "When I tried to kiss her, she went psycho on me. Slugged me. Broke my glasses."

The glasses he wasn't wearing when he tried to abduct Selena and wasn't wearing now. *All these years, just part of his disguise.*

"Sorry to hear that. Must have made you mad."

"Pissed me off royally."

His face contorted, and Sidney caught a glimpse of some emotion so intense it chilled her. "So you decided to teach her a lesson."

"Damned straight. Let karma be my guide."

"You watched her." Her voice sounded hollow, but Jeff didn't seem to notice. He was on a roll.

"Yeah, I watched her. Bided my time. I am a patient man."

A cold knot of dread formed in Sidney's chest. She didn't want to hear the details. She wanted to take a time-out and leave the room. Steady her resolve. Shed the residue of disgust that had crept over her. But she knew she couldn't shatter Jeff's momentum. She might not get it back.

He continued smoothly, convinced he had a rapt audience. A begrudging admirer. "I waited until she was alone at the church one evening. Paid her a visit. It was child's play. So easy to get up close and stick her with the needle. A triumphant moment, I can tell you. The hellcat was tamed." Very much amused for some reason, Jeff met her eyes and smiled. "I left her in the trunk of my car for a couple hours to show her who was boss."

Sidney loathed this man. She controlled herself with effort. "Go on."

"Boy, was Mimi grateful when I took her into the warm cabin."

Cabin. There was the slip Sidney had been waiting for. *Where was this cabin?* "How did you know she was grateful?" *She couldn't move or talk.*

"I understand women in a unique way." His eyes sparkled, as though he was simply sharing details of his prowess at tennis or golf. "What every woman really wants is to be taken care of by a man. Have her role clearly defined. Have a blueprint to follow."

"You mean dominated."

A half-smile. "Semantics."

"What did you do with Mimi to put her in her place?"

"A gentleman doesn't tell." His smile widened. "Saving that for the book. Think it will be a best seller?"

"Where's the cabin?"

"My little secret."

She tried another tactic, hoping for another slip. "You took Bailey with you after you killed Sammy. Why? You soft on dogs?"

"Yeah. I love dogs. I was sorry I had to hit him. After I left Sammy, I carried him to my car. We spent the night together at the cabin."

"His paws were bloody when he got back to Ann's. Looked like he ran about twenty miles. Not very humane of you."

"Not my fault. He escaped. It was only seven miles."

"Must have been through the woods, the way his paws looked. This side of the lake?"

He smiled. Clammed up.

"Seven miles through the woods, this side of the lake..."

Zip.

With a flash of temper, Sidney turned off her recorder. "Interview's over."

His eyes widened.

"No press conference until you're ready to tell me everything. What you did to those women. Where the cabin is." Sidney pushed herself out of the chair and without a backward glance or goodbye, walked out of the room.

She got less than ten feet before she heard his indignant voice call out.

"Chief Becker."

She stopped in the hall, waited.

"Chief Becker!" Voice hoarse, angry now.

Sidney breathed deeply, waited.

"Chief Becker." A touch of humility. "I'm ready to talk."

Sidney just wanted to get away from him. Irritation boiled up inside of her and she took a couple more deep breaths to try to dilute her dark mood. She didn't want to hear any more about Jeff's unspeakable acts and the unspeakable pain he caused.

After taking another deep breath of air, she turned and began walking back to the psychopath's room.

CHAPTER FORTY-FOUR

SIDNEY AND SELENA PREPARED scalloped potatoes, roasted vegetables, and a crisp green salad in the kitchen while listening to the hum of male voices and laughter coming from the porch. Sidney smiled, stealing glances at David and Granger socializing while firing up the grill. Smoke wafted behind them as top sirloin steaks hit the grill and sizzled. Selena had beamed when Granger assured her that the prime cuts of beef, straight from his ranch, were grass-fed, with no antibiotics or hormones.

When the food groups were coordinated, the two couples gathered around the table with a bottle of good Merlot, compliments of David, and dug in, trading flattering remarks about the cuisine. The cats prowled around the table, excited by the company, vying for treats, and finally settling into four bundles of fur decorating the worn Asian rug.

The conversation was dominated by accounts of reporters harassing everyone in town, turning any grain of information into a speculative story. Though some of the townsfolk were miffed by the invasive questions, the money the outsiders were spending—a boost to the town's economy, smoothed most ruffled feathers.

"How's Ann?" Sidney asked Selena.

"She's doing okay. A blanket of doom has been lifted from her shoulders. Noah's gone. Jeff's gone. The whole town is breathing easier. She feels safe enough to be home alone." Selena paused to eat a forkful of potatoes.

"Miko stopped by with a basket of fresh eggs," Granger filled in. "He looked exhausted, and pretty torn up. Bags under his eyes. He apologized to Ann for Noah's behavior."

"He's a decent guy." Selena wiped her mouth with a napkin and continued while Granger stabbed a bite of steak and shoved it into his mouth. "Ann was surprisingly gracious. She told Miko she knew it wasn't his fault. She offered to make quiche Lorraine with the eggs and drop some off to him." Selena shared a smile with Granger before she turned back to David and Sidney. "There's something going on between those two. I wouldn't be surprised if they become an item down the road, after everything cools off."

I could say the same thing about you two, Sidney thought. The lingering gazes, their sparkling eyes and flushed faces, the way they lightly touched each other while talking, were dead giveaways.

After dinner, stomachs full, plates pushed aside, another bottle of wine was opened, and inevitably the topic turned to the homicide investigation, now in its final stages. They all needed to talk about it, try to get some closure.

Warmed by the wine, Sidney found it easier to relate the details of her conversation with Jeff at the hospital, right up to the point where she left his room and returned minutes later after calming herself in the hallway. She paused to sip her Merlot, all eyes on her in anticipation, except for Granger, who knew the whole story. He, Amanda, and Darnel had accompanied her to Jeff's one-room cabin after she left the hospital yesterday. The cabin—a euphemism for a drafty, old woodshed—was located in a remote, wooded area seven miles from the lake. Jeff had been renting it for years as a writing retreat.

"So, what did Jeff tell you when you went back in his room?" Selena asked.

"The location of the cabin and every gruesome detail of the the three murders. He didn't need to go into detail, I discovered later. Just wanted to shock me. We found his video collection when we processed the cabin. He had documented everything, every detail, in cinematic color. The cabin was set up like a love nest. Bear rug in front of the fireplace, silk sheets on the bed. Everything he imagined a woman would want on a dream date."

"Yech." Selena's face paled.

"How did he avoid leaving trace evidence on the women?" David asked.

"He cleaned them up afterwards. Did a thorough job, except for that one pubic hair he left on Sammy."

No one spoke. They didn't need to. Revulsion was etched on their faces.

"Bottom line," Sidney said. "Jeff imagined these incapacitated women welcomed his assaults. Once they were put in what he called 'a submissive role' they became willing partners to his sexual exploitation."

"Demented," Selena seethed.

"His own special kind of crazy," David agreed.

"Got that right. Definitely a psychopath," Sidney said. "He spoke of his atrocities like he was talking about the weather. With a sense of pride, even." For a moment her voice constricted, as the horror of Jeff's actions threatened to engulf her.

She focused on David's handsome face, the deep velvet brown of his eyes, which expressed compassion and support in the soft lighting. She began to relax, like a woman walking on a frozen lake who realizes she's back on dry land. The worst was over. Her sister was safe. The town was safe.

"He showed no remorse?" Selena asked, breaking into Sidney's thoughts.

"None. It's clear he's incapable of remorse, or any kind of real relationship with another human. So, killing them after they met his perverted needs didn't push his envelope out too far."

"So his motivation was sex, after all," Selena said. "Like the paper said."

"Not entirely. The common denominator linking all three victims seems to be Derek Brent."

David and Selena looked surprised.

"All three women were exceptionally pretty. Not the type who would give Jeff a passing glance. But in his mind, all three had been sexually involved with Derek."

"So Jeff built up a fantasy about Derek, and was jealous of him?" David asked.

"Yes. To the point of neurosis. He spoke of Derek with extreme malice. I'm no expert, but he seemed to be obsessed with having what Derek had, at any cost."

Selena's brows came together. "I don't get it. Why did he think Derek was involved with these women?"

"He's delusional." Sidney sipped the last of her Merlot and met David's gaze. He smiled and refilled her glass. "I spoke with Derek last night," she continued. "It appears Jeff twisted things Derek said to him off the cuff. Granted, he did have a thing with Mimi. Impulsive. A quickie in the church, which they both regretted afterwards, and didn't repeat."

"And Jeff may have witnessed Sammy flirting with Derek when the two men ate at Hogan's one night. But she probably flirted with all the male customers. Seeking bigger tips. Jeff was dead wrong about Derek and Samantha having an affair. Derek was actually outraged by her. Apparently, she sold his nephew illegal drugs. Possibly even the heroin laced with fentanyl that killed him. The lover's spat Jeff thinks he witnessed in Barney's parking lot was actually Derek giving Samantha holy hell."

Sidney paused to sip her wine, and then continued. "And Jeff was certainly wrong about Satoshi. In reality, she and Derek were close friends, but not lovers. She was gay. While recovering in Sand Hill, Derek spent a lot of time with her. He was extremely grateful that she befriended him when he was nearly suicidal."

Selena's eyes widened. "Suicidal?"

"Yeah. He was deeply depressed after the accident, and in terrible pain. Thought he'd never walk again. Satoshi spent a lot of time with him. She turned him on to a Chinese spiritual practice that gave him the strength to recover. He feels she saved his life."

Sadness touched Selena's face. "I feel bad we accused him of murder."

"Me, too. But following the evidence in an investigation isn't foolproof. Derek's not holding a grudge. He's just thankful we pulled the mask off Jeff."

"So Jeff believed he was moving in on women that were infatuated with Derek," David said.

"Yes. While Jeff had a history of being rebuffed by pretty women, he watched them 'drool' over Derek. Derek was everything Jeff wanted to be—rich, handsome, highly intelligent, successful—while Jeff came up short in every category."

"Then Derek was in the car accident," Selena said. "His face disfigured."

"When we talked about that, Jeff gloated." The memory chilled Sidney. "He was thrilled about Derek losing his looks and experiencing misery, 'like the rest of us.'" With Derek out of the way, Jeff had the run of his property. He was happy for three years, living a privileged life."

"Interesting," David said. "During that period, there were no murders."

"Yep. Since Mimi. Then Derek started coming back to Garnerville on weekends, and then he told Jeff he was moving back permanently."

"Oh dear," Selena said. "Trouble."

"Big time. Somewhere along the line, Derek raved to Jeff about Satoshi. Brought her art pieces home, and her photo."

"Must have stirred up old feelings of resentment," Granger said. "Even with his face scarred, Derek managed to attract a gorgeous woman."

"Jeff couldn't tolerate the thought of Derek being happy," David said.

"So he had to be punished," Selena said. "By killing Satoshi."

Sidney was silent, staring into her glass.

"What aren't you telling us?" Selena asked.

Sidney looked up and met her sister's gaze. "Strange, but Satoshi affected Jeff differently. He described her as gentle and trusting, while he referred to Sammy and Mimi as loose women who deserved to be punished. He imagined he and Satoshi had some kind of deep romantic connection. Spent two days with her in her little cottage over the bay. Propped her up at the table, ate his meals with her, read her the paper, read poetry to her after 'they made love.'"

"Horrifying." Selena visibly shivered and sadness weighed on her voice. "That poor woman."

"Jeff couldn't bring himself to leave Satoshi out in the woods, exposed to the elements like the other two, but instead he killed her in the lighthouse. Sealed in what he called 'a fitting tomb.' He told me he cried for days after he killed her."

"Cried for himself," Granger said. "Not for what he did to her. He missed his play toy."

There was silence around the table.

"Which leads to me," Selena said, voicing what everyone was thinking.

Sidney had planned to avoid talking about Selena's victimization, but the look on her sister's face told her she needed to air it out. Sidney said, "After moving back to Garnerville, Derek became attracted to you. No doubt, he mentioned you to Jeff. Jeff couldn't let that develop." Sidney cleared her throat, continued. "Jeff was driven to experience whatever good thing Derek experienced."

"A beautiful woman that had always been outside his grasp,"

Granger said, his gentle blue eyes holding Selena's gaze.

"He wanted to gratify his own need and punish Derek at the same time," Sidney said.

Selena drew in a long, ragged breath. "So he invaded our house and planted that filthy little camera in my bedroom. How long was it there?"

"Not long," Sidney said. "A couple days. While you were at Ann's. When we reviewed the footage on his computer, your room was empty. Except for the cats. Chili slept on your pillow the whole time you were gone."

Selena attempted a smile, then swallowed. "Hard to believe that nerdy Jeff Norcross killed three women, just to hurt Derek."

"There's a completely different entity residing in his body. Something with talons and fangs." Sidney sipped her Merlot. "I also think he was responsible for Derek's car accident."

Selena's eyes widened.

"He strongly inferred as much when we talked. Makes sense when you think about it. He tampered with the brakes on your car, Selena, knowing you'd eventually crash. He led me to believe he did the same thing to Derek's car the morning of his accident."

Selena asked, "Was his intent to kill him?"

"I don't think Derek's death would have fazed him, though the end result suited him beautifully."

"Where did this madman come from, anyway?" David asked. "How did he end up in Garnerville?"

"Born and raised here," Sidney said. "Jeff wouldn't talk about his upbringing. But research shows there's a genetic predisposition to antisocial behavior. An unhealthy environment, with abusive parenting, can push an individual with that tendency into extreme, violent behavior. Jeff is six years younger than me, so I never knew him from school, never met his family. His parents moved out of state a few years back, to Wyoming."

"I knew him," Granger said. "We had classes together. I

remember he was very brainy. On the honor roll, the debate team. He had a girlfriend who was just as brainy." He squinted, thinking. "Oh yeah, her name was Marla Gundwich. Thick glasses. As short and round as he was tall and skinny. I remember the jocks and cheerleaders use to poke fun at them. Called them the odd couple; Bean Pole and Melon."

"Cruel," Selena said.

"Mean, for sure. But mostly, Jeff was invisible," Granger said. "He left town to go to Oregon State. Journalist major. Came back and started the *Daily Buzz*. Filled a void. The citizens of Garnerville were tired of being second class citizens, getting the rare mention from the *Jackson Bulletin*."

"He finally came out of obscurity. Got some attention," Selena said.

"Not the kind he craved. He really wanted his name in neon lights," Sidney said. "Now he's got it."

Again, they sat in silence. Sidney became aware of David's gaze on her. His eyes crinkled at the corners and a smile flickered on his mouth. She flashed him a tired smile.

"On a lighter note, who's up for dessert?" Selena asked. "Warm bread pudding with bourbon cream sauce."

There was unanimous agreement around the table.

Over coffee and the delicious bread pudding, they spent the rest of the evening pleasantly chatting about trivialities, conjuring stories of local lore and funny episodes from the history of Garnerville. It went a long way to cleanse their minds of criminal activity.

Granger was the first to say goodnight, citing chores waiting at home. Selena was quick to volunteer to walk him to his truck.

David hung out with Sidney in the kitchen, helping her tidy up and load the dishwasher. She was aware of the smell of him, musky sandalwood, and the clean scent of his shampoo. She took comfort in her growing sense of familiarity with his face and the lines of his body.

Selena swept back into the house, eyes sparkling, face deeply flushed. She excused herself for the night, the four cats bounding after her.

Finally, Sidney and David were alone. He folded the dishtowel, hung it on the oven door, and leaned against the counter.

As she met the brown eyes she'd lost herself in so many times, she isolated a feeling that had been mixed with other emotions all evening—the stirrings of desire. She couldn't help the surge of attraction she felt for this man. "Thank you," she said gently.

"For what? The wine?"

"For being here." She closed the space between them, and he pulled her into his arms.

She winced, her whole midriff deeply bruised from the bullet hitting her vest.

Concern flooded his eyes, and he loosened his hold. "You okay?"

"Yes, just don't press too hard. At least my lip is healed," she teased.

"Is that an invitation?"

They kissed, long and sweet. It was reassuring to feel his warmth against her body, and it was hard to pull her mouth away, but she did.

"You're kicking me out, aren't you?"

"Early morning," she murmured, her lips against his neck.

"It's okay. I have to pick up my son. Dillon's basketball practice ends in about fifteen minutes."

"Time for another kiss."

He obliged, this one deeper, more urgent. She felt it down to her toes. When they pulled away, she couldn't speak.

David filled in the silence. "Dillon is staying with a friend Friday night. I thought I could make you dinner at my place."

"I see. You're a planner."

"Yeah." He chuckled. "You've found my biggest flaw."

"I'm a planner, too." *And I'm planning a different outcome for Friday night than me sleeping alone.* "I'll bring a toothbrush."

"I love how you read between the lines." He pecked her nose, released her, and let out a barely audible sigh, the sound of a patient man summoning up his reserves. "Until Friday."

Sidney stood on the porch in the evening chill and watched David climb into his SUV. The engine started with a plume of exhaust, and she heard the tires crunching gravel as he drove down the driveway to Main Street. After his taillights disappeared, she lingered, rubbing the goose bumps on her arms, listening to the quiet sounds of the night, letting the peacefulness of the small town seep into her soul. In the vast dome of black sky overhead, stars sparkled like diamonds, and the fragrance of the forest lingered in the air. She entered the house, shutting out the mysteries of the night, wondering with a twinge of anxiety what wild and deadly creatures crouched out there in the darkness, waiting to strike.

ALSO BY LINDA BERRY

PRETTY CORPSE

Lauren Starkley, a widowed single mom and beat cop in San Francisco, has a rebellious teen, a night-shift partner with family issues, and a crush on the captain, her boss. When Lauren and her partner stumble on a series of sex crimes close to her own neighborhood, she does a little off-duty detecting. She earns official trouble for her efforts, but the warnings from her superiors don't keep her from tugging at elusive clues. And Lauren finds she's put both her daughter and herself in mortal danger

CHAPTER ONE

October 1999

PATROL OFFICER Lauren Starkley pulled her gaze away from the laptop mounted on the console. Calls had come in nonstop since she and her partner started their evening shift two hours ago. Then for the last fifteen minutes, nothing. Dispatch was directing units to other parts of the city. *Break time.* "I need a java jolt."

The car shifted abruptly as Patrol Officer Steve Santos stepped on the brakes, jerked the wheel to the right, and parked at the curb. She glanced up through the rain-marbled windshield. Peet's Coffee glimmered in the darkness.

"Fast enough, Princess?"

"The whiplash wasn't necessary."

"Sorry. You could've driven."

"Nope. Your turn. Wouldn't wanna deprive you." She'd had her fill of maneuvering on rain-slick city streets. They'd been dodging the downpour all evening and failing. Her uniform was damp, she was chilled to the bone, and the car was warm. Putting on her most charming smile, she asked sweetly, "You running in for me, darling?"

"You know I can't resist when you call me darling." He grinned, opened the door, and strode quickly across the wet sidewalk.

Rolling her shoulders back and forth, she tried to release her growing tension. San Francisco had been under a deluge for days. The storm had momentarily let up, but worse than rain was fog, which had thickened dramatically in the last few hours, drifting into the Mission District from the bay. There were always collisions on nights like this, and they'd already written up three fender benders and two DUIs. So far nothing serious, but it was the witching hour. Prime time for drunks to empty out of the bars.

The smell of wet asphalt rolled into the cab as Steve slid into the driver's seat balancing two cups of hot coffee. He passed her a cafè mocha. "Here's your frou-frou drink. That sugar and cream's going straight to your booty."

"My booty's just fine, thank you very much." Steve thought he was doing her a service by offering dieting tips, which she ignored. They both hit the gym hard almost every day. He was solidly packed muscle, while she always ran five to eight pounds overweight, which gave her a little paunch and forced her to constantly suck in her gut. *To hell with fat.* She removed the lid and sipped, sighing her pleasure.

Steve took his java robust and black, no frills. They drank in silence.

The voice of a dispatcher crackled over the radio. "We've got a 618. Report of a woman's screams in Cypress Park."

"We'll take it," Lauren said into her shoulder mic. "We're three blocks away."

Steve hit the siren and light and the patrol car roared forward. Lauren was pressed back against the seat and hot coffee spilled over her fingers. With a silent curse, she set the cup in the holder. "Where's the witness?" she asked the dispatcher.

"Anonymous call."

"Location?"

"East side. Near the tracks."

"Copy that."

A report of screams could mean anything, but a decade at the busiest station in the city had taught Lauren to prepare for the worst. City streets flew past the window, the patrol car squealed to the curb on Grifton Street, and she and Steve sprinted into the park. As a soccer mom, she had spent hundreds of hours on the fields of

Cyprus Park, but tonight they entered the densely forested east side and she found it unrecognizable. Fog blocked out the glare of streetlights and it was pitch black under the thick canopy. Her flashlight beam steered her around trees and puddles, but bushes clawed her uniform, and a low-hanging branch whipped her cheek. There was no sound except her heavy breathing and her thick-soled shoes making sucking noises in the earth. Thirty feet to her left, Steve's light sliced through the fog in sweeping strides. She heard him stumble and curse. "Where're the damn tracks?" he yelled.

"Over here." Using the faint glimmer of streetlights as a reference point, Lauren reached the rim of the trolley car gulch and swooped her light down to the tracks below, then up the opposite bank. Tattered mist shrouded the steep grades, while to the north the gaping mouth of the tunnel was barely visible. Low hanging clouds muffled everything, muting the persistent roar of the city. She wiped sweat off her face with the sleeve of her jacket and let the silence seep into her consciousness.

Emerging through the mist, Steve's shadowy frame solidified as he joined her. He was breathing hard and tracks of moisture glistened in the folds of his neck. "Damn fog," he said. "Anyone out in this soup is certifiable."

"You should be very afraid," she said in a low, creepy tone. "Vampires and werewolves abound."

"No problem." His handsome Latin features brightened. "My stake's sharpened, and my cross is freshly doused with holy water."

"I feel better now."

"I sure don't hear any screaming," he said. "Someone's getting their jollies screwing with cops."

Turning her gaze to the south, Lauren peered into a dense grove of sycamore trees. "What's that in there? A dumpster?"

He shrugged. "Dunno. Let's take a look."

She felt the temperature drop as they entered the grove. The air was moist and thick and smelled of decay. The drenched tree trunks looked black and oily and water dripped from the branches. Her beam cut across a glistening carpet of dead leaves, scaled the leg of a picnic table to its surface, and froze. An icy shiver raced across her scalp. "What the hell? Give me more light."

"Holy shit," Steve breathed as his beam joined hers. Caught in the crossbeams was the nude body of a woman. Lauren cleared her 9mm Beretta from its holster. Steve did the same. Standing back-to-back, their light splintered between trees and probed the latticework of branches overhead. The grove possessed an eerie stillness.

"Clear," Steve said after several tense moments.

Holstering their sidearms, they approached the body. Lauren shuddered as she viewed the woman lying on her back with her arms crossed over her chest. Her body was graceful and athletic, legs straight and rigid, toes pointing outward. Her fingers pressed a full red rose to her pale breasts, and her dark hair fanned away from her bloodless face like a halo. She made a stunning corpse.

Lauren disliked touching the dead, but ignoring the queasy flutter in her stomach, she pressed her fingers to the woman's carotid artery, and felt a pulse. "She's alive!" Lauren hurriedly shook out of her jacket and draped it across the woman's torso while Steve spread his own over her bare legs.

"We need a 408, Code 3," Lauren barked into her mic. "We're in Cypress Park across from the tracks." With an ambulance and backup units on the way, she turned her full attention to the victim. A cloying floral scent Lauren didn't recognize wafted off the body.

"Christ. She's just a kid." Santos was holding his beam over her face, and they could clearly see that alabaster makeup had been meticulously applied to her face from hairline to chin. Her generous mouth was painted scarlet. "The white makeup makes her look bloodless."

"Just like a corpse." Lauren felt a tightening at the back of her neck as she studied the teenager's face—she was maybe fifteen, sixteen years old.

"What the hell is she doing out here, like this?" Steve asked.

The emotion in her partner's voice matched her feelings exactly. She and Steve both had teenage daughters. Finding this young victim hit like a sucker punch. Lauren's light traveled down to the girl's throat, which was badly bruised and swollen. A bold weave pattern was impressed in the flesh, with tiny puncture wounds evenly spaced throughout. Lauren swallowed, found her voice. "Looks like she was strangled with something that had little sharp edges."

Santos released a quick exhale. "Sick. These little cuts must've been bloody."

"No doubt. Whoever did this had her for a while. Cleaned her up, and then took a lot of time getting this makeup just right. Had to be a man. Someone strong. She was carried in here from the street. Then he took his sweet time staging her like a corpse, fanning out her hair, placing the rose under her fingers. Everything perfect."

Steve's jaw bunched. "A regular Picasso."

"I'm sure he thinks he's a genius."

"One thing's for sure. She couldn't have screamed. She's out cold."

"You're right. The anonymous call must've come from the assailant. He wanted us to find her right away."

"Admire his handy-work."

"Let's see if he left other evidence," she said.

They scoured every inch of the clearing. No sign of the girl's belongings, no disturbance in the leaves. "Didn't expect to find anything," she said, disappointed. "He's too careful."

A low guttural moan brought their attention back to the victim. Her eyelids fluttered open and Lauren gave a little gasp. The whites of her eyes were red. The strangulation, she realized, had to have been brutal to force blood to burst through the eye vessels. The assailant had been a hair away from killing her.

The teen held a fixed stare, then her eyes widened in terror. Lauren placed a hand on her arm and said slowly and deliberately, "You're okay, hon. We're police officers. We're here to help you. Do you understand?"

The girl's expression alternated between dazed and frightened. Her hands jutted out from under the jacket and lightly caressed her throat, fingers trembling. She winced and made a choking sound. Tears filled her eyes and ran down her temples. She tried to rise, but Lauren pressed a hand to her shoulder. "Lie still for now. Help is on the way."

The girl lay back, motionless.

"What's your name?"

No answer. Blank stare.

Lauren repeated the question. "What. Is. Your. Name?"

"Melissa. Melissa… Cox." Her voice was raspy and triggered a spasm of coughing. Her hands moved down to her groin. "It hurts."

Lauren and Steve exchanged a look. His face darkened. Lauren quelled her own anger and spoke in a soothing tone. "Hang in there, Melissa. An ambulance is on the way. You're safe now."

Melissa reached out and grasped Lauren's hand. "Will you… go with me?"

"I'll be right at your side." Noticing Melissa wore a gold band on her left ring finger, Lauren made a mental note to ask about it later. "Melissa, do you know who did this to you?"

The girl shook her head.

"Can you tell me your phone number?" Steve asked. Melissa rasped out a number.

A twig snapped just outside the grove. Lauren froze. Did a shadow flicker in the darkness? An animal? She peered through the mist, only half hearing Steve eliciting personal information from Melissa. The next sound Lauren heard was unmistakable. Muffled footsteps, moving away from the grove. Her partner's voice was interspersed with static as he talked to Dispatch. Lauren met his eyes, signaled. He nodded.

She squeezed Melissa's hand. "I'll be right back." Pulling out her Beretta, Lauren tread cautiously, her beam fanning between columns of trees and veils of mist. Disoriented, she waited until the haze parted and dim lights appeared in windows on King Street, seemingly floating above ground. Footsteps slapped pavement some distance to the east heading for the footbridge crossing the ravine. Lauren bolted through the underbrush and reached the gorge as the hazy figure of a man darted onto the bridge some twenty yards away.

"Stop! Police!"

His outline paused for a second, then disappeared into the fog. Lauren thought she could intercept him if she angled down the embankment and up the other side. The terrain dropped away and she descended the rocky slope in long, careful strides.

Across the grade, the suspect reappeared directly above her, metal glinting in his hand.

Shit!

Loud, thundering shots cracked the night. White sparks bounced off the rails below.

Adrenalin jolted her system. She moved fast, sidestepping on gravel. Her leg skidded out from under her and she felt herself falling. She lurched into a violent tumble, somersaulting once, and came to a jolting stop against the berm of the tracks. She lay dazed, shocked by the fall. A trolley car burst from the tunnel. Caught in its headlights, she made an easy target.

More gunshots. Dirt shot up the hill behind her. The ground exploded an even distance away on either side of her. The shooter was circling her with bullets. Deliberately missing. Playing her.

Blood pounding in her ears, she bent to one knee, took aim at the shooter, and fired off a few rounds before the trolley reached her and rushed passed in a rumbling blur of metal and blinking lights. The tracks cleared. The shooter was gone.

Lauren's nerves felt exposed. Her pulse raced. Sweat dripped down her face. Staying on task, she crossed the tracks and mounted the hill. Gauzy layers of mist swirled over King Street.

Parked cars and houses appeared, then disappeared. Heart punching her ribcage, senses wide open, she scanned the area in slices. No movement. The distant wail of sirens rushed toward her and grew piercingly loud. Vehicles screeched to a halt. Blue and red strobes fractured the night. Car doors opened and slammed. Footsteps slapped asphalt. Uniformed figures approached through the haze.

Hands clammy, Lauren lowered her Beretta. "I'm Officer Starkley. A suspect's at large in this vicinity. Male, lean build, dark clothing, ball cap."

As cops dispersed rapidly into the park and immediate neighborhood, Lauren updated her report to dispatch. A dozen more officers arrived promptly and joined the manhunt. Shots fired at an officer was deadly serious business.

Buy *Pretty Corpse*: amzn.to/2s9d2ha

To learn of new releases and discounts add your name to Linda's mailing list: www.lindaberry.net

Linda loves to hear from you. Follow her at:

Twitter: @lindaberry7272

https://twitter.com/LindaBerry7272

Facebook: https://www.facebook.com/linda.berry.94617

ABOUT THE AUTHOR

Linda's love of the written word and the visuals arts culminated in a twenty-five-year career as an award-winning copywriter and art director. Now retired, Linda writes mysteries and intense, fast-paced thrillers. She currently lives in Oregon with her husband and toy poodle.

CPSIA information can be obtained
at www.ICGtesting.com
Printed in the USA
LVHW01s0529190618
581208LV00025B/184/P

9 780999 853818